CAT SEEING DOUBLE

Also by Shirley Rousseau Murphy

Cat Laughing Last
Cat Spitting Mad
Cat to the Dogs
Cat in the Dark
Cat Raise the Dead
Cat Under Fire
Cat on the Edge

CAT SEEING DOUBLE

A JOE GREY MYSTERY

Shirley Rousseau Murphy

HarperCollinsPublishers

CAT SEEING DOUBLE. Copyright © 2003 by Shirley Rousseau Murphy. All rights reserved. Printed in the United States of America. No part of this book may be used or reproduced in any manner whatsoever without written permission except in the case of brief quotations embodied in critical articles and reviews. For information, address HarperCollins Publishers Inc., 10 East 53rd Street, New York, NY 10022.

HarperCollins books may be purchased for educational, business, or sales promotional use. For information, please write: Special Markets Department, HarperCollins Publishers Inc., 10 East 53rd Street, New York, NY 10022.

FIRST EDITION

Designed by Nancy B. Field

Illustration by Beppe Giacobbe

Printed on acid-free paper

Library of Congress Cataloging-in-Publication Data
Murphy, Shirley Rousseau
  Cat seeing double : a Joe Grey mystery / by Shirley Rousseau Murphy — 1st ed.
    p. cm.
  ISBN 0-06-620950-1 (hc)
  1. Grey, Joe (Fictitious character)—Fiction. 2. Cats—Fiction.
  I. Title.
  PS3563.U355 C34   2003
  813'.54—dc21   2002068481

03 04 05 06 ❖/RRD 10 9 8 7 6 5 4 3 2 1

For Pat, as always.

*And for Jake, weimaraner of many talents
who powerfully touched our lives.*

We have reawakened ourselves to the vital and different roles that animals can play in our lives—sometimes with significant, even life-changing consequences. Veils of mystery and misunderstanding are being lifted. . . .

—BRAD STEIGER AND SHERRY HANSEN STEIGER,
Animal Miracles: Inspirational and Heroic True Stories

CAT SEEING DOUBLE

1

Ryan Flannery had no idea, when she dressed for the wedding of Chief of Police Max Harper on Saturday afternoon, that she would soon face the police not as a wedding guest among friendly uniformed officers, but as a prime murder suspect. No notion that the tentative new friendships she'd made within the department would turn without warning to that of investigators and possible offender.

An hour before the ceremony, half-dressed in a slip and scuffs and the first skirt she'd had on in weeks, she stepped into the kitchen alcove of her studio apartment to nuke a cup of coffee. Through the wide front windows the dropping sun blinded her, reflecting from the village rooftops and repeated as hundreds of brilliant signals across the surface of the sea, as if all the sea creatures held up little mirrors attempting to communicate with the land-bound before evening descended. Nearer, just below her balcony, the mosaic of rooftops among the oak trees was as serene as a storybook hamlet where all promises ended happily-ever-after. No smallest twinge of unease touched her, no sixth sense that early the next morning uniformed attendants to a murder would fill her garage stringing yellow crime tape, the coroner working on poor Rupert taking care not to disturb any evidence among the stack of broken windows with which the body was entangled—her ex-husband lying white and lifeless among shards of colored glass. And Ryan herself facing Detective Dallas Garza answering her uncle's questions as, cold and detached, he recorded her formal statement.

Pouring a cup of cold coffee left from breakfast, a brew that at 3:00 in the afternoon closely resembled crankcase oil, she stuck the cup in the microwave. She needed something to keep her awake. Even at what she considered the tender age of thirty-two she could no longer stay up until 1:00 in the morning and feel human the next day.

She'd driven down late last night from the mountains after paying off her carpenters and wrapping up a construction job, wanting to be back home and have her work squared away in plenty of time for the wedding. She'd pulled into her drive well after midnight dead for sleep, had unloaded the precious stained glass windows she'd found in a junk shop in San Andreas, locked her garage and truck and come upstairs. Pulling off her boots and jeans, she had fallen into bed—wondering only briefly why her tarp, folded behind the stack of windows, had what looked like cracker crumbs and half-a-dozen Hershey wrappers among the layers when she unfolded it.

Someone had been in the truck bed, but she wasn't sure when. Maybe one of the kids hanging around the job site, up there. Well, nothing was missing. Too tired to care, she'd rolled over and known nothing more until nearly dawn.

Waking, she'd lain in bed staring out at the black September sky, then dropped into sleep again like diving into deep, silky water. Awakening again at 9:00 feeling dull, she'd showered, unpacked her duffel, dumped her laundry in the washer, made a peanut butter and jelly sandwich for breakfast, and spent the middle of the day cleaning out her truck, putting away tools and stacking the antique windows more securely in the big double garage. Seven beautiful old windows she'd bought for a song, with wonderful designs of birds and leaves. It was amazing what you could pick up in the little back hills junk shops even today when every tourist was a bargain hunter.

Clyde had left a message on her phone tape, that he'd pick her up at 3:30 for the wedding. The ceremony was scheduled for 4:00 with a casual reception afterward in the garden of the village church. Ryan had helped Charlie pick out her wedding dress, and Charlie's aunt Wilma and several friends had handled the arrangements and the caterer and informal invitations, all of which had given Charlie a prime case of nerves. Charlie Getz, inclined to be a loner, was better at the easel or the typewriter or at housecleaning and maintenance repairs than at sorting out the details of a social function that would change her life as she knew it.

Because Charlie's parents were dead and she had no close male relatives, Ryan's uncle Dallas would give her away. And Clyde Damen, Max Harper's lifelong friend, would be best man. She wondered if he'd show up for his official duties dressed in sweatshirt and jeans. Never one for polish, Clyde was as unlike Ryan's philandering ex-husband as it was possible to be, and that made her like him quite a lot.

As she reached to open the microwave, a scratching sound at her window made her start. Turning, she caught her breath then swallowed back a laugh.

Two cats crouched on the sill peering in at her: Clyde's big gray tomcat and his lady pal, dark-stripped Dulcie. Two bold freeloaders who, before she left for San Andreas, had been at her door every morning.

How could they have known she was home? Or had they come every day for two months, expecting the handout they'd grown accustomed to? Oh, surely not. No cat was that tenacious, and certainly these cats never went hungry—though at the moment, with their noses close to the glass, their whiskers drawing delicate patterns through the dusty surface, they presented the picture of ultimate greed and impatience.

And the tomcat had brought her a gift.

From the gray cat's sharp white teeth dangled a dead mouse.

Joe Grey held his kill securely by its rear, its fur matted and wet from mauling. She stared at it, and looked into the burning yellow eyes of the self-satisfied tomcat, and choked back a laugh. Joe remained staring at her, his expression growing to deeper impatience. He began to shift from paw to paw.

Did he think he was going to bring that thing in the house? Was the mauled mouse a gift? An offering to human gods?

Knowing Joe Grey, she didn't think so. If that cat considered anyone a god in his relationships with humans, the god would be Joe himself.

Both cats cocked their ears, watching her. The tom's short fur was as sleek as gray satin clinging over strong muscles, the white triangle down his nose and his white paws and chest looking freshly scrubbed—no tinge of mouse blood. His yellow eyes were fierce. Clearly he expected her to hurry to the door and to formally accept his treasure.

His tabby lady was more demure. Her brown curving stripes, catching the light of the dropping sun, were as rich as silk batik. Her pink mouth was open in a plaintive little mew that sounded through the glass as thin and wavering as a cry from another dimension. Ryan reached to crack open the window.

"As happy as I am, Joe, to see you kill the mice, as grateful as I am for your efforts, you're not bringing that thing in here."

Joe Grey glared as if he understood, as if this was not an acceptable response.

The tomcat's avid commitment to ridding her garage of mice, an undertaking that had begun several months ago, had left her both puzzled and amused.

Having complained to Clyde about the vermin, about the voracious little beasts that had burrowed into her brand-new rolls of insulation and were nibbling on the electrical cords of her power tools, she hadn't expected Clyde to offer up his own private feline exterminator. She'd have poisoned the mice, but she had feared for the neighborhood pets; and Clyde had insisted that Joe Grey would eradicate them. Of course she hadn't believed him. "Why should they hunt in my garage when they have all the wild hills? You can't *tell* a cat where to hunt, Clyde. I've seen them hunting up the hills. I've seen those two killers dragging rabbits through the grass."

"You feed them when they show up, give them a little snack, and install a cat door into your garage, and I guarantee they'll catch the mice."

"But that's silly."

"Try it. I promise."

"A cat door will only let in more mice."

"The mice are already getting in somewhere," he had pointed out, "despite the fact that you and Charlie went over the garages of both duplexes and patched all the holes. What difference is one more opening? Trust me. Cut the door, and leave a little snack."

Build it and they will come, she'd thought, wanting to giggle.

"Just do it. Joe and Dulcie will clear the place."

Out of desperation she'd followed his instructions, visualizing extended families of mice marching in through the newly cut cat door to set up housekeeping, vast generations of rapacious rodents settling in to gnaw the cords off drills and saws and droplights. Reluctantly she had put in the cat door and then had gotten on with the job at hand, which was the renovation of Clyde's back-yard, transforming his weedy garden and scruffy lawn into a handsome outdoor living area.

After a week, all signs of mice in her garage had vanished.

Maybe this mouse that Joe dangled was the last one. Maybe, she thought giddily, Joe Grey had brought this last mouse to her to receive her final stamp of approval.

Or her final payment? Would he present a bill? Or was this

extermination job in partial exchange for Clyde's yard renovation? Well, Clyde *had* been pleased with the renovation.

Months earlier, when a small, exclusive shopping plaza was built behind Clyde's house, it had turned the property line at the back into a two-story concrete wall that destroyed Clyde's view of the eastern hills. She'd pointed out the virtues of the new wall, how it could be turned from what Clyde considered a negative feature to a positive asset. In the plan she submitted, she'd made every effort to replace the loss of a view with satisfying architectural interest, enclosing the outer limits of the yard with six-by-six pillars that met the smoothly plastered wall and supported a heavy overhead latticework in a simple Spanish style. This structure framed the maple tree and enlarged deck, the new southwestern style fireplace, wet bar, and outdoor grill. Beneath the trellises she had constructed a series of raised planters arranged in different heights among plastered benches. They'd installed tile decorations for the high wall, and had arranged interesting, bold-leafed plants against it. *Voilà*, an eyesore turned into a handsome private retreat.

Soon, now that she was home from the San Andreas job, she would begin the second phase of Clyde's renovation, a second-floor addition, jacking up the attic roof to create the walls of a new master bedroom and study. Here in this small, lovely village of Molena Point, with its high demand for real estate, Clyde's upgrading was well worth the investment. The third phase of his project would complete the transformation as she opened the kitchen to the small dining room, then nudged the face of the Cape Cod cottage into a more contemporary aspect with a Mexican accent. Some people might call that bastardization. Ryan called it good design.

In the five months since she moved to Molena Point, she'd accomplished a lot. Had gotten her local contractor's license and the necessary permits to launch RM Flannery, Construction, had put together two good crews, and had finished three jobs beside

Clyde's: a drainage project for four ladies who had just bought a home together for their retirement, the addition in San Andreas, and the far more complicated Landeau vacation cottage here in the village, which waited now only for the new handwoven carpet that had been ordered from England. The rug wasn't part of the architectural work but was the province of her sister Hanni, who had done the interior design. All in all a satisfying beginning for her new venture.

She had escaped San Francisco for Molena Point the night she finally decided to leave Rupert, had packed her personal possessions into cardboard boxes, loaded them into a company truck and taken off in a cold rage—in a move that was long overdue. Heading south along the coast, for the village she loved best in all the world, for the little seaside town where she had spent her childhood summers, she was filled not only with hurt anger at Rupert but with excited dreams for a new beginning—her own business, totally hers, completely free of Rupert.

But she fully intended to receive in cash her share of Dannizer Construction, which she had helped Rupert to build.

Her sudden decision to leave—when she found another woman's clothes in her closet—had been bolstered by the fact that her uncle Dallas and her sister Hanni had already moved to Molena Point, that both would be nearby for moral support. Dallas had taken a position as chief of detectives for Captain Harper in the smaller and more casual police department, shaking off the heavy stress of San Francisco PD for his last few years before retirement. And early this spring Hanni had opened a design studio in the village, leaving the large city studio where she had worked under too much pressure. Maybe this sudden midlife bid for new directions, this need to pull back and be more fully one's own boss, was in the blood.

When she looked again at the window, the gray tomcat was still staring.

"That's very good, Joe Grey. I'm proud of you. It's a fine

mouse. But you *can't* bring it inside." What did he want her to do, fry it up for supper? At her words, his yellow eyes narrowed with defiance, his stubborn look so droll that she cracked open the door a couple of inches to see what he would do.

The sight that met her made her choke.

On the mat lay five dead mice lined up as neatly as the little toy soldiers she'd marshaled into rows, as a child.

The instant she cracked the door open, the tomcat dropped the sixth mouse precisely beside the others. He didn't try to bring it in; he simply laid it on the mat perfectly aligned, and looked up at her.

Was he grinning? The cat was definitely grinning.

She studied the tomcat, and the six dead mice presented for her review. This was some trick of Clyde's. He must have slipped up the steps and set up the dead mice as a joke. Now he would be watching her, hidden somewhere, like a kid glancing around the corner of the building. Except, what had made the tomcat drop the sixth mouse there?

She looked along the street for Clyde's car and up the side streets as far as she could see. Maybe he'd parked the yellow roadster up the hill on the back street.

But where did he get the mice? How could he have made the cat take part in such a ruse? Make the cat look in the window at just the right moment, dangling another mouse in his jaws, and then lay it on the mat?

Certainly Joe Grey was no trained cat, she thought, smiling. Clyde wasn't even able to train a dog effectively. She'd heard about the fiasco with the two Great Dane puppies that Clyde had raised, a pair of huge adolescent dogs with no hint of manners, two canine disasters until Max Harper and Charlie took over their training.

She wondered idly if Max and Charlie's romance actually began up in the hills at his ranch as they taught two misbegotten puppies some manners and trained them to basic obedience. Charlie had never said. But if that was the case the pups really should be ring bearers, she thought, amused, imagining the two big dogs trotting down the aisle with little satin pillows tied to their noses bearing matched wedding rings.

She had to get hold of herself. She really hadn't had enough sleep.

Charlie had stopped by this morning on an errand despite the fact that it was her wedding day, and they'd had a short, comfortable visit. Ryan had liked the freckled redhead from the moment they first met, had liked that Charlie didn't talk trivia and that there was no friction between them because Charlie had recently and seriously dated Clyde and now Ryan was seeing him.

She admired Charlie for starting her life over after a false beginning, chucking an unsatisfactory career as a commercial artist at which she'd realized she'd never be tops, tossing away four years of art school education. Moving down to Molena Point to stay with her aunt Wilma, Charlie hadn't wasted any time in putting together an upscale housecleaning and repair business, a service that Charlie now ran so efficiently she found time not only to do her wonderful animal drawings, but had launched herself into a brand-new venture writing fiction for a national publisher.

Charlie took the attitude that if you were hungry to do something, give it a try. If you fell on your face, try something else. They'd laughed about that because Ryan had been hungry for such a long time to be free of Rupert and on her own. Charlie's understanding had been very supportive, had sustained her considerably as she established her own firm.

Cracking the door wider for a better look at Clyde's practical joke all laid out on her doormat, she didn't protest when the tomcat immediately shouldered past her into the kitchen—sans mouse. Both cats strolled in with all the pomp of a well-dressed couple stepping from their Rolls-Royce in response to her formal invitation to tea. Even the cats' glances were unsettling, Dulcie's green eyes and Joe's yellow gaze far too imperious and self-possessed. Were all cats so self-assured and bold? Padding past her into the big studio room they lay down in the center of the Konya rug, the most beautiful and expensive furnishing she owned, and simultaneously, as if on cue, they began to wash.

Watching them, she decided the two cats added warmth to the room, as well as a sense of whimsy.

The studio was large and airy, its white walls bathed with late afternoon sun. Only on the north side of the twenty-foot-square room did the ceiling drop to eight feet where one long barrier wall defined the kitchen, bath, and closet-dressing room. The studio's sleek, whitewashed floor showed off to perfection the rich colors of the Turkish Konya rug that she and Clyde had found at an estate sale, its thick pile and primitive patterns glowing in vibrant shades of deep red and turquoise and indigo.

That shopping spree had been their first date. Clyde had brought a fabulous deli basket for an early, presale picnic breakfast along the rocky coast. Sitting on the sea cliff where the salty spray leaped up at them, he had served her wild mushroom quiche, thin slices of Belgian ham, strawberry tarts, and espresso—a very sophisticated meal for a guy who often seemed ordinary, even cloddish. That morning, teasing her about being a lady contractor, he had made her laugh when she'd badly needed to laugh.

After breakfast, returning to the handsome villa, they were among the first group to tour the estate. They'd found wonderful bargains that they loaded into her truck. Her few furnishings had all come from that sale except her new drafting table. The desk that faced her front windows was a handsome solid oak unit with a dull, pewter stain and an ample wing for her computer. The two tomato-red leather chairs occupied the back of the room facing a wide wicker coffee table, and a wicker daybed covered with a handwoven spread and an array of tapestry pillows—all were from the sale, even the carved, multicolored Mexican dining table and four chairs that were tucked into the kitchen alcove. She'd brought nothing with her from the San Francisco house but her clothes and files and books, had wanted as little as possible from her old life, had wanted to start with everything new after what seemed an endless term of enslavement.

Nine years with Rupert. Why had she stayed so long? Cowardice? Fear of Rupert? The forlorn hope that things would get better? Chalk it up to ennui, to lack of direction—to stupidity. She felt, now, that she could whirl in circles swinging her arms and shouting and there was no barrier to force her back into that confining cage—a cage wrought of Rupert's vile rages that burned just on the edge of violence, and of his drinking and womanizing.

No more barriers in her life.

Except that this morning when she ran her phone tape she'd had not only the welcome message from Clyde saying he'd pick her up for the wedding, but a tirade from Rupert, a communication she had not expected, hadn't wanted and didn't understand.

You didn't think you'd hear from me, Ryan. I can't condone what you did running off and trying to take half my business that I owned before we were married. I can't condone what you did to Priscilla but I feel obligated to tell you. . . .

That had made her smile. What *she* did to *Priscilla?* That day before she left him she'd arrived home from a week in north Marin County finishing up an apartment job, had opened the garage door and found, in her half of the garage, a little red Porsche parked next to Rupert's BMW. She'd thought, thrilled and amazed, that Rupert in some uncharacteristic fit of generosity or guilt had bought her an anniversary present two weeks early.

But, opening the unlocked door of the Porsche, she had smelled the stink of cigarette smoke and perfume and seen another woman's clutter in the backseat—hairbrush, pink fuzzy sweater, wrinkled movie magazine. Checking the registration, she'd tried to recall who Priscilla Bloom might be.

And then in the house she'd found the woman's belongings all over the conjugal bedroom, Priscilla's clothes in the closet jamming her own garments to the back. That was the moment she ended the marriage.

Hauling out every foreign item from the bedroom, all of it reeking of cigarette smoke and heavy perfume, she had dumped it all in the little red car. Seven trips from house to garage, then she had backed her truck up the drive, hooked her heavy-duty tow chain to the back bumper of the Porsche, and pulled it out into the middle of the street blocking both lanes and seriously slowing traffic. What she'd wanted to do was move her truck up behind the Porsche and push it right on through the front garage wall, effectively wrecking the structure and the car in one move. Only the legal aspects of such an action had deterred her. She didn't need any further court battles.

The car sat in the middle of the street until the police came to issue a ticket, impound the vehicle, and haul it away. She hadn't answered the door when the officer rang; she'd been busy cleaning out the room she used as an office. When at last she came out to load her truck, the police and the Porsche were gone. Smiling, she'd locked the house and taken off for Molena Point.

The message she'd listened to this morning had badly jolted her . . . *tell you that someone's been asking questions about you . . . about your plans this weekend. Are you going to some wedding? As little feeling as I have left for you, Ryan, I have to say be careful. I don't want anything on my conscience. . . .*

There'd been a long pause, then he'd hung up. She'd sat at her desk staring at the phone trying to figure out what he was talking about. Did his call have something to do with Priscilla Bloom getting back at her? But surely not. Why would the opportunistic Priscilla or any of Rupert's female friends have any connection to Max Harper and Charlie's wedding or even know about it? How would she know them at all?

Maybe Rupert had heard about the wedding and wanted to upset her by implying there was some kind of danger. That would be like him. Innuendo was just the kind of meaningless warning that would highly amuse him. She was so tired of his stupidity. Even the court battle now in process, that Rupert's attorneys had managed to delay endlessly as she fought for her rightful half of the business, even Rupert's testimony in court had been all hot air, all fabrication and lies—silly delaying tactics.

She'd worked hard to help build that business into what it now was. She wasn't dumping it all and walking away from what she'd earned. The Molena Point attorney she'd contacted had recommended an excellent San Francisco firm, and they were handling the case with minimum fuss for her despite the antics of Rupert's slick lawyers.

She rinsed her empty cup and lay it in the drain rack, glancing in at Joe and Dulcie, treating the two cats to a string of rude remarks about Rupert Dannizer. Then she went to finish dressing.

Ryan didn't see behind her the two cats' response to her longshoreman's description of Rupert, didn't see Joe Grey's yellow eyes narrow with amusement, and Dulcie's green eyes widen with laughter at her characterization of the man she so despised.

2

SHE WAS REACHING FOR HER SUIT JACKET WHEN she remembered she'd have to change purses, that she couldn't dress up for a wedding and carry a canvas backpack. Crossing the studio in her slip, Ryan glanced again at the two cats sprawled across the blue-and-garnet rug, admiring Dulcie's chocolate stripes and Joe's sleek silver gleam. Quietly they stared up at her, Joe's gaze burning like clear amber, Dulcie's eyes as bright green as emeralds. But the intensity of their concentration forced her to step back. And as she moved away toward the dressing room she was certain that behind her they were still watching.

Strange little cats, she thought. Why was their interest so unsettling?

"Strange little cats," she had once told Clyde.

"How so? Strange in what way?"

"There's something different about them. Don't you notice? I've never had cats, only dogs, but . . ."

"All cats are strange, one way or another. That's what makes them appealing."

"I suppose. But those two, and the black-and-brown one you

14

call the kit, sometimes they behave more like dogs than cats. The way they follow you around. And all three cats seem so intense, their glances are so . . . I don't know. The way they look at a person, the way the kit looks at you, they're not the way I think of cats." She had watched Clyde, frowning. "Neither Wilma nor you finds your cats odd? Doesn't Wilma ever comment on how different they seem?"

Clyde had shrugged. "I don't think you've observed cats very closely. Cats *are* strange, cats *stare* at you, and every cat is different in some way. Unpredictable," he'd said. "Dogs are more alike, easier to understand."

"I see," she'd answered doubtfully, wondering why he sounded so defensive.

Glancing in the dressing room mirror, she slipped on the beige linen suit without a blouse. The deep V of the neck set off the best of her tan—perfect for cleavage if she'd had any. Well, her tan *was* good. No one could tell it was a farmer's tan, ending where her shirt collars and sleeves began. With jacket and skirt in place, and pantyhose, most of her little bruises and cuts from working construction were well enough hidden.

The thought did nag her that she ought to do something about her general appearance, the most pressing item being her hair, which badly needed cutting. Two months on the job without stopping to get a haircut had left it longer than she liked, and ragged. Her nails were rough too and her skin felt as dry and leathery as an old carpenter's apron. What she could have used was a week at some cushy spa with luxurious daily massages, perfumed oils, professional hairstyling, steam baths, manicure, pedicure—a complete overhaul guaranteed to put all emotional and physical parts back into working order.

It amused her to wonder what those high-class masseuses and beauty specialists would make of her calloused, torn hands and cut thumbs and assorted body bruises—little marks of hard labor earned by toting heavy lumber and plumbing fixtures, and leaning into two-by-fours to hold them in place as she nailed them solid. At least her fancy masseuse could have admired her slim butt and super muscle tone, even if the skinny package was as full of bruises as the dents in an ancient farm pickup.

Fastening on an ivory pendant, she brushed back her dark hair into some semblance of order and sprayed it, and applied lipstick. So much for elegance. She'd leave the pizzazz to her sister. Hanni would arrive at the wedding dressed in something that caught all eyes, something almost too wild, too far out, but that would look great on Hanni, with her prematurely white, wildly curling coiffure, her long lean body and her total self-assurance. Hanni was the show-off of the family, the onstage personality, the would-be model, Ryan thought warmly. She'd missed Hanni and Dallas, just as she constantly missed her dad. She hadn't seen much of him since she left the city, but she missed him more now, knowing he was so far away, on the East Coast. He'd been gone for nearly a month, conducting training sessions; she'd be glad when he was home again.

She found herself looking forward eagerly to the wedding, to a bit of social life, to being with friends, and with at least two members of her family. And looking forward too, to the quiet and meaningful ceremony.

Just because her own marriage had been ugly didn't mean she had to rain on others' bliss.

The marriage of Max Harper, that wry-witted police captain who, Clyde said, had seemed so very alone after his wife died, was a cause of celebration for the entire village—or at least for all those who didn't hate Harper, who didn't fear Harper's thorough and effective response to village crime.

To see Charlie and Max marrying pleased Ryan very much. The two were just right for each other. Two no-nonsense people who, despite their down-to-earth attitudes, were each in their own way dreamers. Though you'd never know that about Max Harper; he'd never let you know that.

16

Charlie and Max had wanted a small, private wedding that better fit their approach to life and was in keeping with Max's low-key style as chief of police. But the villagers were so excited about the occasion, everyone wanted to be a part of the wedding. The couple had settled for a ceremony in the small village church with the wedding guests mostly police officers and their wives and a few close friends, but with all the village crowded around in the adjoining rooms of the church and in the garden, and at the open patio doors where they could hear the couple's vows. The garden buffet afterward would be for the whole village.

She thought about Rupert's message. *Someone's asking . . . about your plans for the weekend . . . Are you going to some wedding? . . . I don't want anything on my conscience. . . .*

She shook her head. That was all talk. She was stupid to let Rupert worry her, that was exactly what he wanted. Rupert's warped sense of the melodramatic was inappropriate and embarrassing.

Finished dressing, she decided to make fresh coffee for Clyde; he was usually early, a quality that had at first annoyed her but that she'd come to find reassuring. Clyde didn't like to be late and neither did she. Having not seen each other for over two months, they could sit and talk for a moment before being swallowed up in the crowd and the ceremony. The coffee was brewing when she heard him double-timing up the stairs. She opened the door eagerly, before he had time to knock, forgetting the mice on the mat.

He stood at the edge of the mat staring down without expression. She remained silent, unwilling to respond to his corny joke, and wondering again how he'd accomplished it.

Looking up at her, he started to grin. His short, dark hair was freshly cut, his shave smooth and clean, making her want to touch his cheek. She loved the scent of his vetiver aftershave. She had never seen him in a suit before, only in jeans and a polo shirt or, for evening, jeans and a sport coat. Today, as best man, he *had* dressed handsomely, choosing a dark navy suit, a pale, pinstriped shirt and a rich but subdued paisley tie. He seemed truly surprised by the dead mice.

"That's what your tomcat brought me."

"He does that," Clyde said casually. "He does that at home."

"Leaves mice on the mat? Lines them up like a pack of sausages? Come on, Clyde."

Clyde looked at her innocently. "All in a row. I haven't been able to break him of it." His look was blank and serious.

She didn't pursue it. Maybe the cat had done it on his own. This was not the day to discuss the vicissitudes of Clyde's cat.

But as she turned to pour the coffee, she glimpsed the look he shot the tomcat. A glare deeply indignant, as if the cat should have used better judgment. And Joe Grey was staring back at Clyde with amused indulgence, with the kind of silent look that might pass between a dog and his trainer. She'd seen Dallas exchange such a glance with his pointers or retrievers, not a word spoken, or maybe a single word so soft that no one but man and dog heard it —a close, perceptive contact between man and animal.

Was such contact with a cat possible?

Well, why not? Maybe cats *were* as intelligent as a well-bred pointer or retriever. Whatever the case, Clyde was apparently more skilled with cats than with canines.

Stepping over the mice and into her kitchen, Clyde fetched a plastic bag from the drawer beside the refrigerator and returned to the deck to dispose of the bodies, shaking them from the mat into the bag, and carrying it down to the drive and around behind the garage to the garbage can. She heard him rinse his hands at the outdoor faucet. She listened to him come up the stairs, still wondering how many cats would line up their mice on the mat, or would think to do such a thing. Maybe she should learn more about cats. The subject might be entertaining. Clyde returned as she poured the coffee. Pulling out a chair, he glanced in once more toward Joe Grey and Dulcie. "The kit wasn't with them?"

"No. Just the two of them."

He shrugged. "She's getting big, growing up. I guess she can take care of herself."

"You and Wilma have to worry about your cats. They wander all over the village. And the hills . . . it's so wild up there. I can hear the coyotes yipping at night. Don't you—"

"How many times have you asked me that, Ryan? Yes, we worry." He looked at her intently. "Cats are not dogs, to be fenced and leashed. I went through this with Charlie. She couldn't believe we let the cats wander. She understands them better, now. You can't shut them in, they'd die of boredom, their lives would be worth nothing. They're intelligent cats. They need to pursue— whatever weird little projects cats pursue. They need to hunt. They're careful. I've watched them crossing the streets; they look, they don't just go barging out."

"But the coyotes. And the dogs—big dogs."

He sipped his coffee. "I'm sure they know when the coyotes are near, they can hear and smell them—and dogs and coyotes can't climb." He gave her a little smile. "Those three cats will chase a dog until he wishes he'd never heard of cats. I once saw the kit ride the back of a big dog, raking and biting him, rode him from Hellhag Hill clear into the village. She was only a kitten, then. I'd hate to see what she could do now."

The tortoiseshell kit had been with Charlie's aunt Wilma and Dulcie for nearly a year while her owners were traveling. Ryan thought she was charming, those round, golden eyes in that little black-and-brown mottled face always delighted her. The kit's looks were so expressive that, more than once, Ryan caught herself wondering what the little animal was thinking.

"You're tan. It was hot up in the foothills."

"Ninety to a hundred. Surveying, laying out foundation, and putting up framing in the hot sun."

She loved the rolling hills at the base of the Sierras, the rising slopes golden with dry summer grass beneath islands of dark green pine trees, the kind of vast grazing country that had fed millions of longhorn cattle two centuries before when California was part of Mexico, and at one time had fed vast herds of buffalo and elk.

Rising, she fetched a pack of photos from her desk, to show him the added-on great room she had just completed. "Job went like a charm. No major delays in deliveries, no really critical battles with the inspectors, no disasters. But I'm glad to be home, after living with those two in that trailer."

Dan Hall was a Molena Point carpenter who had been willing to work on the San Andreas job providing his young wife could come up on weekends. Scott Flannery was Ryan's uncle, her father's brother, a burly Scotch-Irish giant who had helped to raise Ryan and her two sisters after their mother died. Scotty and her mother's brother Dallas had moved in with them when Ryan was ten, a week after her mother's funeral. The three men had kept up the lessons their mother had insisted on, teaching the girls to cook and clean house and sew and to do most of the household repairs. Scotty had added more sophisticated carpentry skills, and Dallas, then a uniformed officer with San Francisco PD, had taught them the proper handling and safety of firearms as well as how to train and work the hunting dogs he raised. While other little girls were dressing up, learning party manners, and how to fascinate the boys, Ryan and her sisters were outshooting the boys in competition, were hunting dove or quail over one or another of Dallas's fine pointers, or were off on a pack trip into the Rockies.

"Guess I'm getting old and crotchety," Ryan said. "That big two-bedroom trailer seemed so cramped, I found myself longing for my own space. The whole time, I didn't see anyone but those two, and a real estate agent who wants me to do a remodel—and a couple of kids underfoot."

Clyde looked at his watch and rose to rinse their cups. "Neighbor's kids?"

She nodded. "I never did figure out where they lived. They said up the hills. Those houses are scattered all over. You know how kids are drawn to new construction."

Clyde picked up Joe Grey, who had trotted expectantly into the kitchen. "So did you take the remodeling job?"

"I think I'll let that one go by," she said briefly.

Slinging the tomcat over his shoulder, Clyde scooped up Dulcie too, cradling the little female in the crook of his arm.

"You're taking them to the wedding," Ryan said. It was not a question. Clyde took the gray tomcat everywhere.

"Why not? It's a garden wedding. If they don't like it, they can leave." He grinned at her. "Max has a thing about cats. I like to tweak him. I thought it would be amusing to bring the cats to his wedding, let them watch from the trees. Charlie will appreciate the humor." They moved out the door and down the steps to his antique yellow roadster, where Clyde dropped the cats into the open rumble seat.

"Bring them up front with me, Clyde. You don't want them jumping out. I'll hold them."

"They won't jump. They're not stupid."

"Bring them up here. They're cats. Cats don't . . ." She shut up, looking intently at Clyde and at the cats. Joe Grey and Dulcie lay down obediently on the soft leather rumble seat, as docile as a pair of well-mannered dogs—as if perhaps they *had* been trained to behave.

"They'll be fine," Clyde said, starting the engine. "It's a nice day, they want a bit of sunshine." And as he headed down the hills, the cats remained unmoving, seeming as safe as if they wore seat belts. Ryan was sure there couldn't be another cat in the world that wouldn't leap out to the street or stand on the edge of the seat and be thrown out. Cats riding in open rumble seats, cats attending weddings.

Dulcie looked up at her with such contentment, and Joe Grey's expression was so smug that she almost imagined they were proud to be riding in that beautiful vintage car.

Clyde had completely restored the '28 Chevy—new, butter-yellow leather upholstery, gleaming yellow paint. Old cars were

Clyde's love, the Hudsons and Pierce-Arrows and old Packards that he worked on in the back garage of his upscale automotive shop. When he got one in perfect condition he would drive it for a while and then sell it. He was paying for the remodeling of his cottage with the profits from one car or another, just as he had paid to renovate the derelict apartment building he had bought. It was clear that he took great joy in acquiring abandoned relics, in making them new and useful again. Maybe that too was why she liked Clyde Damen.

In the bright autumn weather Molena Point was mobbed with tourists, but despite the glut of out-of-town cars Clyde found a parking place half a block from the church. Swinging a U-turn he neatly parked, scooped up the two cats to keep them safe from traffic, and they crossed to the deep garden in front of the Village Church.

The garden paths were already crowded with villagers. Pausing beside a lemon tree, Clyde half-lifted and half-tossed the two cats into the branches away from crowding feet. Ryan watched them climb, as Clyde headed inside the church to his duties as best man.

She saw, across the garden, her uncle Dallas and her sister. Hanni, decked out in outrageous rags, looked like a million dollars. It was the first time in months that she had seen Dallas in uniform and not in his detective's plainclothes. The entire police force had turned out spit-and-polish, everyone in the village was dressed up and in a party mood. In the excitement of celebration on such a lovely day she had no reason to imagine that disaster would, within moments, rock the church and the garden.

But as the wedding guests laughed and gossiped, and inside the church the groom in his captain's uniform paced with nerves, an unexpected event began to unfold, a drama that could alter—or cut short—the course of many lives.

3

At first, no one saw the lone witness. Not even Joe Grey and Dulcie, crouched high among the branches of the lemon tree, saw the tortoiseshell cat on the rooftops across the street. The two older cats had no glimpse of the tattercoat kit hunched on the dark shingles hidden beneath the overhanging oak branches; they had no hint of the panic that would, in a moment, course through the kit's small, tensed body.

The community church was set well back from the street within its garden of flowering shrubs and small decorative trees. The nonsectarian meeting rooms of the one-story Mediterranean building were employed for all manner of village functions besides church services, from political discussions to author readings. The kit had hung around the church all morning watching the cleaning crew performing a last polish and setting up buffet tables on the back patio; and she had watched masses of white flowers being delivered and arranged within the largest meeting room. Only when the wedding guests began to arrive had she trotted across the narrow residential street, to be out of the way of sharp-heeled party shoes and the hard black oxfords of the many uniformed

23

officers. Swarming up a jasmine trellis to the roof of a brown clap-
board cottage, she had stretched out where an oak tree's shadows
darkened the weathered shingles. Here, she had the best seat of
all, with a clear view across the garden and through the wide glass
doors to the lectern where the bride and groom would stand,
exchanging their sacred vows.

She had watched Charlie and Wilma arrive, Wilma carrying
the bridal dress in a long plastic bag and Charlie carrying a small
suitcase. What a lot of preparation it took for humans to get married, nothing like the casual trysting of the feral cats she had run
with when she was small. The two women entered the south wing
of the church through a back door, where the bride would have a
private office in which to dress. The kit was watching the growing
crowd when, below her, the bushes stirred with a sharp rustle, and
a man spoke.

He must be standing between the close-set houses. The timbre of
his gravelly voice suggested he was old. He sounded bad-tempered.
"Go on. Boy. Get your ass up there, you haven't got all day."

No one answered, but someone began to climb the trellis,
slowly approaching the roof. The kit could hear the little cross-
pieces creak under a hesitant weight. Padding warily away across
the shingles, she crouched beneath overhanging branches out of
sight, where she could see.

A young boy was climbing up. A thin dirty boy with ragged shirt
and torn jeans, his face smudged, but pale beneath the dark smears.
His black eyes were oblique and hard, his hands brown with dirt.
One pocket bulged as if maybe he'd stuffed a candy bar in it, forti-
fication against sudden hunger. The kit knew that feeling.

Peering over, she studied the man who stood below. He was
equally ragged, his faded jeans stained, his face bristling with a
grizzled beard, his gray hair hanging long around his shoulders.
Both man and boy stunk of sharp scents that made the kit's nose
burn. The boy had gained the roof. He didn't swing up onto it, but
stopped at the edge, turning to look down.

24

"Go *on*, Curtis. They'll be filling the church in a minute."

"I don't . . ."

"Just lie under the branches, no one'll see you. Wait till Harper's in there and the girl and them cops, then punch it and get out. I'll be gone like I told you, the truck gone. You just slip away, no one'll see you."

Clinging in the vines, the boy looked both determined and scared, like a cornered rat, the kit thought, trapped in a tin can with nowhere to run.

"Just punch it, Curtis. Your dad's in jail because of them cops."

Swinging a leg over, the boy gained the roof, crouching near the kit beneath the oak branches. She didn't think he saw her, he seemed totally centered on finding a vantage where he would be hidden but could best see the church.

When he'd chosen his place he removed from his pocket a small smooth object like a tiny radio, and laid it on the shingles beside him. The kit puzzled over it for some time before she understood what it was, this small, plastic, boxlike thing that the boy could hide in one hand. Wilma had one, and so did Clyde. And the old man's voice echoed, *Just punch it and get out*. She didn't understand—there was no garage door in the church to open. Why would . . .

Just punch it and get out. . . .

What else could a garage-door opener do, the kit wondered, besides open the door for which it was intended? With its little battery inside, its little electrical battery, what could it do?

Just punch it and get out . . . Wait until Harper's in there, and the girl . . .

That little electrical battery, that little electric signal . . .

All the wonders of electrical things that had so astonished the kit when she first came to live among humans: the dishwasher, the refrigerator, the warmth of an electric blanket, the magical lifting of the garage door while Wilma was still in the car, its signal leaping from that opener—its electrical signal leaping . . .

25

She remembered cop talk about triggering devices. She stared across the street into the church where someone had left a gift for the bride and groom, a silver-wrapped package tucked down into the lectern where Charlie and Max Harper would stand to be married. She had seen it earlier as she watched the workers, had thought it was a special present hidden just where the preacher would stand, where the bride and groom would stand, a gift all silver-wrapped with little silver bells on the ribbon. . . .

A special present. . . .

A gift that was not a gift, she realized with a quaking heart, and the kit exploded to life, racing at the boy, leaping on his back, raking and biting and forcing him away from that electric signal-maker, that plastic box that could send its message across the street into the church, could send its triggering message . . .

She might be wrong. The boy's actions might be innocent. But . . . *Your dad's in jail because of them cops. . . . Punch it and get out. . . .* Terrified and enraged, she clawed and raked and bit, driving the boy away across the roof, forcing him toward the trellis. Nearly falling, he swung away down the trellis, the kit clinging to his back.

Before he hit the ground she dropped clear and ran flashing across the street between cars. . . .

There . . . there was Clyde hurrying out of the church toward his car as if he had forgotten something. As he leaned into the open convertible, reaching, she leaped to his back nearly shouting in his ear, only remembering at the last instant to whisper. . . .

"Bomb, Clyde. There's a bomb in the church in that oak stand, in the lectern. A boy on the roof . . . garage door opener to set it off . . . tell them to run, all to run . . . I chased him, but . . ."And she bailed to the ground again and was gone, racing back across the street causing Clyde to shout after her. The street was thick with cars letting people off.

But then seeing her appear at the far side and swarm up a tree to the rooftops, he spun away, never questioning the kit's warning.

26

Not daring to question, not this small cat. Never daring to question her any more than he would question Joe Grey. . . .

MOMENTS EARLIER, DULCIE HAD BEEN LICKING BLOOD FROM her paw where she'd cut herself on a thorn of the lemon tree. She sat among the branches licking at her pad and looking across the garden into the church, admiring the big meeting room with its high, dark-raftered ceiling and white plastered walls and its two long rows of glass doors looking out on the front and back gardens. Vases of white flowers were massed at both ends of the room, and someone had tucked a gift down inside the lectern. She could see a corner of the silver paper, maybe something special to be presented at the ceremony, though that did seem odd.

Imagining the ritual of the wedding, she was filled with purring happiness. No matter what ugliness might happen elsewhere in the world, no matter what hideous events occurred outside their own small village, here, today, human love ruled.

Behind her Joe Grey hissed, "What's she doing?"

She turned on the branch, never doubting from Joe's distraught tone that he was talking about the kit, this kit to whom disaster clung like needles to a magnet.

He was staring across the street at a dark-shingled roof. Dulcie could just see the kit crouched on the edge of the roof beneath overhanging branches.

There was a boy on the roof. The kit watched him intently, rigid with anger—and the next instant she leaped, clawing the boy and raking him. He swatted at her and ran. The kit rode his back, scratching and biting, forcing the boy off the roof, riding him down then leaping away to race across the street.

The kit hit Clyde, flying up clinging to his shoulder. They could see her poke her nose at his ear, whispering . . . lashing her tail and whispering . . .

In the church office provided for her use, the bride dressed slowly and carefully in her simple linen gown, trying not to fall apart with nerves. In the mirror her freckles looked as dark as paint splatters across her pale cheeks.

Charlie's kinky red hair was pulled back and smoothed, as much as it could be smoothed, into a handsome chignon and clipped with a carved ivory barrette loaned to her by her aunt Wilma. Wilma, tall and slim and white-haired, stood behind Charlie buttoning her dress. The starched-lace wedding veil and crown of white flowers sat on a little stand, on the office desk.

For something blue, Charlie wore blue panties and bra printed with white roses, a private joke between her and Max. Over this, a white lace half-slip and camisole. The "something old" was her mother's wedding ring, one of the few mementos she had from her dead parents. The *new* something was her long white linen gown with its low embroidered neckline and embroidered cap sleeves. Charlie's calloused and capable hands shook both from nerves and excitement and from a sense of the unreal. Time seemed out of kilter, as if in some strange fantasy, the wedding preparations of the preceding few days swirling around her, each moment warped in time and place by her own disbelief.

She was no child bride. At thirty-something she had almost abandoned the idea of falling truly in love and being married. Now that it was happening, and seeming so inevitable, she felt as if she had stepped into a different world and different time, or maybe stepped into someone else's life.

For a while she'd thought Clyde was the one, and that they might marry, but she'd never had this totally lost and committed and ecstatic feeling with Clyde. She and Clyde had ended up no more than good friends, the best of friends. Her feeling for Max was totally different. Her love for Max was the kind of nervous oneness that *made* her hands shake, made her tremble sometimes, and turned her terrified because he was a cop, terrified that he would be hurt, that she would lose him.

"Is that a tear?" Wilma said, watching Charlie in the mirror. Wilma was dressed in a long, pale blue shift, her gray-white hair done in a bun bound low at her neck.

"Of course it's not a tear. I'm not the weeping sort. Steady as a rock." She knew she'd have to get over her fear for Max, that a cop's wife couldn't live like that or she would perish; but right now it was all she could do to keep herself together and get to the altar with Wilma's help and not collapse in a fit of uncontrollable nerves.

"You're not steady at all. Are you this nervous on the firing range?"

"I'm not on the firing range. I'm getting married." She stared at her aunt. "This *is* different than the firing range. Tell me it's different. Tell me . . ." She collapsed against her aunt, shivering, her head on Wilma's shoulder.

Wilma hugged her and smoothed Charlie's hair. "It's different when you're marrying someone like Max Harper. You're having a perfectly normal case of nerves. And maybe second thoughts?" She held Charlie away, looking deeply at her, then grinned. "A simple case of premarital hysteria. I expect Max is having the same. You'll be fine."

"Not second thoughts. Not ever. It's just that . . . If I worried about him before, what will it be like after we're married?"

"He's sharp enough to have lasted this long," Wilma said brusquely. "If something were to happen . . . just give him everything you can. Just fill what time he has—what time we all have. You *must not* fear the future, no one can live like that."

Wilma looked deeply at her. "You know what to do—you prepare as best you can for the bad times—then live every moment with joy." She touched Charlie's cheek. "Law enforcement and protecting others, that is his life, Charlie. You can't change what he wants from his life."

"And there's Clyde," Charlie said, her perverse mind wanting

29

to dredge up every vague cause for unease. "No matter what he says, I feel . . ."

"Guilty."

"As if I dumped him. But he . . ."

"Not to worry," Wilma said. "Not only is he bringing Ryan Flannery to the wedding, he's still pursing Kate Osborne, trying to get her to move back down from San Francisco. I don't think with two women to sort out, trying to pay attention to both, that Clyde is going to spend much time grieving."

"Well, that's not very flattering," Charlie said, grinning. She smoothed the tendrils of her hair that would keep slipping out from the carefully arranged chignon.

"Quit fussing. You look like an angel, a curly-haired, red-headed angel. Now hold still and let me finish fastening. Where are your shoes? You didn't forget your shoes?"

"On the desk. Now who's fussing?"

"It isn't every day my only niece gets married—my only family." Turning to fetch the shoes, Wilma moved to the window and slid the drapery back a few inches to look out into the garden where their friends were gathering. The afternoon was bright and serene. "What a lovely crowd. And people still arriving. Even . . ." Wilma held out her hand. "Come and look."

They stood together peering out, two tall, slim women, the family resemblance clear in their strongly sculpted faces. "Look in the lemon tree. Two of your most ardent admirers, all sleeked up for the occasion."

They could just see Joe Grey and Dulcie peering out from among the leaves, watching something across the street, Joe's white paws bright among the shadows, Dulcie's brown tabby stripes blending into the tree's foliage so she was hardly visible.

"What are they up to?" Charlie said. "They look . . ."

"They're not up to anything, they're waiting to see you and Max married. They have a perfect view, they'll be able to see, above the crowd, right in through the glass doors."

"Where's the kit?"

"I don't see her, but you can bet she won't miss this ceremony."

Charlie turned from the window, reaching for her veil. Wilma, watching her, thought that her niece seemed as close to an angel as it was possible for a flesh-and-blood person to look. She willed the day to be perfect, without a flaw, a golden day for Charlie and Max, with not a thing to spoil it. Charlie was fussing with her veil when the door flew open and Max burst in grabbing her, pushing her toward the door and reaching to Wilma. "Get out! *Now*! Away from the building. Run, both of you—blocks away. *Go, Charlie. Bomb alert.*"

Wilma grabbed Charlie, pulling her away as Charlie tried to follow Max into the garden. Charlie turned on her with rage. "Let me go. Let me go! I can help."

Max spun back, grabbing her shoulders. "Go now! Get the hell out of here!"

She fought him, trying to twist free. "What do you think I am! I can help clear the area!" Her green eyes blazed. "I'm not marrying a cop I can't work beside!"

He stared, then turned away with her into the garden. "That woman in the wheelchair, those women around her—get them off the block and down the street." And he was gone among his officers, keeping order as tangles of wedding guests moved quickly out of the garden, and a few confused elderly folks milled together in panic. Charlie grabbed the wheelchair as Wilma corralled half a dozen frail ladies.

THE CATS DIDN'T SEE CHARLIE AND WILMA COME OUT. THEY were watching the kit where she had fled back across the street and up the trellis. The boy had climbed again too. Running across the roof, he knelt, reaching for something. But again the kit landed on his shoulders raking and biting. What was the matter with her? Then suddenly all the cops were running, fanning out across the street, staring up at the roof. The boy snatched something from the roof and spun around, racing across the shingles, trying to dislodge the kit. He slipped and fell, and seemed to drop in slow-motion, falling and twisting.

He hit the ground and an explosion rocked the garden. A sudden cloud of smoke hid the church and trees, smoke filled with flying flecks of plaster and torn wood and broken shingles—as if the church had been ground up and vomited out again by a giant blower.

The side of the church was gone. There was only a jagged, smoking hole where the wall of the church had been.

Ragged fragments of the building, and of broken furniture and wedding flowers lay scattered across the bricks and clinging to trees and bushes, and still the sky rained debris.

The two cats crouched clinging to the branches choking with smoke and dust, shaken by the impact. Had it been a gas explosion? Maybe the church furnace? But it was a warm day, and the furnace would not be running. They stared down at a young woman staunching a child's bloody arm, at a young couple holding each other, an old woman weeping, at officers clearing the area. A bomb. It had been a bomb.

But no villager could do this, not now when the very thought of a bomb was so painful for every human soul.

They saw no one badly hurt, no one was down. "The kit," Dulcie said. "Where is the kit?" She hardly remembered later how she and Joe reached the kit, where she clung in a pine tree across the street. She only vaguely remembered racing between parked cars and people's legs, scorching up the pine tree and cuddling the kit against her, licking her frightened face.

Below the pine, officers surrounded the boy. Had that small boy caused the explosion? He couldn't be more than ten. A ragged child, very white and still.

That was why the kit had jumped him! To stop him! Then she had raced to Clyde. Dulcie licked the kit harder. What kind of child *was* that boy, to do such a thing? *He's just a child,* Dulcie thought, shivering. But then she saw the boy's eyes so cold and hard, and she felt her stomach wrench.

Sirens filled the air. Dulcie looked around for Charlie and Wilma. *Don't let anyone be dead, don't let anyone be badly hurt.* What kind of sophisticated electronic equipment did this little boy have, to set off such an explosion? He seemed just an ordinary, dirty-faced kid, handcuffed now and held between two cops. Just a boy—except for those hard black eyes.

But as Dulcie and Joe peered down from the pine tree with the kit snuggled between them, the boy looked around as if searching for someone. His gaze rose to the roofs and surrounding trees—and stopped on the three cats.

He looked straight at the kit, his eyes widening with rage.

And the tattercoat kit dropped her ears and backed away, deeper among the dark, concealing branches.

4

THE DEBRIS-FILLED SMOKE TWISTED AND BEGAN slowly to settle. The dropping sun sent its deep afternoon light streaming down through the torn roof of the church, illuminating airborne flecks like falling snow through which officers searched the rubble for wounded, and quickly moved shocked onlookers away, in case of a second blast.

No one seemed badly injured; but the miracle of escape was slow to instruct the villagers. They stood in little clusters holding one another, the shock of the deed reverberating in every face, beating in every heart.

Charlie looked around her at the white petals of the wedding bouquets scattered across the detritus—as if some precocious flower girl had thrown a tantrum flinging her pretty treasures. Near her an old woman stood with her handkerchief pressed to her bloody forehead. As Charlie moved to help her, she heard Ryan shout for a medic, and saw Ryan supporting Cora Lee French, Cora Lee's dark arm around Ryan's shoulder. Holding the old woman, Charlie wanted to run to Cora Lee.

Pressing her handkerchief to the old woman's forehead,

Charlie got her to sit down on the sidewalk. It was not a deep cut, only a scratch in an area that would naturally bleed heavily. As the woman rested against her, Charlie looked at the church where she and Max were to have been married. Where, if they hadn't been alerted, she and Max, Clyde and Wilma and the minister would have been standing with nearly the whole village crowded around them.

The three standing walls of the church bristled with shards of debris embedded in the cracked plaster. The rows of velvet-padded chairs that had awaited the wedding guests lay splintered into kindling and blackened rags. One side of the carved lectern lay whole and apparently untouched, smeared black and dotted with silver-bright specks. The corner of a cardboard box lay near it, still covered with silver paper. How odd, that the center had remained nearly undamaged. Sirens screamed again in the narrow street as two more ambulances careened to the curb beside squad cars whose trunks stood open, officers snatching out first aid equipment.

No villager could have done this. No villager could have performed such an act. Not now . . . No one could have wanted to destroy . . .

Destroy Max . . . ?

Destroy Max as someone had tried to destroy him last winter, setting him up for murder? Charlie began to shiver, she was ice-cold. She turned her eyes to Max across the garden where he stood talking with two officers. Was this what their marriage would be like, this icy internal terror? Would she go through all their life together ridden by this terrible fear, so that fear touched every smallest joy, turned all their life ugly?

Fury filled her, hot rage. She wanted to pound someone, pound the person who had done this. She looked across the street at Clyde and the officers, handcuffing that young boy. And she turned away, not wanting to think a child had done such a thing.

She watched the two medics arguing with Cora Lee until at last Cora Lee obediently lay down again on the stretcher. She watched Max talking on his field phone as his officers cleared the street, sending people home. She walked the old woman to the open door of Cora Lee's ambulance and saw her settled inside. As she turned away, the squad car carrying the boy passed her, the kid scowling out from behind the grid, his face all sharp angles and angry. So very angry.

THE CATS WATCHED A SQUAD CAR TAKE THE BOY AWAY, THE child crouched sullenly in the backseat behind the wire barrier. Officer Green had taken the broken garage door opener from the boy's pocket. The small remote had looked badly smashed where the kid had fallen on it. They could see, within the torn church, detectives Davis and Garza photographing the scene, Juana Davis holding the strobe lights down among the dark rubble so Garza could shoot close-ups of scraps of splintered wood and torn carpet and shattered plaster and bits of silver gift wrap. Dulcie shivered. That prettily wrapped box that they had glimpsed and ignored. That innocent-looking box.

She didn't understand humans, she didn't understand how the bright and inventive human mind could warp into such hunger to destroy. She didn't understand how the human soul, that in its passion could create the wonders of civilization, could allow that same passion to warp in on itself and burn, instead, with this sick thirst for destruction.

Evil, she thought. *Pure evil. That kind of sickness is part of the ultimate dark, the dark power that would suck all life to destruction.*

"Well, there *will* be a wedding," Dulcie said softly, lashing her tail, looking at the kit, then looking down at their human friends, at Charlie in her blood-splattered wedding dress holding two children by the hands as their mother tried to calm a screaming baby. "There *will* be a wedding." That boy had destroyed the wall of the church, but he hadn't destroyed anyone's spirit. He had not destroyed love, or human will.

She watched officers stringing yellow crime tape, securing the area. She had heard Captain Harper calling for a bomb team, she supposed out of San Jose. She knew that those forensic technicians would spend hours going over the area, photographing, finger-printing, bagging every possible bit of evidence. But once the team arrived, when the work at hand was organized, would there be a wedding? Surely somewhere within the village, Charlie and Max Harper would be married.

Beside her, the kit was hunkered down among the branches looking so small and miserable that Dulcie nosed at her with concern. "What, Kit? What's the matter?"

The kit shut her eyes.

"Don't, Kit. Don't look *sad*. You saved lives. You saved hundreds of lives. You're a hero. But how did you know? How did you know what he planned?"

"I heard them. I heard that old man telling the boy what to do, an old man with a beard and a bent foot. He shook the boy and told him to wait until everyone was in the church, the bride and groom and minister and everyone, then to punch the opener. I didn't know what he meant. He said to punch it and run, to get off the roof fast and get away. The boy was angry but he climbed up to the roof and the old man hobbled away. I didn't mean for the bomb to explode, I wanted to *stop* whatever would happen, I didn't mean for a bomb to go off," the kit said miserably.

Dulcie licked the kit's ears. "If you hadn't jumped that boy, then warned Clyde, then jumped the boy again, he would have killed everyone. You're a hero, Kit. Do you understand that? Who knows how many lives you saved."

Dulcie twitched an ear. "To those who know, to Clyde and Wilma and Charlie—to all of *us*, Kit, you'll forever be a hero."

"Absolutely a hero," Joe Grey said softly, nudging the kit. "But where did the old man go? Did you see where he went? Did he have a car?"

The kit shook her whiskers. "I didn't see which way. I didn't see him get in a car, but . . ." She paused, thinking. "He said to the boy, 'The truck will be gone.' And there was an old truck parked down the side street, a rusty old pickup, sort of brown. And when . . . when I jumped the boy and the man ran, I think . . . I *think* I heard a rattley motor."

Joe's eyes widened, and immediately he left them, backing down the tree and streaking for Clyde's open convertible. He would not, among a crowd of humans, ordinarily be so brazen as to leap into the car and paw into the side pocket, hauling out Clyde's cell phone. But he had little choice. Looking up over the car door, seeing no one watching him, he punched in a number.

Dulcie and Kit heard Max Harper's cell phone ringing, across the garden. How strange it was that Joe's electronic message could zip through the sky who knew how many miles to some phantom tower in just an instant, and back again to Harper's phone where he stood only a few feet away.

Harper answered, listened, and gave an order that sent officers racing away on foot through the village, and sent squad cars swerving out fast to cruise the streets looking for an old brown truck and for the old man who was the boy's accomplice. And above the searching officers, Dulcie and the kit raced away too. Flying across the rooftops they watched the sidewalks below, peering down into shadowed niches and recessed doorways where a hidden figure might be missed; and soon on the roofs two blocks away they saw Joe, also searching.

For nearly two hours, as dusk fell, and as the police combed the streets and shops below, the cats crossed back and forth along balconies and oak branches and across peaks and shingles, peering into dark rooftop hiding places and in through second-floor windows looking for the bearded, crippled old man.

There was no sign of him. When at last the search ended, below in the darkening streets the entire population of the village joined to move the site of the wedding. Men and women in party clothes hauled tables and chairs from dozens of shops, carrying them for blocks, setting them up in the center of the village. And when the cats returned to the church garden, it was lined with cars again—the bomb team had arrived.

Within the barrier of yellow tape, grid markers had been laid out. Five forensics officers were down on their hands and knees under powerful spotlights working with cameras and small instruments and collection bags, carefully labeling each item they removed. The process seemed, even to a patient feline hunter, incredibly tedious. Watching from the roof across the street, the cats were overwhelmed by the work that must be accomplished. Clyde found them there, intently watching, perched on the edge of the roof like three owls in the cool and gathering dusk.

"Come on, cats. It's time for the ceremony. Come on, or you'll make us late."

5

IN THE DARKENING EVENING, OCEAN AVENUE'S two lanes were closed off by rows of sawhorses; and its wide grassy median beneath spreading eucalyptus trees was filled with wavering lights; lights shifted and wandered and drew together in constellations. Nearly every villager carried a candle or battery-operated torch or, here and there, a soft-burning oil lantern retrieved from the bearer's camping supplies.

Down the center of the median a narrow path had been left between the crowd, for the wedding procession. The long grassy carpet led to a circle of lawn before a giant eucalyptus whose five mammoth trunks fanned out from the ground like a great hand reaching to the star-strewn sky. Within the velvet-green circle ringed by wedding guests, the pastor waited, holy book in hand. Beside him, the groom looked more than usually solemn, his thin, lined face stern and watchful.

Tall and straight in his dark uniform, Max Harper was not encumbered with the cop's full equipment, with flashlight, hand-cuffs, mace, the regulation array of weapons and tools; only his loaded automatic hung at his hip. His gaze down the long green aisle where the bride would approach was more than usually watchful; and along the outer limits of the crowd, his uniformed officers stood at attention in wary surveillance. This was what the world had come to, even for an event as simple as a village wedding—particularly for such an event. Harper's nerves were raw with concern for Charlie.

She stood a block away at the other end of the grassy path waiting, apparently demurely, between her aunt Wilma and Dallas Garza, her red hair bright in the candlelight, her hands steady on the bridal bouquet of white and yellow daisies—she had chosen his favorite flowers. No stain of blood shone on her white linen dress or on Wilma's blue gown, as if the two women had diligently sponged away the slightest hint of trouble.

Charlie did not look up along the grassy path at him but glanced repeatedly to the street watching for Clyde's arrival. Max got the impression that the moment the best man's yellow roadster appeared, at one of the side-street barriers, she meant to sprint down the lane double-time and get on with the wedding, before another bomb rent apart their world.

But then when Clyde's car did race into view, parking in the red before the sawhorses, Max saw Charlie laugh. He couldn't see what she found amusing, but among the guests who had turned to look, several people smiled.

Only when Clyde and Ryan came across the street, did he catch a flash of movement along the ground—three small racing shadows almost immediately gone again from view, among the wedding guests. He wasn't sure whether to laugh, or to swear at Clyde. Buddies they were, but there were limits. Watching his best man push through to take his place, Max fixed him with a look that would intimidate the coldest felon.

Clyde's sly grin told him that indeed cats were among the wedding guests; and the faintest scrambling sound behind Max told him those guests were now above his head, in the branches of the eucalyptus tree—doing what? Cats did not attend weddings, cats

41

did not know about weddings. Max looked down the long grassy aisle to Charlie, needing her commonsense response to such matters. This business of weirdly behaving cats left him out of his element, off-center and shaky, as nothing else could do.

THE INSTANT CLYDE PARKED, THE THREE CATS HAD LEAPED OUT of the open convertible and streaked across the empty eastbound lane hoping not to be noticed on the dark street. Slipping into the crowd, swerving between shoes and pant cuffs and silk-clad ankles they stormed up the far side of the giant eucalyptus. Concealing themselves among its leafy branches, they looked down on the crowd below, massed in the falling evening among the sheltering trees.

"Oh," Dulcie whispered. "Oh," said the kit. The faces of the villagers were lighted from beneath by candles and torches like the faces of children carrying votive candles in solemn procession. The scene put Dulcie in mind of some ancient woodland wedding performed in a simpler time, perhaps a Celtic ceremony in a far and magical past.

The minute Clyde took his place beside the groom, Wilma began her measured walk up the grassy aisle, her step dictated not by wedding music, for there was none, but by the rhythm of the sea that broke some blocks away on the sandy shore, the surf's eternal hush deep and sustaining. Behind Wilma, the bride approached on the arm of Dallas Garza between the flickering lights, her dress gleaming white. "She'll have sponged it," Dulcie whispered.

Some of the wedding guests sported bandages; but only Cora Lee French was in the hospital. "For observation," Clyde had said. Cora Lee's lack of a spleen after her attack and surgery last spring prompted her doctor to keep close watch on her. Very likely, the cats thought, Cora Lee was fully prepared to enjoy the wedding secondhand from her friends' eager descriptions and from the plates of wedding cake and party food that would be carried over to the hospital.

As Charlie, Wilma, and Dallas took their places, Dulcie felt a tear slide down her whiskers. The ceremony was simple. At, "who gives this bride to be wed?" when Detective Garza led Charlie forward to stand beside Captain Harper, Joe Grey muttered a little prayer that in all the confusion Clyde hadn't lost the rings. Only when Clyde slipped his hand in his coat pocket and the ring boxes appeared, did the cats relax, watching with fascination as the traditional words *to love and to cherish* formed a deep and solemn promise. Dulcie's eyes were indeed misty. Looking down through the branches, the cats watched Max Harper place the gold band on Charlie's finger. As Charlie slipped Max's ring on, another tear slid down Dulcie's nose, a tear that no ordinary cat could shed. Joe looked at her intently. "What's to cry about? This is the *start* of their new life."

"A tomcat wouldn't understand. All females cry at weddings, it's in the genes."

But in truth all three cats were touched by this human ritual. The kit snuffled into her whiskers; and as the villagers gathered around the bride and groom kissing and hugging them, the cats moved higher up the great tree, easing out along a wide branch through the softly rustling foliage, where they had a wider view of the village street. As Max and Charlie mingled with their friends, and someone's CD player brought alive the forties swing that Charlie and Max loved, Ryan and her Uncle Dallas left the party hurrying in the direction of the police station.

"To have a look at the boy," Joe said. "To see if Ryan *does* know him."

"That seems so strange," Dulcie replied, "to think that she saw him all that far away, in San Andreas."

Earlier, at the bombed church, coming down from the roof and allowing Clyde to carry them to the car, they had crowded gratefully onto Ryan's lap, even Joe Grey with no show of macho independence.

"Do you mind holding them? I think they're scared."

"We're all scared. They can comfort me." Ryan had hugged the cats, crushing them gently together; they had ridden the few blocks to the wedding like three furry prizes she might have won at some carnival booth, three rag animals held tight by a fearful little girl. "Does anyone know the boy?" Ryan said. "Know who he is?"

Clyde turned to look at her. "Detective Davis thought she recognized him. I got the impression Garza might know him, but he wasn't saying much."

"I might know him. Or he's a dead ringer for one of the boys hanging around the trailer, in San Andreas."

"That would be pretty strange. I got the feeling he's local, that he might be involved with that last bust Harper made, that meth lab up the valley. I think the guy they sent up had a kid."

"I think it's the same boy, Clyde."

He looked over at her. "Was there an old man with him, up there?"

She shook her head. "I saw only the boy. Tell me again how you knew about the bomb, what made you run shouting for everyone to get out. Through a *phone call*?"

"I'd gone into the church with my phone in my suit pocket, and someone said it made a lump. I went back to the car to leave it. When it rang I wasn't going to answer, I don't know what made me pick up. It was a woman, whispering. Said there was a bomb, that a boy on the roof had the trigger, a garage-door opener." Clyde shrugged. "You know the rest. I didn't dare *not* believe her."

Clyde was, Joe thought, improving his lying skills. At least he had, apparently, convinced Ryan.

Now, below the cats, the bride and groom drifted away among a tangle of friends, heading for the party tables. Only Wilma remained beneath the eucalyptus tree lingering in the grassy circle. Looking up, she spoke softly—anyone who knew Wilma Getz knew that it was not unusual to hear her talk to her cats.

"Come on, Kit. I'm going to the hospital."

The kit's eyes widened.

"Taking Cora Lee some party food."

Kit scooted down at once, so eagerly that she nearly fell backward into Wilma's arms. The cats knew the kit had been worried about the Creole woman. The two of them were fast friends. Though Cora Lee had no notion of the little cat's true nature, the kit was special to her. This last spring, they had spent six weeks onstage together charming their audiences. No actress and her protégé can star together bringing down the house every night without forming an indestructible bond.

CARRYING THE KIT ON HER SHOULDER, WILMA HEADED AWAY through the crowd. "I have a shopping bag in the car that should hide you, should get you into her room." Reaching her car, she turned so they could both look back, watching the bride and groom dancing the first dance in the westbound lane of Ocean, the tall, handsome couple laughing as their shoes scuffed on the rough asphalt.

"They are happy," Wilma whispered. "Safe, Kit, thanks to you. Thanks to their guardian angel, they are safe and happy. Very, very happy."

The kit smiled, and snuggled closer. How strange life was, how strange and amazing. She never knew, one moment to the next, what new wonder would fill the world around her, dazzling and challenging her—and sometimes terrifying her.

The inside of the car smelled deliciously of the party food that Wilma was taking to Cora Lee. But as the kit settled down on the front seat beside her friend, extravagantly purring, neither she nor Wilma imagined that the day's events would not be the last ugliness to twist this weekend awry and leave its ugly mark.

DESCENDING THE GREAT EUCALYPTUS TREE, DULCIE AND JOE Grey backed precariously down the slick bark below the branch line, slipping, dropping the last six feet, and headed directly across the street to the long buffet tables set up in front of the village shops.

At the center table where bottles of champagne were being popped, Max and Charlie stood cutting the cake, exchanging bites, smearing white icing across each other's faces as the occasion was duly recorded by a dozen flashing cameras. The cats glanced at each other, purring. A gentleness filled the crowd, a gentleness in people's voices and in their slower movements, an extra kindliness washing over the village, born of the near-disaster.

They saw Ryan and Dallas coming up the street, returning from the station where Ryan must have had a look at the young bomber. As she joined Charlie at a small table, Dallas stood conferring with Harper, then headed away toward the church to oversee the bomb team. And Harper himself headed quickly for the station, leaving Charlie to the first of the endless separations and delays that would accompany her life married to a cop. The cats trotted near them, to listen, settling down on the sidewalk between some potted geraniums.

Ryan sat down, touching Charlie's hand. "You look pale."

"I'm fine. Was it the same boy?"

"Same kid. Dallas knows him; he's Curtis Farger."

"Son of the guy Max and Dallas busted?" Charlie said. "He's supposed to be down the coast with his mother. Maybe she's not too reliable."

The trial of Curtis's father had ended just three weeks before. Gerrard Farger was doing six years on the manufacture of an illegal substance, and two years each on three counts of possession. The meth lab he'd put together had been in the woods below Molena Point, a shed behind a two-room cabin, the property roped off now with warning signs, and stinking so powerfully of drugs that it would likely have to be destroyed. Though the chemicals and lab equipment had been removed, the walls and floor and every fiber of the building still exuded fumes as lethal as cyanide.

"I had a look at him through the one-way mirror," Ryan said. "When I was sure it was the same kid, Dallas took me on in. Kid looked at me like he'd never seen me. I told him I'd cleaned up my truck, found the cracker crumbs and Hershey wrappers in my tarp."

"I'm missing a beat, here."

Ryan laughed. "I didn't know what had happened in my truck, only that someone had been in it. That had to be on my way down from San Andreas, or that night after I got home. But then when I saw the kid . . . well, it fit. I asked him if he'd hitched a ride down from the mountains. He just stared at me. When I pushed him, he said, 'What of it, bitch? I don't weigh nothin'. How much gas could it take?'"

Ryan shook her head. "Not a bit like the nice, polite, innocent kid he let me think he was, hanging around the Jakes job."

"You're *sure* it's the same boy?"

"The same. Same straight black hair, with a cowlick—big swirl on the left side. Same big bones, square-cut dirty nails. Same coal-black eyes and straight brows with those little scraggly hairs." Ryan gave Charlie a wry smile. "He was so eager and polite when he and his two friends showed up around the trailer.

"And just now in jail, underneath his hateful stare and rude mouth, I think the kid was scared."

"He should be scared," Charlie said. "He's in major trouble."

"Dallas called Curtis's mother. She said the boy wasn't there right then, that he'd gone to a movie. A ten-year-old boy going to a movie alone, at this time of night? Dallas asked her what movie. She didn't know, said she'd forgotten what the kid told her. Said whatever was playing in town. That there was only one theater, and one screen. Said she guessed he'd be home by midnight." Ryan shook her head. "A ten-year-old kid running the streets at midnight. Dallas plans to go down in the morning, have a talk with her."

Charlie nodded. "If that old man is Gerrard Farger's father—Curtis's grandfather . . . They've had a warrant out for him. Max and Dallas were sure the two ran the lab together, but when they busted Farger the old man was gone, not a trace. Now, if there's a connection to San Andreas, that's a whole new track to follow. We may not make it to Alaska."

"I'm sorry."

Charlie shook her head. "Whatever Max decides is okay. We can take the cruise later. That old man needs to be stopped. At the time of the drug raid, the second bedroom in the Farger cabin had been cleaned out, where he might have bunked with the boy. Nothing but a bare cot against the wall and an old mattress on the floor, and the kid's clothes. Juvenile officer picked those up after the bust, when he took the kid down to his mother. Not a sign of the old man, and during the trial Gerrard wouldn't say a word to incriminate his father."

Ryan shrugged. "Nothing like family loyalty. Were they part of a bigger operation?"

"Max doesn't think so. More of a family business," Charlie said wryly. "Farger apparently thought he could run a small operation without alerting the cops or the cartel."

Ryan laughed. "Sooner or later the cartel would have known about it—would have destroyed the lab or taken it over, made Farger knuckle under and follow their orders." Both young women were very aware of the powerful Mexican drug cartel that operated in the Bay Area. "He's lucky Max made the bust, he's safer in jail. Was he farming marijuana too?"

"DEA is investigating," Charlie said. The cartel used its meth profits to bankroll marijuana operations across the state—a behemoth of criminal activity as dark and invasive, in the view of law enforcement, as if the black death were creeping across California destroying families and taking lives. In the national forests and other remote areas, the marijuana patches were guarded by gunmen who shot to kill, so intent on protecting their crops that a deer hunter or a hiker venturing into the wrong area might never be heard from again.

And the toxic waste from meth labs was dumped down storm

drains so it went into the sea, or was poured into streams so it got into the water supply, or was poured on the ground where it could stay for years poisoning fields and killing wildlife. Whoever said doing meth didn't hurt anyone but the user didn't have a clue.

"You *are* pale," Ryan said softly. "We shouldn't be talking about this stuff. You want to get out of the crowd, go somewhere quiet and lie down?"

"I'm fine," Charlie said crossly. "I don't need to lie down."

But she wasn't fine, she couldn't get over being scared. She'd thought she was okay until, walking up the grassy aisle, with all their friends, everyone she knew and cared about, standing like a wall to protect her, she kept imagining the grass exploding in front of Dallas and Wilma, exploding with all those people crowding close.

She felt ice-cold again. Her hands began to shake.

Ryan put her arm around her, hugging Charlie against her shoulder.

Charlie shook her head. "I'm sorry. Delayed reaction."

"I guess that's allowed. You don't have to be stoic and fearless just because you married a cop."

"It would help."

They looked at each other with perfect understanding; but they glanced up when Clyde and Wilma approached their table.

Wilma was wrapped in a blue cashmere stole over her pale gown, against the night's chill. She carried a woven shopping bag that bulged and wriggled.

Clyde carried two paper plates heaped with canapés and salads and sliced meats. As he set one in the center of the table and the other underneath, Joe and Dulcie slipped beneath the table; and from Wilma's shopping bag the kit hopped out, strolling purposefully under the table to claim her share.

"Cora Lee's fine," Wilma said. "Apparently something hit her in the head, but no concussion. They want her overnight, though." When, early in the spring, Cora Lee had walked into the middle of a robbery and murder, she had been hit by such a blow to her middle that her spleen had ruptured and had to be removed. The dusky-skinned actress told them later she was terrified she would never sing again. But she had sung, the lead in the village's little theater production of *Thorns of Gold*. With the kit as impromptu costar during the entire run, the play had sold out every night.

"Dallas is trying to get Curtis Farger remanded over to juvenile," Clyde said. "But since the fire, with their building gone, they're not eager to take any kids. Kids scattered all over, in temporary quarters, and not great security." He looked at Charlie. "Max would be smart to get a move on, before you decide to enjoy the cruise without him."

"Maybe we'll just do a few days in San Francisco, and book the cruise for next spring." Their reservation at the St. Francis gave them three days in the city before boarding their liner for the inland passage. At the moment, that sounded pretty good to Charlie.

"Can you cancel a cruise like that?" Wilma said. "Even Max . . ." She watched Charlie, frowning. She wanted her niece and Max to get on that ship and be gone, to be away from the Farger family.

"Max knows someone," Charlie said. "When he made the reservations, that was part of the package, that if something urgent came up, we could cancel." She glanced beneath the table where the cats feasted, Joe and Dulcie eating fastidiously, the kit slurping so loudly that Ryan looked under too, and laughed.

WHEN THE CATS HAD DEMOLISHED THEIR QUICHE, SEAFOOD salads, rare roast beef, curried lamb, and wedding cake, they stretched out between the feet of their friends for a leisurely wash, grooming thoroughly from whiskers to tail. They could have trotted over to the jail and had a look at Curtis Farger, but they were too full and comfortable. And Joe didn't think they'd hear much.

Very likely Curtis had already been questioned as much as he could be, until a juvenile officer arrived in the morning to protect the kid's rights. Sleeking his whiskers with a damp paw, Joe Grey thought about the legal rights of young boys who set bombs to kill people.

No one liked to believe that a ten-year-old child had intended, and nearly succeeded in, mass murder. In the eyes of the law, Curtis and his grandfather were innocent until proven guilty. But in Joe Grey's view they were both guilty until proven otherwise. If you attacked innocent people with all claws raking, you should know that your opponent would retaliate.

Charlie said, "This afternoon at the church—before the bomb—I felt like I was nineteen again, so scared and giddy. And then after the bomb went off, it was . . . I wasn't nineteen anymore, couldn't remember ever having been so young." She chafed her hands together.

"There was some reason," Ryan said, "some profound reason, why that bomb went off prematurely. What made the kid turn and run? What made him trip and fall? You couldn't see much under those overhanging trees. He was lucky he didn't break something, falling off that roof. Just bruises—and those scratches on his face from the branches." She looked at Clyde. "Do you think he *would* have set off the bomb if he hadn't fallen? Do you think he *would* have pressed that little button?"

Clyde and Charlie and Wilma avoided looking at each other. All were thinking the same. Had no one seen Kit attack the boy?

"The boy went to a lot of trouble," Clyde said, "to suddenly abandon the idea. Whether he made the bomb or the old man did, don't you think a ten-year-old would do what he was told to do? If the old man forced the kid to go up on the roof, if he threatened Curtis . . ."

"You're saying he *would* have done it," Ryan said. "But then fate stepped in—as if Max and Charlie's guardian angel was looking after them, looking after all of us."

Wilma lifted her champagne glass. "Here's to that particular angel. May our guardian angels never desert us." And Wilma did not need to look beneath the table to know that the guardian angel was pressing against her ankle. That particular angel purred so powerfully that she shook both herself and Wilma.

6

THE PLATTERS OF PARTY FOOD WERE EMPTY, THE wedding cake had all been eaten or small pieces wrapped in paper napkins and carried away as little talismans to provide midnight dreams of future happiness. The empty champagne bottles had been neatly gathered and bagged, the tables and chairs folded and loaded into waiting trucks. In the quiet night the grassy, tree-sheltered median was empty now and silent and seemed to Ryan and Clyde painfully lonely. As they headed for the few parked cars, Ryan took his hand.

The bride and groom had left for San Francisco, for the bridal suite at the St. Francis, the loveliest old hotel in the city. They had joked about arriving in Max's Chevy king cab, and had talked about renting a limo but considered that extravagant. The pickup wasn't fancy but it was safe on the highway, and in the city they would put it in storage during their cruise. They had three days to enjoy San Francisco before they moved into the stateroom of their luxury liner and sailed for Alaska—or before Max realized that he couldn't leave, with the bombing case working, that they'd have to head home again.

"Maybe only a three-day honeymoon," Ryan said sadly, already certain of what Max would do.

"Whatever they do," Clyde said, walking her to Dallas's car, "they're happy." He gave Ryan a hug by way of good night, watched her settle in beside Dallas, then swung into his yellow convertible to drive the three blocks home, leaving Ryan and her uncle heading for her place to collect what little evidence might remain in the bed of her truck. Strange about the kid hitching a ride, hiding under the tarp where he couldn't be seen through the rear window—he had to know exactly when she'd be leaving San Andreas. He had made his way into the town itself, maybe hitch-hiking, to wait for her there.

Clyde drove home thinking uneasily about Joe, and about the kit and Dulcie. The cats would be into this case tooth and claw.

A bombing was a different game than shoplifting, or domestic violence, or even domestic murder. A bomb investigation of any kind could be more than dangerous—and you could bet Joe Grey would be onto it like ticks on a hound.

Short of locking the cat up, there wasn't much Clyde could do to stop him.

Joe claimed he had no right to try. And maybe Joe was right. As much as Clyde wanted to protect Joe, the tomcat was a sentient being, and sentient beings had free choice. Joe could always argue him down on that point.

Parking in his drive, Clyde took a few minutes to put up the top of the antique Chevy. Following the slow, cumbersome routine, pulling and straightening the canvas and snapping the many grommets in place, he thought how strange and amazing, the way his life had turned out. Who would have imagined when he was living in San Francisco walking home from work that particular evening, when he paused to kneel by the gutter looking at that little bundle of gray fur among the trash and empty wine bottles. Reaching to touch what he was sure was a dead kitten, who could imagine the wonder that lay, barely alive, beneath his reaching hand?

When he took up the little limp bundle and wrapped it in his wool scarf and headed for the nearest vet, who could have dreamed the off-the-wall scenario that would soon change his life? That he was holding in his hand a creature of impossible talents, a beast the like of which maybe no other human had ever seen, at least in this century.

No other human, except Wilma.

It didn't bear pondering on, that Joe Grey and Dulcie had ended up with him and Wilma, who had been fast friends ever since Clyde was eight years old and Wilma was in graduate school. Through all of Wilma's moves in her career as a parole officer, and through Clyde's own several moves, they had remained close.

But how and why had the two cats come to them?

Dulcie said it was preordained. Clyde didn't like to think about that stuff, any more than Joe did. The idea that some power totally beyond his comprehension had placed those two cats where they would meet, not only kept him awake at night but could render him sleepless for weeks.

And yet . . .

Fate, Dulcie said.

Neither Clyde or the tomcat believed in predestination, both were quite certain that your life was what you made it. And yet . . .

Entering the living room and switching on the low-watt lamp by the front door, he found Joe fast asleep in his well-clawed arm-chair. The gray tomcat lay on his back, snoring, his white belly and white chest exposed, his four white feet straight up in the air. Obviously over-full of party food. He must have left the reception early and hiked right on home and passed out, a surfeited victim of gluttony. Clyde turned on a second lamp.

Joe woke, staring at up Clyde with blazing eyes. "Did you have to do that? Isn't one lamp enough? I was just drifting off."

"You were ten feet under, snoring like a bulldog. Why aren't you hunting? Too stuffed with wedding cake? Where's Dulcie?"

"She took the kit home, she doesn't want her out hunting." Joe flipped over. Digging his front claws into the arm of his chair, he stretched so deeply that Clyde could feel, in his own spine, every vertebrae separate, every ligament loosen. "She's worried about Kit, afraid that old man saw her jump the boy and will come back to find her."

Clyde sat down on the couch. This thought was not far-fetched. Already Joe and Dulcie had been stalked by a killer because of their unique talents. If the kit had foiled the old man's plans, wouldn't he wonder what kind of cat this was? Wouldn't his rage lead him back to her? Clyde looked intently at Joe. "So where are you going to hide her?"

"I was thinking about Cora Lee French, when she gets home from the hospital. Since the play, she and the kit are fast friends. And that big house, that the four senior ladies bought for their retirement, has a thousand hiding places. Sitting there on the edge of the canyon, it would be a cinch for a cat to escape down among the trees and brushes—that old man would never find her, it's wild as hell in those canyons."

"Right. She can just slip away among the bobcats and coyotes, to say nothing of a possible cougar."

Joe shrugged. "We hunt that canyon now and then, we've never had a problem."

Clyde headed for the bedroom, pulling off his suit jacket and loosening his tie. You couldn't argue with a cat. Behind him Joe hit the floor with a thud, and came trotting past him into the bedroom. Glancing up at Clyde, he clawed impatiently at the sarouk rug, waiting for Clyde to turn back the spread.

Share and share alike was okay, cat and man each claiming half the bed. But one couldn't expect a poor little cat to turn back the covers.

Grumbling, Clyde pulled off the spread. At once Joe leaped to the center of the blanket and began to wash, waiting in silence for Clyde's inevitable lecture. *You don't need to take your half in the middle.*

And as to that canyon, you can't possibly foresee all the dangers in that canyon. You do remember the mountain lion? And we can all hear the coyotes at night yipping down there. And those bands of raccoons . . .

When Clyde's words of caution were not forthcoming, Joe stopped washing to look at him.

Clyde said, "You are very cavalier when it comes to the kit's tender young life."

"That isn't fair. That is really insulting—to me, and to the kit. Kit can smell another animal, she knows how to slip away."

Clyde didn't answer.

"What would *you* do," Joe said, "if you were out on the hills and a cougar came prowling? You would simply keep your distance, use a little common sense."

"I'd get the hell out of there. And I'm not seven inches tall." He glared at Joe. "You can be so—cats can be so . . .

"Irritating," Joe Grey said, smiling. *"Cats can be so maddening and unreasonable."* Turning his back, he pawed his pillow into the required nest shape for absolute comfort. He was just settling down, warm and purring, when Clyde pulled off his shirt. Joe sat up again, staring at Clyde's bare back, at the dried blood and raw, red wounds. "What happened to you? You look like you had a really wild night."

"Don't be crude." Clyde twisted around pressing against the dresser to look in the mirror. "That's the kit's handiwork—when she jumped on me to warn us about the bomb."

Joe watched Clyde dig through his top dresser drawer searching for the medication he used when one of the cats, or their elderly retriever, Rube, had a scratch. Clyde found the salve and, twisting and straining, began to spread it on the scratches.

"Dr. Firetti would be interested to know how you're using his prescriptions. Aren't you afraid of picking up something from old Rube or one of us cats? A touch of mange? Ringworm? Poison oak? Some ancient and incurable—"

"Cool it, Joe. This is all I have. I don't handle this stuff carelessly. I don't . . ." He stared at the open tube, and at his fingers, and turned a bit pale.

"There's iodine in the medicine cabinet," Joe said helpfully. "You used it on Rube when he cut his foot, but you poured it in a cup."

Recapping the tube, Clyde went into the bathroom. Joe heard the shower running as if Clyde were scrubbing off the dangerously infected salve. When Clyde came out again he smelled sharply of iodine. Refraining from comment, Joe turned over and closed his eyes. He was soon deeply asleep while Clyde lay in the darkness worrying about ancient and unnamed diseases.

Two floodlights washed across Ryan's drive, shining down from the roof of the duplex onto her new red pickup—not new from the factory, the vehicle was a couple of years old, but new to her, in mint condition and with really low mileage. A handsome new workhorse with locked toolboxes along both sides, and a strong overhead rack to hold lumber and ladders.

In the six-foot truck bed Dallas knelt examining the tarp that she had so carefully shaken out the night before and neatly refolded, unwittingly destroying all manner of evidence.

A few long black hairs remained, which Dallas removed with tweezers, and there were some short gray hairs, that Dallas hoped might have come from the old man. "I'll need to take the tarp to the lab."

"I have another." She watched as Dallas finished up. As he packed away his fingerprinting equipment and locked the truck, she went up the outside stairs to make fresh coffee. Filling the coffeepot, she wasn't sure how much information she could supply about Curtis Farger or about his two friends. She tried to recall the other boys' names, tried to remember which direction they came from when they arrived at the trailer, and to remember any chance remarks that might help Dallas know where Curtis had been staying. It was nearly midnight. With so little sleep the night before, it was hard to keep her eyes open. As the coffee brewed she stepped into the closet and took off her suit and high-heeled pumps, pulling on a warm robe and slippers. The idea that that boy had hitched a ride for two hundred miles, and she'd never known, both angered and amused her. You had to give him credit.

Had the boy set that bomb? Had he *wanted* to set it, or was he forced to do it?

The kid was old enough to know right from wrong, old enough to have refused to take part in such a deed, even when he was ordered by a grown-up. What kind of boy was this? A child terrified of crossing the old man? Or a twisted child, excited by the thought of murdering hundreds of people?

That was a hard thought to consider. A child warped and crippled by those who had raised him? She didn't like to think about that.

Returning to the kitchen, she watched Dallas pull a box of shortbread cookies from her freezer. He had his uniform jacket off, his collar loosened, and had poured the coffee and set the sugar and cream on the table. They sat comfortably together the way they had when she was little, when she'd had a problem at school or when she wanted to hear for the hundredth time the old family stories about her dead mother, the tales about Dallas and her mother growing up on the little family acreage in the wine country east of Napa.

They remained talking until after 1:00, discussing the boy, and Ryan describing the Jakeses' mountain cabin where she had added a new great room, turning the old living room into a master bedroom. They both knew the foothill area well, the rolling slopes that were green in winter until the snows came, green again in spring until the summer sun burned the hills to the golden brown of wild hay, broken by the dark green stands of pine. Scattered vacation homes were tucked among the hills along with pockets of older shacks down in the gullies where the drainage was poor and there was no sweeping view. There were a few large estates too, back away from the main roads, like that owned by Marianna and Sullivan Landeau, the couple whose weekend house she had recently finished, here in the village. The Landeau's San Andreas estate was huge, the house overbearing with its excessive use of marble. Not at all like the simple Molena Point cottage that Ryan had designed for them.

"Must be nice to have that kind of money," Dallas said. "What, three houses—one in San Francisco?"

She nodded. "Nice, I guess. But they don't seem all that happy."

Dallas broke a cookie in half. "And the boy—you have no idea where he lived, where any of those kids lived?"

"They came up the drive, but you can't see the road from the house. I never did see which direction they came from." She named the other two boys but she didn't know their last names, she was certain she'd never heard them.

"The kids didn't talk about their families. They hung around the way kids do, showed up after school as if they were on their way home, and once or twice on the weekend. They seemed open enough, and friendly.

"Right in the beginning Curtis *was* sort of nosy, asking questions about where I was from, and did I do this kind of work for a living." She glanced wryly at Dallas. "He looked . . . when I told him where I lived he did a little double-take, then immediately covered it up. We were busy surveying and laying out the addition, I didn't think any more about it."

She looked at Dallas. "Right then, did he decide to hitch a ride, when he knew where I lived? Did he have it all planned, weeks ago?

"And what was he doing up there? How did he get there, in the first place? And did the old man hitch too? That would make me feel really stupid, if those two were both in the truck." Ryan shook her head. "Did I give them both a ride so they could set that bomb?"

"Soon as we get a lab report, likely we'll start checking stores in the San Andreas area—hardware, drugstores, feed and grocery. That might be where the meth supplies were coming from. We sure didn't turn up with big purchases here on the coast. That raid on the Farger shack netted us a hoard of antifreeze, iodine, starter fluid, fifty packs of cold tablets, just for starters. To say nothing of the mountain of empties buried in a pit. But no record—or no admission—of increased sales locally. Could be they got their bomb makings up there too."

She looked at him. "I wasn't carrying their bomb supplies! In the back of my truck!"

Dallas shrugged. "That could be hard to sort out. Ammonium sulfate, for instance. The bomb wouldn't have taken much, compared to what a farmer might use."

"That would be sick, Dallas. If I was hauling their bomb makings for them."

"What time did you leave San Andreas? Took you about four hours to get home?"

"About seven in the evening. Took me five hours. I stopped in town to load some stained-glass windows I'd bought from an antique dealer. He'd said he'd wait for me. Then halfway home I pulled into a fast-food place for a burger." She imagined the kid hunkered down under the tarp, cold in the wind and nearly drooling at the smell of greasy fries and burgers. "Why didn't I see him? How could I have loaded the windows without . . ." She stopped, and sat thinking, then looked up at Dallas.

"When I loaded the windows, the guy had given me some cardboard to buffer them, so I didn't need the tarp. I tossed it near the tailgate, still folded. There was no one in the truck, then."

"When you'd loaded the windows, what did you do?"

"I went back inside to give the shopkeeper a check."

"Was there any room left in the truck bed?"

"The windows were lined up in the front, riding on several sheets of foam insulation, and tied and padded. The back half of the truck bed was empty."

Dallas kept asking questions. Yawning, she went over every detail she could remember. The hitchhikers could easily have dropped off the back of the truck when she pulled into her drive. In the dark, she wouldn't have seen them.

"What other contacts did you have up there?"

"Lumber and building-supply people. Building inspectors. The furnace guy. A local realtor wanting me to do a remodel—a Larn Williams. Has his broker's license. Works independently."

"You take the job?"

"He wants to talk with his clients." She yawned. "I think I may skip that one. He seems interested in more than the work."

Dallas rose. "You're beat. I'll cut out of here."

She grinned up at him. "You never get tired, when you're on a case." She got up too, and hugged him, and saw him out the door. But the moment he pulled out of the drive and headed down the hill, she turned off the light and fell into bed, dropping immediately into sleep—she was definitely not a night person.

BUT OTHERS IN THE WORLD LOVED THE NIGHT, OTHERS FOUND the small hours after midnight filled with excitement. While Dallas and Ryan sat in her studio trying to get a fix on Curtis Farger, Joe Grey woke from his nap in the double bed beside Clyde, woke hearing Dulcie and the kit at his cat door banging the plastic flap.

Leaping down and trotting out through the living room, he found the kit on the porch slapping at the flap, and Dulcie stretched out on the mat beside her enjoying the cool night breeze. Within moments they were racing through the village past the dimly lit shops, dodging around potted trees, streaking through sidewalk gardens. Ocean's wide median and one-way lanes were empty now and deserted, the wedding party vanished as if all the people and lights and tables of food had been sucked up by the sea wind. The cats didn't pause until they were high in the hills where the tall grass whipped in long waves—they ran chasing one another, clearing their heads of too many voices, too much laughter, too many human problems. Alone in the night racing blindly through the tangles caring nothing tonight for caution, they laughed softly and taunted one another.

"Gotcha." Then a hiss and a playful growl, humanlike voices no louder than a whisper. *"Not me, you can't catch me." "Alley cat! You're an alley cat!" "Last one up the tree is dog meat!"*

Dulcie scorched up the branches of a huge oak that stood on the crest of the hill, a venerable grandfather flinging its black twisted arms out across the stars. Racing and leaping within the great tree, riding its wind-tossed branches like sailors clinging to a rocking masthead, the cats looked down the hills that fell away below them. Ancient curves of land that, just here, were still totally wild, empty of human civilization. And out over the sea the new moon hung thin as a blade. The stars among which the moon swam were, Dulcie liked to imagine, the eyes of spirit cats who had passed from the world before them.

The wind died. The cats paused, listening.

The night was so still they could hear each other breathing; and in the new silence, another sound.

Something running the hills, trampling the dry tall grass. A big beast running; they could hear him panting.

High above the ground, they were safe from dogs and coyotes. But cougars could climb. And now in the faint moonlight they could see the shadow running, a beast as big as a cougar, large and swift, dodging in and out among the hillside gardens.

It did not move like a cougar.

"Dog," Joe hissed. "Only a dog."

But the plunging beast ran as if demented, and it was a very big dog. Was it tracking them? Following the fresh scent of cat? In the still night, its panting implied a single-mindedness that made them climb quickly higher among the oak's dark foliage.

Contrary to common perception, some dogs could climb quite

63

handily up the sprawling branches of a tree such as this. They had seen such picures, of coon hounds on a passionate mission. Dulcie glanced at the kit worriedly because the kit was young and small.

But she wasn't small anymore, Dulcie realized.

The little tattercoat wasn't a kitten anymore. She was as big as Dulcie herself and likely was still growing. And Dulcie knew too well, from their mock battles, that this kit was as solid as a rock. Beside her on the branch the kit sat working her claws into the rough bark, staring down at the racing dog with eyes burning like twin fires. As if she couldn't wait to leap on that running back clawing and raking.

It seemed only yesterday that Dulcie and Joe had found the kit up on Hellhag hill, a little morsel of fur and bone so frightened, so bullied by the bigger cats that she never got enough to eat. Such a strange little cat, vastly afraid one minute, and giddy with adventure the next, filled with excitement and challenge.

But that had been a year ago. A year since Joe saw that car plunge over the sea cliff and found the driver dead inside, a year since Lucinda Greenlaw buried her murdered husband and fell in love with his uncle Pedric. A year since Lucinda and Pedric married, and adopted the kit and set out traveling with her. The kit had been so excited, setting off to see all the world, as the kit put it—only to turn home again very soon, the little cat dreadfully carsick. Three times the Greenlaws had tried, three journeys in which the Kit became deathly ill.

Nearly a year since Lucinda brought the little tattercoat back for good, to stay with Wilma while the elderly newlyweds traveled.

She's grown up, Dulcie thought sadly. That fact, coupled with the kit's wild and unruly temperament, made Dulcie feel not simply lonely suddenly, but sharply apprehensive.

Once the kit realized that she was a grown-up cat who need not necessarily obey her elders, what might she do then?

Crouching among the branches watching the big pale hound racing along with his nose to the ground eagerly following their scent, Dulcie's head was filled with a cat's natural fear of the unfamiliar beast, and filled as well with all the fear that had accumulated during this strangest of days. With the terrible tragedy that might have been. And with the kit's boldness in preventing that disaster.

And suddenly life seemed to Dulcie overwhelming. She felt totally adrift, she and Joe and the kit. Alone in the vast world, three cats who were like no other—not totally cat, and not human, but with talents of both. Were they, as Joe had once said, the great cat god's ultimate joke? Three amusing experiments invented for His private and twisted amusement?

She did not believe that.

And why, tonight, did her thoughts turn so frightened?

That terrible explosion had upset her more than she'd imagined.

"He's leaving," Joe said, peering down the hill where the dog had swerved away. They watched the animal disappear between cottages, causing housebound dogs all along the street to bark. Block by block, barking dogs marked his progress until all across the village, dogs bored with their dull lives chimed together delighted at any new excitement.

When the dog had vanished and the barking died, the cats dropped out of the tree and headed across the slope to hunt. Prowling in the still night, it was no trick to start a rabbit among the tall grass, to corner and dispatch it. Wedding party food was lovely, but it didn't stay with one like a nice fresh rabbit. At three in the morning, by the chimes of the courthouse clock echoing across the hills, they were crouched in the grass sharing their third rabbit when two gunshots cut the silence.

Distant shots echoing back and forth across the hills.

The cats stopped eating.

The noise could have been backfires, but they didn't think so. They hadn't heard a car purring along the streets. And when they reared up to look above the high grass, they saw no reflection of headlights moving through the dark village. And the sounds had been sharper, more precise than the fuzzed explosion of a back-fire—the cats knew too well the sound of a handgun, from listening outside the police station to cops practicing on the indoor range. And Joe and Dulcie knew, from being shot at themselves, an experience they didn't care to repeat.

The echo bouncing among the houses had made it impossible to pin the exact location, even for sensitive feline ears. But certainly the shots had come from the north end of the village. Watching the few scattered lights in that direction, looking for a house light to go on or to be extinguished, they saw no change.

When no further shots were fired, the cats headed down the hills toward home and safety. They might love adventure, but they weren't stupid. But then as they crossed the little park above Highway One, they heard a car somewhere off to their right, its progress muffled among the cottages.

Racing up a pine tree they spotted a lone car, its lights glancing across buildings and through the trees' dark foliage, shafts of intermittent light bright and then lost, then appearing again. They heard it gear down, heard it rev a little as if it had turned in somewhere. Then silence. And the moving glow was gone. They waited for some time but it did not reappear.

It had vanished maybe ten blocks to the north. They couldn't tell which street. Climbing higher up the pine they watched the dark configurations of cottages and dividing streets. No light came on in any house. The car didn't start out again but they heard a car door open and close, the soft echo bouncing along the quiet streets.

They waited a long time, sprawled uncomfortably in the pine tree. The thin, prickly branches were not as accommodating as the easy limbs of a eucalyptus or oak; and the pine was sticky too, its pitch clinging in their fur in hard masses that couldn't be pulled out and that were impossible to lick out. The only thing to do about pine pitch was to let Wilma or Clyde cut away the offending knots, an operation the cats abhorred. The darkness seemed lonely and frightening, now, to these cats who loved the night. Over on Ocean, where only hours before the streets had burned with candlelight and rung with music and laughter, now all was deserted and still and, after the two shots, the silence seemed laced with threat.

Quickly Joe backed down the rough trunk. "That car's in for the night. Probably had nothing to do with the shots—if they *were* shots." Yawning, he watched the sleepy kit above them turn to make her way down headfirst. "Wake up, Kit! Don't do that." How many times did they have to tell her. "Watch what you're doing! Turn around. Dig your claws in."

The kit came down in a tumble, clawing bark and leaping to the sidewalk. She might be grown big, but she still pummeled out of a tree like a silly kitten. Righting herself, she looked at the older cats with embarrassment.

Dulcie winked at Joe and glanced away in the direction of Jolly's alley. She had meant to part from him and head home with the kit, to a warm bed beside Wilma. But maybe a few minutes behind Jolly's Deli would cheer the kit and smooth away her fears.

Joe twitched a whisker, grinning, and headed for Jolly's.

But, padding up the sidewalk staying close to the kit, Dulcie's skin twitched at every shadow and at every patch of darkness. Things were not right, tonight. What *were* those shots? One culprit was already at large, his bombing attempt gone awry. And now, gunshots? What if the attempted bombing was just the tip of the iceberg? One move in some larger criminal entanglement—a tiny lizard tail that when seen in full, would turn out to be a rattlesnake?

7

RYAN WOKE BEFORE DAWN, BUT WOKE NOT eagerly looking forward to her day as had been her habit lately, not leaping up to turn on the coffeepot and pull the curtains back to look out at the first hint of morning. Instead, an unnatural heaviness of spirit pressed her down; a sense of ugliness made her want to crawl into sleep again. Darkness and depression filled her. And an inexplicable fear. She felt as she had so many nights waking in the small hours to see Rupert's side of the bed still empty, to wish wholeheartedly that she was somewhere else, in some other life.

But now, she *was* somewhere else. This *was* another life. She was free of Rupert.

So what was wrong?

The pale room rose pleasantly around her, its high, white beams just visible in the near-dark. On the west wall the white draperies over the long bank of windows were starting to grow pale with the first promise of dawn. Before the draperies, her new desk, her drafting table and computer stood waiting for her just as she had arranged them for ultimate efficiency and pleasure. She was here in her private nest. Nothing could be wrong. Squeezing her eyes closed, she tried to get a fix on her powerful but unfocused dread.

A cloud of swirling smoke and churning flying rubble. Black, angry eyes staring at her. People running and screaming. The side of the church gone, the sky above filled with flying pieces of broken walls and with white petals falling, falling. Senseless fragments, borne of senseless hatred.

She lay shivering, seeing the black, hate-filled eyes of that boy. She sat up in bed, driving his image away. Deliberately she brought into vision the lovely bridal procession in the cool night, down the narrow grassy carpet between hundreds of friends all holding up fairy lights, or so it had seemed to her, ephemeral candles burning to mark the bride's way. Charlie approaching her groom stepping to the rhythm of the sea's music and to the rustle of the giant trees that stood guard over her.

Nothing, *nothing* could have been more filled with joy and closeness. No ceremony could have better demonstrated Charlie's and Max's and the villagers' stubborn defiance of evil.

Rising, she pulled on her robe and padded into the kitchen to fill the coffeepot, dumping out the grounds from last night. As the coffee brewed, she opened the draperies that ran the length of the studio.

Out over the sea, dawn's light was somber. Impatiently waiting for the coffee, she imagined Charlie rising this morning to let in room service, or to fetch in the elegant breakfast cart herself, where it had been left discreetly outside the door of the St. Francis bridal suite. Charlie and Max were safe. They were safe.

Ryan poured her own first cup of coffee not from a silver server into thin porcelain, as Charlie would be doing, but into an old earthenware mug, breathing in its steamy aroma. She was deeply soothed by the absolute seclusion and calm of her own quiet space. And after two weeks of hot weather, of eighty- and ninety-degree temperatures in the California foothills, she was pleased to see a heavy mist fingering in from the sea, to chill the day. Opening the window, she breathed in the cool, damp breeze that smelled of the sea at low tide. Only as she turned did she imagine someone stirring in the apartment behind her.

But how silly. Moving into the empty studio, she could see into the bath and dressing room, could see from their mirrors' reflections that she was quite alone. Her head must be muzzy from the late hours. Certainly her mind still rang not only with the explosion and the sirens and with her friends' frightened cries, but with the forties music and laughter that had come later.

Strange how sounds stayed with her. When she was working a job, her dreams would ring, each night, with the endless whine of the Skilsaw or with the incessant pounding as she drove nails in a rhythm which, even in dreams, was so real that she would wake to find her arm twitching with tension. Or in her sleep she would hear the repeated *thunk, thunk* of the automatic nailer like a gun fired over and over. Those measured *bangs* were with her now, a delayed but strangely insistent residue from days ago, from her long hours' work on the San Andreas job.

Sipping her coffee, she decided to take herself out to breakfast before she tackled her mail and some phone calls, give herself a little treat. Maybe breakfast at the Miramar Hotel, sitting on the terrace watching the sea and enjoying a Spanish omelet—a small celebration to welcome herself home. She was never shy about tendering herself fancy invitations. Seven weeks in a cramped trailer sharing that tiny space with her two carpenters, and she deserved a little pampering. Particularly since their nights had been purely platonic, about as exciting as curling up with the family picture album. Scotty was one of her two second fathers. And young Dan Hall was happily married, his wife coming up every weekend, further crowding the cramped, two-bedroom rig. On those nights when Dan needed a place of his own rather than bunking with Scotty, she had given him her room, and she had slept in the main house among stacks of lumber and torn-out walls. Dan Hall was a hunk, all right, and so was his beautiful wife, a slim girl with a body to kill for. Dan had lived from weekend to weekend in a haze of sickening longing, a yearning so palpable it was at times embarrassing.

It must be very special to know that your husband wouldn't cheat on you, to be absolutely certain that he lived only to be with you, and would never play around or lie to you.

Ryan sighed. She had never believed for a minute that Rupert wouldn't cheat. She had known better.

Why she had stayed with him so long was just as much a mystery to her as to everyone else. Both Scotty and Dallas, and certainly her dad, had been more than pleased when she left him. Through all the years she procrastinated, they had stood by her—and most of the time they had kept their mouths shut.

Scotty, her father's big, redheaded brother, had inherited all the bold, blustery genes of the Flannery family. Her dad was quiet and low-keyed, his humor far more subtle—a little quizzical smile, and crow's feet marking his green eyes. Michael Flannery enjoyed the world fully, but with little comment. Her uncle Scott Flannery took hold of life with both hands and shook it, and laughed when life banged and rattled.

But her dead mother's brother, Dallas, was the rock. You had to know the stern, silent cop for a long while to enjoy the warmth and humor underneath.

She refilled her coffee mug and sat at the kitchen table, her bare feet freezing. The fog was moving in quickly, the sky turning the color of skimmed milk; she could hear the waves pounding the shore and the seals barking from the rocks, but the ocean itself was hidden in fog. Too restless to be still, she tied her robe more securely and went out along the front deck and down the long flight to get the paper.

The wooden steps were rough under her bare feet, the chill dampness of the fog stroking her ankles. The concrete drive was icy, the Sunday paper damp where it had been tossed against the bushes.

The church bombing covered the front page. A montage of

pictures, the ragged, torn-out wall. The more severely wounded, the pictures taken at angles that magnified the seriousness of cuts and the size of bandages. She didn't need to look at this. Refolding the paper, she turned back up the drive.

But, brushing by her pickup that Dallas had gone over last night collecting evidence, she stopped, frowning.

She had left the truck relatively clean yesterday, much to Dallas's chagrin. Now it wasn't clean, but smeared with mud and with huge paw prints.

She'd had the truck only a month, had traded in the old company model for this reliable baby that made her work so much more fun. It had everything, king cab, lockable toolboxes down both sides, a bull-strong overhead rack. At this particular time in her life, no husband or lover could have given her the same ego trip, the same sense of self-worth, as that shiny new truck.

But now, the vehicle was filthy. Some dog as big as a moose had been all over it, some bad-mannered neighborhood beast had hopped up into the truck bed and apparently walked along the tops of the lockboxes too, rendering her shiny red paint a mess of dried, flaking mud and paw marks. Circling the truck, she headed around the side of the garage to the pedestrian door to fetch some rags and the hose. She didn't realize until she was through the door that she'd left it unlocked last night, that, preoccupied with Dallas's search for evidence she'd forgotten to punch the lock.

Switching on the light she dug under the sink for the box of rags she kept there, pulling out a handful of threadbare towels. Rising, she turned toward the frail, vintage windows that she'd brought down from the foothills, glad the mutt hadn't been able to get into the garage to trash the antique stained glass.

She caught her breath and stepped back, banging into the sink.

The windows stood leaning away from each other, each set of four supported by a heavy box of plumbing fixtures, leaving an empty V space between. A man lay there, jammed between the windows, his face turned away.

The side of his cheek was very white, the blood on his neck and cheek dark and dry. His black hair was tossled and scattered with broken glass, as was the black stubble on his jaw and the black hair on his arm. His blood splattered the broken window and his shirt.

Rupert. *It was Rupert.*

Involuntarily she reached out a hand, but then drew back.

Not quite believing that this was her husband, not quite believing that anyone at all lay there, she moved around the windows to an angle where she could see his face, and stood looking down at him.

His skin was too white even for Rupert. He looked, in death, no more solemn than he had in life. His eyes were open and staring, his face grayish, like the melted paraffin that her mother had used long ago to seal jelly glasses.

The wound in his chest was dark around the edges, the hole in his forehead dark and ragged. Surely both were gunshot wounds.

When was he killed? She had heard no shots. Staring at the bone of his skull, her stomach turned. She badly wanted to heave.

The drying blood that had run down his face and stained his blue polo shirt was so dark it must surely be mixed with the black residue of gunpowder. His ear against the shattered glass was covered with tiny blue fragments. His dark hair was so mussed he looked almost boyish, though in life Rupert had never looked boyish. His broad gold watchband shone from his pale wrist pressing the white skin, nestled among thick black hairs. She thought of Rupert naked, the black hairs on his arms and chest and belly over the too-white flesh. She'd come to hate hairy men. She leaned to grab his feet to drag him out of there, get him away from the frail windows before his weight shattered them further but then, reaching, reality took hold and she backed away, chilled.

But the next moment she knelt. She felt compelled to touch him, though she knew he was dead. Reaching to his thigh, she jerked her hand away again at the feel of lifelessness, at the icy chill that shocked her even through the cloth of his chinos.

Kneeling over him, she didn't know the fog was blowing away until the newly risen sun shot its rays in through the small high window at the back of the garage, a bolt of morning light that lay a glow across her hands and, gleaming through the colored glass, threw a rainbow of colors across Rupert's shattered face. She rose, needing to be sick.

Getting her stomach under control, she stood staring down at the man she'd spent nine years alternately loving and hating until the hate outdistanced all else. And she realized that even in death Rupert had the upper hand.

That even in death, he had placed her in an impossibly compromising position.

She had no witness. He was dead in her garage. She would be the first, prime suspect. Maybe the only suspect.

Dallas could vouch for her until one o'clock this morning. No one could speak for her after Dallas left. She'd seen no one; no one had been in her house. What time had Rupert died? How could he have been killed here in the garage, not ten feet from her, and she had not heard shots?

And what was he doing in Molena Point? Why had he come down here from San Francisco? He had no friends here.

Had he come to confront her in person over the lawsuit where she was claiming her half of the business? She'd started proceedings five months ago. And who had been with him, to kill him? Even if the shooter had used a silencer, why hadn't she at least heard glass breaking when Rupert fell? That sound should have waked her, occurring just beneath the floor where her bed was placed.

She glanced at the unlocked side door, trying to remember if she *had* locked it last night. Moments ago it had been unlocked. And she realized that when she turned the knob she had very likely destroyed fingerprints or perhaps a palm print.

She had to call Dallas.

The thought of calling the station, of calling for the police, of calling for Detective Dallas Garza, both comforted and sickened her.

She needed Dallas; she needed someone.

Dad would be out of town for two more weeks. And Scotty— big strong guy that he was, she was afraid that Scotty would do nothing but worry.

She needed Dallas. Needed, even more than Dallas's comforting, the facts that he would put together. Fingerprints. Coroner's report. Ballistic information. Cold forensic facts that would help her understand what had happened.

She wondered what the neighbors had seen. Her nausea had fled, but she felt shaky and displaced. Nothing made sense. Staring at Rupert, she found herself swallowing back a sudden inexplicable urge to scream, a primitive guttural response born not of pain for Rupert or of empathy, but an animal cry of fear and defiance.

What had someone done? What had someone done not only to Rupert but to her?

Glancing to the back of the garage, into the shadows around the water heater and furnace she realized only then that the killer might still be there, perhaps standing behind those appliances silently watching her.

Backing away, she stared into the dim corners where the light didn't reach, expecting to see a figure emerge, perhaps from behind the stacked plywood or from behind one of the old mantels she'd collected or the stack of newel posts. She had no weapon to defend herself, short of grabbing a hammer. She studied the low door beneath the inner stairs that opened to a storage closet. She breathed a sigh when she saw that the bolt was still driven home.

She longed for her gun, which was upstairs in her night table. How many times did one need a .38 revolver to fetch the Sunday paper? Frightened by the shadows at the back of the garage behind what Dallas called her junk pile, she turned swiftly to the pedestrian door and, using the rag in her hand to open it, she retreated to the open driveway.

If she'd had her truck keys she would have hopped in and taken off, made her escape in her robe and called the department from some neighbor's home. Her cell phone of course was in her purse, by the bed, near her gun. Her truck keys were on the kitchen table. She felt totally naked and defenseless. Scuffing barefoot over the dried mud the neighbor's dog had left across the concrete, she hurried up the outside stairs. She paused with her hand on the knob.

She'd left the front door unlocked behind her. Now, when she entered, would Rupert's killer be waiting?

But why would someone set her up as if she'd killed Rupert, then destroy the scenario by killing her as well? That didn't make any sense.

She could imagine any number of estranged and bitter husbands who would like to see Rupert dead, but why would they make her the patsy? What motive would any of them have— except to put themselves in the clear, of course? And why not? What better suspect than an estranged and bitter wife?

Moving inside, glancing through to the night table at the far end of the room, she slipped her truck keys into the pocket of her robe and eased open a cutlery drawer, soundlessly lifting out the vegetable cleaver. Then stepping to her desk, she dialed the department, using the 911 number.

The dispatcher told her that Dallas was out of the station. She told the dispatcher who she was and that there was a dead man in her garage.

"I'm going to search the apartment, if you'd like to stay on the line." Laying the phone down as the dispatcher yelled at her not to do that, to get out of the apartment—and warily clutching the cleaver—she moved to the night table to retrieve her gun.

Pulling the drawer open, she stopped, frozen.

Empty.

Notebook, pencils, tissues, and face cream. No gun.

Her face burned at her carelessness. The gun was in her glove compartment. She hadn't brought it up last night or the night before; it had been there since she left San Andreas. She hadn't touched it since she packed up the truck and headed out, day before yesterday.

The wedding, and all the picky details of coming home and lining up her crew to start Clyde's job tomorrow had totally occupied her. She told herself she *wasn't* careless with a gun, that Dallas had taught her better than that.

Yes, and Dallas had admonished her more than once for keeping the .38 in her glove compartment, which was against the law, and in her unlocked nightstand, which was stupid.

Approaching the bath and closet, most of which she could see from their mirrors, holding the cleaver behind the fold of her robe, she moved against all common sense to clear the area. This wasn't smart. Even from the closet she heard the dispatcher shouting into the phone. And, louder, she heard a siren leave the station ten blocks away. Passing the door to the inner stairs, she saw that the bolt was securely home, blocking that entrance. As the siren came screaming up the hill she flung the closet door wider, to reveal the back corner.

8

THE BACK OF THE CLOSET WAS EMPTY, ONLY HER clothes and shoes. A second siren started to scream from down the hills. She moved into the bath, clutching her cleaver, jerking the shower curtain aside. In her inept search of the premises she couldn't stop her heart pounding.

The shower was empty. There was nowhere else for anyone to hide. Slipping out of her robe, she hastily pulled on panties and jeans and a sweatshirt as a squad car careened into the drive cutting its siren, and two more units squealed brakes as if pulling to the curb. Grabbing her sandals she moved across the studio to the front windows. Leaning her forehead against the glass, waiting for Dallas to emerge, she watched three officers get out of their two units, and behind them two medics from the rescue vehicle.

Dallas wasn't with them. Officers Green and Bonner moved up the drive on the far side of her pickup. Green was a wizened, bearded veteran, Bonner a young, new officer as fresh-faced as a high school kid. Detective Juana Davis, dressed in jeans and a sweater, skirted the truck on the near side. All three had their hands on their holstered weapons. Shakily Ryan pulled on her sandals and went out on the balcony where they could see her. Looking down at Davis, catching her dark gaze, she couldn't read what the detective might be thinking.

"In the garage," Ryan said, her voice raspy, the way she'd sound if she had a sore throat. She watched the medics halt to wait until the officers had entered and cleared the garage. She couldn't quell her fear, it was a gut reaction beyond reasoning, she was the only possible suspect, she was in exactly the position the killer had planned. Deeply chilled, she looked to the officers for direction. "Do you want me down there?"

"No," Davis said. "Stay on the deck while we have a look."

"Could I go inside to get my coffee?"

Davis nodded. Ryan returned to the kitchen to refill her cup, then stood on the deck again setting the mug on the rail, trying to stop her hands from shaking, thinking guiltily about Rupert.

The year they were married, he had been so enthusiastic about her joining the construction firm, taking a full-time job in the business. It had all seemed so wonderful, an opportunity for her to use her design education though she didn't have a degree as an architect, an opportunity to learn some basic engineering from the firm's structural architect. From the beginning Rupert had handled the business end, the hiring and bookkeeping and sales, while she assisted the architect and did more and more designing. When the architect moved on to a practice of his own, she had been able to take over all the designing with the help of a consulting engineer. Their clients had loved her work. She had served as a carpenter's helper too, adding to the skills she'd mastered working with her uncle Scotty in the summers and weekends since she was a child.

She had gotten so good at the job that soon she was filling in for the three foremen. But then the trouble began. Rupert hadn't liked that she was on the job alone with a bunch of men, even though she had saved them money. She had never drawn a salary, either as head designer or as a foreman; everything went back into the firm. She'd never wanted to know how much might go for Rupert's personal pleasures. She guessed Scotty had tried to tell her, but she hadn't wanted to listen.

Now Scotty was working for her, her dear, gruff, philosophical Scotty who loved carpentry and cabinetwork, who had never wanted to move into the management end of the business. Who had joined her immediately in Molena Point, no questions asked, her first carpenter and foreman. Moving in with Dallas, into their family summer cottage, Scotty had been as happy as she to be away from Dannizer Construction.

When she left Rupert there was never any question where she'd go. She'd loved Molena Point since she was a child. The evening she left Rupert she'd hauled out of San Francisco, taking the oldest company pickup loaded with most of her worldly possessions packed nattily in an assortment of liquor boxes from the local market. It was an easy two-hour drive. Arriving in the village, she had picked up a deli sandwich and a couple of cold beers, checked into the only motel with a vacancy, and called Dallas. When she told him what she'd done he couldn't hide his happiness. She had told him she wanted to be by herself for a few days to lick her wounds, and he'd understood. She'd taken a long hot shower and tucked up in bed with her beer and sandwich trying to relax, trying to deal sensibly with her conflicting emotions, seesawing back and forth between victory in finally making the move, and fear of what lay ahead. Thinking one minute that she was crazy to go out on her own, that she couldn't make a success of her own company, and wondering the next instant why she hadn't done this sooner—knowing that if she sued him for half the company, Rupert would fight her, maybe so successfully that he would deplete her personal bank account and leave her destitute. Knowing that she had to find an attorney. And that the lawsuit would be incredibly stressful, but that half the business was rightfully hers and she meant to have her share, that she would need that money to get started.

Wondering if she *could* make a go of her own business, if she had it in her to do that, she'd sat in bed trying to calm her nerves, so stressed she hadn't even called her sister, though Hanni would have turned out the guest room, popped a bottle of champagne to toast her wise decision and her coming success.

Hanni had moved down to the village some months before Dallas made his own job change, and Ryan could have stayed with either of them; but Hanni was so positive and sure of herself and would tell her exactly what to do, would cross all the t's and dot the i's to make life easier for her. It would have been hard to explain to Hanni the illogical pangs that were mixed with her wild sense of euphoria at being free—almost free. Alone in her motel room she'd gone to sleep hugging her pillow, congratulating herself that Rupert was out of her life, and scared silly of what lay ahead.

Now, standing at the rail watching Juana Davis come around the side of the garage and look up, she set her cup on the rail and went down to answer the detective's questions.

IN THE EARLY DAWN, JOLLY'S ALLEY WAS SOFTLY LIT BY ITS decorative lights and by the gentle glow from the leaded windows and stained-glass doors of its little back-street shops. The charming, brick paved lane, lined with potted trees and tubs of flowers, was not only a favorite tourist walk, but was the chosen gathering place for the village cats—for all the nonspeaking felines who knew nothing of Joe and Dulcie and Kit's human speech nor, in most cases, would have been impressed. If the occasional cat looked at them with fear or with wonder, these moments were few and fleeting.

Entering at the eastern end of the block-long retreat, they found an old, orange-tabby matron beneath the jasmine vine, licking clean the big paper plate that George Jolly had set out. Joe knew the matron well, they had once been more than friendly but that was long before he met Dulcie. Probably the old girl didn't

81

remember those hasty trysts, and certainly Joe didn't care to. He was a different tomcat now, totally faithful to his true love—though he still liked to look. No harm in a glance now and then.

The matron, finishing her breakfast, lay down on the bricks precisely where the first thin rays of morning sun would have gleamed, if the dawn sky had not been low with fog. Dulcie glanced at her absently, her mind on San Francisco and on Charlie and Max Harper awakening this morning in that beautiful city.

"Breakfast at the St. Francis," she said softly, "looking down on the city." Such a journey, to the city by the bay, had long been Dulcie's dream. But at Dulcie's words, the orange cat widened her eyes then turned her face away with disgust, tucking her nose under her tail. Such un-catlike behavior was both alarming and patently beneath her notice. Squeezing her eyes shut she refused to move away from them, though the skin down her back rippled with wary annoyance. Down at the end of the lane a homeless man ambled by, then two young lean women jogged past, their long hair pulled through the backs of their caps.

"Breakfast in bed," Dulcie whispered, still dreaming, "then to wander that elegant city, to ride the ferries to Sausalito and to Oakland, to visit the museums and galleries."

Joe looked at her and sighed. Sometimes it was hard to understand the shape and depth of Dulcie's longings.

Though Joe was just as different from other cats as was Dulcie, he didn't suffer from her exotic hungers and impossible yearnings. He didn't steal his neighbor's cashmere sweaters and silk teddies, for one thing, and haul them home to roll on like some four-pawed Brigitte Bardot. He didn't imagine wandering through Saks, or Lord and Taylor. He had no desire to dine at the finest restaurants with views of San Francisco Bay. Joe Grey liked his life just as it was—as long as Dulcie was a part of it.

The two cats stirred suddenly. Their ears pricked. Their bodies went rigid as sirens screamed from the station four blocks away.

Swarming up the jasmine vine to the roof where the kit sat

welcoming the dawn, they watched two whirling red lights racing north among the cottages where some hours earlier they thought they'd heard the two shots fired—and like any pair of human ambulance chasers, Joe and Dulcie took off across the roofs, intent on police business.

The kit trailed along halfheartedly, her mind on other matters.

Racing across the rooftops and crossing above two streets on spreading oak branches, Joe and Dulcie scrambled down a trellis and galloped along the damp morning sidewalks and through fog-wet gardens, eagerly following the sirens. A screaming rescue vehicle passed them. And somewhere in their mad race the kit vanished. Glancing around, Joe and Dulcie fled on; there was no keeping track of the kit. Up the next hill, the rescue vehicle and squad cars were parked in the drive and at the curb of Ryan Flannery's apartment. The cats paused, slipping ahead warily, rigid with their sudden apprehension.

Though the dawn was now bright, a light burned around the edges of Ryan's closed garage door. The voices that issued from within were low and muffled. The cats could hear Ryan, her voice taunt and upset, and could hear Detective Davis and Officer Bonner speaking solemnly. Davis, a longtime department veteran, was solid in her ways, businesslike and reassuring. The cats were still evaluating young Bonner. As they trotted up to the big, closed door and pressed against it to listen, the coroner's green sedan pulled into the drive. Filled with curiosity, the cats slipped into the shadows beneath the stairs.

Stepping from his car, Dr. John Bern headed around to the side door. Bern was a slight, skinny man with a round face and a turned-up nose so small it seemed hardly able to support his wire-rimmed glasses. As he entered the garage, the cats padded through the shadows as silent as the fog itself and as innocent as any neighborhood kitty out for a morning stroll, and moved in behind him through the pedestrian door, to hide behind some leaning sheets of plywood.

A body lay among a stack of stained-glass windows, as if shrouded by them in some weird religious ritual. Where the windows formed a tall V shape, the cats could see the man's feet sticking out at one end, clad in expensive Rockports. At the other end his head and one shoulder were visible. There was a small hole through his forehead. His neatly trimmed brown hair was soaked with blood. Dr. Bern opened the electric door to give more light, and knelt over the body, making certain the victim was dead. There was not much blood pooled beneath him. When soon the coroner rose again, he began taking photographs. Twice he glanced across the garage to the far, back wall as if tracing the line of trajectory that might have occurred if the victim had been standing when he was shot. Detective Davis, fetching a ladder from beside a stack of old doors, climbed to photograph at close range the twin bullet holes in the Sheetrock. She took pictures from several angles, then told Bonner to cut out that section of wall. "Allow plenty of board, we don't want to pull on it if there are nails near the shots. You may have to saw through the nails or slice out part of the stud."

"Do we have the tools?"

"Ryan has."

The cats could see, when Dr. Bern lifted the man's head, how the shot had left the back of the skull with a wide, ugly tear wound and fragments of bone sticking out. As John Bern dictated his notes into a small tape recorder, he was hesitant in this assessment, offering several possible scenarios as to the sequence of events. When he had finished dictating, Detective Davis spent a long time herself photographing the scene, shooting the body from all angles, laying a ruler here and there around the corpse to show distances. She photographed most of the garage, the floor, the stored tools and plywood, the stacked paneling and newel posts, the furnace and laundry area, and the inside stair that led to the upstairs apartment. Only Joe Grey and Dulcie escaped documentation, crouching silently behind the plywood then moving behind some stored boxes then a mantel, on around the garage as Davis's strobe light flashed. They froze in place when young Bonner glanced at the paw prints in the dust then at the cat door that Ryan had installed. As the officers worked, Ryan stood outside by her truck, pale and silent.

At last Davis put down her camera and began to collect small bits of evidence, threads, slivers of wood, hairs that she picked up with tweezers and dropped in evidence bags. It was late morning, just after 10:00 by the distant chimes of the courthouse clock, when she finished picking up the last nearly invisible bits, then went over the area again with a tiny and powerful hand vacuum. This part of an investigation always amazed the cats. Talk about tedious. They knew by now that the corpse was Ryan's husband.

Once Ryan had answered Davis's questions she sat in the garage on the inner steps, keeping out of the way, her hands folded on her knees, her expression closed and glum, so distressed that, across the garage in the shadows, Dulcie reached an involuntary paw to comfort her. But soon the sound of a car in the drive sent Ryan eagerly out the side door. The cats followed, slipping into a jungle of pink geraniums as Detective Garza swung out of his Chevy Blazer next to the coroner's car.

9

DETECTIVE GARZA STOOD WITH HIS ARMS AROUND Ryan but looking past her at Rupert Dannizer's body. He studied the stacked windows, the garage itself, the drive and Ryan's truck and the front of the building, his photographic detective's mind recording every smallest detail, though he would record it all again in careful notes and perhaps in photographs of his own. Dallas Garza was, the cats had come to learn, a meticulous investigator, his nature as stubbornly prodding as that of any feline.

Yet despite the detective's thoroughness, there was sometimes information to which a human cop had no access, private doors he couldn't legally enter, crannies and niches a human couldn't squeeze into—clues, in short, that a clever cat might snatch from the shadows. Joe Grey's fascination with police investigation was not in lieu of human talent, but was adjunct to that talent.

They watched Garza move inside the garage where he conferred with Davis and the coroner, carefully observing the victim and asking Dr. Bern questions. Garza's position was indeed awkward, with his niece as prime suspect.

"Will he have to stay off the case?" Joe said softly. "Apparently not, or he wouldn't be here at all."

"The papers are going to love this," Dulcie said dourly. "Even the *Molena Point Gazette*. I can just see it: *Police detective's niece arrested for murder.* If they put a reporter on it who doesn't like Garza, he'll have a field day."

Joe flicked a whisker. "And from what Clyde says, Rupert Dannizer was well known in San Francisco. This will be big news, with Dannizer dead before the property settlement, with Ryan standing to inherit . . ."

"No one would believe that!" she hissed

"We don't believe it. And the papers don't have to believe it; they'll print what sells. Their readers will eat it up."

"If Ryan wanted to murder him, would she do it in her own garage?" Dulcie laid back her ears, her green eyes narrowing. "Question is, who hated Rupert Dannizer *and* Ryan enough to kill him and frame her for the crime?"

They watched Officer Bonner string crime tape around the garage and yard, while the coroner sat in his car making additional notes. But when Bonner and Detectives Garza and Davis escorted Ryan upstairs for a look at her apartment and for questioning, the two cats scorched around the building, to slip inside.

The steep hill at the back rose four feet away from the wall of the garage apartment. Crouched in the tall grass looking across to Ryan's bathroom window, Joe Grey leaped. Hanging from the sill, he scrabbled with his hind claws while, with one white forepaw, he finessed open the sliding glass.

The cats had discovered this access when young Dillon Thurwell was kidnapped and they had rescued her from the garage below, from the little airless storage closet beneath the stairs. Because the window was too small to accommodate any human, no one had ever thought to lock it. Now, dropping down into the bathroom, they slipped past the tub and into Ryan's closet-dressing room, to crouch among her jogging shoes and work boots.

The room was large enough for a chest of drawers, a bench with storage underneath, and a six-foot clothes rod that held little more than jeans and work shirts. A single, zippered garment bag appeared to hold a few dress clothes. Her good shoes, like the strappy sandals that she had worn to the wedding, must be tucked away in the plastic boxes they could see atop the closet shelf. The closet smelled faintly of rose perfume. They could hear Ryan and Dallas in the kitchen, talking. But Davis and Bonner were quiet. Very likely they were there as witnesses to prevent the close relationship between uncle and niece from any taint of collusion. At some point Davis would, the cats thought, have to take over the investigation from Detective Garza.

There was a flash of light from the studio, and another, and the cats peered out of the closet to see Davis photographing the apartment, seeking to record any smallest detail that might later fit into a jigsaw puzzle of evidence. As Davis turned toward the closet they drew back behind Ryan's boots, closing their eyes so not to catch a flash of light, Joe ducking to hide his white face and paws and chest; all that remained was a gray mound. Davis took several shots in the closet causing the cats to pray that a stray paw or tail wouldn't show up on the film—not that it mattered, Dulcie kept telling herself. *We're only cats.* What if they were in a photograph, or if Davis did spot them? Dulcie could never overcome her fear of being discovered, never shake the feeling that the truth about them would be as clearly detectable as fresh blood on whiskers. Her need for secrecy overpowered all reason. Such fears were so foolish. After all, Ryan did have a cat door in the garage. If they were discovered, Clyde's mouse hunters were simply on the premises doing their appointed job.

From the kitchen they heard a cup rattle as if Ryan had poured the coffee that had, from the smell of it, steamed in the pot for some time. Dallas asked, "When did you see Rupert last?"

"I haven't—hadn't seen him since early July. I caught sight of him here in the village. That startled me, he never came down here. I don't think he saw me. I'd had dinner with Clyde—Clyde Damen. We were coming out of the grill when I saw Rupert at the bar with a tall, sleek blonde. Long, gleaming hair. I didn't see her face but Rupert turned and I saw his profile. I have no idea what he was doing down here, he has no friends in the village that I know of."

"And he didn't see you?"

"I don't think so. I practically dragged Clyde out of there. We . . . a divorce and lawsuit are not pleasant. Rupert hadn't been very pleasant."

The cats listened to Ryan describe when and how she had found the body, and what she had done afterward, how long it took her to go upstairs and call 911.

"Did you touch the body?"

"I touched his leg. I just . . . reached out before I thought. I was sure he was dead, the dried blood, and he was so white, but I . . . something in me had to be sure—that there wasn't life there, that there was nothing I could do. He . . . he was so cold. . . ."

"And what would you have done if you'd thought he was alive?"

"The same as I did, call the department—unless I'd thought CPR would . . . I suppose I would have tried that."

"What did you tell the dispatcher?"

"That a man was dead in my garage. And I answered her questions."

"You came upstairs to call?"

"Yes."

"Do you own a gun?"

"Yes."

Behind Ryan's boots, the cats glanced at each other. Of course Dallas knew she owned a gun, but he was committed to asking all the necessary questions. He made her describe the black .38 Smith

89

and Wesson, made her tell him where she kept it, where it had been that morning and where it was at that moment. The cats didn't need to watch him to know he was carefully recording her answers both on tape and in his log—recording not to incriminate but to protect, to have the record straight.

"I forgot to bring my gun upstairs when I got back from San Andreas. Normally I would have put it in my nightstand. It . . . it's been locked in my truck since I got back, night before last. I . . . just forgot about it."

"Forgot about it?"

"I don't feel the need, in Molena Point, to keep a gun with me at night the way I . . . the way one might in an isolated trailer."

"You left it locked in your truck, where?"

"In the glove compartment."

"I'll need your keys."

The cats heard keys jingle. Dallas said, "Are they all here? None have been removed?"

A pause, then, "Yes. All there. Apartment door, garage, truck keys, side lock boxes, glove compartment. Key to the house in San Francisco, which is still officially half mine."

The cats glanced at each other. She was just a bit defensive. But surely she didn't like being questioned this way, even by her uncle, even though she knew it was necessary.

"Last night, what time did you go to bed?"

"The minute you left here. Just before two."

"Did you hear anything during the night, any noises?"

"No."

"Nothing downstairs?"

"No."

"Did you hear gunshots."

"No I didn't. I don't understand why not."

"What is your opinion about that?"

"That whoever killed him used a silencer. Or that he was shot somewhere else and brought here."

"Does that strike you as rather improbable?"

"It's improbable to find Rupert down there, dead in my garage. I only know that I didn't hear shots. And it seemed to me there was very little blood, for a head wound."

Joe Grey frowned, the white strip down his face squeezing into wrinkles. In the dim closet his yellow eyes shone black as obsidian. His whisper was soft. "If those two bullets, that went into the back wall, had been a couple of feet higher they could have come up through the floor directly where Ryan was sleeping."

Dallas said, "Did you see any indication that the body had been moved to that location? Any blood trail? Any drag marks down the drive or in the yard?"

"No. You would have seen them too."

"But there was a tire mark," Dulcie said softly. "A little thin tire mark, like a bike, just at the edge of the drive."

"I didn't see that," Joe hissed. "How could I miss that?"

"You were watching the coroner. I saw Detective Davis photograph the ground there, but the mark was really faint. I thought it went along the drive, maybe to the side door."

"You heard nothing after you went to bed?" Dallas repeated. "You didn't hear a shot fired." The cats pictured Officer Bonner silently observing the detective, witness to the fact that Dallas was detached and objective and didn't lead Ryan's answers.

"I'm sure I'd have waked to gunshots," Ryan said. "Unless there was a silencer."

"And you heard nothing during the night?"

"Not that I remember. I was dead asleep, I was very tired." But the cats glanced at each other. Ryan sounded as if she wanted to tell Dallas something more. As if perhaps later when they were alone, when she was not on record, she would share with him something that was bothering her?

"Those stained-glass windows," Dulcie said softly. "How could the killer have wedged the body in like that? To lift a dead weight, pardon the pun, at that angle and ease the body down between the windows . . . That would be like standing on your hind legs lifting a dead rabbit as heavy as you, hoisting it way out at an angle and slowly down without dropping it. The killer had to be strong. But why bother? What was the point of leaving the body there?"

"You don't think he was shot there?" Joe said.

"Nor do you," she said, cutting her eyes at him. "Those windows are old and frail. You heard Ryan last night telling Clyde. That glass has to be brittle, and those strips of lead fragile. Those old stained-glass windows in the English Pub, the way if you rub against them, the glass will push loose from the leading? If Rupert had fallen there he'd have smashed those windows to confetti."

Dallas said, "We'll have to take your gun." The cats heard chair legs scrape, then the front door open, heard the officers and Ryan going down the stairs.

Leaping from the bathroom window and down the hill, they were just at the edge of the drive when the officers and Ryan came down; and the medics set down their stretcher, prepared to take Rupert away. Slipping into the bushes, they watched Dallas unlock Ryan's truck door then unlock her glove compartment. Flipping the glove compartment open, he turned to look at her.

"You said your gun was here?"

Ryan stared in past Dallas. She reached, but drew back.

Dallas pulled out a thin folder, and laid it back again. "Empty. I've never known a woman to keep an empty glove compartment."

"I keep stuff in the console, you know that. Except my gun. Where's my gun!"

"You didn't take it upstairs?" he said sternly.

She shook her head, scowling. "No. I didn't."

"Let's go over it again. You got home Friday night around midnight."

"Yes. Unloaded the windows, unloaded a few tools, closed and locked the garage door. Went upstairs and fell into bed, dead for sleep."

"And the next morning—Saturday morning?"

"Got up, made coffee. Came down and finished unloading, hauled my trash bags around the side of the garage. I'd bought a mantel up there, as well as the windows, and some carved molding. I stacked those better, along the back wall, and shook out the tarp and folded it, put it back in the truck bed where I keep it. It had crumbs and Hershey wrappers in it, and was folded differently than I'd left it. I learned Saturday night after the wedding, the Farger boy hitched a ride down from San Andreas without my knowing." All this was for the record, for the tape that was surely running.

"And before we came upstairs last night, I locked the side door. I know I did. But this morning when I first went in, it was unlocked. And there were muddy paw prints in the truck bed as if one of the neighbors' dogs got in during the night. My truck wasn't muddy Saturday night when you examined it. It was when I went in the garage to get some cleaning rags that I . . . that I found Rupert."

"Did you drive the truck anywhere Saturday?"

"No. I rode to the wedding with Clyde Damen. And you brought me home that night to look at the truck in regards to the Farger boy. It was clean then. It hasn't been out of the drive since I got home Friday midnight."

"Was there any mud in the garage yesterday when you cleaned up?"

"No, I'm sure. And it hasn't rained. But behind the garage, to the side . . . I hosed down a shovel and rake back by the faucet, tools I'd used at the last minute, at the jobsite to set some stakes. It was muddy back there."

They looked up as Officer Bonner came around the side of the garage carrying a black handgun by a stick through the trigger guard. The clean-shaven, neat young man did not look at Ryan, only at the detective.

"Found it in a trash bag, along with some wet, stained rags and stained bedsheets. Dark stains that could be blood."

Ryan studied the gun. "It appears to be mine. If it's mine,

you'll find the trigger guard is worn, the bluing worn off." She began to shiver. Dallas didn't touch the stick or the weapon. He looked at Bonner. "Has it been fired?"

Bonner's shiny black shoes and the pant cuffs of his uniform were muddy. He sniffed the barrel briefly, as if he had already made a determination. "It smells of burnt gunpowder. I'd say it's been recently fired. The trigger-guard bluing is worn off."

"Bag it," Garza said, and turned to Ryan, his face unreadable, that reined-in cop's expression bearing no discernible message of love or familial closeness, offering her no support or encouragement.

Ryan looked back at him, very white. "How did this happen? That gun was locked up! You yourself unlocked the cab door after you collected evidence about the boy. Just now, you unlocked the glove compartment. How could—?"

Neither mentioned that such storage of a gun was not legal, that in California one had to have a special lockbox that could be removed from the car, a law that had never, to Joe Grey and Dulcie, made any sense. What good was a lockbox if it could be removed by a thief?

"Who else has keys to your truck?" Dallas asked.

"Scotty has a set because we used it on the job, but he's family. I've only had this truck three weeks—I bought it in San Andreas." She looked hard at Dallas. "Could someone in the truck sales, someone . . . ?"

"Not likely, but we'll check. Has anyone else driven it, besides your uncle Scott?"

"Dan Hall, once or twice. He used Scotty's keys or mine. There was no one else up there but Dan and Scotty."

"No one?"

"No one to drive the truck. Some kids were hanging around, the Farger boy and his friends, but they weren't . . . they couldn't . . ." She looked at him, shaken. "They had no chance, they couldn't have taken my keys."

"The kids were in the house trailer where you were staying?"

"A couple of times, but I was with them. They were never alone. I let them make sandwiches one day, while we were eating. They . . . well . . . there was one time," she said faintly. "They . . . when I was surveying one day, they wanted to use the bathroom. I was right there, down the hill," she said lamely.

"And your keys?"

"Either in my purse or on the table. I kept my purse in the bedroom closet." She stared at Dallas. "That boy . . . why would he take my keys? Anyone," she said more forcefully, "anyone could have gotten into the truck with a door tool, then used a lock pick on the glove compartment."

"Could have," Dallas agreed. He hesitated, glancing at the tape recorder. Then: "That boy very likely set a bomb, Ryan. Set it or helped someone set it. You think that was innocent, that bomb?"

She said nothing.

"Did you use the truck every day?"

"No, sometimes not for several days if we could get a lumber delivery in good time. But if he did take my keys," she said softly, "what was the connection? Between the boy and Rupert?"

The two cats looked at each other. *You are, Joe Grey thought. At the moment, Ryan, it looks like you're the connection.* The tomcat shivered. *If someone wanted to harm the Molena Point police, first with the bombing that, lucky for everyone, hadn't come off as planned, maybe they'd meant to ruin reputations, too, as a backup move.*

So they chose Ryan, Detective Garza's niece, as the patsy. Pin a murder on Ryan, they'd put Garza in an embarrassing position.

And, the tomcat thought with a soft growl, *this scenario was far too much like the vicious attack earlier in the year when Police Captain Harper was set up as a killer.*

Were Rupert Dannizer's death and yesterday's bombing connected to that other murder? Were all three crimes part of some planned vendetta against Molena Point PD? The possibilities rattled around in Joe Grey's head as wildly as those little plastic balls in some diabolical pinball machine. He felt he was racing back and forth across the glass top swatting uselessly at unrelated facts, the little bright spheres forming, as yet, no logical configuration.

10

THE IMAGES OF DEATH REMAINED WITH RYAN long after Dallas and his officers left the crime scene. Rupert's torn face, the coroner working over him, the strobe lights reflecting shatters of raw color across his body from the broken windows. The coroner wrapping Rupert in a body bag as if he were trussing up a side of beef, the emergency van hauling Rupert away through the village with no final ceremony, no tenderness, no one in attendance.

So what did she want, banks of roses strewn in his path embellishing his journey to the county morgue? Roses scattered by his former lovers? She imagined the coroner sliding Rupert into a cold gray storage locker, to remain forever alone. But the vision that clung most vividly was Rupert's shattered face, his bloody broken face. That picture would remain with her for all time, generating a distressing internal response to every hurtful thought she'd ever entertained about Rupert Dannizer, to every angry wish she'd ever made about Rupert's ultimate fate.

When all the vehicles had gone, she stood in the empty drive feeling small and scared. Wishing Dallas could have stayed with her, feeling like a child in need of strong male support and assurance.

But Dallas had been shaken too. He would never show it, but he was upset and worried for her.

He would do everything possible, he wouldn't give up until he had unraveled the facts and put them in their proper order. Even if he had to step off the case, and surely he would, he'd remain in the background making certain that everything was done right, seeing that no clue was ignored, no investigative procedure disregarded.

She stood thinking about death, wondering if Rupert, as he lay in her garage gazing blindly up toward the rafters, might have experienced some final metamorphosis of the spirit, wondering if he'd perhaps undergone some sudden change of view. If Rupert, transformed into the eternal state, had awakened to face the error of his ways.

She was not a churchgoer. But she'd never doubted that there was more to the spirit than this one life.

However, given Rupert's earthly performance, she really didn't imagine that in some great toting-up he would be a candidate for a medal in exemplary behavior. More likely Rupert had, in his final moments, felt the searing heat and witnessed his first glimpse of the eternal flames. And that was all right with her.

Turning to go upstairs, she looked across the street at the neighbors' blank windows imagining people peering out from behind their curtains wondering what kind of woman had moved into their neighborhood bringing murder, neighbors already certain that *she* had killed the victim, neighbors wondering who he was and what kind of stormy relationship had led to this particular act of violence.

Well, they'd know soon enough. The papers would have it all, every dirty aspect of hers and Rupert's marriage. Some reporter would dredge up every harlot and married woman Rupert had ever bedded, every incident that would throw suspicion on her, his estranged and bitter wife.

Heading for the stairs, she stopped to inspect the truck again, and to brush some of the mud from its sleek red paint. Even her nice new truck, this solid and reliable symbol of her new and independent start in life, had become a part of the mess. Dallas and Officer Bonner had dusted it inside and out for fingerprints, a thorough job that had taken them the better part of an hour. Now, moving to the cab, she looked in at the red leather upholstery that puffed luxuriously over the two bucket seats. No hint of mud there. The day she bought the truck she had promised herself that the soft seats and pristine red carpet were going to stay as clean as her kitchen sink. No sawdust, no candy wrappers or greasy hamburgers or leaking Coke cans dripping their long sticky trails. No open tubes of caulking, no getting in the cab with wet paint or plaster on your jeans.

She had not imagined a strange dog tramping mud all over the truck bed—nor some evil little boy hiding under the tarp planning his sickening crime. She was incredibly tired from the morning's adrenaline-heavy emotions. And scared of what lay ahead.

Innocent or not, if another suspect wasn't found, the next few months would be ugly. And now that Dallas had taken away her gun, she had no protection against whoever was out there.

Did Dallas really think the killer wouldn't return, that he'd have no further interest in her? She leaned on the truck, lightheaded.

She needed a hot shower and some breakfast. She needed food, needed to get her blood sugar up, dump some protein into the system. Needed to get away from the house for a while.

As she started up the stairs she saw movement across the street in a window, the slats of a venetian blind shifting. Scowling at the snooper she beat it up the steps, her face burning.

Her door wasn't shut, it stood ajar. And a sound startled her, a soft hush through her open window that made her wrists go cold.

The stirring came again, a shuffling noise.

But she knew that sound, it was only the breeze through the

open window rifling the papers on her desk, disturbing the stack of letters and bills and junk mail that had collected.

While she was gone, Hanni had come in every few days to go through her mail, to call her with anything important, but had left the rest for Ryan to clean up at her leisure. The mail blowing, that's all the soft sound was.

But why was the door ajar?

Very likely she hadn't closed it tightly when she and Dallas went back downstairs. It had a tendency not to want to latch. Certainly there was no one in there, no one would be dumb enough to enter with cops all over the place. Moving inside she thought she'd take a long hot shower then head out again and treat herself to a nice breakfast, try to get hold of herself, to get centered. She thought of calling Hanni, see if she could join her. Hanni wouldn't let her get the shakes, she'd put a positive spin on any disaster. A few smart retorts, a touch of twisted humor. *So you cut the cost of the lawsuit, so quit bellyaching, you've inherited the whole enchilada.*

Shivering, she decided against calling Hanni. Stepping into the kitchen to turn off the coffeepot, she stopped.

She was not alone.

He stood beside the breakfast table, a muddy dog so big his chin would have rested easily on the tabletop. His short silver coat was smeared with dried mud. His pale yellow eyes watched her with a look so challenging that she stepped back.

He was bone thin, deep jowled and with long floppy ears. Built like a pointer, his tail docked to a length of six inches. The tail wagged once, a brief and dignified question. He had left a trail of flaking mud across her kitchen and into the studio, had tracked to her unmade bed then back to the drafting table and desk, apparently quartering the room in a thorough inspection. While she stood looking at where he had wandered, his gaze on her turned patronizing, as if she was very slow indeed to make him welcome.

And certainly she should welcome him, she had done so several times before but not in Molena Point. Up in San Andreas he had in fact been far more welcome than the three eager children with whom he had sometimes come to the trailer.

The kids said he was a stray, that he roamed all over the hills. That had seemed strange and unlikely for such a handsome pure-bred. But surely he'd been very thin, and though she'd reported him lost to the sheriff and had run an ad in the paper, no one had claimed him. She'd seen him only with the children, happy to be running with kids—kids didn't demand that a dog follow rules, they themselves were rule breakers. Kids, still young animals in spirit, made fine companions for a wandering canine.

There was no question that this was the same dog, there could not be another weimaraner exactly like him, not with the same challenging look in those intelligent yellow eyes nor with the same small, lopsided cross of white marking his gray chest and the same notch in his left ear. The same old, cracked leather collar without any tags. She thought there could not be another dog anywhere with quite this insolent air. She knew that if she were to stroke his side and shoulder she would feel the little hard lumps where buckshot, sometime in his unknown past, must have lodged beneath his skin, gunshot likely administered by some angry farmer not wanting a hungry dog nosing around his chicken coops. She held her hand out to the big weimaraner, wondering what she had in her bare cupboards to feed him.

The dog stood assessing her, gauging her intentions.

"Hungry?"

His yellow eyes lighted, his long silky ears lifted, his short tail began to move slowly back and forth in a hesitant question.

She found a jar of peanut butter in the nearly empty cupboard and spread it on some stale crackers. When she held them down, he didn't snatch them, he took each gently from her fingers. But he gulped them as if truly starving, and when she filled a bowl with water, he drank it all, never lifting his head until the bowl was empty. She stood considering him.

Looked like Curtis had a companion when he hid in her truck. She could just see Curtis climbing in and calling to the dog, the big weimaraner eagerly joining him. This had to have happened in the small town itself when she stopped to pick up the windows. She could imagine Curtis slipping into the truck after she loaded up, while she was inside paying her bill, and coaxing the dog under the tarp with him. What did Curtis think would happen to a nice dog like this running loose in the city? The kids had called him Rock, because of his color like an outcropping of gray boulders, though when clean his coat was more like gray velvet.

The dog was, in fact, exactly the same color as Clyde Damen's tomcat, she thought, amused. Not only the same color, but both animals had docked tails that stuck up at a jaunty angle, and both had wise yellow eyes. How droll. Even their expressions were similar, bold and uncompromising.

The silly humor of dog and cat look-alikes helped considerably to ease her stress. She gave him all the crackers and peanut butter. There wasn't anything else in the cupboard that would interest a canine, only a can of grapefruit. When she picked up her truck keys, thinking to go buy some dog food, he brightened and headed for the door looking up at her with eager enthusiasm, as if they did this every day.

OUT ON THE DECK BEHIND RYAN, THE TWO CATS SAT ON THE windowsill looking in, watching with fascination this amusing relief from the morning's events. They had watched the dog earlier as he approached the police cars, trotting silently down the sidewalk, his tongue lolling in a happy smile as he headed for all the busy activity.

But then he had paused suddenly, testing the air, and abruptly he had turned aside, slipping into the tall bushes. There he had lain down out of sight, remaining still, only lifting his nose occasionally then dropping his head again to rest his nose on his paws—something about the crime scene, perhaps the scent of death, made him keep his distance.

When he had first pushed into the bushes the cats had tensed to race away to the nearest fence top. But the dog, sniffing idly in their direction and making eye contact, had only smiled with doggy humor and turned his attention to the human drama; he had exhibited no desire to haze or lunge at cats, had shown no inclination to snap up a cat and shake it—not at the moment. Though maybe another day, another time. One could not always be certain.

He had remained hidden and watchful until the officers' attention was concentrated around the tailgate of Ryan's truck, then with no humans watching to shout at him, he had moved from the bushes up the stairs casually sniffing each step. Within seconds he was nosing the door open to disappear into Ryan's apartment. Soon they had heard the soft click of toenails on hardwood. And now through the window they watched Ryan feed him crackers and peanut butter, then pick up her truck keys.

"He's beautiful," Dulcie said. "He's the same color as you."

"What?"

"Exact same gray. And your eyes are the same color." Her own eyes slitted in an amused cat laugh. "Even your tails are docked the same." She looked at Joe and looked in at the big dog. "Except for size, and his doggy face and ears, he's a mirror image."

Joe Grey scowled; but he peered in again, with interest. He had to admit, this dog was unusually handsome.

WONDERING WHAT TO DO WITH THE DOG, RYAN GLANCED TO the window and saw the two cats staring in. They didn't seem afraid, only interested. Benignly the dog looked up through the window, giving no sign of wanting to chase.

When she had left San Andreas, and Scotty stayed on in the trailer to put in some landscaping, he had planned to feed the dog and continue to look for his owner. Both she and Scotty had wanted him, but neither had a decent way to keep him. She would be working eight and ten hours a day, and she had no fenced yard and none that could be properly fenced. The front lawn of the duplex was only a narrow strip, broken by the two driveways. Her side yard was six feet wide, not nearly big enough for a dog like this. And at the back, the hill went up far too steeply even for a billy goat. No place to keep a dog and no time to devote to this animal. Weimaraners needed to run, they needed to hunt or to work, that was what they'd been bred for. Without proper work, a dog like this could turn into a nightmare of destruction, fences chewed up and furniture reduced to splinters.

And Scotty had no home at all, at present. When he returned to Molena Point he'd be staying with Dallas, who already had two elderly pointers that he was boarding until he could build a fence of his own, aged dogs who were past the need to run for miles. Dogs that had never known the consuming needs of this more active breed.

The dog had appeared the first time, without the boys, on a moonless night as she and Scotty and Dan sat in the trailer eating supper. A soft movement at the open door, a pale shape against the dark screen so insubstantial and ghostly they thought it was a young deer stepping inexplicably up onto the tiny porch. Then they saw the dog peering in, sniffing the scent of food.

Of course Scotty invited him in. The dog had come willingly, staring at their plates but he didn't beg or charge the table. He stood silent and watchful, observing them and their supper with those serious yellow eyes, studying each of them in turn. Scotty had hesitated only a moment, then blew on his plate to cool the hot canned stew, stirred and blew again, and set it on the floor.

Not until Scotty stepped back did the dog approach the plate. He paused, looking up at Scotty.

"It's okay. It's for you."

The dog inhaled the stew in three gulps. They had fed him all their suppers and opened another can. After an hour they fed him again, bread and canned hot dogs. Over the period of several hours they cleaned out the cupboard. The dog had slept in the trailer that night, and the next morning they called the sheriff, thinking he'd gotten lost from some hunter. From then on the dog would show up every couple of days, usually with the kids, but always starving. The boys had no notion where he lived, nor did the sheriff or his deputies.

Now as Ryan opened the door the cats came alert, prepared to leap from the sill and away. The dog trotted out quietly looking them over but making no move to approach. Ryan, with a handful of paper towels, stood on the deck wiping the dried mud from his coat. But then as she started down to the truck, she paused, frowning, and turned back inside. The dog followed her, staying close, looking up at her begging her to get a move on.

PICKING UP THE PHONE AND DIALING THE STATION, SHE WAS relieved to be put through at once to Dallas. "Have you gotten Curtis Farger to talk? Gotten a line on where he was staying in San Andreas?"

"Nothing yet. Why? Officers searched the old man's shack again this morning, but no sign that a bomb had been put together there—and no sign of Gramps and no fresh shoe tracks or tire tracks, no indication anyone's been back there."

"I think I might have something. I'd like to come talk with Curtis."

"This hasn't anything to do with Rupert?"

"No, it hasn't."

He waited, not responding.

"There was a dog up there around the trailer, hanging out with those kids. He's in my kitchen now, looks like Curtis brought him along for company. Looks like when he got to Molena Point Curtis never thought to take care of the animal, but just let him run loose."

"You didn't mention a dog when we talked."

"I had a reason."

"Which was?"

"I'll tell you later. It hasn't anything to do with Curtis."

"You sure it's the same dog?"

"Same dog. A fine big weimaraner. There aren't two like this one. Scotty and I tried to find his owners. We both wanted to keep him, but . . ."

"So what's the secret?"

"When you see him, *you'll* want him."

Dallas laughed. "You think if you bring the dog in, you can soften Curtis up?"

"I think it's worth a try. He seemed to really like the dog, maybe he would open up. When the dog was around, Curtis was always hanging on him, hugging him."

"And you're all right, about this morning?"

"I'm fine," she lied.

"Come on in."

"I need to get him some food, first. And feed myself, I'm dizzy with hunger. Have you eaten anything?"

"As we speak. Enjoying the last bite of a double cheeseburger."

Hanging up, she got a bath towel and, down on the drive, gave the dog a thorough rubdown, sleeking his coat to a shine. Amazing how good he looked despite his half-starved condition. Laying another, clean towel over the passenger seat of the cab, she told him to load up.

He knew the command, hopping right up into the bucket seat, sitting as straight and dignified as if he'd spent his life riding in the best vehicles.

Considering only briefly her promise to herself about no mud in the cab, she closed the passenger door, slid into the driver's seat and headed for the market. Some promises, at certain moments in your life, were indeed made to be broken.

She was inside the market and out again breaking all records, her mind filled with stories of hyper-energetic weimaraners who had torn up the insides of a car or travel trailer with amazing speed and efficiency. In one instance involving a brand-new RV, a weimaraner with tooth-and-claw enthusiasm had created 20,000 dollars' worth of damage in less than half an hour while the dog's family grabbed a quick lunch.

Tossing a fifty-pound bag of dog kibble into the truck bed, and dropping the bag containing her deli sandwich next to her on the bucket seat, she headed for the little park at the bottom of her street where she and the dog could share their breakfast. In a fit of possessiveness she had bought, from the market's pet section, a new leather collar, a leather leash, a choke chain, and a long retractable leash that would make Dallas laugh. No competent dog trainer would be caught dead with such a contraption, but for the time being she thought it might be useful. She had not seen behind her as she headed down the hill from her duplex, the two cats taking off on their own urgent errand, racing across the neighbors' yards and down the hill in the direction of Molena Point PD.

Nor would she have paid any attention. She would have no reason to think that the cats were headed for Curtis Farger's cell, to wait for her and Rock. That they would soon be crouched outside the high cell window which, on this bright morning, should be wide open, secured only by its heavy iron bars. She would have no reason to imagine that four-legged spies would be waiting, intent on any scrap of information she might glean from the young bomber.

11

NEWS OF A MURDER IN MOLENA POINT TRAVELED
swiftly through the village, flashing from phone to phone, to on-the-
street conversation, to phone again to gossip passed on by waiters,
customers, shopkeepers, in short from friend to friend. Clyde
Damon listened to the details as related to him by his supervising
mechanic while Clyde inspected the engine of a '96 BMW. Turning
away from the sleek convertible, he went into his office to call Ryan.
When her phone rang ten times and no answer, he called Wilma.

Wilma had heard about the murder from the tortoiseshell cat
when the kit came running home. The kit had heard about the
death as she lingered beneath a table of the Courtyard Café. Kit
would have been a witness to the police investigation except that
early that morning she had veered away from Joe and Dulcie as
they raced down the hills toward Ryan's duplex following the
sirens like a pair of cheap ambulance chasers.

The kit, heading into the village, had trotted along the sidewalk sampling the aromas from half-a-dozen restaurants. She had
paused before the Swiss House patio examining the fine scent of
sausages and pancakes. With whiskers and ears forward and her

fluffy tail carried high she padded into the brick patio to wind around friendly ankles, smiling up at tourist and local alike, at whoever might feel generous.

The kit was not an opportunist. But having spent most of her short, transient life running with bigger cats who took all the garbage, leaving her with none, she viewed the matter of food seriously. Not until she met Joe and Dulcie and her first human friends, did realized she could stop snarling over every morsel, that some cats and humans enjoyed sharing.

Now in the café's patio she soon bagged a fine breakfast of sausage and fried eggs and thin Swiss pancakes, all laid out on a little saucer by a kind tourist. Life was good. Life was very good. The kit's purr reverberated beneath the table like a small and busy engine.

But then, having eaten her fill, she slipped away before her benefactor knew she'd gone. Prowling the village, nipping into shops, wandering among antique furniture and displays of soft sweaters, she soon entered a rug gallery where she paused to have a little wash on an expensive oriental carpet. Wandering out again, she slipped into a gift shop, drawn by the scent of lavender. Then down the street threading between the feet of tourists and in and out of shops, alternately petted or evicted according to the shop-keeper's temperament. When the sun had warmed the rooftops she wandered there, across the tilting shingles and peaks until she was hungry again, then followed the aroma of broiled shrimp to a nearby patio restaurant. It was here that she heard the news of a body in Ryan Flannery's garage.

As the kit gobbled shrimp from a little plate beneath the table, rubbing against the ankles of the gallery owner who had provided the delicacy, that lady remarked to her companion, "He was a womanizer, you know. Rupert Flannery. It may be crude to speak so of the dead, but Ryan's lucky to be rid of him."

"Maybe that's only gossip," whispered her friend. "Maybe he . . . *Do* you think she killed him? Right there in her own garage?"

"If she did, I wouldn't blame her. You know, my dear, one of my gallery clients is Ryan's sister, decorator Hanni Coon. Well, of course Hanni never said anything, but her office manager told Bernine . . . You know Bernine Sage, she worked for Beckwhite's until after *he* was killed, then she worked for the library for a while. Well, Bernine knows some friends of the Dannizers in San Francisco, and she told me all about Rupert. She says he does like to sample the herd, as my husband would so indelicately put it."

The kit wasn't sure what that meant, but she certainly understood about the murder in Ryan's garage. As soon as she'd finished all the handouts that seemed forthcoming she galloped down the street three blocks to the library and in through Dulcie's cat door, and leaped to Wilma's cluttered desk.

She waited in Wilma's office for perhaps three minutes before she grew impatient and trotted out into the reference room. Hopping onto a library table, then to the top of the book stacks, drawing smiles from several patrons who were used to seeing her and Dulcie among the books, she trotted along the dusty tops of the stacks looking down on the heads of patrons and librarians until she spotted Wilma behind the checkout desk. Wilma stood shelving reserve books. Her long silver hair, bound back in a ponytail, shone bright against the dark bindings. The kit, hanging down over the shelves above Wilma's head, mewed softly, the kind of small mutter she would use when speaking to another cat.

Looking up, Wilma reached to take the kit in her arms. She didn't speak, the kit was too impetuous; Wilma was always afraid the little tattercoat would forget and say something back to her, blurt out some urgent message in front of other people. Certainly the kit had something vital to say, she was all wriggles, she could hardly be still.

But Wilma was not to be hurried. With the kit settled across her shoulder she finished her shelving, stroking the kit's back and scratching her ears to keep her quiet. Taking her time, she at last headed for her office.

The moment the door was closed the kit launched into her story of murder, into every smallest detail she'd overheard. ". . . and Ryan hasn't been arrested yet, but that woman who gave me the shrimp thought she would be. She said Ryan's husband liked to sample the herd. What does that mean? Is that why someone killed him? Oh, Ryan didn't kill him, Ryan wouldn't kill anyone."

Setting the kit on her desk, Wilma held her finger to her lips, and immediately she called the station. As the phone rang the kit jumped to her shoulder and settled down with one tortoiseshell ear pressed against the headset. She tried not to wriggle or purr as she listened.

When Dallas came on he gave Wilma the particulars of the death. Ryan had not been arrested. She was on her way to the station to interview the Farger boy. Wilma had hardly hung up when Clyde called from the shop. As they talked, the kit left quietly again, through Dulcie's cat door, and galloped over to the police station to hear what she could hear. That boy in jail didn't need to see her, that boy she had jumped on and made to set off his bomb. She would just slip into the station past the dispatcher, she would be just a shadow, no one would see her.

IN RYAN'S TRUCK THE DOG SAT CUTTING HIS EYES AT THE PAPER bag that lay on the console between them, sucking in the scent of charbroiled hamburger and fries. He made no move to touch it, and Ryan stroked his head. "You have lovely manners." She studied him as she waited for a stoplight. "Where *did* you come from? How could anyone abandon you?" This was a valuable dog, not one of the registered "backyard bred" animals whose owners had given no thought to what such a mating would produce. That happened too often when a breed became popular. This big, strong fellow was far above those ill-planned mistakes. He looked like he could hunt from dawn until dark and never tire. His breed had been developed for all-around work and stamina, to retrieve on land or on water, to point, to track, to hunt big game, to work by

111

both sight and by scent. Watching him, Ryan was more than smitten, she was overboard with desire. This was a fine, intelligent animal, a hunter's dream.

But she couldn't keep him. When would she hunt him? When would she work him? It wouldn't be fair to the dog.

Pulling up beside the little park she dropped the choke chain over his head, fastened on the leash, snatched up her sandwich bag as she stepped out, and gave him the command to come. He was immediately out of the truck sitting before her as she closed the door, then moving to heel.

Oh, yes, a dream dog, a treasure.

Leaning over the truck bed she opened the kibble bag and scooped a large serving into one of the two bowls she had bought. Carrying the bowls and a bottle of water and her own breakfast she headed for a sprawling cypress tree near the edge of the park, settling down beneath it on the grass. The cool fall morning was silent except for the cries of the gulls and the faint *whish* of a few passing cars. The dog lay down beside her alertly watching the kibble bowl that she still held. At the other end of the park some children were playing catch, their voices cutting the silence. A few tourists wandered across the grass or sat on the scattered benches, and a pair of joggers passed her. When she put the bowls down, the kibble vanished quickly, as did half the water. She didn't offer more food, she didn't want him throwing up. Their alfresco picnic apparently presented an interesting study because several cars slowed to have a look. She savored her hamburger and fries, wondering if she was stupid to take the dog over to the jail. *Would* his presence encourage Curtis to talk, or was that wishful thinking?

Whatever she thought of the kid, up in San Andreas he had seemed so tender toward the dog. But knowing now what he was capable of, that he had tried to kill half the village, maybe this visit was futile. And she wondered if, when she faced Curtis again, she could keep her anger under control.

Still, if Dallas didn't find the old man, Curtis was the only lead they had to unraveling the full story of the bombing. Her preoccupation with that urgent matter served very well to ease her own fears, to put in perspective her own precarious position. This boy, son of the man Max Harper had helped prosecute for drug making, had nearly killed Max and Charlie and maybe the entire wedding party.

The silence of the early Sunday afternoon was broken suddenly by Dixieland jazz blaring from an approaching convertible, and a pale blue Mercedes pulled to the curb, parking illegally in the red zone, the top down, her sister Hanni behind the wheel. Hanni's short silver hair was styled to a flip of perfection, her long silver earrings caught the sunlight, her million-dollar grooming made Ryan feel, as always, all ashes and sackcloth, made her snatch uselessly at her uncombed hair and stare down at the stain on her sweatshirt.

Hanni remained in the car quietly observing the dog in a way that made Ryan bridle with possessiveness. Then she looked up at Ryan with such concern that Ryan knew she'd heard about Rupert, that probably Dallas had called her. Hanni would know every detail: Ryan's gun found in the trash, the bullets embedded in her garage wall, the fact that Ryan had no witness to her own whereabouts during the time that Rupert was killed.

"Private picnic?" Hanni called, turning the CD down to a soft rhythm and swinging out of the car. Her long, thin legs were encased in faded blue jeans that matched exactly the blue of the Mercedes, her slim, tanned feet cosseted in expensive handmade sandals. Above the denims she wore one of numerous handmade sweaters, this number a bright rainbow of many colors that set off Hanni's prematurely gray hair. She stood looking at the dog with wide-eyed admiration.

"Where did he come from? He's beautiful. Dallas didn't mention a dog." She waited impatiently for an explanation, watching Rock, not Ryan. Then seeing that no answers were forthcoming she sat down on the grass oblivious to dirt or grass stains—she wouldn't have any, and Ryan didn't know how she did that. Watching Ryan, Hanni searched gently for an exact reading to the morning's events, making Ryan's throat tighten. Sympathy always made her cry.

"You can tell me the bad stuff later," Hanni said. "Except, is there anything I can do?"

Ryan shook her head. "It . . . I don't think I want to talk about it." She looked up at Hanni. "The dog isn't mine. Well, maybe he is if I can't find the owner. If I could figure out how to keep him," she said hastily. "He showed up this morning, he was up in San Andreas."

"You brought him back with you?"

"No, I told you . . . he showed up on his own. He was in the kitchen when I went up after . . . after Dallas left."

Hanni frowned, puzzled.

"He was hanging around up at the trailer, with those kids. They said he was a stray."

"A dog like this?"

"We tried to find his owner." She told Hanni the story, and how she thought the dog had found his way to Molena Point.

"And now you're going to reunite him with that Farger boy? See if you can get the kid to talk?" Hanni stared at her. "You think you can soften up *that* kid? You think if he joined that old man in setting a bomb, you can get the kid to spill on him?"

"I need to try. The dog *might* make a difference."

Hanni just looked at her; but then her gaze softened. "If I can help, I'm here." Rising, she rubbed the dog behind the ears then opened his mouth with easy familiarity and looked at his teeth. "Young. Maybe two years old." She gave Ryan a clear, green-eyed look. "If you can't find the owner, you have a real treasure. He's some handsome fellow." She rose and backed away watching him move as he followed her. When she sat down again the dog dropped down beside her stirring a hot surge of jealousy in Ryan. To look at her and Hanni, anyone would pick Ryan as the rough-

and-tumble dog person, not impeccably groomed Hanni Coon. Yet it was Hanni who seemed able to train the roughest dog and still look like she was dressed for a party, not a smear of dirt, not a hair out of place.

Hanni lifted the dog's silky ears and looked inside, checking for ear mites and for a possible tattoo. She avoided mentioning Rupert directly. They both knew Ryan would be under investigation for his murder and that Ryan too might be in some danger. Picking up Ryan's purse Hanni opened it, reached into her own purse and, shielded by the dog and by Ryan, she slipped an unloaded revolver into Ryan's bag with a box of shells. She looked up at Ryan. "Until this is over, until you get yours back."

"Did Dallas . . . ?"

"No. He doesn't need to know," she said, ignoring the intricacies of California gun laws that gave a person a carrying permit for only specified models. Hanni patted Ryan's hand with sisterly tenderness. "I'm headed for the Landeau house. You have time to come along?

"I . . ."

"The rug arrived from England, it's in San Francisco. It will be down by truck, a day or two. I went over this morning to see if the gallery had delivered the sculpture for the fireplace. The floor's wet, I guess from last week's rain."

"Wet? How can it be wet?"

"The Landeaus have already installed the sculpture, I don't know when they were down. Not there now, and I can't get them on the phone. I nearly sank in water, the floor's soaked. That temporary rug under the skylight. We need to find the leak, we can't put down the new rug, with a leak."

"There is no leak. I didn't build a leaky house. What did they spill?" Ryan could feel anger heat her face. "I installed that skylight myself, Scotty and I. It couldn't have leaked, it has a huge lip and overhang and it's all sealed, you saw how it's made. That's the top-of-the-line model. It's molded all in one piece, absolutely leak-proof. We checked with the hose, Hanni! Did you call the Landeaus? What did they say?" The idea that an item she'd ordered and checked out might be shoddy infuriated her.

She had finished the Landeau remodel shortly before she left for San Andreas. The Landeaus had bought the place as a tear-down, meaning to start from ground up, but she'd talked them into gutting and refurbishing the well-built old cottage, turning it into a small and elegant Mediterranean retreat. She had torn out walls to create a flowing space for living, dining and master bedroom, and removed the old ceilings. The high, angled roof beams rose now to an octagonal skylight directly over the sunken sitting area.

She had covered the concrete floor, which was broken into three different levels following the rising hill, with big, handmade Mexican tiles the color of pale sandstone. Only the sunken sitting area was to be carpeted, with the rug that Hanni had designed, a thick, deep wool as brightly multicolored as Hanni's sweater, a rug to lie on reading, to sink into, to make love on. Hanni had ordered the handmade confection about the time Ryan started work on the house. The Landeaus had waited months for that rug, using a temporary brown shag that could be discarded when the new one arrived. And now that area was wet? The shag rug wet? She looked intently at Hanni. "The skylight did not leak. Marianna must have been down. What did she spill? Sullivan's blood?"

"Be nice, Ryan. You don't have to like the woman to do right by her professionally."

"I am doing right by her professionally. The skylight didn't leak."

She had a satisfactory enough business relationship with Marianna Landeau but she wasn't fond of her. Hanni jokingly said she was jealous of Marianna's beauty, but it was more than that. Marianna was a difficult woman to warm to. The pale-haired ex-model of nearly six feet—fine-boned, slim-waisted, as broad-shouldered as a Swedish masseuse—was as cold as an arctic sea.

Marianna dressed in silks with tangles of gold jewelry, and wound her flaxen hair in an elegant chignon so perfect that no ordinary woman could have mastered its construction on a day-to-day basis. Over the years that Ryan had worked with the Landeaus on their San Francisco house, she had never seen Marianna really smile, had *never* heard her laugh with pleasure, only with sarcasm. Marianna Landeau was beautiful ice, a client who paid on time, but a woman Ryan didn't understand and didn't care to know better.

Hanni gave the dog a pat. "It must have been awful this morning." She waited quietly, watching Ryan, hoping that Ryan might unburden herself. Ryan scowled at her, and they sat not speaking. The dog sighed and stretched out. Hanni said, "What are you going to name him?"

"Why would I name him? The kids called him Rock."

When Hanni reached to unbuckle the dog's collar, Ryan said, "No ID on that, I just bought that collar. I have to get moving, Hanni. I told Dallas I'd be over before the juvenile authorities get there—I can meet you at the cottage in an hour or so."

Hanni hugged the dog, and rose, one easy twist from flat on the ground to her full five-six, a movement like a dancer, the result of her passion for yoga. When Hanni got up, the big dog rose with equal grace and started to follow her. Ryan grabbed his collar. He gave her a sly sideways glance and sat down quietly beside her. It did cross her mind that they were both con artists.

"See you in an hour," Hanni said and headed for her Mercedes where a New Orleans trumpet was entertaining the neighborhood of cottages that edged the small park.

"Hour and a half," Ryan called, picking up her trash. Walking back with Rock to the truck, the dog turned puppyish, dancing around her, his tongue lolling. Loading him up, she headed for the police station wondering again if she was doing the right thing to approach Curtis Farger, if this was a smart move, trying to out-con that deceitful boy.

12

THE PARKING LOT OF MOLENA POINT COURTHOUSE was shaded by sprawling oak trees that rose from islands of flowering shrubs. The building, set well back from the street, was of Mediterranean style with deep porticos, white stucco walls, and tile paving. The police department occupied a long wing at the south end that ran out to meet the sidewalk. Recently, Captain Harper had remodeled the department to afford increased privacy and heightened security. The jail was in a separate building, at the back, across the small, fenced parking lot reserved for police cars. Within the station itself one holding cell was maintained, opening to the right of the locked and bulletproof glass entry. The seven-by-eight concrete room had an iron bunk, a toilet and sink and one tiny window high in the east wall secured by bars and shaded by an oak's dark foliage. The oak's three thick trunks angled up from the garden as gently as staircases. Joe Grey and Dulcie were set to race across the garden and up into the branches that covered the cell window, when whispers from above them in the tree sent them swerving away again, to crouch among the bushes.

A man clung high above, among the dark leaves, his shoes and pant cuffs just visible, his balance on the slanting trunk seeming unsteady. He wore high-topped, laced shoes, old man's shoes. Moving to a better vantage, the cats could see one gnarled hand reaching out to grip at the bars for support as he peered down through the little window. It must have been hard for the old boy to climb up, they could imagine him teetering, grabbing the surrounding limbs.

If this was Gramps Farger, he had plenty of nerve to come right to the station when every cop in the state was looking for him—or maybe he thought this was the last place they'd look. Joe wanted to shout and alert the department. His second, more studied response, was to shut up and listen.

The old man's faint quarrelsome whispers and the boy's hissing replies through the open window were so soft that even from within the police department, maybe no one would hear them, not even the dispatcher from her electronic cubicle; the whispers would be easily drowned among the noise of her radios and phones.

Slipping closer, where they could hear better, the cats began to smile.

"Them big mucky-mucks don't care," the old man rasped. "The way you muffed this one, Curtis, I'm sorry you showed up at all. You should've stayed in them mountains. Well, the deed's done—you blew it, big-time. Your pa sure ain't gonna be pleased."

The kid's reply slurred angrily against the rumble of a car engine starting in the parking lot. And not for the first time, Joe wished he had one of those tiny tape recorders, wished he was wired for sound.

"Your uncle ain't gonna like it neither. You know Hurlie don't tolerate sloppy work. And your ma . . ."

"None of *her* business."

"Them cops're gonna ask you plenty. You see you don't mention Hurlie or them San Andreas people. You don't tell no one you was up there. Pay attention, Curtis. You don't know nothing about where Hurlie is, you don't know nothing about where your old gramps is. You understand me?"

"What you think I'm gonna do," the kid snapped. "Why would I tell the cops anything?"

Apparently, Joe thought, the old man didn't know that Curtis had hitched a ride with Detective Garza's niece. What a joke. Maybe Curtis himself didn't know who she was.

"Keep your voice down. Don't matter I'm your grampa, I cut no slack if you mess up again."

"*Mess up!* That rabid damn cat near killed me. You don't give a damn about me, you don't give a damn if I die!"

"You ain't gonna die. From a cat scratch? And you sure as hell didn't see me over at that church, no matter what they ask." The old man peered down into the cell. "I'm out of here, Curtis. Meantime, you keep your mouth shut." And Gramps started shakily down the tree snatching at branches, putting his unsteady feet in all the wrong places. Nearly falling, stumbling down the last few feet he tumbled into the geraniums so close to Joe and Dulcie that they spun around, melting deeper into the bushes.

The old man rose, apparently none the worse for the spill, and turned toward the parking lot. The cats followed him out across the blacktop, staying under parked cars when they could, slipping along in the river of his scent, which was so overripe they could have trailed him blindfolded. This old codger needed a bath, big-time. A Laundromat wouldn't hurt, either. Pausing beneath a plumbing repair truck, they looked ahead for an old pickup, as the kit had described, for some rusted-out junker. The old man was passing a black Jaguar convertible when he whipped out a key.

It was not a new-model Jag but it was sleek and expensive. The top was down, and several celluloid kewpie dolls hung from the rearview mirror. The bucket seats were fitted out with tacky zebra-patterned covers as furry as an Angora cat. A very nice car, royally trashed.

Unlocking the driver's door, Gramps slid in and kicked the

engine to life. Pulling on a tan safari hat, he tucked his long shaggy hair under, and wriggled into a khaki jacket straight out of an old B movie. The attempted disguise was so ludicrous the cats wanted to roll over laughing. This old man wasn't for real, this old man was dotty.

But, in fact, he had changed the way he looked. As the old man sat at the wheel tying a white scarf around his throat, Joe glanced tensely back toward the station, his heart thudding with urgency. The old boy would be gone in a minute, he was going to get away, and all they had was the license number. Crouching to scorch up the tree thinking to shout through the holding-cell window and alert the dispatcher, get some muscle out there, Joe paused.

If he knew where the old man was going . . .

The tomcat crouched, tensed to leap in. Dulcie stopped him with a swipe of her paw, ears back, eyes blazing. "Don't, Joe!"

He backed off, hissing.

Gramps put the car in gear, revving the engine like a teenager—and at the same instant, Gramps saw Joe. Staring down at Joe, his expression said this guy was not a cat lover. Joe's paws began to sweat. Gramps cut the wheels suddenly and sharply toward the tomcat and gave it the gas—and the cats were gone, scorching under the plumbing truck, the Jaguar headed straight for them. Maybe, since the aborted church bombing, Gramps Farger hated all cats.

Safe under the big yellow vehicle, but ready to run again, they cringed as, at the last instant, Gramps swung a U just missing the truck and screeched off toward the street.

Coming out shakily, they fled up the nearest oak. Staring out, they could see the Jaguar heading north and then east, up into the hills. They watched until the car disappeared over the next rise.

At least they had a general direction, and they had the make and license. Who would be dumb enough to drive such an easily identifiable vehicle? Talk about chutzpah. And the old boy might as well have driven the Jaguar right on into the station, every cop in the village was looking for him. Did he think his stupid disguise would fool anyone?

But maybe it had fooled someone. Turning out of the lot, Gramps had passed two young officers returning on foot to the station. Both had looked right at him. With the scarf tucked up around his beard, and his grisly long hair out of sight, Gramps looked like just another eccentric, another tourist. The rookies looked at him and kept walking, no change of expression, no glance at each other, no quickening of their walk to hurry into the station. Complacent, Joe Grey thought. Harper needed to talk to those guys, shake them up.

But the two cops weren't the only ones to miss something.

Though the two cats couldn't have seen her, and with Gramps's overripe scent they would never have smelled her, the kit passed within feet of them crouched on the floor of the Jaguar. They had no hint that she was huddled behind the driver in the escaping car, shivering with excitement and with fear.

The kit knew Joe and Dulcie were there. From deep in the garden she had watched the old man pull into the lot and had watched him climb to the kid's cell window, had watched the two older cats approach to listen. Downwind from them, she had listened, too, then had beat it for the Jaguar, leaping in while Gramps was still precariously descending the tree. And now she was being borne away who-knew-where, in a car racing way too fast and she couldn't jump out and she was getting pretty scared. Was regetting, not for the first time, what Wilma called her impetuous nature.

"Who from San Andreas?" Joe said, feeling defeated and cross. "Who else besides this Uncle Hurlie? Who was the old man talking about?"

"I don't . . . There's Ryan's pickup, just pulling in."

As Ryan parked and swung out of the truck, the gray dog leaped out too, coming to heel. And Dallas stepped out of the station as if he had been waiting for them.

The detective looked the dog over. "You *found* this animal? How long was he running loose—five minutes?" The dog watched Dallas brightly, his yellow eyes alight as if he recognized a dog man, a kindred and understanding spirit. Only when Dallas put his arm around Ryan did the weimaraner growl.

Grinning, Dallas stepped away. "Looks like he's found his home." He looked down at Ryan. "You doing okay? You all right about what's ahead of you?"

"I guess. There's nothing I can do about it. Have you . . . You haven't been in touch with Harper?"

"He called, the murder's been on the San Francisco news. He and Charlie are coming back, canceling the cruise."

"Oh, damn! Because of me. Because of Rupert—and the bombing. Why does this have to spoil their honeymoon?"

Dallas squeezed her shoulder. "One of life's nasty tricks. One big, double calamity, sandwiched in with the good stuff." He knelt and beckoned the dog to him. Not until Ryan released him with a command, did Rock approach, sniffing Dallas's hand. The detective looked up at her. "You're going to keep him."

"I can't, Dallas. I don't . . ."

"He's pretty protective already, a little work and he could be useful."

"I don't need protection."

He just looked at her.

"Hanni—Hanni loaned me a gun."

"I don't need to know that. You could build a fence up that back hill for him, I'm sure Charlie wouldn't mind."

"Let's go in. I told Hanni I'd meet her up at the Landeau place in an hour, there's some kind of water problem. Leaky skylight, Hanni said."

"You've never installed a leaky skylight."

She tugged on his arm, heading for the station. "I'm losing my nerve. I'm not looking forward to this."

By the time they entered through the bulletproof glass doors, the cats were high in the oak outside the boy's window. Hidden among the leaves, they listened to the *scritch* of metal against metal as the cell door swung open.

No one spoke. They heard a sudden intake of breath and a doggy huff, then the scrabbling of claws on concrete. Warily they peered down through the bars.

Ryan sat alone on the end of the boy's cot. The boy stood rigid, his back to the wall, staring at her with rage as he held up an arm halfheartedly fending off the dog who, wild with joy, was leaping and pressing against him, his whine soft, his short tail madly wagging. Ignoring him, Curtis's cheek was touched with shine. Was the kid crying—or was that dog spit?

Ryan watched him evenly. "What's his real name, besides Rock?"

"How would I know? He's a stray. Why did you bring him here? What do you mean, his real name?"

"He rode down in the truck with you."

"So he got in the truck. What was I supposed to do, shove him out? And what difference? He don't belong to no one—he don't belong to *you*."

"He's a beautiful dog. I can see he's your buddy."

"Do I look like he's my buddy? What do you want?"

"He rode down with you, so I figure you're responsible for him. You want him running the streets, hit by a car on the highway? That would be ugly, Curtis."

"So take him home with you."

"I can't keep him. I live in a small apartment, I have no yard for a dog."

"Feed him, he'll stay around."

"I can't let him run loose. If I knew where he lived . . ."

Curtis just looked at her.

"I could take him back to San Andreas, to his owners, or to the people you were staying with."

No answer. The dog licked Curtis's face then looked past him through the bars, watching someone. In a moment there was a stirring at the cell door, and the air was filled with the smell of hamburgers and fries.

The blond, matronly dispatcher, glancing in at Ryan, handed a large paper bag through the bars. Boy and dog sniffed as one, eyeing the grease-stained bag.

Tearing open the bag, Ryan spread it out on the bunk, revealing four burgers, a box of fries, a large box of onion rings and a tall paper cup that, when the boy began to drink, left a smear of chocolate across his lip. Curtis didn't wait to be asked. Gulping most of the first burger, he slipped a few bites to the dog. Ryan said, "If you can't tell me where he lives, I'll have to take him to the pound."

Curtis glanced around the tiny cell as if thinking the dog could stay there.

"I work all day, Curtis. I can't keep him. Maybe the pound will find him a home before they have to gas him."

For the first time, the boy's defiance faltered. "You looked all over up there for his owner. There's no way you'd take him to the pound."

"I have no choice, unless I can find his owner. I'd drive him back up to San Andreas, to people who'd take care of him, if you'll tell me where. Otherwise it's a cage at the pound and maybe the gas chamber."

"You won't do that."

"Try me. I can't keep him, and I don't know anyone who can. I'd rather take him home. If I have to, I'll call the weimaraner breeder's association. They'd have the name of the registered owner."

The boy nearly flew at her. "You can't! They'll kill him."

"Who would kill him?"

The boy reverted to glaring. Beside him, the dog's brow wrinkled as he looked from one to the other, distressed by their angry voices.

"You want to fill me in, Curtis? Tell me where he belongs?"

"The dog's a stray. I meant—the place I was staying, they . . . they don't like dogs. They ran him off."

"Where were you staying, Curtis? Who were you staying with?"

Curtis turned his back, and said no more. The cats were nearly bursting, wanting to shout the name Hurlie, burning to tell Ryan about the uncle that the old man wanted so badly kept secret.

Ryan stayed with the boy for perhaps half an hour more, but nothing was forthcoming. She gave up at last and left the cell. The cats could hear her talking with Dallas, out near the dispatcher's cubicle, then their voices faded as if they had headed back to his office. "Maybe," Joe said, "Ryan's cell phone is in the truck, and we can fill them in about Hurlie?"

"She'll have locked it," Dulcie said. "But she's meeting Hanni. Hanni leaves her phone in the car with the top down."

Joe Grey smiled.

Dropping from the oak tree, they crossed the parking lot running beneath parked cars and leaped into the back of Ryan's truck, settling down beneath the tarp ready for a ride up the hills.

A cat, at best, is not long on patience. Ask any sound sleeper whose cat tramps across his stomach at three in the morning demanding to be let out to hunt. Joe Grey was fidgeting irritably by the time they saw Ryan coming. Burrowing flat as pancakes beneath the folded tarp, they were glad that Rock had taken over the front seat, that he wouldn't leap into the truck bed nosing at their hiding place.

But as it turned out, it would be Rock who would nose out, for the cats, the connection between the church bomber and Rupert Dannizer's killer.

Ryan was pulling out of the parking lot when a horn honked. The cats didn't peer out from beneath the tarp, but when she slowed the truck they heard Clyde's voice over the sound of the idling antique Chevy.

"Can I do anything?" he said quietly.

"Thanks, but it's all in hand—at the moment."

"You okay?"

"So far. Just on my way over to the Landeau place to meet Hanni."

Clyde's car moved ahead a little. "Free for dinner?"

"Matter of fact, I am. That would be nice—something early? Burgers and a beer? And we can go over some last-minute details on tomorrow's work. Could I come by for you, and put this fellow in your yard?"

"Sounds good, and you can tell me about him. Around six?"

"See you then."

Clyde pulled out, shifting gears. As he drove away, and Ryan turned into the street, Joe's thoughts returned to the Farger clan, to Curtis's uncle Hurlie. Riding beside Dulcie half-smothered by the tarp, he was all twinges and prickling fur, the San Andreas connection compelling and urgent. Did Gramps get the makings for the bomb up in San Andreas with the help of Hurlie? Hurlie gave that lethal package to Curtis, and Curtis carried it down to Molena Point in the back of Ryan's truck? Curtis delivers the gunpowder or whatever in Ryan's truck, Gramps makes up the bomb, then sends Curtis up on the roof to set it off.

Of course the law would be onto it. Now that Ryan had found a connection between Curtis and San Andreas, Garza and Harper would be onto it like pointers on a covey of quail.

But was the law missing one piece of vital information? As far as Joe could tell, they had no clue yet about Hurlie Farger. Or, if they knew that Hurlie existed, they apparently didn't know that he was in San Andreas, that *he* was the San Andreas connection.

But Joe forgot Hurlie as Ryan turned into the drive before the Landeau cottage. As she pulled up to park, the big dog began to lunge at the window, leaping at the half-open glass roaring and snarling, pawing to get out.

13

THE OLD MAN WAS A FAST DRIVER. HE TOOK THE winding road at such a pace that, on the floor behind the driver's seat, the kit had to dig her claws hard into the thick black rug. The Jaguar fishtailed and skidded around the tight curves swaying and twisting ever higher into the hills. Against the late afternoon sky, she couldn't see any treetops but sometimes she could glimpse the wild, high mountains toward which they were headed. Behind the car, the sun was dropping, shifting its position as the road turned. She had no notion where he was going or how she would get home again; she was sorry she'd hidden in the old man's car. She'd started to be sorry when she heard him come across the parking lot and open the car door but already it was too late, he was starting the engine. Now the cold wind that swooped down to the floor of the convertible snatched at her fur and whistled inside her ears, and the sharp chemical smell that clung inside the small space burned her nose so that tears came. When the car began to climb even more steeply she felt her stomach lurch until soon she thought she'd have to throw up as she always did when riding in cars. But she daren't, he would hear her retching.

Soon, above the ugly stinks, she could smell sage and mountain shrubs. At every squeal of tires she hunched lower. When at last he skidded to a stop on dirt and gavel, she thought she must be a hundred miles from home. Even Joe Grey would not have been foolish enough to get in the car with this man. She could smell dry dust, and the rich scent of chickens, and more chemical smells. She was terrified he would look in the backseat and find her.

But he didn't look, he got out and slammed the car door. She heard him go up three wooden steps and into a house or building and slam that door too. She waited, shivering. When after a long time she heard nothing more she slipped warily up the back of the furry zebra seat and poked her nose over the edge of the door, looking.

She was so high up the hills that only the jagged mountains rose above her, tall and rocky and bare, their thin patches of grass baked brown from the heat of August and September, brown and dry. Down below her, the road they had taken wound sickeningly along the side of the cliff. The rough clearing where the car stood was only a shelf cut into the bank, just big enough to hold an unpainted cabin and two sheds, all so close to the edge that she imagined at the slightest jolt of earthquake the buildings sliding off into the chasm below.

She could see, farther down the cliff, three rough chicken pens made of wire, with plywood roofs, and though she could smell the dusty scent of chickens, she could not hear them clucking or flapping.

When she looked toward the shack she could see through a dirty window the old man moving around in there, she could hear him opening cupboards or shifting furniture, making some kind of dull thudding racket. Had that boy lived here with him? Curious to see more, she hopped to the back of the front seat. She was rearing up on her hind paws when the old man came out again suddenly. In panic she dropped to the ground beneath a clump of dry sage—leaving pawprints etched in the dust behind her.

Maybe he would think they were the tracks of ground squirrels or rabbits. Hiding among the bushes she watched him carry out four black plastic garbage bags tied at the tops, their bulging sides lumpy with what looked like boxes and cans, bags that stunk like a hundred drugstore chemicals spilled together or like the garden center of the hardware store with all its baits and poisons where she had wandered once and been scolded by Dulcie and Joe, smells that made her want to back away sneezing. Was this the bomb stuff? She tried to remember what Clyde and the police had said when they were talking about the bomb. She wasn't sure what she remembered and what she'd imagined about that terrible day. She remained frozen still as the old man loaded the dirty bags into his nice car. When he started the car she fled away deeper among the tangled growth that edged the yard.

He turned the car around in the clearing, its wheels just inches from the drop-off, and headed away down the twisting road leaving her alone. As the car descended snaking along the edge of the ravine she reared up looking at the land, hoping to see the way home. She could have been on the moon, for all the feel of direction she had after that blind and twisting ride.

Though anyone would know east by the rising mountains, and west by the dropping sun. The sun *was* dropping, fast. She did not want to be caught here at night. The kit loved the night, she loved to roam in the night, but up here in the wild high ridges where bobcats and cougar and coyotes hunted, night was another matter.

Standing at the edge of the clearing, her ears and her fluffy tail flattened by the wind, she looked west down curve after curve of summer-brown slopes, far down to the shifting layers of fog and to the tiny village, so far away.

Well, she wasn't lost. Cats didn't get lost. Not when they could see the mountains and the sun hanging low in the sky and the wide fog-bound Pacific. *I'm a big cat now.* And, scanning the falling hills for possible places to hide when she was ready to make her way home, she spotted the best of all refuges.

Far below among the tree-scattered hills stood the dark tangle of broken walls and crumbling buildings that marked the Pamillon estate where she had hidden from the cougar, and from a human killer. Where she had once, as the cougar slept in the sun on the cracked brick patio, almost touched him, until Joe snatched her away. There among the Pamillon ruins were all manner of caves and crannies.

Now that she knew where to hide in the falling night, she didn't hurry. First she would do as Dulcie and Joe Grey would do. She was about to approach the cabin when, way down on the winding road, she saw a car moving fast toward the ruined estate, a black, open convertible.

Why would the old man go there? It would soon be too dark for humans in that place. What was he doing? Did he mean to dump his plastic bags there? Was the Pamillon estate, with all its mystery, nothing more to that old man than a place to get rid of his garbage?

Turning away with disgust, trotting up the steps to the cabin and hearing no sound within, she considered the ill-fitting door. Standing on her hind legs, then swinging on the knob, she forced it open and quickly she slipped inside.

The floor was dirt, tramped hard, and the wooden walls were so rough that when she pressed her nose against the planks their splinters stuck her. Nor was there much furniture. Two rough wooden armchairs with ancient dusty seats, a scarred aluminum dinette table with two mismatched aluminum chairs, a small old bookcase filled with jars of peanut butter, pickles, baked beans, and a half loaf of bread that smelled stale.

Attached to one wall was a plain laundry sink and next to it a tiny old refrigerator whose motor sounded sick. A second room led off the first, a niche no bigger than Wilma's bathroom, just enough space for two cots at right angles and a wooden chair with a pair of man's shoes tossed underneath. Every surface was rimed with dust, even the plank walls. Big nails in the wall held some wrinkled shirts and pants, some of a small size that might belong to the boy. Certainly the old man slept here, she could smell him. No cat would let himself get so rank, only a dog and some humans would tolerate that kind of stink on themselves. She could still smell the nose-burning chemical smells too, so strong she could taste them. Something about those smells rang alarms for her, something that came from police talk. Nosing along the walls she looked for a closet to investigate, but there was none.

Slipping outside again panting for fresh air she circled the small, crude building, padding quickly around it even where it hung out nearly over the ravine; and the chemical smell led her down the steep canyon toward the chicken pens.

She had no notion how long the old man would be gone. The cages all looked abandoned. Longing to head down the hills into fresh air and into the golden light of last-sun, instead she trotted closer, approaching the wire enclosures.

HEADING FOR THE LANDEAU COTTAGE, RYAN'S THOUGHTS were still on Clyde, comforted by his easy ways and quiet reassurance; just their few brief words, in the parking lot of the station over the sound of their idling engines, had eased her tension. Maybe she'd call him early, see if they could take Rock for a run before dinner. Maybe with Clyde she could sort out the fear that had shadowed her ever since she found Rupert's body.

She didn't ordinarily confide in new acquaintances, but Clyde was Max Harper's lifelong friend. Dallas trusted him; and Clyde had stood steadfastly by Harper when the captain was accused of murder. And better to burden Clyde with her fears than Dallas. Her uncle wasn't in an easy position. New man in the department, appointed chief of detectives over someone with more seniority, and now his niece was under suspicion of murder. No need to lay more stress on him

She supposed she wasn't very trustful of men anymore, not

since marrying Rupert. Not trustful as she had once been when she was young, growing up in a household nurtured by three strong men. Those associations, and spending her weekends bird hunting with her dad's and Dallas's friends, or hanging around San Francisco PD waiting for Dallas, or at the probation office with her dad, she had always felt easy and confident. Though, in fact, in that law-enforcement atmosphere she *had* developed a wariness too. A wait-and-see view of outsiders that some folks would call judgmental, but that a cop would call sensible. More than once that mind-set had served her well, though it sure had deserted her when she met Rupert.

She wondered if, after you died, you had the chance to look back and assess the way you'd lived your life. She couldn't seem to leave that thought alone.

Even after seeing Rupert cruelly torn she could feel nothing generous toward him. That fact distressed her, that she was thinking about Rupert as heartlessly as Rupert himself had thought about others. This was not a time to be bitter. Maybe Clyde could help her put these last few days into a kinder framework—a friend she could lean on, someone not family and not part of law enforcement, someone who need not be careful of his conversation with a frightened murder suspect. Just someone steady to help her sort through the tangle. And, turning into the drive of the Landeau cottage, thinking about Clyde, Ryan had no idea that other friends were ready to help her, friends so near to her at that moment that she could have stepped back and touched them, two small friends ready to assist in their own quiet way.

14

THE LANDEAU COTTAGE STOOD AMONG LIVE OAKS in the rising hills north of the village, its leaded windows set deep into white stucco walls, reflecting the mossy, twisted branches. A ray of late-afternoon sun shone down through the trees illuminating the domed skylight and tile roof. The clearing in front of the cottage was planted with a variety of drought-resistant native shrubs artfully arranged among giant boulders. Beneath a grandfather oak a wide parking bay was paved with granite blocks, and a granite drive led back to the garage, which was hidden behind the house in the style of 1910 when cars had just begun to replace horses and were put in the barn at night like their predecessors. The neighboring houses were hardly visible, just a hint of roof to the north between the dense trees, and on the south a few feet of blank garage wall; a private and secluded retreat, for an undisturbed weekend. As Ryan pulled her truck onto the parking next to Hanni's blue Mercedes, Rock went rigid, sniffing warily through the partially open window, his gaze fixed on the house, and the next moment leaping at the glass, barking and fighting to get out.

Easing open her door, Ryan meant to slip out and leave him inside until she knew what was the matter, but he exploded past her jamming one hard foot into her thigh, half knocking her out of the truck. He hit the drive roaring. She piled out behind, hanging onto his leash. He lunged again, up the drive, charging ahead with such force that she had to turn sideways jerking the leash tight across her legs to keep from being pulled to her knees.

The cottage door opened. Hanni stepped out watching the dog and glancing toward the back of the house where Rock was staring as if to launch for someone's throat—the dog looked toward the house too, his lip curled over businesslike teeth, but then returned his attention to whoever stood, out of sight on the drive. Ryan thought of Hanni's gun tucked in her purse, which she'd tossed on the seat of the truck when Rock bolted past her.

But this was a small, quiet village, not the streets of east L.A. Even with Rupert's murder and the church bombing, as horrifying as both had been, Molena Point wasn't a crime zone. Yet, watching Rock, watching the drive, she was deeply chilled.

FROM THE WOODS WHERE THEY HAD HIDDEN WHEN THEY dropped out of Ryan's truck, Joe Grey and Dulcie watched the big dog too, the fur on their backs rigid, every muscle tense, ready to scorch up a tree out of harm's way.

But then suddenly Rock relaxed, raised his head and cocked his ears and gave a questioning wag of his short tail. And as Ryan eased back, seeming to let out her breath, Rock trotted eagerly forward, all smiles and wags.

The old man who came up the drive was tiny, dressed in faded work clothes and carrying a stack of empty seedling flats. He seemed not much taller than the hound; and surely Rock's teeth were sharper. What dog would think of growling at Eby Coldiron? The cats slipped closer toward the drive as Ryan hugged Eby. Eby stroked Rock then backed away to have a look at him.

135

"This is a fine animal, Ryan. When did you get him? Will he hunt?"

"It's a long story, Eby. Complicated—the kind of story for over a cup of coffee when Louise is here too."

Eby grinned at her and nodded and continued to pet Rock, who wriggled and danced under the small gardener's hand. Typical canine behavior, Joe thought. So hungry for acceptance. Eby and his wife were Ryan's landscaping contractors and they worked with Hanni, as well. The Coldirons were in their eighties, Eby no bigger than a twelve-year-old boy, white-haired and frail-looking, but as strong as coiled steel. The skilled landscaper shared Ryan's liking for native plant environments in an area where water was often scarce. He was dressed this morning in his usual khaki shirt, his jeans rolled up over muddy jogging shoes. Eby bought his clothes in the boys' department of Penny's or Sears.

"Where's your truck?" Ryan said. "Where's Louise?"

"She took the truck, went to shop. Said she'd bring back a pizza but she gets in those stores, forgets the time."

Eby's wife was as minute as he, and nearly as wiry. Like Eby, she bought her clothes in the children's section, size ten-to-twelve. Eby maintained a capable gardening crew, but he and Louise liked to do the new landscaping themselves. They might be old and wizened, the cats thought, but Ryan said she had never seen a happier marriage. The Coldirons not only handled the landscaping for half-a-dozen builders, but now and then they purchased a decrepit old house and refurbished it, doing much of the work themselves. And they took a nice cruise every winter to Hawaii or to Curacao or the Bahamas. As Eby stacked his flats at the curb and returned to the back of the house, and Ryan and Hanni disappeared inside, Joe leaped into Hanni's open convertible looking for her cell phone.

It wasn't there. Not on the seat, not under the seat, not in the console that he managed to flip open, nor in the glove compartment.

Dropping out of the car again, he headed for the house beside Dulcie. On the porch the dog lay obediently, his leash hooked around the six-by-six stanchion that supported the sweeping line of the roof. Ryan had left the door open, apparently so she could watch him.

Seeing neither Ryan or Hanni inside, the cats padded casually across the stone porch, facing the big weimaraner, ready to run if he lunged at them.

Rock looked at them with doggy amusement, not offering to attack in a sudden game of catch-the-kitty. Quickly they slipped inside, to crouch behind a carved Mexican chest beside the front door.

The room was big and open, the floor on several levels. The seating area was the lowest, with glass walls on three sides, a glass cube set against the oak woods. Its fourth side stepped up to the tiled entry. Its high rafters rose to the skylight, where the mid-morning sun sent diffused light down across the tall fireplace. The built-in, raised seating was covered with bright pillows tossed against the glass walls. With the woods crowding in from outside, the sunken room was like a forest grotto, the embroidered pillows brilliant against the leafy background. Ryan knelt before the fire-place examining the wet rug.

She glanced up at the skylight, and studied the face of the fire-place: the plain white slab that rose from floor to vaulted ceiling showed no sign of water stains. Its surface was broken by three tall rectangular indentations, painted black inside, each holding a stainless-steel sculpture of abstract design.

From behind the Mexican chest, Dulcie drank in the beautiful room with twitching tail and wide eyes. The tiled entry stepped up again to the raised dining area, which gave the impression of a cave. To the right of that, and two steps higher, rose the master bedroom, its bank of white, carved doors standing open, its bright bedspread mirroring the colors of the sitting-room pillows. Looking and looking, Dulcie had the same rapt expression on her tabby face as when she made off with a neighbor's cashmere sweater, the same little smile in her green eyes—a greedy female joy in beauty, a hunger for the lovely possessions that no cat could ever truly own.

KNEELING IN THE SITTING-WELL EXAMINING THE WET RUG, Ryan wondered who Marianna had sent down to install the three pieces of sculpture. Maybe the sculptor himself? He lived fairly near, some miles south of San Francisco. The job wouldn't have taken long. One didn't have to drill, just install and tighten the tension brackets, but certainly it wasn't like Marianna to lift a hand. Marianna had left no message on Hanni's tape, as she might if she'd been down. When Ryan felt the rug, it was wet all along the fireplace and back about three feet. Already it smelled of mildew. Using a screwdriver, she pried up a corner to feel the pad beneath.

The pad was sopping. Looking up at the skylight, she studied its pleated shade that had been drawn across the transparent dome. Not a sign of water stain, nor were the white walls of the skylight-well stained.

Rising, she fetched the pole with which to open the shade. When she accordioned it back, there was no spill of water, only sunlight fell more brightly into the room. Fetching a ladder from the truck she covered its ends with clean rags so not to mar the wall, and climbed to examine the Plexiglas dome at close range.

Finding no tiniest streak or discoloration, she frowned down at Hanni. "There's no leak, never has been."

Hanni stared up at her. "But the Landeaus haven't been here. And it did rain last week. Go up on the roof, Ryan. Have a look up there."

"When you called them, told them the rug was wet, what did they say?"

"My god, I didn't *tell* her it was wet. I just casually asked if they'd been down. She said *no*. I should tell that woman the roof leaks? You want her all over you?"

"But it hasn't leaked. Either they've been down or someone else has been here. Did you check for a break-in? Call her again. Make her tell you when they were here, and what happened, or if they loaned out the key."

"*Make* Marianna tell me?" Hanni stared up at her, then went to check the windows. Soon the cats could hear her phoning. Ryan came down the ladder, telescoped it, and carried it outside where she extended it full length against the house.

SWINGING ONTO THE ROOF, SHE REMOVED HER SHOES AND LAID them in the gutter. Walking barefoot across the glazed clay tiles, she knelt beside the skylight. She examined every inch. There was no way this baby could leak. She checked the installation of roof tiles over its two-foot apron, where the roof slanted down. There was no hairline crack in either the Plexiglas bubble or in the casing. Intending to develop irrefutable proof, she went down to the backyard, got a plastic pail from the garage, filled it with water, carried it up, and slowly poured it over the unoffending skylight while Hanni watched from inside.

Only after four bucketfuls of water and no leak was Hanni willing to call Marianna again. She came back from the phone shaking her head.

"Not home. I got Sullivan. They haven't been down. Maybe it's from underneath the floor, maybe a broken water line."

"There is no water line there," Ryan said irritably. "The water lines, Hanni, are under the kitchen and bath."

"Waste line?" Hanni said lamely.

"For a top interior designer, you awe me with your ignorance."

"Just trying to be helpful."

Ryan knelt, sniffing at the rug at close range, moving to smell several places. She looked up at Hanni. "I smell wine. Call her, Hanni. Asked her if she spilled wine. My god, if she tried to mop it up, with that amount of water—she must have spilled the whole bottle."

"I don't want to call again. Let's take the rug up."

Within ten minutes they had the wet rug up. Moving the car and truck, they spread it across the parking apron as if carpeting the driveway for royalty. While they were thus occupied, and Joe watched from the living room windows, Dulcie found Hanni's purse in the kitchen and pawed inside searching for Hanni's cell phone.

Not there.

The Landeau phone stood on the kitchen counter right above her, but she daren't use it. Even as Joe stood watch, Ryan and Hanni returned to the house.

"They *were* here," Ryan grumbled, coming in. "And they spilled something. Did you tell Sullivan we're laying the new rug tomorrow?"

"I told him."

"Why didn't he tell you what they did? We can't lay the rug until we know for sure what this is. The only other possibility is groundwater, and I have a deep trench clear around the hillside. Maybe Marianna came down alone and didn't tell Sullivan."

Hanni raised an eyebrow.

"Have you checked your tape again? Maybe she left you a message."

Hanni just looked at her, her short white hair catching a gleam through the skylight.

"Call your tape. Where's your cell phone?"

"Forgot to charge it last night," Hanni said. "Left it home in the charger."

"If you'd get another battery . . ."

Hanni shrugged, and headed for the kitchen as Ryan stepped outside to stroke Rock. The dog glanced in toward the space behind the carved chest where the cats crouched, but then he grew rigid, looking nervously around the room and pulling to get inside. Hanni returned, looking at her watch.

"Marianna called my tape half an hour ago. Said she just woke up, said she was down day before yesterday and spilled a bottle of pinot noir, that she came down to tend to some errands and to arrange a birthday surprise for Sullivan—that it was too late to call me, that she hadn't told Sullivan she was down here and she knew I wouldn't spoil the surprise. She took a lot of time explaining it all," Hanni said, amused.

Ryan laughed. "So. Cold-blooded Marianna has a lover?"

Dulcie glanced at Joe, her green eyes equally amused. Sullivan Landeau was out of town a lot, was on the boards of half-a-dozen companies. She had heard Ryan and Clyde speculating on what Marianna did for entertainment.

"She said the wine bottle spun and fell before she could grab it, that there was wine everywhere, that she sopped it up with towels, and sponged the rug."

"Can you imagine Marianna Landeau sponging a rug?"

"Dallas was on my tape too. He has the report from ballistics. He wants you to go on back to your place, he'll meet you there."

Ryan had knelt to examine the wood floor. Looking up at Hanni, she stiffened. "Why my place, why not the station when it's only a few blocks away? Why doesn't he want me to come to the station?"

"He said he'd let himself in. Shall I come with you?"

"Why do I feel so cold? I have no reason to fear the ballistics report."

"You didn't kill him, so what's the big deal?"

Ryan rose, biting her lip. As they turned to leave, the cats slipped out past them and dropped into the bushes, moving so close to Rock they brushed against his leg, startling the big dog. They were concealed among the lavender bushes when Ryan undid Rock's leash.

Crossing to her truck as Hanni locked the house, Ryan was just getting into the cab when the Coldiron truck arrived, Louise driving. Hanni waved to her. "Good shopping?"

"Awesome," the little woman said, laughing.

"You want a rug for one of your rentals?" Hanni gestured toward the ten-by-ten square of beige shag. "It's nearly new. A bit damp. It smells like pinot noir."

"Added bonus," Louise said as Eby came up the drive.

The cats watched Ryan turn out onto the street as Louise and Eby and Hanni rolled up the rug. And still they hadn't called Dallas to tell him they'd seen the old man, to give the detective the make and license of the unlikely car Gramps was driving.

"SENIOR CITIZENS," RYAN TOLD THE BIG SILVER DOG AS SHE turned out of the drive, glancing back at the Coldirons. "Tough as old boots." Of the half-dozen older people she had met since she moved to the village, the Coldirons were not unusual. Theirs was a tough generation. She wondered if her own age group could half keep up with them, or with Charlie's gray-haired aunt Wilma who walked miles everyday, and could hold her own on the pistol range. Or with Cora Lee French or with sixty-some Mavity Flowers who still did forty hours a week cleaning houses. "Those folks were the depression children, the children of war, the survivors," she told Rock. "Tough as alligator hide." And she kept talking to the big dog to avoid thinking. She did not want to go home and face Dallas's ballistics report.

"SHE'S SCARED," DULCIE SAID, WATCHING FROM THE BUSHES as Ryan's red truck pulled away. "Scared to go home, afraid of what Dallas has found. If Rupert was shot with her stolen gun . . ."

"So someone set her up. Question is, what other contrived evidence did they leave for the police to find?" Joe watched Hanni help the Coldirons load the rug. When the truck and Hanni's Mercedes pulled away, he rubbed his face against a warm boulder then leaped atop the smooth granite, looking around the garden. "What was the dog on about? What did he smell?" He stood looking, then dropped down again and trotted back along the drive sniffing at the concrete.

He picked up Eby's scent, then that of Hanni and of the dog. He found the fainter scent, perhaps days old, of a woman, most likely Marianna Landeau. Nothing else. Whatever the dog had smelled, escaped him. His mind still on getting access to a phone and calling Dallas, he turned to look at Dulcie.

"It's only ten blocks to Ryan's place, and the day's getting warm. Maybe she'll leave the truck window down for a few minutes—right there in her own driveway. Maybe we can call Dallas while he's still at her apartment."

"Just a nice run," Dulcie said, and she took off through the woods heading downhill toward Ryan's duplex. Leaping bushes or brushing beneath them, she was thankful that she and Joe had been given more than the usual amount of feline stamina; most cats were sprinters, your average housecat was not made for long-distance running. Careening down the last hill to the back of Ryan's apartment and around to the front, she wasn't even panting hard.

A squad car sat in the drive beside Ryan's truck. The cats smelled fresh coffee. They circled both vehicles, but all the windows were up; and the covered door handles were beyond a cat's ability to manipulate. Joe leaped at them, trying, but it was no good. There was no chance of using either phone to call the detective. Joe gave her a sour look and they fled around the side of the duplex to the back, where the tiny bathroom window waited.

15

LEAPING AT THE SILL, JOE SNATCHED AND CLUNG, hanging by his claws, peering down into the empty bathroom, then dropping to the sink and to the linoleum. As Dulcie followed, faintly they heard Ryan and Dallas talking, their voices so solemn that Dulcie shivered.

She liked Ryan Flannery; the young woman was bold and bright. She liked her because Clyde did, and because she was Dallas Garza's niece. Liked her because Ryan had taken hold of her life and straightened out the kinks, exercising an almost feline degree of sensible independence: If you're not welcome, if you're badly treated, make a new start on life.

Now that Ryan was just into her new life, she didn't need this malicious attempt to ruin her.

From behind, Joe nudged her. "Get a move on." She'd been crouched as still as if frozen at a mouse hole, overwhelmed by her own thoughts. Trotting into the studio, out of sight of the kitchen, they slipped beneath Ryan's daybed.

The hardwood floor was admirably clean, no sneeze-making dust, not a fuzz ball in sight. That was another plus for Ryan.

There was something really depressing about finding the under-side of a couch thick with stalagmites of ancient, congealed dirt, the dusty floor littered with bobby pins, lost pencils, and old gum wrappers, with tangles of debris that clung to the whiskers or was gritty to the paws.

Looking across the big room to the front windows, they could see neat piles of papers stacked on Ryan's desk but they couldn't see much of the kitchen, just the end of the table and Dallas's shoulder. They could smell, besides fresh coffee, the greasy-sugar scent of doughnuts, and could hear the occasional cup clink against a saucer. Dallas said, "I wish your dad were here."

"Please don't call him, there's no need for him to think about the murder just now, to take his mind off what he's doing. I'll tell him when he gets home, when he's done with this training. You're my dad too, you and Scotty. Except, *you* can't play that role just now."

"I can play any hand I like. But it would be nice to have Mike here. You sure you don't want to stay with me or with Hanni, not be alone?"

"I'm fine. If the killer had wanted me dead, he'd have come after me instead of Rupert. I need to do a ton of desk work, clean up a stack of letters, pay my bills. I did manage to do the Jakeses' billing, I have that almost ready to mail."

"I'm glad you've got this big guy." The cats heard Dallas pat-ting the silver dog.

"What did Captain Harper say when he called, when you told him there'd been a murder? I can imagine he wasn't happy."

"He didn't say much, took it in stride. Said he and Charlie are having a great time in the city. They're taking a couple of days to drive home, through the wine country. And before they leave San Francisco he's going to make a contact for me. Something I'd rather he did in person."

"About Rupert?"

"A couple of guys on the force owe me. Good friends. You remember Tom Wills and Jessie Parker."

"Of course. They were partners. Tom's wife teaches second grade."

"I'm giving them a list of the women I know Rupert was involved with. They can do a rundown on them, and on their husbands and boyfriends. Here's the list. Anyone you'd care to add? Or any facts that would help?"

The cats heard paper rattle, then a little silence. Then, "You were very thorough, all these years. I don't know half these names. Barbara Saunders? Darlene Renthke? June Holbrook? Martie Holland? I haven't a clue, I never heard of these women. My god. How many were there? And you never told me. This makes me feel so unclean. Well here are five I know, all right. And you can add Priscilla Bloom. She drives a little red Porsche with, very likely, marks from a tow chain on the rear bumper, and a citation on record for blocking traffic on the street in front of my house."

Dallas laughed.

"So Max will spend his honeymoon getting that line of the investigation started," Ryan said. "And on the way home, they'll swing through San Andreas to check on the Fargers? I'll bet Charlie's thrilled, having to cancel a dream voyage."

"I imagine they made that decision before they left the village. Doesn't matter," Dallas said. "Those two will have a long and happy honeymoon no matter where they are."

There was longer silence, broken by doggy chuffing as if someone was feeding the weimaraner doughnuts. Ryan said, "I feel so stupid not to have heard anything that night, not to have waked up. You're going to make him sick with doughnuts."

"Why don't you call Charlie on their cellular, see if she'll let you put up a fence out back. It's not the optimum yard but it'll do."

"I told you, I don't plan to keep him."

"Of course you'll keep him. I wouldn't want to try to take him away. When I touch him, you're jealous as a hen with chicks."

"Why does everyone in the family always know what I'm thinking! And what I intend to do!"

"He's a stray, Ryan. He's been abandoned. You going to take him to the pound, like you told Curtis? If he'd been lost, the owner would have been looking all over San Andreas for him."

She sighed. "You look tired. Have you eaten anything this morning besides doughnuts? Did you have breakfast?"

"Eggs and bacon. I'm fine. Davis took the evidence up to the county lab herself, the casts of footprints, the dried mud she bagged, the garbage. She wasn't happy with Bonner walking through the mud behind the garage. Between the gun and bloody rags in the trash, of course the footprints were important."

The cats had heard that before, that police officers were too often the biggest contaminators of a crime scene. Cops walking through the evidence, maybe in a hurry to apprehend a prowler. It just went to show, life wasn't perfect. What was a cop supposed to do, fly around on little angel wings?

"Davis did a good job photographing the prints," Dallas added. "*She* stayed out of the mud."

"You're stalling. Was it my gun that killed him?"

"It's Sunday, Ryan. I had to get a ballistics man off his fishing boat. He wasn't happy. The only reason I did was to keep from having to arrest you and set up an arraignment."

"If it wasn't my gun, you'd have told me right away."

"I'll have the full report tomorrow. But ballistics turned up enough to keep from booking you."

"*What*! It *wasn't* my gun? Why didn't you tell me!"

"The two bullets in your garage wall were fired from your gun, but ballistics doesn't think they killed Rupert. There was no blood or flesh on them."

"But how . . . ? Those holes in the wall were so small. They couldn't be my loads, mine would have done more damage. The holes in the back of his head . . ." she said sickly. "What am I missing here?"

"Forensics says Rupert was shot at about six feet by a hard case thirty-eight bullet or maybe a thirty-two."

147

"But I load hollow points. You know that."

There was a long silence.

"What?" she said. "You know I load with hollow points."

Another silence. They heard the dog's toenails on the linoleum. Dallas said, "Are you sure of your load? Are you certain what you loaded?"

"Of course I'm sure."

Another heavy pause as if each word took great effort. "Your thirty-eight, registered to you, with your prints on it, was loaded with hard case. Four rounds and two empty cylinders."

"No. I loaded hollow point, that's all I use except on the range."

"Maybe you forgot to reload out there? Left the . . ."

"You know I use wad-cutters for practice. You know I wouldn't leave those loads in."

"Anyone can make a—"

"Didn't," Ryan said. "I remember reloading—with hollow point."

The cats well understood about hollow-point ammo and why Ryan used it. If she ever had to shoot in self-defense, a hard shell could travel an incredible distance, the bullet might go right through the intended and hit someone beyond. They'd read about such cases. But a hollow point would stop in the object or person hit, and would be more certain to halt an attacker—and that was what defensive shooting was about. The only reason Ryan would shoot someone was if her life were threatened and she had no choice.

"Someone not only took my gun from the locked glove compartment," she said in a shaky voice, "they reloaded it."

"You want the last doughnut?"

"Eat it. Don't give Rock any more, you know better."

"We searched every inch of the garage again, came back while you were with Hanni, went through every piece of that damned stuff you have stored down there. Did you ever think of taking that clutter to the dump?"

"That's stuff's valuable, sooner or later I'll use every piece of those wonderful old details. I'll use it if I . . . if I'm still in the free world to use it."

"Come on, Ryan. Your prints weren't on the trigger of the Airweight, though it had been fired."

"Whose prints . . . ?" she began excitedly.

"None. No prints on the trigger. Your prints were on the smooth parts of the grip and on the holster we took from the glove compartment."

"I cleaned the Airweight last week, Scotty and I spent the afternoon at the San Andreas range, while we were waiting for the plumber. Cleaned it, loaded it with hollow point and holstered it. I did not," she said as if Dallas was staring at her, "reload with practice ammo."

"And what did you do with the gun?"

"Dropped it in my purse, kept it with me in the trailer, put it in my glove compartment when I started home. Locked the compartment when I left the truck to load the windows, and again when I stopped to eat."

"It was there when you left the restaurant and hit the road again? Did you look?"

"No, I didn't look. The truck was locked. I could see it from the restaurant. No one bothered it. But I . . . I left the gun in the truck that night and the next—in the locked truck in the locked glove compartment. When I got home I was so tired, I just unloaded the windows and came up and fell into bed. And the next night, after the wedding, you were all over the truck. No one had bothered it."

"I wasn't into the glove compartment, wasn't in the cab."

"Someone," Ryan said softly, "someone unlocked my truck the night I got home, or the next night. Down there in the drive. Unlocked the glove compartment, took my gun, reloaded it, and either carried it away and killed Rupert, or killed him here, after you left—while I was right here asleep. Not ten feet from him.

"And where," she said, "was Rock, that night? Where were you, big boy, while all this was happening? Out running the neighborhood chasing the ladies?"

"The better question," Dallas said, "is what would he do if it happened again? He has a strong feeling for you, now.

"Except, you don't know his background or training. You don't know what he's trained to do. I'd feel better if you'd move in with me for a while."

"You can't baby-sit me twenty-four hours a day. Whoever killed Rupert could break into your downstairs in the middle of the night, just as easily as into my truck and garage—even if Scotty's back, staying with you. He sleeps like . . . he wouldn't hear anything. Rock," Ryan said softly, "Rock and I will do just fine."

Joe glanced at Dulcie. Had Rupert's killer also prowled around the Landeau cottage that night? Was that what Rock had smelled this morning that sent him snarling and ready to attack?

Maybe the killer had been after Marianna too? Did he have some vendetta against Marianna Landeau as well as against Rupert and Ryan?

But what vendetta? What was the connection? Did the killer plan to murder Marianna, as well, and incriminate Ryan for that crime?

More puzzling still, Ryan had seen how the dog behaved at the Landeau cottage, but she hadn't told Dallas. Did she think the dog's wariness wasn't important, that he had simply been startled by Eby Coldiron, by the sound of someone unseen approaching up the drive?

And that was only one crime, one set of players. What about the bombing? The cats needed urgently to pass on to Detective Garza the information about Curtis's uncle Hurlie who had perhaps sheltered the boy when he ran away to San Andreas, who had perhaps been involved in the bomb-making. They needed to call Dallas, or call Harper himself on his cell phone before he arrived in San Andreas, let him know about Hurlie, and that the address

Curtis gave Dallas was probably as fake as a rubber rodent stuffed in a mouse hole.

The cats could see, from beneath Ryan's daybed, Ryan's phone sitting on the desk, its summons so strong that Joe was tempted beyond reason to creep across the room and try phoning Harper. With his voice drowned by Ryan and Dallas, could he make a quick call?

Oh, right. And see his entire life and Dulcie's irrefutably hit the fan.

Dallas said, "You're starting Clyde's job tomorrow, you'll be too busy to worry while we get on with the investigation."

"I'm thinking of putting Clyde off. I don't want to start ripping into the roof, then have to leave him with the house torn apart."

"Have you told him that?"

"No. We're having dinner. I'll tell him then."

"Is your crew ready?"

"Two good men. But I don't like to . . ."

"Can you call Scotty? Does he have to stay up there?"

"He's just doing some landscaping, putting in some sprinklers and walks. I guess he could—"

"Call him," Dallas said. "Get him down here and get on with the Damen job. I wish your dad was here. Call Scotty. You need to stay on schedule. Clyde's easy," he said, his voice lighter, "he'll understand if we throw you in jail, if he has to live for a few weeks with the roof off his house."

"'Specially if it rains." Ryan returned his laugh shakily, sounding close to tears.

Chair legs scraped as if he had risen. "Hang in there, honey. We'll get it sorted out. We'll do our work, and you do yours, and it'll come out all right."

The cats heard him leave, and watched Ryan at the window following the detective's progress as his car headed down the hill. Beyond the windows the setting sun hung like a third-degree spotlight blazing in at her, and forcing the cats' pupils to the size of pinpricks. The sun would be gone soon, pressed into the sea by the dark clouds that hung heavy above it.

Ryan worked at her desk for some time. The cats napped lightly. So did the weimaraner, who must be very full indeed, of sugar doughnuts. As the sky dimmed, only the desk lamp and the light of the computer brightened the darkening room. Ryan didn't pull the curtains. When her phone rang she answered abruptly, as if irritated at being disturbed.

"R. Flannery."

As she listened, a smile touched her face. "Yes, I'm about ready, I just want to finish up some billing. We need to go over the time schedule too and rethink a few details."

The call had waked Rock. Sniffing the scent of cat, and not preoccupied with sugar doughnuts, the big weimaraner trotted across the studio to where Joe and Dulcie were hidden, and poked his nose under the daybed.

"Get back!" Joe hissed in the faintest voice. "Get back!"

The silver dog, having no experience with obedience commands from a cat, flashed him a look of disbelief and hastily backed away.

"Sit," Joe breathed.

Rock, his yellow eyes wide with amazement, sat down on the hand-woven rug.

Ryan, still talking to Clyde, was punching in a program. "They're open on Sunday? Mexican food sounds like heaven. See you in a few minutes."

As she hung up the phone, behind her the big dog was trying, from a sitting position, to scoot closer to the daybed for a better look at the amazing talking cats.

"Stay," Joe told Rock. "Stay!"

Frowning and perplexed, Rock settled back on his haunches. Ryan did some final addition, hit the print button, and headed for the bathroom. The cats could hear her brushing her teeth, then the little crackling sounds, barely audible, as she brushed her hair. She appeared again when the phone rang, smelling of dusting powder and mouthwash. She was wearing lipstick.

Standing by the desk she lifted the papers from the printer and picked up the phone. "Flannery," she said shortly. "Oh . . . Hi, Larn." She didn't sound pleased. As she listened, she glanced over the printed sheets, then laid them on top of what was probably a stack of bills. "You did? No, I haven't run my messages. I left San Andreas very late. Did your remodel client get in touch?"

Balancing the phone between shoulder and cheek, she tamped the papers to align them. "Looks like I'm booked for a few months, picked up another couple of jobs. And as for tonight, I'm sorry but I have a date. I was just going out the door."

She hung up and turned, looking relieved that she had a ready excuse. She looked at Rock, frowning. He was still in the sitting position, hunched down staring fixedly under her daybed. As she started forward, the cats tensed to run.

"What are you staring at?"

The big dog turned to look at her.

"What?" she said softly. She looked at him and at the daybed which had only five inches of space underneath, not enough to accommodate any prowler. She glanced toward the closet and bath, and toward the door that led to the inside stairs, and silently she moved to try its bolt.

"What is it?" she asked Rock. "What's the matter? Come, Rock," she whispered. Again she glanced toward the closet and bath. But she had just come from there. She turned, looking into the empty kitchen. "*Come*, Rock."

Rock seemed torn between the two commands. When Ryan knelt, the cats backed out from beneath the daybed on the far side.

But she wasn't looking underneath. She reached out to Rock from his level as if she thought he needed that face-to-face reassurance. Rock went to her at once.

"You want to go for a romp with Rube, in Clyde's yard?" At the word *go*, Rock began to dance. Ryan endured several minutes of wagging, leaping delight before she got him settled down.

Turning on the copier, she made a second set of bills, addressed a large brown envelope and tucked the copies inside with her printout. Weighing the envelope, she slapped on some stamps, picked up her purse, spoke to Rock again and they headed out, Ryan carrying the envelope and key-locking the door behind her.

The minute they heard her descend the stairs, the cats leaped to her desk. In the darkening evening, they watched her truck lights come on. Waiting to be sure she wouldn't forget something and come rushing back, Joe nosed at the San Andreas bills for lumber, electrical and plumbing supplies, and miscellaneous hardware. Dulcie sat admiring Ryan's business cards. "*R. Flannery, Construction.* Very nice. Home phone and cell phone." Quickly she memorized the numbers.

But Joe, reaching a paw to the phone, stared out through the window hissing with surprise, watching a gray hatchback pull out without lights, following Ryan's car; and before Dulcie could say a word Joe was pawing in the number of Ryan's cell phone. The cats caught one glimpse of the driver as the car moved under a streetlight.

Ryan answered at once.

"This is a friend. It appears that a car is following you, a block back, without lights. A gray hatchback."

"Who is this?"

"A neighbor, just happened to look out and see you leave in your red truck, saw this guy pull out from up the hill and take off following you. You might want to see if you can lose him. I didn't see the plate number."

"How many people in the car?"

"One man," Joe said. "Tall and appeared to be thin. Seemed to have a relatively short haircut. That's all I could see."

"Where do you live? A neighbor? How did you—"

Joe hit the disconnect, then punched in another number, accessing Max Harper's cell phone. Dulcie sat quietly listening, washing her paws and whiskers. She liked watching Joe at work. He'd told her about the first time he had ever used a phone, how scared he was. In the village drugstore, crouching behind the counter, he had used their business phone to call Clyde. That had been a big-time emotional trip, a milestone trauma for both the tomcat and Clyde.

It was different now. Joe had developed a really professional telephone presence.

When Dulcie heard a woman answer, she put her face close to Joe's, to listen. He'd gotten Charlie. Dulcie gave him a stern sideways glare, a *don't you dare play games* look. *Don't you dare draw Charlie into a conversation in front of Harper*—if indeed the captain was present. Knowing Joe, the temptation had to be great, and she watched him with a warning gleam.

"Captain Harper's number," Charlie repeated.

"Charlie? It's . . . This is . . ." Joe swallowed. "I have information for Captain Harper."

"May I take a message?" The cats could hear in Charlie's voice a desperate attempt to hide a guffaw of laughter. This was a first for her, taking a call from Joe Grey for the captain. Passing on a secret feline communication that, if Harper knew the identity of the caller, would send him right over the edge. "I . . . he's driving," she told Joe shakily. "Wait, I'll turn on the speaker."

There was a pause as if she was looking for the speaker button. "Go ahead."

"Captain Harper? That boy, Curtis Farger—I think he gave you a no-good address in San Andreas."

"Wait a minute, you're cutting out," Harper said. There was a long pause. Then, "Okay, go ahead."

"Apparently Curtis was staying with his uncle up there, a Hurlie Farger. I think Hurlie is Gerrard's brother. I don't know where he lives. I get that the Fargers have friends or a contact of some sort in San Andreas, maybe friends of Hurlie's."

"Do you have something more specific?"

"At the moment, that's all I have, that was all I could pick up, and you'll have to run with that."

"Where did you hear this?"

"I . . . a discussion between the boy and the old man."

"A discussion where?"

"The old man was talking through the kid's cell window. I'm sure Detective Garza will want to know that the old man is still in the village. Will you fill him in?"

"I'll do that." Was Harper laughing? Joe didn't know how to take that. Laughing at what? He turned an alarmed look on Dulcie.

But maybe Harper was only laughing because the snitch was telling the captain what to do.

"Maybe someday," Harper said, still with a smile in his voice, "you'll have sufficient trust in me—as I've learned to trust you—to share your sources with me, and share your identity."

Joe hit the disconnect, his paws tingling with nerves, his whiskers twitching. He looked at Dulcie, frowning. "I think I'll tell Garza myself."

She shrugged, amused at him because Harper had made him nervous.

Dialing a third number, he looked at Dulcie's grin and pushed the headset across the blotter. "It's your turn, miss smarty. You talk to Garza."

"I can't. What . . ." Taken off guard, she was silent when Garza came on the line.

"Detective Garza," he repeated.

She swallowed. "That old man," she said in the sultry voice that she saved for these special calls, "that old man that bombed the church. Are you looking for him?"

"We are," Garza said, dispensing with unnecessary questions.

"He's in the village, or he was around noon today. He's driving a black Jaguar convertible . . ." She allowed herself a little laugh. "Done up real classy with zebra seat covers. California license two-Z-J-Z-nine-one-seven.

"He talked with the boy, through that high little window into the holding cell. He climbed up that leaning oak trunk, and nearly fell. He's pretty crippled. They have—the boy has an uncle in San Andreas. Hurlie Farger, apparently Gerrard's brother. That's where the boy was staying. We've already informed Captain Harper. He was in his car, so they may already be on their way to San Andreas." And before Garza could ask any questions, Dulcie hit the disconnect and collapsed on the blotter.

Joe watched her, grinning. "That should shake things up. Let's hit for Lupe's Playa, before we miss the action—and miss supper."

16

THE AROMAS OF GARLIC AND CHILIES DREW RYAN like a benediction. The enticement of a spicy, delicious meal, the hot Mexican music, the soft light cast by the swinging lanterns, all the rich setting of Lupe's Playa seemed to cosset and comfort her. On the brick patio beneath the gently blowing oaks, they had their favorite table in the far corner beside the brick wall. This was where she and Clyde had first met, when she first arrived in the village and Dallas brought her here for dinner. Now, seated beside Clyde, ordering a beer, she took his hand, comforted by his strong presence. Ever since taking the call on her cell phone she had felt even more uncertain, even more raw and exposed.

She hadn't told Clyde about the call, hadn't wanted to spoil their evening. Now, she tried not to keep glancing out through the pieced-brick patio wall, to the street, to see if she *had* been followed. Yet she couldn't help watching the host's desk, through the patio doors, studying each new arrival, wondering . . . a thin man, the caller had said. She had no idea whether she would know the person—*if* she'd been followed, if this wasn't some hoax, someone wanting to harass her. Who could have made such a call?

Certainly Max Harper received some strange phone calls. But she wasn't a cop, she was a private citizen. How could this call tonight have any connection to a police informant?

Whatever the truth, that anonymous call, just after the murder, had given her a deep and lasting chill.

It wasn't as if she knew her neighbors, as if any of them would be concerned about her safety. Certainly none of them would have her phone numbers handy.

"So, you have another date? You want to hurry on through dinner?"

She looked at him blankly.

"You've been staring out at the street like you're waiting for a lost lover."

"I had a phone call, coming down. He wouldn't give a name. Said that when I left the apartment I was followed. I didn't want to tell you, and spoil the evening. He described a slim man driving a gray hatchback, said he'd been parked above the apartment apparently waiting for me. It's probably some nut call, but . . ."

Clyde's expression startled her. His face flushed but he didn't seem exactly surprised. "What the hell. You don't need crazy phone calls on top of everything else."

"It made me a little nervous, that's all," she said quickly. She wiped some water from the table with her napkin and unrolled the blueprints, weighting them down with the chip and salsa bowls. Clyde leaned over, studying the drawings. She had presented the floor plan and several elevations. The vaulted ceiling of the new room was impressive, both from the street and from within.

But even with the excitement of the promised addition, Clyde's mind remained on the phantom snitch. His thoughts about the tomcat were not charitable. Did Joe have to upset Ryan? Probably the car Joe saw had been some neighbor or visitor pulling away, and Joe had let his imagination run. Damn cat had to mind everyone's business. And what was he doing near Ryan's place? Or, *in* Ryan's place? Involuntarily Clyde glanced out through the pierced wall, himself, at the slowly passing cars, wondering if someone *had* followed her—and that message to Ryan wasn't the only phone call Joe had placed tonight.

Just before Clyde left the house Max had called, on his way from San Francisco to Sonoma. The snitch had been in touch, the same unidentified voice that contacted Harper periodically. Max always filled Clyde in because those calls made Max nervous. The snitch had never been identified, the caller refused to give his name, and he did not fit the profile of most snitches—he sure never asked for payment.

The bottom line was, Joe Grey could not stay off the phone.

And now, tonight, had the snitch gone too far? He had told Harper that the San Andreas address for Curtis Farger was a fake, that Curtis had been staying with an uncle up there. How could the tomcat know such a thing, so soon after the bombing? Know more about the young prisoner than did either Garza or Detective Davis, both of whom had questioned Curtis?

This time, Clyde didn't see how Joe could have a solid source, for either call. So he saw someone driving down Ryan's street behind her. Probably some guy running down to the store for a bottle of milk or a six-pack. Joe had to be snatching at whirlwinds, clawing at unreliable "facts" that would only serve to muddy the investigation. Clyde didn't like to think that of Joe.

Certainly he'd underestimated Joe in the past; but these calls just seemed too far out—scaring Ryan, and maybe sending Harper on a wild-goose chase. And there was nothing that he, Clyde, could say to Harper to stop him from wasting his time. *That was my tomcat calling, Max, and this time, I gotta say, he was way off base.*

Right.

Clyde did not stop to examine his perplexed anger, or to consider that it grew precisely from his own increased respect for the small hunter's skill. Deeply irritated with Joe, wanting only to dismiss the matter, he concentrated on the blueprints.

The first stage of the work to update his modest Cape Cod

cottage called for converting the smaller of Clyde's two bedrooms into a stairway and storage closet, the stairs to lead to the new second floor. Ryan planned to jack the tilting roof straight up to form two walls of the new upstairs. She said this was the fastest and most economical approach, and it was a concept that made sense to Clyde. The new master bedroom would have a fireplace, two walk-in closets, a compartmentalized bath, and a large study with a second fireplace. Both fireplaces would have gas logs but could be converted easily to burning wood. Neither Clyde nor Ryan had mentioned that the suite was admirably set up for a couple.

The waiter appeared. As they ordered, Clyde glanced out through the wall again, to where Ryan's truck was parked. Several tourists were passing, glancing into the cab as people seemed compelled to do, peering into empty vehicles.

"It'll take only a day to raise the roof," Ryan said, "once we have the end walls off. A few days to build and sheath the new roof and new end walls. Then we'll be dried in and it won't matter what the weather does." *Or if I go to jail,* she thought. "My uncle Scotty will be coming down to work on the job. My dad's brother."

Clyde nodded. "Dallas calls him a red-faced rounder of an Irishman with a Scotch name and the mind of an insanely talented chess player."

She laughed. "Scotty loves analyzing the smallest detail, sorting out every possibility. It was from Scotty I learned to love all kinds of puzzles—that's what made me want to be a builder. When I was little he taught me about space, the uses of space. I learned to design from Scotty—silly games a kid loves, that teach you to look for all possibilities in how you arrange and use space."

She looked at him solemnly. *He didn't teach me about finding a dead body in your space. What kind of puzzle is that?* She said, "Dallas called Harper. He and Charlie are coming back, canceling the cruise."

"Yes, Harper called me just before I left the house. They were on the road, going to stay somewhere in the wine country tonight then spend a day or two in San Andreas, see if they can get a line on what the boy was doing up there."

"Some honeymoon."

"Dallas said you talked with the kid again, in jail. What do you make of him, now?"

"He's difficult to read. Maybe scared, maybe just hard-nosed defiant. It's ugly to think about a ten-year-old kid without conscience, but it can happen. Or maybe," she said, "maybe he's trying real hard to protect his grampa."

"You think the old man set the bomb?"

"His son's in prison for running a meth lab. The fact that Harper couldn't make a case against Grampa may have left the old boy feeling like he had to do a little payback."

"Pretty heavy payback. Have you wondered if the kid, when he was up in San Andreas, had anything to do with copying your truck keys?"

"It's possible. That was the first thing Dallas asked me. We both had keys, Scotty and I. I suppose mine could have gone missing for hours, and I wouldn't notice. But that's . . ." She shivered. "If that's the case, who got him to steal them?"

Clyde buttered a tortilla. "Whatever they find out about the boy, looks like the department's stuck with him for a while. Harper said juvenile hall can't take him, he'd just talked with Dallas. The fire they had last month destroyed most of the building, and the temporary quarters aren't that secure. Juvenile authorities want Curtis to stay where he is."

"When Max called, did you talk with Charlie too?"

He nodded. "She had lunch with Kate Osborne yesterday in the city while Max made some phone calls and kept an appointment—a couple of Dallas's buddies on San Francisco PD," he said softly. "They'll be checking, unofficially at this point, on Rupert's connections in the city."

"The girlfriends," she said. "That's encouraging."

He nodded. "The girlfriends, and their male companions.

Maybe they'll turn up a jealous lover or two, find something they can run on."

"I hope." She touched his hand. "I feel shaky about getting through your job without the grand jury coming after me. If you want to . . ."

"Will you quit that? You didn't kill him and you're not going to jail." He took her hand. "You figure a month to do my upstairs. You were right on schedule with my patio construction, so I'm guessing you will be with this. Long before that, Dallas and Harper will have Rupert's killer behind bars."

She just looked at him.

"Believe me. You have no faith in those guys? In your own uncle?" He winked at her. "You'll have to stay out of jail if you mean to be on time, so you can get on with the next project." They had agreed early on that ripping out one downstairs wall, opening Clyde's seldom-used dining room to the kitchen to make one big space for casual entertaining, fit Clyde's lifestyle. Clyde and his friends played poker in the kitchen, and enjoyed their potluck meals there, or on the new enclosed patio.

"And you still want the little tower at one end of the new upstairs?"

"Absolutely. Joe would feel slighted if he didn't have his own place."

Ryan laughed. "You don't spoil your animals."

"Of course not." *A private cat tower,* Joe Grey had said, *with glass all around. Sun warmed, with an ocean view. A private feline retreat, off-limits to humans.*

But as he joked with Ryan and tried to reassure her, Clyde kept wondering if the cats had called her from her apartment. And wondering if someone *had* followed her. Wondering if they might have doubled back when they were sure the apartment was empty, maybe used a duplicate key? And that worried him. If someone was in there, he prayed the cats had left.

THE GRAY HATCHBACK DID RETURN TO RYAN'S PLACE WHILE the cats were still crouched on the desk. They were poised to leave when the same car passed below the windows, coming slowly up the hill, and parked half a block up the street.

A tall man emerged moving swiftly toward the building and silently up the wooden stairs. He was maybe forty, with soft brown hair in a handsome blow-dry and, in his right hand, a small leather case the size of a cell phone. As he approached the door the cats dropped off the desk and under the daybed. They were beginning to feel like moles, or like a pair of fuzzy slippers abandoned beneath the mattress. He knocked, knocked again, waited a few minutes, knocked a third time. Then faint scratching sounds began.

"Picking the lock," Joe said.

He was inside within seconds, moving directly to Ryan's desk. Pulling the curtain across the broad windows, he switched on the lamp to low and reached to a pile of files. But then he shoved them back, laughing softly, and picked up the bills and the copy of her billing for the Jakes job, that lay on the blotter. Chuckling, he turned on her computer. The cats glanced at each other. What had these no-good types done before the invention of computers? Seemed like every kind of villainy, these days, required electronic assistance.

But Dulcie couldn't be still, she kept fidgeting and glancing away toward the bathroom window, thinking about going home, thinking about the kit. Joe laid his ears back, hissing.

"Will you cut it out? She's fine."

"We don't know that. We don't know where she is. I don't like when she's gone for hours and hours. We haven't seen her since breakfast."

Joe hissed again gently to make her shut up, and watched their burglar bring up Ryan's bookkeeping program. He went immediately to the Jakes account.

He made a disk copy of the pages, then changed the figures on her hard drive, making them higher, adding several thousand dollars to the bill. Cooking Ryan's books, setting her up for some kind of swindle. Turning on her copy machine, he made two sets of her lumber and supply bills. He put one set in his pocket, and worked on the other with an eraser and Wite-Out, apparently inserting new figures to match the higher numbers in her computer. He made fresh copies of these. As he ran a printout of the doctored billing, the cats could only puzzle over where this was leading. Ryan had taken her completed bill with her, ready to mail. Had the guy guessed that? Had he seen her through the window working at her desk? Did he plan somehow to intercept the envelope after she mailed it?

Or had she not had time to mail it? Was the envelope still in her truck? If he had followed her to the restaurant, he'd know she didn't stop at a mailbox. Maybe he'd strolled by her truck and seen the envelope lying on the seat.

Shutting down the machine and slipping his various sets of bills and the printout into his pocket, he was out of there quickly, locking the door behind him. The cats fled to the desk watching him descend the stairs, walk the half block up the hill, and swing into the gray hatchback. He headed back toward the village.

"What now?" Dulcie said. "If she's already mailed her bill, what's he going to do with that stuff? Do you think that was Larn Williams? That he called earlier just to see if she was going out this evening?"

Joe didn't answer. Knocking the phone off the cradle, for the second time that night he pawed in the number of Ryan's cell phone.

RYAN WAS ENJOYING THE LAST OF HER FLAN WHEN HER CELL phone rang. She didn't want to answer, she pushed it across the table to Clyde.

"R. Flannery, construction," he said between mouthfuls.

"May I speak to R. Flannery? I called earlier, I have an urgent message for her."

"I can take the message," Clyde told Joe, trying not shout with rage.

At the other end, Joe sighed. "All right," he said. "I *think* the guy who followed her is going to break into her truck, within the next few minutes. It's kind of complicated."

Clyde stared at the phone. "Just a minute." He handed the phone to Ryan. "You'd better take this." But he leaned close to listen.

"It's me again," Joe said. "I believe someone is intent on falsifying your billing for the Jakes addition in San Andreas. Have you mailed that bill?"

"I . . . who is this? How do you . . . ? What are you talking about?"

"Have you mailed the bill or is it still in your truck?"

"No. Yes. It's in my truck. What . . . ?"

"The person who followed you earlier returned to your apartment and broke in. With lock picks. While you've been having dinner he changed the billing on your computer and made copies of the original bills and doctored them. He ran a new printout, made copies of the doctored bills, and left. I'd guess he's headed your way."

"*Who is this? How could you know such a thing?*"

"He prepared the new statement for considerably more than your original cost-plus numbers. If you've mailed the bill, probably no harm done—unless he is able to intercept it at the other end. If you haven't mailed it, I think he'll try to break into your truck, open the envelope, and switch billings. In other words, he wants to set you up, add embezzlement to the possible charge of murder."

"Why would he bother? Isn't murder enough?"

"Maybe he thinks embezzlement would in some way strengthen the murder charges."

"What does this guy look like, who's supposed to be doing all this?"

Listening to the caller's description of the burglar, she felt all warmth drain from her hands and body.

"Don't let him get that envelope," the caller said. "There isn't much time." And he hung up.

Hitting the disconnect, Joe dropped to the floor and headed for the bathroom window. Ahead of him Dulcie, balanced on the windowsill, said, "I'm going home first, see if the kit's there. She . . ."

"There's not time," he said, leaping past her. "We'll miss the action."

"Can't help it. Go watch Ryan's truck. I'll be along when I know the kit's safe."

"But . . ."

Dropping from the window she fled around the building and raced down the sidewalk heading for home, filled with worry.

17

THE RUSTY WIRE NETTING OF THE CHICKEN HOUSES was half falling down like those the kit had seen long ago in her travels when she was small. She longed to push inside and have a look but the smell stopped her, burning and stinging her nose. The stink came strongest where the dirt floor of the pens was covered with sheets of rotting plywood. In the darkening evening she could see that one of those had been shifted aside. A black emptiness loomed beneath, a hole big enough for a man to slip through. Why would a man want to go down there? Padding around the side of the pen, she could see down into the pit where heavy timbers stood against the earthen walls. Rough steps led down.

Backing away sneezing and coughing, she knew she had found something important. What was the old man up to? She wanted to look closer, but she daren't creep down into his stinking cellar, that smell was like something that would reach up and grab her. Tales filled her of human people dying, of skin and eyes burned, of lungs rotted, and even their brains turned to dust, and she hurried away, afraid clear down to her paws.

But she could follow the old man, if she kept her distance. She could see what that was about, dumping his bags of garbage down there among the ruins.

Hurrying away from the ugly, deserted cabin, she raced down the narrow road and down the scrubby, empty hills as fast and silent as a hawk's shadow. But she ran scared. Traveling the darkening, empty land so far from home, alone, was not like when she slipped through the night shoulder to shoulder with Joe Grey and Dulcie feeling bold and safe. Watching the falling blackness around her for prowling raccoons and coyotes or bobcats, she ran pell-mell for the Pamillon estate.

DULCIE HURRIED THROUGH THE VILLAGE BENEATH POOLS OF light from the shop windows heading home, praying the kit was there, an uneasy feeling in her stomach, a frightened tremor that drew her racing along the sidewalks brushing past pedestrians' hard shoes and dodging leashed dogs, running, running until at last she was flying through Wilma's flowers and in under the plastic flap of her cat door. Mewing, she prowled the house looking for the kit, mewing and peering behind living-room furniture and under the beds, unwilling to speak until she was sure Wilma didn't have company.

Determining at last that the house was empty of humans and of the kit as well, she called out anyway, her voice echoing hollowly. "Kit, come out. Kit, are you there? Please come out, it's important." All this in a voice that was hardly a whisper though her calls would reach feline ears.

There was no answer, not a purr, no soft brush of fur against carpet or hardwood as she would hear if the kit sneaked up on her, playing games.

At last, leaving the house again, she scented back and forth across the garden, and searched driveway and sidewalk for a fresh track. She raced up a trellis and sniffed all across the roof too and up the hill in back through the tall dry grass where hated foxtails leaped into her fur. Finding no fresh scent of the kit she grew increasingly worried. Kit hadn't been home at all.

Well, she couldn't search the whole world, one couldn't search *all* the hills though she and Joe had tried to do just that when the kit disappeared for three days last winter.

But the kit had been smaller then, and more vulnerable. She was a grown-up cat now. And, as Kit was far more than an ordinary cat, Dulcie thought stubbornly, she would have to take responsibility for herself.

Hurting and cross but giving up at last, Dulcie headed for Lupe's Playa. *I must not worry, I hate when Wilma worries about me. The kit is big now and can take care of herself.* But Dulcie was so unsettled that when she saw Joe on the low branch of a cypress tree outside Lupe's Playa she scorched up the trunk ploughing straight into him, shivering.

He hardly noticed her; his entire attention was on Ryan's red pickup parked just across the street.

The passenger door stood open. A man sat inside, poised with one foot on the curb and watching the restaurant through the window, as if ready to slip away at any sign of Ryan.

Joe Grey glanced at her, and smiled. "He opened the envelope. Removed Ryan's billing." They watched him fill Ryan's large brown envelope with the sheaf of papers from his pocket. "He opened the door with a long, thin rod. Only took a second. Opened the bottom of the envelope, peeled it back as slick as skinning a mouse. He doesn't see Ryan and Clyde watching." He looked toward the patio wall where the bricks were spaced in an open and decorative pattern offering passersby a teasing view of the garden and diners. In the restaurant's soft backlight Dulcie could just see Ryan and Clyde with their heads together, peering out through the wall's concealing vine. Talk about cats spying.

"I wonder if Ryan called Detective Garza," Dulcie said, glancing along the street as if Garza or Detective Davis might have hurried over from the station to stand among the shadows.

"I don't think so. She means to lead the guy on—that's Larn Williams, all right." Joe flicked an ear. "I was on the wall when he approached the truck. She told Clyde she can make a second switch, print a new, correct bill and mail it. Let Williams think he was successful, let him wait for the Jakeses to hit the roof because the bill's so high, wait for them to maybe file a lawsuit. She thinks he might tell the Jakeses that she cooked the books, even before the bill arrives, make up some story about how he found out."

"Would they believe him?"

"Are Larn Williams and the Jakeses close friends? We don't know a thing about them." Again Joe smiled. "One more phone call. Who knows how much Harper can pick up about Williams, while he's in San Andreas?"

"You're going to ask *Harper* to gather information for *you?*"

"Turnabout," the tomcat said softly, looking smug.

Dulcie stared at him for a long time. She did not reply.

Williams sealed the envelope and laid it on the seat. "Same position as he found it," Joe said. Quietly Williams depressed the lock, shut the truck door and slipped away up the street, disappearing around the corner. The cats heard a car start. He was gone when Ryan and Clyde emerged.

Ryan drove slowly away as if she had no idea the truck had been broken into. Clyde, parked in the next block, followed her.

"What will they do now?" Dulcie said.

"She'll swing by our place, I guess. She left Rock there. I'm betting that when they finish going over tomorrow's work Clyde will follow her home. Check out her apartment. Maybe try to talk her into staying at her uncle's for a few nights."

"She won't, she's too independent. And if Larn Williams wanted to kill her, why would he bother setting her up for a lawsuit?" Dulcie backed quickly down the tree and headed up the street toward home. "Maybe the kit's back, maybe she's raiding the refrigerator right now."

And Joe, his stomach rumbling with hunger, galloped along

beside her. Within minutes they were flying through Wilma's garden among a jungle of chrysanthemums and late-blooming geraniums, the flowers' scents collecting on their coats as they approached the gray stone cottage.

Padding up the back steps and in through Dulcie's cat door, entering Wilma's immaculate blue-and-white kitchen, Joe headed directly for the refrigerator but Dulcie never paused, off she went, galloping through the house again searching for the kit.

The first time Dulcie ever brought Joe here, she had taught him to open the heavy, sealed door of the refrigerator, to leap to the counter, brace his hind paws in the handle and shove. Now, forcing it open, he dropped to the floor catching the door as it swung out. The bottom shelf was Dulcie's, and Wilma always left something appealing; she didn't forget half the time the way Clyde did. Joe might find on his own refrigerator shelf a fancy gourmet selection from Jolly's Deli, left over from the last poker game, or the dried up end of a fossilized hot dog.

Dulcie's private stock tonight included two custards from Jolly's, sliced roast chicken, a bowl of apricots in cream, and crisply simmered string beans with bits of bacon, all the offerings stored in Styrofoam cups that were light enough for a cat to lift, and with easily removable lids that were gentle on feline teeth. He had them out and was opening them when Dulcie returned.

"Kit's not home. And Wilma's still gone. I think she said there was some kind of lecture tonight on the changing tax picture."

"Sounds deadly. Why does she go to those things?"

"To reduce her taxes, so she can buy gourmet food for us." She nosed at the array of delicacies that he had arranged on the blue linoleum. "I wish the kit would come home."

But the kit did not appear. Joe and Dulcie feasted, then Joe retired to Wilma's desk to call Harper. He punched in the number but there was no answer. He tried again half an hour later, and again.

"The phone's turned off," Dulcie said. "Leave a message."

Joe didn't like to use the phone's message center, but he did at last, then curled up on the blue velvet couch beside Dulcie and fell quickly asleep. Curled next to him, Dulcie lay worrying. The kit's propensity for trouble seemed so much worse at night, when Dulcie imagined all kinds of calamities. She dozed restlessly, jerking awake when Wilma came in, and again at 6:00 in the morning when she heard her cat door flapping.

She leaped up, fully alert as the kit galloped into the living room, her tail high, her yellow eyes gleaming. Above them, the windows were growing pale. Hopping to the couch, Kit nosed excitedly at Dulcie. "I found the old man. I found where he lives. I smelled chemicals so maybe it's where he made the bomb. I found where he dumps his trash. Why does bomb-making leave all that trash?"

"Trash?" Joe said, sitting up yawning. "What kind of trash?"

"Boxes and cans that smell terrible of chemicals."

He rose to stand over her. "Where, Kit? How much trash? Where did you find it?"

The kit looked longingly back toward the kitchen where she had raced past the empty plastic dishes. "Is there anything left to eat?"

"We left a custard in the refrigerator," Dulcie said, "and some chicken."

The kit took off for the kitchen. Following her, they watched her jump up to force open the heavy door. The minute it flew back she raked out the cartons, fighting open the loosely applied lids, and got down to the serious business of breakfast. She ate ravenously, gobbling more like a starving hound than a cat, making little slurping noises. She didn't speak or look up until the custard and the chicken had disappeared and the containers were licked clean.

"All right," Joe said when the kit sat contentedly licking her paws. "Let's have it."

"I need to use the phone," the kit said softly. "Right now. I need to call Detective Garza."

Joe and Dulcie stared at her. "Come in the living room," Joe said. "Come *now*, Kit."

Cutting her eyes at Dulcie, the kit headed obediently for the living room and up onto the blue velvet couch.

"Start again," Joe said, pacing across the coffee table. "From the beginning."

"I found where the old man lives. Up the hills above the Pamillon estate in a shack on the side of a cliff above that big gully and a chicken house hanging—"

"Kit. *How* did you find him?"

"I hid in his car. A black Jaguar with the top down. He drove so twisty it made me carsick again. An old shack and the chicken houses hanging on the edge of the cliff and I could smell chemicals and there weren't any chickens, maybe the chemicals killed them all. He filled his car with stinking garbage bags and went away and then I saw his car far down in the old ruins and—"

"Kit," Joe said, "slow down. This is all running together. What are you leaving out?"

The kit stared at him.

"For starters, where did you find his car?"

"At the police station. After he talked to that boy. He drove like fury. I didn't know why he had such a nice car or why he would load it down with garbage. I—"

Dulcie licked Kit's ear. "Go slower. Tell us slower."

The kit started over from where she had slipped into the old man's black Jaguar. She described the shack and how she had gone inside. How he had loaded up his trash and driven down into the Pamillon estate. "I went there. I ran and ran."

The hills had loomed below her black and silent, and her head was filled with unfriendly beasts hunting for their supper. She ran listening for every sound, watching for any movement among rock and bushy shadow. Ran flying down the hills as night fell, trying to make no noise herself in the dry grass, ran terrified until the half-fallen mansion loomed against the darkening sky, and ancient dead trees rose up with reaching arms.

Slipping into the ruins among the old oaks she had padded

among fallen walls into the empty mansion with its rooms open to the stars. She could smell where the old man had walked, his scent thick, his old-man stink mixed with the nose-burning chemical odors. His trail led through the half-fallen parlor and through the kitchen and down into the cellars, his sour trail clinging along the walls.

The cellars were too black even for a cat to see. She had to travel by her whiskers alone, by the little electric messages telegraphed from muzzle and paws. Warily jumping at every imagined movement, she drew deep beneath the mansion. A thinnest light came at last seeping in from a great crack in the cellar wall. And smells exploded suddenly, as loud as a radio blaring on. She could barely make out, ahead in the blackness, a looming form like a huge misshapen beast. It was silent and still, and it stunk: the garbage bags, black and lumpy. Imagining the old man standing there too, she spun and ran again back and up through the tunnels until at last she could see starlight once more, above the open rooms.

Hiding behind fallen stones panting and staring out at the night sky, she had crept up the broken stairs to the nursery and into the old chest beside the fireplace where once her friend Dillon Thurwell had hidden. There, hungry and frightened and very tired, she had curled up in a tight ball trying to comfort herself, and soon she slept.

She had awakened when the first hint of dawn shone in one long pale crack beneath the lid of the chest. Pushing up the lid with her nose, and crawling out, she had padded across the second-floor nursery to where the wall fell away. There she stood looking down at the heaps of rock and dead oaks that bristled like some gigantic devil's garden, stood looking past the ruins to the hills that dropped away below her. Wanting to be home right then, right that minute, wanting breakfast, wanting most of all to telephone Dallas Garza and tell him where that old man was, who had tried to kill half the village. Was she the only one in the world who knew where that old man was hiding? Consumed by her need she had leaped down the ragged stairs flying over heaped stones and through tangled bushes running for home, running.

"And here I am," said the kit, licking a last smear of custard from her whiskers. "No one else knows where that old man is. No one but the boy because the boy's clothes were in the shack but that boy will never tell anyone." And she sailed to the desk and pawed at the phone, her ears and whiskers sharp forward, her long fluffy tail high and lashing—this kit who was scared of the phone but who, right now, was more full of herself and more eager to confide in the law, or at least to confide in Detective Garza.

18

"Very smooth," Joe said, leaping on the breakfast table, landing inches from Clyde's plate.

"What's smooth?" Clyde said, wiping up the last of his fried eggs. "Where've you been? Your breakfast's getting cold."

"Up on the roof, watching them put up the platform and stairs. Pretty fast workers."

"Scaffolding. It's called scaffolding." Clyde glanced at his watch. "They got here before seven, one of the carpenters had the lumber on his truck. They're expecting another delivery at eight."

"I gather Ryan's not a union member. She'd never get away with starting work so early." Already Joe's ears felt numb from the thunder of hammers and the rasping scream of the electric saws. He might boast superior knowledge and skills, for a tomcat, with none of the normal feline fears, but the sound of a Skilsaw or an electric drill still sent shivers up his furry spine.

The scaffolding that Ryan had constructed along the side of the house, with a temporary stairway from the front sidewalk, was indeed a platform large and strong enough to support any number of carpenters plus a considerable weight in lumber and building materials. The men wouldn't have to enter the house except to connect the plumbing and, at some point in the job, to build the inner stairway in half of Clyde's small guest room. Clyde's present bedroom would become the new guest room, without his desk and weight equipment that now cluttered the little space. That would all be moved upstairs.

"They plan to have the shingles off the roof this morning before the lumber arrives," Clyde said. "There'll be roofing nails all over the yard. I'm taking the morning off to vacuum them up, but you cats stay out of the way. Watch your paws. Stay inside when the truck gets here, until they've dropped that load of lumber. Be sure the kit is inside."

"Anything else? Don't pick up any fleas? Stay away from barking dogs?"

Clyde gave him a long, patient look. "I am only a human. You can't expect me to be as intelligent or perceptive as a feline. But because I am human, I worry about you. That is what humans do. You are going to have to make allowances. If you want to keep me healthy and happy and keep me bringing home the kippers, you will have to humor me. Stay out of the way of the truck. Is that clear?"

"There is no need for early morning sarcasm. I already told Dulcie about the lumber. And I laid down the law to the kit. You don't need to write a script and do a two-minute stand-up."

Clyde glared.

But Joe Grey smiled. "A load of lumber in the yard will be the end of that patch of scruffy grass you euphemistically call the front lawn."

Ignoring him, Clyde rose to rinse his plate. Joe nibbled at his own breakfast. "Very nice omelet." Savoring the Brie-spinach-bacon-and-cheese concoction, he pawed open the morning paper.

DETECTIVE'S NIECE PRIME MURDER SUSPECT

San Francisco contractor Rupert Dannizer was found shot to death Sunday morning in the garage of local contractor Ryan Flannery, niece of newly appointed police detective Dallas Garza.

178

Rupert's death had not come to the attention of reporters until the Sunday edition was already on the street. This Monday morning it filled the front page above the fold. There was no photograph of the body or of Ryan; likely Dallas had seen to that. Joe scanned the article, which said nothing that he didn't already know. The press had made clear that the murdered man's widow, in whose garage the body had been found, was not only police detective Dallas Garza's niece, but was the sister of local interior designer Hanni Coon. And that Ryan's father was Michael Flannery, chief U.S. probation officer for the northern district of California, based in San Francisco. The article pointed out that Ryan had filed for divorce from Dannizer six months earlier when she moved to Molena Point to open a separate contracting business. It gave the name of her new business and some interesting details about the lawsuit in which she was suing Dannizer for half the value of their San Francisco firm, Dannizer Construction. That lawsuit was now unnecessary. The paper made it clear that, with Rupert's death, Ryan would be a wealthy woman. Joe scanned, as well, the *Gazette*'s latest article on the church bombing, but it was only a rehash of previous reports, except for information on those who had been treated for minors wounds or shock, and that Cora Lee French had been released from the hospital.

Now that Cora Lee was home, Joe thought, it was time to take the kit up to stay with her. The kit could have gotten herself into all kinds of trouble, up at that old man's shack. Cora Lee would love playing hostess to her favorite cat, and until this bombing business was cleared up, the unpredictable tattercoat would be safer—and Dulcie wouldn't be wound in knots. Joe was more than curious to see if Garza would run with what the kit had told him.

It did occur to the tomcat that, in worrying over the kit, he was behaving exactly like Clyde and Wilma. But he immediately dismissed that thought. This was an entirely different circumstance. The kit was still young, innocent, and totally unpredictable.

Abandoning the newspaper and his empty plate, Joe dropped

off the table. If the police had further information about the bombing, it wasn't in the *Gazette*. But, of course, Garza would keep any new leads strictly within the department. Nipping out his cat door and up a neighbor's pine tree, he stretched out on a branch where he could watch Ryan tear up the roof, and could think over the two cases.

As to evidence in the church bombing, he knew the county lab was backed up for months and that they made very few exceptions. But couldn't they try, for a case such as this? Harper said every department and every court had to wait its turn. So why wasn't there more staffing? Joe scratched an itch that was definitely *not* a flea. All kinds of people were out of work, yet these high tech jobs were going begging. Why? Humans were adaptable, they were smart. If a cat couldn't catch rats, he'd go after other game.

Still, he guessed it was hard to made a change in your life.

He watched Ryan and a young, long-haired carpenter cut and nail plywood flooring. Above them on the attic roof the other carpenter knelt, ripping off shingles, dropping them down to the yard and sidewalk. In a moment Clyde wandered out of the carport with a rake and went to work down at the end of the yard where shingles already littered the grass and cement. Sometimes, all the banging and hustle that accompanied busy human endeavor wore a cat right out.

Dulcie would say all that hustle was what humanity was about. Build, invent, improve, and move on. Push the envelope. The ingenuity of the human mind was no longer involved simply with hunting. A billion possible scenarios now waited, to be deftly harnessed. She would say, only when that eager creativity was twisted into negative channels, into destruction, did mankind falter and slide back to the cave mentality.

Now that old man, old Gramps Farger. *There* was a cave mentality, with his bombs and drugs.

Gramps had disappeared completely from the little house where he and Curtis's father had run their original meth lab.

Harper's men hadn't found a sign of life when they went back after the bombing, again looking for Gramps. The lab had been out back, a quarter mile away from the house, in a rough shack. Harper said it stunk so bad that the officers had to wear masks. Those chemicals got right in your lungs. Maybe the house would have to be burned down, Joe thought, and the earth turned under like some atomic waste.

And now Gramps was running free, letting the kid take the rap, letting a ten-year-old boy cool his heels in jail.

Joe watched the carpenters tearing out the two end walls, preparing to cut loose the apex of the roof. Eight huge, businesslike jacks stood ready to lift the long halves of the roof straight up, turning them into walls. He wondered how dangerous that would be, jacking up those two forty-foot sections. Wondered how Ryan was going to secure them in place while she built the new roof on top and built the end walls. He'd hate to be underneath if one of those mothers gave way. Talk about a cat pancake.

But watching the dark-haired young woman swing her sledgehammer knocking out two-by-fours, Joe didn't doubt that Ryan's plan would work, that it was efficient and professional, and as safe as any construction operation could be.

Still, though, he thought he'd keep his distance during the jacking up. He was just wondering if Ryan planned to do that after lunch, when Rock's booming challenge filled the morning, echoing from the backyard where Rock had been confined with old Rube.

Leaping to the next tree between the neighbor's house and his own, Joe watched Rock cavorting and dancing around Rube trying to get the old black Labrador to play. The two elderly cats and the young white female looked on from atop the trellis, not yet comfortable with the big energetic weimaraner. Poor Rube seemed willing to romp, ducking his gray muzzle and pawing at the paving but his limbs and joints didn't want to cooperate. Joe mewed softly, knowing how much Rube hurt and feeling bad for him, knowing that even with the wonders of modern medicine Dr. Firetti couldn't turn off all the pain of arthritis.

At least Rube had a nice backyard. And the patio's heavy Spanish-style trellis provided fine aerial walkways for the cats. To say nothing of the warmth—the high stucco wall at the back trapped the afternoon sun so the patio was warm as a spa, holding the heat well into evening where an animal could stretch out for a luxurious nap.

Ryan had even provided a decorative tile border around old Barney's gravestone. The golden retriever, Rube's lifelong pal who had died last year, was buried just beyond the oak tree. Ryan had, with tenderness, retained the small sentimental elements that were important to their little family while, in more practical terms, pursuing a remodeling regimen that would make the house worth twice its present value.

Clyde's "building money" for this project had been, just as when he bought the old apartment house, cash earned from the sale of his restored antique cars. The latest vehicle, a refurbished 1942 LaSalle, Clyde had purchased in a shocking condition of rust and neglect. Now, renewed nearly to better than its original state, the antique car had sold almost at once for more than enough to complete the upstairs project, a sum hard to comprehend in terms of kitty treats or even in confections from Jolly's Deli.

Watching his contented housemates, Joe was glad Clyde hadn't sold their little home. As for the house next door, it had not been turned into a restaurant after all, but had been sold again. The one property alone, apparently, hadn't been large enough to make the venture cost-effective.

Listen to me, Joe thought, alarmed. Cost-effective? Worth twice its present value? Sometimes I worry myself, sometimes I sound way too much like a human. Next thing you know, I'll be buying mutual funds.

IT WAS WELL PAST NOON WHEN **R**YAN AND THE CARPENTERS broke for lunch, when Clyde's car pulled in. The sudden silence of the stilled hammers and power tools was so profound it left Joe's ears ringing. Any sensible cat would have left the scene hours before to seek a quiet retreat, but he didn't want to miss anything—and now he didn't want to miss lunch. He watched Clyde come up the steps toting a white paper bag that sent an aroma of pastrami on rye like a benediction, watched Ryan hurry down the makeshift stairs and around to the backyard to see that Rock had water and a few minutes of petting, before she ate her lunch. As she returned, Joe settled beside Clyde, where he sat on the new subfloor, opening the white paper bag. He felt sorry for the household cats, that they couldn't have gourmet goodies. The vet had warned Clyde long ago about the dangers of such food to felines. Dr. Firetti had no idea of the delicacies in which Joe and Dulcie and the kit indulged, apparently without harm. They all three checked out in their lab tests and exams with flying colors. "Healthy as three little horses," the doctor always said, congratulating Clyde and Wilma on their conscientious care. "I see you're sticking to the prescribed diet." And no one told him any different.

Listening to Ryan's soft voice, Joe tied into his share of Clyde's sandwich, holding it down with his paw. Far be it from Clyde to cut it up for him. Glancing above him, he saw that Ryan hadn't yet cut loose the roof along the peak. All was solid up there over their heads. The two carpenters sat at the other end of the room, their radio playing some kind of reggae, turned low. Both were young and lean and tanned, one with a rough thatch of hair shaggy around his shoulders, the other, Wayne, with dark hair in a military trim that made Joe wonder if he was moonlighting from some coastal army camp. Ryan's uncle Scotty hadn't yet arrived.

Ryan was saying, "When I got home last night, Rock took one sniff at the stairs and the door and charged into that apartment roaring. He knew someone had been in there. He raced around looking for him, pitching a fit. Took me a while to get him settled.

183

I didn't want to discourage him from barking but I sure don't want the neighbors on my case."

"Neighbors ought to be happy to have a guard dog in residence. Put it to them that you had a prowler and you're sure glad the dog ran him off."

"I wonder if the neighbors saw Larn, if anyone saw him come in. You'd think if they had, they'd have called the station."

"Did you tell Dallas?"

"Yes. He's checking for prints, something for the record." She looked at him solemnly. "My dad called early this morning from Atlanta, he'd heard about the murder on the news."

"He didn't know?"

"I asked Dallas not to tell him. There's nothing he can do and I thought it would only distract him. Don't those TV stations have anything to fill up their time besides a murder clear across the country? They gave it the same spin as the San Francisco papers, contractor's money-hungry wife."

Clyde handed her a container of potato salad, glancing across at the carpenters. The two men were deep in conversation, paying no attention to them. "What are you going to do about Williams?"

"Wait and see what he does. I sent a correct bill this morning to the Jakeses by registered mail. Put the doctored billing in my safe deposit box with a note about the circumstances."

Clyde raised an eyebrow.

She shrugged. "Just being careful."

"Your dad was upset when he called?"

"Mad as hell, ready to kick ass. I told him it would be okay, I told him Dallas would get it sorted out. He'd already talked with Dallas. He'll be back at the end of the week, plans to catch the shuttle on down here."

"You told him about Larn Williams, about the billing switch?"

"Yes. He agreed with me, that I should wait to see what Larn will do."

Clyde was quiet.

"If Larn wanted . . . he could have killed me the night he killed . . ."

She stared at him, her eyes widening at what she had said, what she'd been thinking. They were both silent.

"I have no way to know that," she said quietly. "That just slipped out. I . . . it will be interesting to see if Larn calls me again. Maybe to see if his switch of the billing worked." She smiled. "Maybe I can lead him on, maybe learn something."

"What does that mean? You wouldn't go out with him."

"That would be foolish."

"That's not an answer."

She was silent.

"Would you call me if you decide to see him? Let me know where you're going?"

She just looked at him.

"Will you call me? I make a good backup. Like the safe deposit box."

She grinned. "All right, I'll call. If you'll stay out of the way."

"Totally invisible," Clyde said. They were finishing their lunch when Dallas showed up wearing scruffy clothes and driving a rusted-out old Chevy. He stood in the yard watching Ryan descend.

"On my way up the hills, see if I can find Gramps Farger. A tip that he's living up there in some old shack." Dallas looked at Ryan. "We have some blowups of the murder-scene photos. Found the hint of a tire mark, thin tire like maybe a mountain bike. Lab is doing an enhancement."

He put his arm around her. "From the small amount of blood and the condition of the body, and the angle of the shots, coroner says Rupert wasn't killed in your garage."

Ryan relaxed against him, letting out a long sigh. "I didn't know any news in the world could sound so wonderful."

Clyde said, "What's this about Gramps Farger?"

Dallas moved toward the back patio out of range of the two carpenters. "I got a tip, early this morning, a young woman. She said the old man's living in a fallen-down shack up along that ravine above the Pamillon estate." The detective leaned over the gate to pet Rock who had come racing up. Rearing, the big dog planted his front feet on top the gate and reached to lick Dallas's face.

Dallas rubbed behind the dog's ears. "That old place was sitting vacant. We check on it every couple of weeks—he could have moved in right after our last run up there. A guy can make a lot of mischief in two weeks. Informant said he's dumping bags of trash down among the ruins."

Clyde nodded. "Like maybe drug refuse?"

"Maybe." Dallas smiled. "If I can lay my hands on Gramps Farger, he'll be out of circulation for a while, you can bet."

"You going up there alone?"

"Davis is meeting me. If we can corner Gramps, we'll go on down to the Pamillon place, have a look. Whoever the caller was, I hope she's right on this one."

Joe glanced at Clyde's scowl and looked away. The kit would be pleased, would be all puffed up with triumph.

But until Gramps Farger was in fact behind bars, how safe was she?

He waited until Dallas left in the old surveillance car, then he took off before Clyde thought to stop him. Clyde would think he was headed for the hills to get in the middle of the potentially dangerous arrest of Gramps Farger. When, in fact, he was only going to have a talk with Dallas's young, female informant.

19

Rocky Face Inn outside San Andreas fea-
tured private patios with a wide view of the pine-covered Sierra
Nevada Mountains, and the best pancakes and home-smoked
ham in Calavaras County. Even the coffee tasted wonderful to
Charlie, though maybe that was owed in part to the fresh mountain air and the scent of pines, and the fact that they had been
driving since 6:00 in the morning, heading inland from Sonoma.
Charlie was an early riser but she'd never match Max. If he wasn't
up well before sunrise he felt that the day was half gone. Having
checked in at 8:00 in the morning and enjoyed a leisurely breakfast, she didn't welcome the sight of Max picking up his jacket
and reaching for his truck keys.

"You could stay here," he said. "Lie by the pool."

"Only if you stay with me."

Max picked up her chair with her in it, and tilted her out. "Get
your coat, we're burnin' daylight," he said in his best John Wayne
imitation.

She made a face at him. "Don't need a coat. It's going to be
ninety."

187

Slapping her on the rump, he nudged her out the door. "I want to get over to the Jakeses' house before Ryan's uncle leaves for the coast, spend the rest of the morning talking to the local shopkeepers, see if they've had any unusually large chemical sales. We'll grab a bite of lunch somewhere then have a look for Hurlie Farger. Probably a wild-goose chase, but who knows. And maybe we can get a line on this Larn Williams."

He had, in San Francisco, made contact with Sergeant Wills and Detective Sergeant Parker, and had given them the names that Dallas wanted checked out. Within a few hours of Max's meeting with them, Parker had called to say that two of the women were out of the country, Barbara Saunders and Martie Holland, or appeared to be, at this juncture. June Holbrook was working down in Millbrae and had, several months ago, left her husband. Tom Wills would go down there this morning to see what he could find.

Max ruffled her hair and opened the truck door for her. Settling in the cab, he unfolded the local map, took a quick look then pulled out to the highway.

With the information the two officers supplied, Dallas would work what he could from Molena Point, doubling back to Parker and Wills with questions they could best handle. Charlie had never before been so fully aware of the cooperation among law-enforcement officers. Of the women that the two officers were unofficially investigating, had the jealous husband or lover of one of them killed Rupert and set up Ryan, as a handy alibi?

Driving north from the inn, they turned onto a newly laid granite-block driveway before a peak-roofed, rustic house that had, on the north side, a pale new addition, its fresh cedar siding and shingles reflecting the morning sun. At the side of the garden a man rose from his knees, a big, wide shouldered, redheaded man, his jeans splattered with mud and his hands wet where he had been working on a sprinkler pipe.

He stepped up to the car, wiping his hands on a clean hand-kerchief. "Scott Flannery. You two are up early." He winked at Charlie. "Nice to meet you both. Come on in." His neatly trimmed hair was, if possible, a brighter red even than Charlie's own. His voice was deep and soft as it had been last night on the phone when he returned Max's call—a comforting sort of man, Charlie thought. A reassuring kind of man to have helped raise Ryan and her sisters after their mother died.

"Those kids showed up this morning," Scotty said, ushering them into the house. "There's something about cooking pancakes and bacon with the windows open that draws wandering kids same as it draws bears. Come in, come in, I just made a fresh pot of coffee. The Jakeses moved the house trailer yesterday, to the far side of the pasture."

Seated at the breakfast table in the large, high-raftered family kitchen, Charlie breathed in the scent of new cedar lumber, and, through the wide, open windows, admired the dark mountains that rose in the distance above the golden hills.

"Kids' names are Andy and Mario," Scotty said. "I stuffed them with pancakes, and we talked about the dog. I said I missed seeing him, said maybe the dog was with their friend Curtis, that I hadn't seen him, either. They weren't quick to answer. Maybe they don't have a clue that anything's wrong, and maybe they do. They said sometimes Curtis doesn't show up for a while, that sometimes he goes off with his uncle, cutting timber."

"Did they mention Hurlie by name? What did you learn about him?"

"One of them slipped and mentioned his name, then tried to cover up. They referred to him as Curtis's uncle. Said he works odd jobs around the area, some up in the larger estates. The way this land lies, the wealthy areas are shoulder to shoulder with the rundown little farms, depending on the drainage and on the view.

"The kids claimed they didn't know where Curtis lived, that

they just saw him at school, or 'around' as they put it." Scotty made a wry face, not buying that. "The boys could live in a little shacky area just east of here, Little Fish Creek. I'd look for Hurlie there too. You talk with the sheriff?"

Harper nodded. "He mentioned Little Fish Creek as a transient area, and several other places. Said Hurlie works odd jobs, including some of the larger estates. After some prodding, he suggested the Carter place, the Ambersons and the Landeaus."

"He left you wondering," Scotty said.

Max nodded. "A bit reluctant. Particularly regarding the Landeaus. As if he gave me those names to cover himself, in case I got information from other sources. You see a problem, there?"

"Possibly. I've heard hints, from our lumber people, but nothing specific. A sense of things unsaid, an unease." He laughed. "If I were a local, they'd talk more. You asked about Larn Williams. He and Ryan had dinner to discuss a possible remodel. I don't think she considered it a date. He had come around to look at her work, seemed to like it. Small-time realtor. Works on his own, I gather. She wasn't real taken with him."

"Have you heard anything . . . *off*, about him?"

"Nothing. I see Williams sometimes in town when I go for lumber. I've seen him a couple of times talking with Marianna Landeau. Once on the street, once in the door of his office. They seemed—easy with one another. And the Landeaus *are* into real estate, or at least her husband is. Apparently a big-time operator."

Charlie watched Scotty with interest. Everything he said was soft-spoken, but he wasn't shy, he seemed bursting with male energy. She liked this "second father" of Ryan's, already she felt comfortable with him. She could imagine growing up under the humorous eyes of a man like this, so different from her own reserved and austere father whom she had known only until she was nine. As Scotty refilled their coffee cups, she rose. "Could I take a quick look at the new wing?"

Scotty waved his arm toward the large living room that she

could glimpse beyond the kitchen, and she moved on through, into a space that took her breath away.

The room was the size of a triple garage, but with a high-raftered ceiling that made it seem much larger. It was still empty of furniture. The north side was dominated by a river-rock fireplace that rose from the pine floor, soaring ten feet up to the cedar beams. To her right, the floor-to-ceiling windows looked at the mountains, but to her left the tall glass panes embraced a view of the yellowed hills against the sky, hills dotted with dark oaks and with a scatter of grazing cattle. Stepping out onto the stone terrace, she could see a fence line far below, and as she watched, three deer wandered across the pasture among the black Angus steers and stopped to graze.

Turning back inside, she imagined the room furnished with Navajo rugs and soft leather couches and, in the shelves that lined the back wall, hundreds of books. Through an alcove into the dining room she could see a rough-hewn table set before another fireplace and, on the plain white wall, a collection of small framed landscapes. For a long moment she imagined herself and Max there having supper by the fire, watching their horses down in the pasture.

Oh, the stuff of dreams.

But she and Max had what they wanted, they had a nice home and plenty of room for the horses, and soon, probably under Ryan's skilled hand, they would add a studio where she could work. But, most wonderful of all, and amazing, was that she and Max had each other.

Slipping into the older part of the house she admired the way Ryan had converted the original living room into a handsome master bedroom and turned the old, smaller dining area into an ample dressing room. There were fireplaces everywhere. The original rough-stone fireplace now faced the bed beside window seats where one could look down on the hills. Charlie wondered how Ryan would approach their own building project. Maybe they could turn part of the existing house into studio space, and build a new great room. That possibility was even more exiting.

As she returned to the kitchen, Max was saying, "You're guessing the kids know about the bombing, know that Curtis is in jail?"

"Those kids are secretive about something," Scotty said. "But maybe only about their own situations. There's a lot of petty crime back in these hills, a lot of guys with small marijuana patches. Whatever the problem, the kids sure wouldn't open up about Hurlie. I hope you turn up something more at Little Fish Creek."

Harper nodded, and rose. Charlie touched his arm. "Can you take a minute? To walk through the house? It's quite wonderful."

"Guess I'd better," he said, grinning, "if we're going to hire this gal."

Charlie sat with Scotty, letting Max look on his own without her comments. She told Scotty about Max's ranch and the studio they planned to add.

"A studio," Scotty said, "where you will draw animals. Ryan says you're the best she's seen. You'll be wantin' to draw that big dog that hitched a ride with her, he's a fine, well-bred fellow. He should be hunting. Someone's a fool to have lost a dog like that, and not look for him." Scotty frowned. "Those boys know more about that dog too than they're saying. Maybe something they're ashamed of?" He gave her a puzzled look. "Can't figure out what it might be. The dog was sure easy with them all, not like they'd hurt him."

Charlie watched him a moment, wondering, then Max returned. Rising, Scotty held out his hand to them. "You have the kids' descriptions. Sorry I didn't learn more. I'll be headin' back for the coast mid-afternoon. Ryan's ready to jack up the roof, in the morning, and that takes six men—five men and Ryan. She's got a couple of off-duty officers coming over to help out—for pay of course," Scotty said, watching Max.

Max nodded. "Nothing wrong with that. They earn little enough. I hope they do good work."

"She'll see they do," Scotty said. "I'll be staying with Dallas down there, if there's anything I can do. You want to take my old truck? You'd be less conspicuous up in the Little Fish neighborhood than with that late-model king cab."

"Thanks for the offer," Max said, shaking his head. "But we'll stick with this one. At least it's respectably dusty."

Scotty walked to the truck with them, lifting his hand as they backed out then bending again to his sprinkler pipes. Pulling down the drive, Max glanced at Charlie. "I like the new addition, like what Ryan did. You want to talk to her about enlarging our place?"

"I'd like that. And I'd like to work with her on the project. That could save us a little money, and would be good for my carpentry skills. What if we find Hurlie Farger? Do you have cause to arrest him?"

"I don't have a warrant, but I sure have one for Gramps Farger. Maybe Gramps is in Molena Point as Dallas was told, and maybe he's not. And if I have cause to think Hurlie had something to do with the bombing, I can get a warrant in a hurry. Now watch for Little Fish Road. I'd like to bundle up the whole Farger family and take them out of circulation."

At his words, the same icy chill touched Charlie as when she'd heard the blast and saw the church wall broken out. She was filled again with fear for him. And with cold anger. Because Max had done his job well, had seen Gerrard Farger sent to prison, the Fargers had begun this nightmare.

But she'd known the shape of their future together. Had known it far too well after the Marner murders last winter, when she realized the killer had set up Max to take the rap. She knew what Max's life was about. She meant to be a part of his world, exactly the way he wanted to live it, and she didn't intend to back off. She would not let herself cringe from what the future might hold.

She spent the rest of the morning, and midday, sitting happily in the cab sketching whatever she found of interest, as Max made his calls at every general store, feed supply and hardware, returning to the truck to fill out his field sheets. They ate lunch at a ma-and-pa café of questionable cleanliness, but with wonderful berry pie. Around 2:00 they headed for Little Fish Creek, on a road that dropped suddenly down between steep hills, through tall yellow-dry grass.

Below them, little shacks were scattered among animal pens and old car bodies, the small wooden houses and sheds bleached pale, the fences wandering and leaning. The occupants had been creative, though, fashioning some of their fences from rows of old bedsprings wired together, or old camper covers placed on their sides, each concave interior floored with scattered straw as a shelter for pigs or chickens. The whole settlement looked bone-dry and scrubby, except for the vegetable gardens. These were dark with rich earth and green with luxuriant crops, though some of the rows were fading to brown now, in the September heat. Each property boasted a mixed collection of mongrel dogs and nondescript farm animals too, with scruffy, dust-dulled coats. Charlie glanced slyly at Max. "Which is the honeymoon cottage? Did you make reservations?"

"You can take your choice." But his tone was cool. Something about her remark didn't sit well, and she was sorry she'd said that. Max didn't like that kind of sarcasm. As a matter of fact, neither did she. Not everyone in the world had a choice about where they lived, certainly the children didn't. When she glanced at Max, he looked back at her grinning, knowing very well what she was thinking.

Sitting in the truck while Max went from door to door talking with different families trying to get a line on Hurlie, she watched the mangy dogs and dirty children and thought about Curtis living there and wondered uncomfortably about his life. If Curtis *had* run away from his mother, what had his life been like, with her? And as the afternoon dulled and began to dim, Charlie felt sad, and unaccountably angry.

20

At each small, paintless shack, Max stepped out, hallooed the house, then asked the same questions of the occupant, about where he might find Hurlie Farger. He had already found Hurlie's farm, from the directions the sheriff gave them. The place seemed deserted. No sign of anyone home, no resident animals, no recent footprints across the dirt yard, the garden dried to the color of scorched paper. Though Max had not been fully satisfied that Hurlie wasn't living there among the rubble he could see through the uncurtained windows. He had continued to look, wading through the dust of countless yards making nice to a motley assortment of suspicious dogs, and cajoling their scowling masters who didn't trust a stranger and could smell a cop ten miles away even when he was wearing jeans and wrinkled boots. Charlie sat in the truck watching Max and making quick sketches of the assorted livestock, pausing only to wipe sweat from her forehead; the thermometer was in the nineties.

Far above them, up the last dry hill of Little Fish Creek, Hurlie Farger sat in his old truck looking down the falling land watching Harper ply the narrow roads and switchbacks. He had been there

195

for three hours, killing a six-pack of beer and wagering with himself how long would it take the tall skinny cop to grow discouraged and leave, not accomplishing what he had come for. Knowing cops, he expected Harper might keep looking until nightfall, until it was too dark among the hills for any cop with good sense to hang around, when he was out of his own jurisdiction.

Hurlie Farger, at thirty-eight, was the spit'n image of how his gramps had looked at that age. And he could almost be the twin of his younger brother Gerrard. Certainly anyone running across Gerrard down in San Quentin, and knowing Gramps Farger from the old man's sojourns in various California prisons, would see at once that the sullen, wiry inmate with the muddy brown eyes and pitcher ears was a Farger, and they'd know Hurlie just as easily. All the Farger men had the same chicken-thin neck, the same narrow bony shoulders and lank, muddy hair. Maybe the Farger clan wasn't handsome, but the family genes were strong. In the long haul, Hurlie knew, it's blood that counts.

Watching the newlyweds ply the Little Fish Creek neighborhood, Hurlie had eased down comfortably in his old, rusted-out Ford truck drinking a warm Coors and cradling his cell phone, following Harper's progress not only with binoculars but via the wonders of modern electronics. From his good neighbors he had received a running account of all conversations. He had watched Harper circle his own place peering in the windows, and knew that Harper had gotten the address from Sheriff Beck. But Hurlie had made very sure that the visiting law would find nothing of interest.

Though Harper had the rural-route mailbox numbers of Hurlie's two cousins, he learned nothing from either, or from their kids. Hurlie spoke with and laughed with each of them after Harper left the premises. When Harper drove out of Little Fish Creek, surely hot and thirsty and short-tempered, and headed up the mountain in the direction of the Landeau place, Hurlie tucked the phone on the seat under his folded jacket, started the rattling Ford and headed down the road to meet him.

"THEY'RE COVERING FOR HIM," MAX SAID WITH AN AMUSED grin as he turned onto the upper road the sheriff had described. "The laughter hidden down behind those sour faces. Hurlie's cousins nearly busted a gut trying not to laugh at me." He glanced over at Charlie. "See that occasional flash of sunlight up there atop the hill, see where that old truck's sitting?"

"You've been watching it."

"I'd say that's Hurlie up there." Max eased the truck steadily up the rutted, one-car road. Five turns later he slammed on the brakes.

The rattletrap truck sat in the road crosswise. Hurlie stood beside it resting on the fender like the heavy in an old B movie, a small-caliber rifle leaning beside him. Max touched his holstered Glock, wishing he'd left Charlie at the inn. He stepped out of the pickup. "Good morning, Hurlie. You want to move your truck out of the way?"

"I heard you was looking fer me. Thought I'd save you any more driving around, in this hot weather. What exactly did you want? You some kind of law?" Hurlie glanced in at Charlie with an insolence that made Max step closer to him.

"Right now I want you to move your truck. You're blocking the road."

Hurlie stared, his chin jutted out, his eyes on Max but glancing down at the Glock. "You were lookin' fer me you musta had a reason. I do somethin' wrong?" Gently his hand eased toward his pants pocket.

In one move Max grabbed Hurlie, spun him around and shoved him against the rusted truck, kicking his rifle into the dust. Pressing the Glock into Hurlie's ribs he patted him down, removing a snub-nosed Saturday night special from his pants pocket, two hunting knives and a straight razor from various pockets.

Hurlie, facing the cab of Max Harper's pickup, his hands pressed against the vehicle's roof, looked around at Harper. "So what's this about. I ain't done nothin'."

Max glanced at Charlie where she sat with her hand on the phone. He nodded.

As Charlie called the sheriff, Hurlie's expression remained one of puzzled innocence. Max arrested him for impeding the duties of a police officer, and cuffed him. "Sit down on the ground, Hurlie."

"It's dusty. Dust makes me cough."

"Sit down now."

Hurlie sat, stirring a cloud of dust.

"Why were you waiting for me? Why were you blocking the road?"

"You're that police captain from over to the coast."

"So?"

"So I heard you wanted to talk to me. I was just being cooperative, waiting here."

"Where's Gramps Farger?"

Though Dallas had a lead on Gramps, he hadn't found him yet, and there was no harm in shaking Hurlie up, see what he could jar loose. "Gramps staying with you, Hurlie? You'll feel better if you don't lie to me."

"What you want with him?"

"Is he living with you?"

"I ain't seen him since you sent my brother to prison."

"I don't believe that. And I know Curtis has been living up here with you."

"Ain't seen neither one. Can I get up? Like to smother in dust down here. Ain't no call to make me sick."

"Your shack is full of dust. You have everyone in that hollow covering for you. If I find Gramps up here, I'll lock your ass up for good, along with his. How long was Curtis here? Why did he go home? Be straight with me, Hurlie."

"You can't lock me up for nothin'."

"Harboring a delinquent, for starters. How long was Curtis here? What was he doing up here?"

"He wasn't here. I ain't seen him."

"You working up at the Landeau place?"

"What'd I do up at that fancypants place? Polish the silver? Where'd you get that notion?"

"Are you working for them up there?"

"Doing what?" Hurlie snapped. "Them high mucky-mucks wouldn't have me." As he scowled up at Max, a dust cloud appeared down the hill, the sheriff's car at its center winding up the twisting road.

THE KIT MIGHT BE IN EXILE, BUT HER LUXURIOUS ACCOMMODA-tions quite suited her. Wilma had left work at the library early in order to get her settled, and to visit with Cora Lee. She had brought Dulcie along for the ride, though Dulcie wouldn't be staying.

Following Cora Lee through the big, high-ceilinged living room, Wilma looked around with pleasure. The tired old hillside house, under the ministrations of its four new owners, was more charming each time she saw it. The four senior ladies were doing wonders, most of it by their own hard work.

The two women made an interesting contrast, both tall and slim, both in their sixties. Wilma's gray-white hair was done in a long, thick braid wound around her head. She was dressed in jeans, a red turtleneck T-shirt and red blazer. Cora Lee wore pale cream chinos and a mocha sweater that complemented her dusky complexion. She never understood why women of her coloring liked to wear plum and purple, the very shades that picked up all the wrong highlights. Moving toward the stairs, she was eager to see Wilma's reaction to how she had decorated her own room. The four ladies had drawn straws to choose their rooms, but Cora Lee suspected the outcome had been fixed. The upstairs room was the only one that offered a large alcove off the bedroom, which she could use as studio space.

The house belonged in part to Wilma; she and the other four ladies of the Senior Survival Club had bought the property together as a private retirement retreat. The structure was large enough to give each a spacious room and bath, and to accommodate as well a housekeeper and perhaps a practical nurse or caretaker when that time arrived. It hadn't yet, for any of the ladies. While each woman's room was designed to her own taste, the common living, dining, and kitchen areas were a triumph of compromise, a fascinating eclectic mix that the ladies had put together with a minimum of harsh words. In their intelligent cooperation Wilma found great encouragement against the time, far in the future, when she would sell her own home and move in with them.

The raftered great room with its raised fireplace and long window seat was done in a combination of wicker and leather, with contemporary India rugs, white plantation shutters and, scattered among the books in the wall of built-in bookcases, a collection of local, hand-thrown ceramics. Whoever had built the house had loved fireplaces; there was a raised wood-burning fireplace in nearly every room. Following Cora Lee up the stairs, Wilma was not prepared for her friend's decorating approach to her own large bedroom.

Because the apartment Cora Lee had recently vacated had been all in shades of cream and white and café au lait, Wilma expected the large, sunny upstairs retreat to be much the same.

But this room was wild with color, as bright as the Dixieland jazz that Cora Lee and Wilma loved. The walls were a soft tomato red. The long, cushioned seat that filled the big bay window, the wicker armchairs, and the bed, were piled with patterned pillows brighter than the artist's paints that Cora Lee favored. The room was a medly of reds and greens and blues and every possible color, all in the smallest and most intricate patterns. Pillows like jewels, like flower gardens; and Cora Lee's paintings on the walls were just as bright.

The kit, crouched on Cora Lee's shoulder, looked and looked, then leaped into the heap of cushions on the window seat rolling and purring.

"I think," Wilma said, "that she likes it. *I love it!*"

Cora Lee stood in the center of the room caught between

laughter and amazement. "She does like it. Well, new things always smell good to cats. But . . . look at her pat at the brightest colors. Cats don't see color?"

"Maybe they do," Wilma said uneasily. "The world of science hasn't discovered everything yet." She glanced at Dulcie who stood beyond Cora Lee admiring every detail, and the two shared a look of delight. The private chamber was jewels set in cream, flowers scattered on velvet. The minute Cora Lee sat down on the window seat the kit stepped into her lap, nuzzling her hand, looking from her to Wilma so intelligently, so much as if she meant to join in the conversation, that Wilma stiffened, and Dulcie leaped to the cushions to distract her.

But the real distraction was the tea that Cora Lee had set out on the coffee table before the blazing fire. As the two women made themselves comfortable, the cats looked with interest at the lemon bars and shortbread; and Wilma fixed her gaze on the kit. "This is your home for a little while, Kit. You are to behave yourself, you are to mind your manners."

Cora Lee grinned at Wilma's stern tone, but Wilma's look at the kit was serious and cautionary. *Don't speak, Kit. Don't answer by mistake. Don't speak to Cora Lee. Don't open securely closed doors or locked windows. Don't under any circumstance forget. Do not talk to Cora Lee or to anyone. Keep your little cat mouth shut.*

The kit understood quite well. She smiled and purred and washed her paws. Certainly she was content to behave herself, at least until late at night. Only then, if her wanderlust grew too great, who would know? If, while Cora Lee slept, she lifted the window latch and roamed, who was to see her?

Meanwhile the bits of tea cake that Cora Lee fixed on two small plates were delicious. The kit, finishing first, eyed Dulcie's share but she daren't challenge Dulcie. She listened to Wilma's half-truths about how she had had a prowler and was worried about the kit because of her reputation as a highly trained performing cat, how she thought it best to get her away for a while.

Early this summer when the kit's surprise appearance onstage with Cora Lee had turned out to be the sensation of the village, Wilma had gone to great lengths to make Kit's appearance seem the product of long hours of careful training. But even trained cats were valuable.

"I'll keep her safe," Cora Lee said. "We all know the doors must be kept shut. I have no theater sets to work on now, not until close to Christmas. I'll be right here most of the time, working on the house. We still have the two downstairs apartments to paint and recarpet. Kit will be up here, two floors away from the paint fumes, and with the windows just cracked open—she can't get through those heavy screens. I've hidden some toys and games for her around the room, that should keep her entertained. Well, she's already started to find them."

The kit, exploring the bedroom, had discovered an intricate cardboard structure with many holes where, within, a reaching paw could find and slap a Ping-Pong ball. Next to it, hardly hidden but blending nicely in the fanciful room, stood a tall, many-tiered cat tree that led up to a high, small window. She found a tennis ball beneath Cora Lee's chair, and a catnip mouse under the bed.

"You will," Wilma told the kit again, sternly, "behave as we expect you to do. You will mind Cora Lee and stay inside this room, you will not slip away on some wild midnight excursion."

Cora Lee laughed. "I'll see that she behaves."

But the kit's look at Wilma was so patently innocent that all Wilma's alarms went off—alarms just as shrill as when, during her working career, she had assessed a parolee's too-innocent look and listened to his honeyed lies.

THE SHERIFF PULLED UP BESIDE MAX'S PICKUP, DROWNING them in dust. He was a heavy man, maybe six-four, with a prominent nose and high cheekbones, and in Charlie's opinion an overly friendly smile. He loaded Hurlie into the backseat of his unit, behind the wire barrier. "What charges?"

"Interfering with the duties of a law-enforcement officer," Max said. "Harboring a felon."

"Fine with me."

"And obstructing justice. I'll want his prints."

The sheriff nodded. "You want to toss his place? You have a warrant for the old man. Or I can do it on the way down."

Max considered. "Let's run down together and have a crack at it."

The sheriff made Hurlie hand over his keys, and moved Hurlie's truck onto the shoulder; Max and Charlie followed him down toward Little Fish Creek. As the two men entered the cabin, Charlie waited in the truck. Max had parked where she could see in through the window of the one-room shack. A single bed, covers in a tangle. An easy chair so ragged that not even Joe Grey would tolerate it, far scruffier than Joe's clawed and hairy masterpiece. One plate and cup on the rough wooden sink drain. A door open to a fusty-looking little bathroom that she imagined would be dark with mold. Max and Sheriff Beck were in the shack for nearly half an hour; she watched them going through the few cupboards, checking under the mattress, pulling off wallboard and ceiling tiles in various locations. They performed similar searches in the two scruffy outbuildings. The sheriff's unit, parked directly in front of the shack, afforded prisoner Hurlie Farger a direct view of her. She sat sideways, with her back to him, but she could feel him staring. Max came away from the search looking sour. He stood a moment in the dusty yard beside the truck, with the sheriff.

"You ask questions around those estates," Beck said softly, "you might want to watch yourself. DEA seems interested in that area. They took out two small marijuana plots up in the national forest, day before yesterday, and they still have a plane up. I haven't *heard* of anything on those estates, but they're all big places and there's sure plenty of money up there."

"I'll be careful." Max said, studying Beck. He nodded to the sheriff. And the officer stepped into his unit and pulled away, chauffeuring Hurlie Farger to a cleaner bed than he was used to.

Swinging into the pickup, Max grinned at Charlie. "What?" he said, seeing her uncertain look.

"I half thought you were going to ask me to ride back with the sheriff. So you could run this one alone."

"Would you have gone?"

"I wouldn't have gotten into that patrol car with Hurlie Farger, even with the sheriff there, if you gave me a direct order to that effect."

Max studied her with a small, twisted smile. "I don't think I'd want to try giving you a direct order, Charlie Harper." And he headed up the hills and across a forested plateau approaching the Landeau estate.

But sitting close beside Max, Charlie was quiet, trying to rearrange her thinking. Hurlie Farger had scared her. Something in his eyes, as well as his bold challenge of Max's authority, had left her chilled. And the sheriff's attitude hadn't helped.

Well, she had to learn to live with this stuff, learn to accommodate the ugly, adrenaline-packed moments. In fact, she guessed maybe it was time for a down-to-earth assessment of the way she looked at the world.

She had never been hidebound in what she expected of life. Life was what you made of it, and you sure didn't have to knuckle under just because there were bad guys around. But marrying Max had made her far more aware of that element. Had shoved people like Hurlie Farger right in her face.

Well, she'd experienced some unsettling changes in her thirty-two years. And every one had called for a change in attitude. The adjustments she must make now would be the hardest—but every one would be worth it.

She just wanted, right now, to get through this visit to those estates, to the Landeau place, get through the day and be alone again with Max.

Maybe the aftermath of the church bombing was still with her. The pain of the last few days mixed with Hurlie's attitude had hit home unexpectedly. Laying her hand on Max's knee and leaning to kiss his cheek, she looked ahead to the tall, marbled-faced Landeau mansion with its high forbidding wall. This was just a routine visit. It would soon be over. They'd soon be alone again cuddled before the fire at the inn, ordering in a hot, comforting supper.

21

CLYDE'S ATTIC, ONCE A DARK TOMB FOR GENERA-
tions of deceased spiders, was now free of cobwebs and dust and
ancient mouse droppings, and swept clean of sawdust. The last
rich light of the setting sun gleamed in where the end wall had
been removed, and a soft breeze wandered through, sweet with
the scents of cypress and pine. The attic was silent too, the power
tools and hammers stilled, the carpenters gone for the day—it
was Joe's space now. He lay stretched out across a sheet of plywood that was propped on two sawhorses, lay relaxed and
purring, digesting a half-bag of corn chips that had been abandoned by one of the carpenters. The wind off the sea caressed
him. The buzz of a dispossessed wasp distracted him only faintly,
humming among the rafters. He was nearly asleep when foot-
steps on the temporary stairway forced him to lift his head—
though really no action was required, he knew that step.

Clyde's head appeared at the north end of the attic silhouetted
in the bright triangular space. Rising up the last steps, Clyde
ducked beneath the apex, walking hunched over. By this time
tomorrow evening he would be able to stand tall, would be able to

reach up and not even touch the ceiling—barring some delay in construction, Joe thought. Barring some accident. What if, tomorrow morning, the roof-jacks didn't hold until the newly raised walls had been secured? What if . . .

But such thoughts belonged to the more human aspect of his nature. Humans loved to fret over the disaster that hadn't happened and likely wouldn't happen. Joe's more equitable feline persona lived for the moment and let the future fall how it might, pun intended.

Yawning, he considered Clyde with interest. Clyde stood with his back to Joe, looking out toward the sea, his short black hair mussed up into peaks the way it got when he was irritated. Was he not seeing Ryan tonight? Certainly he wasn't dressed for an exciting evening or even a casual dinner. Arriving home, he had pulled on his oldest, scruffiest polo shirt, the purple one with the grease stains across the front and the hole in the sleeve. And when Clyde turned to look at him, his scowl implied, indeed, an incredibly bad mood. Joe licked his whiskers. "You look sour enough to *chew* the roof off."

No response.

"This is more than a bad day at the shop. Right?"

Nothing. Clyde's body was rigid with annoyance.

"You have a fight with Ryan? But she's doing a great job, the new room will be something. I love that you can see right down to the beach, between the roofs and trees."

A slight shifting of shoulders.

"And the new tower," Joe said. "That's going to be some kind of elegant cat house."

Clyde continued to glare.

"What did you fight about?" Joe studied Clyde's ruddy face trying to read what exactly that particular scowl might mean. "She's too hardheaded and independent?" he asked tentatively— as if he were Clyde's shrink drawing him out. "She wants to install pink flamingos in the front yard with fake palm trees?"

Clyde sat down on a carpenter's stool, a boxy little bench used for tool storage, for cutting a board, for scabbing two boards together, to stand on, or to sit on while eating lunch, a very clever little piece of furniture. He glared. "She's going out with that guy tonight. Out to dinner. The guy who broke into her truck and switched her billing. She's going *out* with him."

"Why would she do that? The guy's a crook. He tried to set her up. Why would she . . ." He stared at Clyde. "She's going to set *him* up? But what does she . . . ?"

"She wants to see what else he might try. He doesn't know she switched the billing back to the original, he'll think the fake bill is in the mail. She wants to see what he'll talk about, what questions he might ask her. She thinks she can figure out what he's after."

"Oh, that's smart. What if *he* killed Rupert? Say he murdered her husband. Shot him in the head. So she goes out to dinner with him." Joe looked hard at Clyde, assessing his housemate. "You couldn't stop her short of locking her up. And you're scared for her."

Clyde nodded, looking miserable.

"So, follow them."

"She figured I might. She said that would blow it, said maybe he knows me and would certainly know my yellow roadster. That I might put her in danger."

Joe sighed. He licked his paw, waiting. But Clyde was silent again—far be it from Clyde to come out and *ask* for help. "So, where are they going?"

"She's meeting him at the Burger Basher at seven. She called me at work, broke our date for dinner. Asked if I'd keep Rock for a couple of hours. I thought I'd . . ."

"What? Just happen in for a beer? That'll fix it."

"I plan to wait outside. In case she needs someone. In case he tries to strong-arm her, get her in his car."

"That's so melodramatic."

"And a dead body in her garage is not melodramatic."

Joe washed his right ear. "And that's why you drove that old brown Hudson home. I wondered what that was about."

"She's never seen that car, and certainly Williams wouldn't have seen it."

Clyde had in his upscale automotive shop, in a private garage at the rear of the complex, enough rare old cars to run surveillance in a different vehicle every night for a month. Clyde's assortment of classic and antique models, all waiting to be restored, might seem to some a monstrous collection of junk. To Clyde Damen those old cars were CDs in the bank, gold under the mattress.

Clyde looked at him a long time.

Joe licked some crumbs from inside the ripped-open corn chip bag. "Burger Basher. Seven o'clock. Okay. So you owe me one."

"How would you go about it without getting—without them seeing you?"

"Feeling guilty already?"

"Burger Basher is all open, just that little low wall around the patio, then the sidewalk. And Ryan knows you. If she sees you schlepping around there, she'll have to wonder. She already thinks you're a bit strange."

"Strange in what way? Why would she think me strange? And what's she going to wonder? If I'm running surveillance? Oh, right."

"That little trick with the mice on her doorstep, you think I didn't have to stretch to make that little caper seem even remotely unremarkable? What made you . . . . ?"

"Do you want my help or not? I have a hundred ways to spend my evening."

Clyde shrugged, looking embarrassed.

"And," Joe said, eyeing Clyde closely, "I have a hundred ways to listen to those two without being seen. In return, if you want to contribute a little something tasty to my supper plate before I undertake this risky venture . . ."

"*Tasty* is such a crass word, even for a cat. It isn't a word. I've never heard you use such a common expression."

Joe smiled. "Dulcie couldn't agree more. She thinks that word is incredibly crude. Let's put it this way. I'm hungry. I'd like something for my dinner that is in keeping with my elevated status as your newly hired private investigator."

Clyde moved toward the stairs. "I just happened to bring home some filet. I'll go on down and slap it in the skillet."

Clyde's skillet-broiled steak, rare and juicy in the middle, crisp and dark on the outside, suited Joe just fine. Leaping past Clyde down the stairs, he headed for the kitchen to sit in the middle of the table as Clyde put supper together. "What time is he picking her up?"

"They're meeting there, at seven. She wanted it to seem as little like a date as possible, just friends meeting for dinner."

"You better park a block away. If she's in immediate danger I'll slip out and alert you. I wish, at times like this, that I had access to a walkie-talkie or a small and unobtrusive cell phone."

"Don't you think a cat carrying a phone around the village is going to attract attention?"

"Not if an enterprising firm would make one that looks like an electronic flea collar. It wouldn't have to ring, it could just vibrate. And . . ."

Clyde turned away to dish up supper.

And Joe, savoring his steak, looked forward with great anticipation to the evening. There was nothing, absolutely nothing as satisfying as sharing your professional skills with those who were less talented.

AT SEVEN IN THE EVENING BURGER BASHER'S PATIO WAS crowded to overflowing: people had gathered out on the sidewalk and sat on the two-foot high wall of the patio, waiting for their names to be called. Ryan and Larn sat on the wall, drinking beer from tall mugs. Half a block away, Joe watched them through the windshield of Clyde's old Hudson. Beside him Clyde had slouched down in the seat with a cap pulled over his eyes, a real B-movie heavy, so ludicrous Joe nearly choked, laughing.

"So what are they doing?" Clyde said, his voice muffled.

"Still waiting for their table. From the looks of the crowd, I'd say about twenty minutes. Williams parked just down the street. He's driving a white SUV, not the gray hatchback."

"Hope they don't decide to take a walk. Maybe I should move the car."

"Don't fuss. No one's going to spot you, you look like an old wino gearing up for a big night of panhandling. Turn on the radio. Listen to a tape. Play some nice hot jazz and let me concentrate. I need to figure where I want to land, in there—the place is about as accommodating as an airport terminal at rush hour."

"I told you it was too open. And why would I turn on the radio? I can hear the restaurant tape just fine. How about that little service counter? You could hide behind the coffeepots."

"And if I suffer third-degree burns? We don't have pet insurance." Studying the crowded dining patio, Joe picked out four possible refuges, none of which looked adequate to hide a healthy mouse. Listening to the sweet, rocking runs of Ella Fitzgerald, he considered the layout.

Maybe the best method was the direct one. The in-your-face approach. Why not? A mew and a wriggle. *Well, hello, Ryan, fancy seeing you here.* A good loud purr. *So what are you having for supper?*

The moment Ryan and Larn were shown to their table, Joe slipped through the open window of the Hudson, dropped to the sidewalk, and headed for the jasmine vine that climbed to the roof beside the kitchen.

The couple was seated nearly in the center of the patio, not his preferred location. From high up within the vine, he watched them peruse their menus. He could feel Clyde watching him—the same sense of invasion as if Clyde were looking over his shoulder while he worked a mouse hole.

Ryan was wearing a handsome pair of faded jeans, a pearl-gray

211

sweatshirt, expensive-looking leather sandals, and gold earrings. Her color was high, her makeup more skillfully applied than Joe had before seen, her dark hair curling fresh and crisp. A nice balance between the casual and self-assured village look, and feminine charm. A very effective statement: *I don't care*, but still a come-on designed to intrigue Williams.

Williams, in contrast, had made a conscious and awkward effort to impress. He was not an attractive man, and his too-careful attire didn't help. He might be thirty-five or so. It was hard to tell, with humans. He was thin-shouldered, his hair mousy and lank around his shoulders, his thin face resembling a particularly sneaky rodent. He wore crisply pleated brown slacks of some synthetic fabric that had an unpleasant shine, and an expensive paisley print shirt beneath a brown tweed sport coat—all just a bit too much, particularly in Molena Point. His shiny brown shoes were meant for the city, not for a casual village evening. As a waiter approached the couple, Joe slipped down the vine, meandered across the bricks in full sight between the crowded tables, stepped beneath their table, and lay down.

Staring at Ryan's sandals and at Williams's hard, cheap shoes he sniffed the heady aroma of charbroiled burgers. If Ryan was aware of him she gave no sign—until suddenly, startling him, she draped her hand over the side of her chair and wiggled her fingers.

Maybe she did understand cats, Joe thought, grinning. He rubbed his face against her hand, wondering why she didn't make some joke to Williams about the freeloading cat. Wondering, as he listened to them order, if he might be able to cadge a few French fries.

WHILE JOE RAN SURVEILLANCE ON RYAN FLANNERY AND LARN Williams, and Clyde sat in the old Hudson with his cap over his face ready to leap out and protect Ryan, or maybe even protect a certain tomcat, two hundred miles away Max Harper, standing in the high-ceilinged white marble entry of the Landeau mansion, was kept waiting for nearly twenty minutes after the short, stocky, white-uniformed housekeeper admitted him.

According to the Landeaus' sour-face maid, Mrs. Landeau was out of town but Mr. Landeau would soon be with him. She did not invite the captain in past the cold marble entry, but motioned with boredom toward a hard marble bench. As if he were one of an endless line of door-to-door hustlers selling magazines or some off-beat religion.

Accompanied by a white marble faun and two nude marble sprites, Harper waited impatiently, wondering at the architecture and decor the Landeaus' had chosen in selecting this particular mountain retreat. There was no hint of the natural materials that one expected in a country setting, no wood or native stone to give a sense of welcome. He had cooled his heels for seventeen minutes and was rising to leave when Landeau made an appearance.

Sullivan Landeau was tall and slim, with reddish hair in a becoming blow-dry, an excellent carriage, a moderate tan that implied tennis and perhaps sailing but some concern for the damages of the harsh California sun. He was dressed in immaculate white slacks, a black polo shirt and leather Dockers. His gold Rolex, nestled among the pale, curly hairs of his wrist, caught a gleam from the cut-glass chandelier. His smile was cool, faintly caustic. "Mrs. Landeau is not at home. As a matter of fact, she's down in your area, on business. Staying in Half Moon Bay tonight, then on down to Molena Point early in the morning to attend to some rental property. I hope you are not here because of some problem with one of our tenants."

"Not at all," Max said, looking him over.

Landeau waited coolly for Harper to state his business, his expression one of tolerance with which he might regard a slow bank teller or inept service-station attendant.

"Perhaps I should be speaking with an estate manager," Max said. "Someone who would be familiar with your employees."

"I am familiar with my employees."

"I'm looking for information about Hurlie Farger, I'd like some idea of his work record, what kind of service he's given you, how long he's been with you."

Landeau looked puzzled. "I'm afraid I don't know the name. Are you sure this person worked here? When would that have been? We've had the estate only three years. In what capacity would he have been employed?"

"My information is that he works here now, part-time, odd jobs on the grounds crew and filling in as a mechanic."

Landeau shook his head. "We don't have a *Farger*. You had better speak with my estate foreman. He's working east of here about four miles, up that back, dirt road. They're cutting timber." He glanced at his watch. "But of course they'll have quit for the day."

Max slipped a mug shot of Gerrard Farger from his pocket. The brothers so closely resembled each other that a person would have to know them very well to see a difference. "You may not recall his name, but as owner of the estate you would remember the faces of those who serve you." Max smiled. "I see he looks familiar."

Landeau had let down his guard for an instant, lowering his eyes as if deciding which way to play his response.

"My information," Max said, "is that he's worked for you for several years."

"The face, yes," Landeau said smoothly. "I believe I recognize this man. If I'm correct, if I have the right man, I believe he was fired six months ago. Something, as I recall, about an arrest, which I won't tolerate. I believe he got into some kind of trouble down in San Andreas. Burglary or shoplifting, or maybe it was something to do with a woman, I don't recall." Landeau looked levelly at Harper. "We don't condone that kind of behavior, it leads to trouble for the estate. Has he been into more trouble? I hope nothing too serious. But it must be serious," Landeau added, "for a chief of police from the coast to come all the way up here."

"Not at all," Harper said. "We're on vacation, heading home. Thought it expedient to collect what information we could, not lay more work on your sheriff." He had no way to know whether Landeau was aware of the bombing in Molena Point. "You say Hurlie Farger hasn't worked for you in six months."

"To the best of my knowledge."

"Would you say that if we show otherwise, you would be open to a charge of obstructing justice?"

"I certainly wouldn't want that," Landeau said. "It may have been less than six months."

"Or perhaps you only considered firing him? Perhaps you changed your mind and let him stay on?"

Landeau shook his head. "It's possible my wife may have done so, in a fit of charity. You know how women are."

"What can you tell me about Farger?"

"If you would care to come into my study, I'll see what I can remember."

Harper moved with Landeau through a vast sitting area whose windows overlooked the top of the darkening pine forest. The mirrored walls reflected chrome-framed chairs, chrome-surfaced tables, and chrome-framed couches upholstered in silver-dyed leather, all straight from some futuristic space movie. The white marble fireplace boasted a huge gas log that either had never been lit, or was scrubbed clean after each use. The black marble floors were unadorned except where the furniture formed "seating areas," each set off by an ice-blue shag rug that made the chrome above it look blue.

"This is my wife's part of the house," Landeau said, watching Harper. "The portion reserved for entertaining." He led Max into a cypress-walled study furnished with natural-toned leather couches, framed antique maps, and a dark oriental carpet, a room that seemed to Max equally posed and out of character, planned for effect, not for any personal preferences. There were no papers on the desk, nothing of a personal or business nature visible, no photographs, no books, no shelves to put books on. Even Landeau's offer of brandy seemed a tired line from a tired old movie. Declining a drink, Max couldn't decide what kind of man Landeau might be. Everything about him seemed studied and timed for effect.

Stepping to a walnut credenza below the window, Landeau poured himself a Scotch and water, and turned to regard Max. And as the two men faced each other, outside on the large parking apron Charlie sat in the pickup studying the house and listening for any smallest sound from within. To her right stood five tennis courts, the heat from their green paving rippling across their chain-link barriers. She could see behind them a pool and ornate pool house in the Grecian style, set against the heavy pines in an idyllic tableau. She could imagine bathers there, beautiful women with figures as sculptured and polished as marble themselves, each woman's skimpy bikini costing more than her entire wardrobe. In the dimming afternoon, the carefully trimmed lawns and precisely shaped bushes seemed as artificial as the house. The six-foot concrete wall that encircled the acreage gave her not a feeling of security but of confinement. Far to her left stood ten dog runs with a kennel at the back of each. The three dogs she could see pacing behind their fences were German shepherds. Maybe the guard dogs had been acquired after the break-ins the sheriff had mentioned to Max.

And Ryan had told her that the Landeaus entertained some high-powered investors up here too, that apparently they had bought the mansion to accommodate Sullivan's real-estate clients. The timbering and whatever else the estate was involved in, Ryan had thought, was secondary to its prime purpose as an elegant business write-off.

Max said the Landeaus had had more than break-ins. That there'd been some trouble from local groups who didn't want them to raise and cut timber, that they had in fact suffered considerable loss from arson. Charlie supposed if she were rich and someone burned her property, she'd have guard dogs too. As she idly studied the kennels, two rottweilers appeared pacing inside their runs, their blunt heads down like bulls ready to charge. All five dogs watched her more intently than she liked. She'd feel easier when Max was out of there, when, safe together in the truck, they were headed back to the inn to a nice private supper before the fire, to a night of lovemaking and let the rest of the world go hang. She was watching for Max, watching for the black-lacquered front door to open, when behind the pool house a white van appeared moving along a service road or drive, parking behind the house.

At that distance, in the falling light, she couldn't read its logo; she could see a crown, with dark lettering beneath. They had passed two vans as they came up the narrow country road, both heading down, one belonging to a dry cleaner, one to a catering service, both seeming out of place in the backwoods setting. Max had handed her the field book to jot down company names and license numbers. She had a sudden desire, now, to slip out of the car and take a look at this vehicle.

But something stopped her. She wasn't sure what Max would want her to do. This was not the kind of home where one was welcome to wander about the gardens for a friendly assessment of the flower beds. She imagined walking along the side of the mansion setting off some kind of electric eye that would open the kennel gates and bring that brace of hungry mutts charging out in a timed race to see who got the juiciest supper. She heard car doors open, and in a few minutes close again, and she watched the van head away, up a back road into the woods until soon it was lost from view. She sat looking after it, disgusted at her own hesitancy.

She wouldn't tell Max she'd been afraid and uncertain. She hadn't spent time with a dozen police wives, at various backyard cookouts and parties, hadn't seen how laid-back and cool those women were, not to be ashamed of her sudden timidity—surely there was nothing that would so seriously cool their romance, as to let fear intervene.

Though Max was the most monogamous and straightforward of all possible husbands, she knew that. She knew a lot, from Clyde and from the people in the department, about Max and Millie's marriage, which had ended with Millie's death. She knew enough to be certain that she had a lot to live up to, in that hard-shelled and loving lady detective.

She could never replace Millie. But she could give Millie the compliment and respect of trying, and in so doing maybe she could make Max happy.

A figure moved behind the house where the van had disappeared. Charlie, turning the key that Max had left in the ignition, hit the window button and rolled down the glass, to listen.

There was no sound. The early evening air was heavy with the scent of pine and with a less pleasant smell from the kennels. Somewhere behind the house a car started, she heard it move away, the scrunch of tires on gravel and the engine hum soon fading. She thought of Hurlie Farger and his old truck, but this vehicle was newer, purring softly. Anyway, this wasn't her business. This was department business. She was a civilian, she needed to behave like a civilian. Max had collected some valuable information today concerning larges sales of bleach, fertilizers, iodine, antifreeze, glass bottles and jars and propane, among the local stores. She didn't need to do anything to distract him or to complicate his work.

But, *Come on, Max. Come out of there. I want you safe. I want you to myself for a little while, and safe.*

22

THE BRICK-PAVED PATIO OF BURGER BASHER WAS lit by lanterns placed along the perimeter and by shifting washes of moonlight beneath fast-running clouds. Though the sea wind was brisk, the forty-by-forty-foot space was comfortably warm, heated by six outdoor gas burners suspended on poles overhead. Joe Grey, sitting beneath Ryan's table, tried not to lick his whiskers at the scent of broiling burgers. Though he'd had filet for supper, who could resist a Basher's double? Encouraged by Ryan's petting, he stood up on his hind paws, looking as plaintive as a begging beagle into her amused eyes.

"Come on, Joe Grey. You want to sit up here? We have an empty chair."

Larn Williams looked disgusted. But Joe was aware of other diners watching him and smiling. Beneath a nearby table, a springer spaniel whined with interest. Leaping into the chair, Joe watched appalled as Williams slopped on mustard, ruining a fine piece of meat. Ryan, sensibly waving away the condiments, cut off a quarter of her burger and dissected it carefully into cat-sized bites.

Placing these on a folded paper napkin, she set the offering on the chair before him. "There you go, big boy. See what you can do with that."

Rewarding Ryan with a purr and a finger-lick, Joe sampled the char-grilled confection. This was the way surveillance should be conducted, in plain sight of the subjects while one enjoyed life's finer pleasures. He tried to eat slowly but he didn't come up for air until every morsel had vanished. Yawning and stretching, again he fixed his gaze on Ryan, licking his whiskers.

She cut her eyes at him as she devoured her own burger. "No more. You'll get fat, lose your handsome tomcat figure."

Williams watched this exchange coldly. "I didn't ask you out to dinner—such as it is—to watch you feed some alley cat."

"He's not an alley cat, I know him very well."

"When did you get home? I swung by the Jakeses' place up there but you'd already left. I didn't know you were leaving. One of your carpenters was still there, that old redheaded guy with the beard."

"I don't consider Scotty old. I consider him handsome and capable. I got home Saturday night, in time to go to a wedding on Sunday, and start a new job this morning."

Williams nodded more amiably, seeming actually aware of his surliness. "Seems like, if you're gone a few weeks, everything piles up, the laundry, the junk mail."

When she didn't respond, he began asking questions about the new job she had started. Her answers were as vague as she could politely make them; Joe hid a pleased smile. Somewhere in the conversation, Williams edged his way back to his primary interest.

"It's that backlog of paperwork I really hate. Every real-estate sale—a landslide of forms to be filed. I don't have to tell you, the paperwork gets worse every year. That, and the billing. And then it's time for taxes."

If, Joe thought, the evening was to be filled with such gems as this, he might as well be home eradicating the front lawn of gophers. Stretched out across the chair, he yawned so deeply that he almost dislocated his jaw; and he lay observing Williams. The guy had a face as bland as yogurt, his pale brown eyes soft-looking and seeming without guile. Gentle, submissive eyes—as if there was no way this good soul could bear to swat a fly. The kind of expression that made any sensible cat uneasy.

And when Joe glanced at Ryan, she was watching Larn with the same distaste, her dislike thinly veiled—though she appeared to take the bait. "At least," she said, sipping her beer, "I caught up with my billing, and got it in the mail. Didn't have any choice. No money coming in, the creditors will be at my throat."

Williams didn't turn a hair. "The building-supply people in San Andreas are pretty good about letting a contractor ride over a month or two."

"That's nice, but I don't do that, I don't work that way. And the Jakeses are good about paying, they were very prompt on the two San Francisco jobs that Dannizer Construction did for them. I expect I'll see their check before the end of the week."

No change of expression from Williams. "I never quite trust people who *always* pay *all* their bills on time. Makes me wonder why they're so careful."

Ryan made no reply. Was he trying to be funny? Joe had never heard any of Clyde's friends talk that way. Certainly not Clyde himself, Clyde valued his prompt-paying customers, and he let them know it.

"Did you say your father was on the East Coast? I imagine you miss him just now, with this unfortunate murder to deal with. I was sorry to hear about your husband's death, in that ugly way. I hope things have—not been too rocky."

"He's on the East Coast, yes," Ryan said, smiling. "I'm doing fine. Thanks for asking." She was trying hard to be nice to Larn. Joe wondered that Williams didn't detect her veiled effort—or didn't seem to.

"Hot weather back there just now. I hope he took something

light. Cotton's best, in the humidity. But I suppose he knows all about that."

Joe narrowed his eyes, studying Williams. This guy was strange.

"Do the police have any line on a suspect? On who would do such a thing?"

Ryan just looked at him.

"I don't understand much about the circumstances, but I hope they've made some progress in locating the killer. What a terrible shock, to find . . . Well, I am sorry."

And you *are* going on about it, Joe thought, curling up with his back to Williams.

"I hope they have enough evidence so you are no longer a suspect. I would hate to be suspected of a murder, even though everyone knows better. It would be so . . . demeaning." Williams was not keeping his voice down. People at the nearby tables had begun to watch them. Ryan looked increasingly uncomfortable.

"Do they have fingerprints, or anything on the weapon? That would certainly make you feel easier."

"I really can't discuss these matters, Larn. And we're attracting attention."

"I only meant . . ." He looked suitably stricken. "I only thought . . . You know, hoping there was something to ease your mind, to take the pressure off," he said, lowering his voice. "Hoping you're able to feel more comfortable about this ugly mess."

"I was told not to discuss it."

"Well, if there's anything I can do to be of help, I just want you to know you can call on me."

"Nothing that I know of."

"When will your father be home?"

This guy was so damned nosy Joe wanted to claw him. Or, he wasn't quite steady in the attic.

"I really don't know, Larn." Her voice was decidedly cooler, as if she were sorry she had come tonight.

But Larn didn't seem to get the drift. "He has a good reputation in the city. I don't know many folks in law enforcement, but people say he does a good job. *I* certainly don't believe the gossip, I don't pay attention to that kind of thing."

Ryan had stopped eating. "What gossip?" she said softly. "What are you talking about?"

People at the surrounding tables had turned away making an effort not to stare. Williams lifted his hand in embarrassment, as if he realized he'd made a blunder. But Joe could see under the table Williams's left fist on his knee beating a soft, energetic rhythm, his body language laying out all too clearly his cold deliberation.

"What gossip?" Ryan repeated, her eyes never leaving Williams. "You'd better explain what you're talking about."

"Well, I *am* sorry. I thought of course you'd heard it like everyone else. . . . It's common . . . Oh, hell, I thought . . . Can we just drop it? Forget I said anything?"

"Of course we can't drop it," she said raising her voice, not caring if people turned to look. "What is this about? *What* have you heard about my father?"

"It's only gossip, it doesn't mean anything. Let's forget it."

Joe didn't need to look up into Ryan's face to see her rage. Every angle of her body was tense and rigid. She waited unmoving for Williams to explain.

"Well," he said reluctantly. "It's just—the women . . . you have to know about the women."

Her silence was like thunder, so volatile that Joe thought the air around her might explode. "*What* women? *What exactly are you talking about! And where did you hear such a thing!*"

Larn sighed, his pale eyes shifting. "Don't be so loud. People are staring." This guy was far more than a nut case.

"Well?"

"It's common gossip in the city, Ryan. I can't believe you never heard it."

"*What, exactly*, is common gossip? You'll have to spell it out."

He sighed again, implying that this was all very painful. "You have to know that Flannery had plenty of women."

Ryan only looked at him.

"And that . . . Well, *call* it gossip, that Flannery had affairs with more than a few of his female parolees. Most of that, the way I hear it, was before he was appointed chief. I thought of course you'd heard this. But gossip doesn't make . . ."

Ryan was white. "That is so patently a lie. I have never heard a hint of such a story. I certainly would have heard that from Rupert, he'd have been the first to pass on such a tale, would have been delighted to repeat that." She was almost shouting at Williams. "This is not a story that anyone in San Francisco has ever heard. Why are you telling me this?" People around them were growing uncomfortable. Two couples, hurrying through their meals, rose to leave. "Where did this come from? What is your purpose in saying such a thing?"

Larn looked totally apologetic, really crushed. Joe was so fascinated he had to remind himself to stop staring. Turning away, he began to wash again, watching Williams with occasional sideways glances.

"I don't know where I heard it. Everywhere. And then just this week I heard it in conjunction with the murder," Larn said embarrassedly. "The implication was that . . . that maybe Rupert had been talking about one of Flannery's affairs, spreading around names and details, and Flannery had—"

Ryan gaped at him then was out of her chair jerking Larn up—he came up under her grip as limp as a doll, looking shocked but making no effort to resist her. She spun him around with surprising strength, forced him between the tables and out through the patio to the street, his arm bent behind him. Forced him down the sidewalk away from the restaurant. As Joe leaped to follow them the thought did cross his mind that someone ought to pay the bill. Well, he sure couldn't. One of the perks of being a cat, you never got stuck with the bill.

Half a block down, she shoved Williams into an alley. Joe glanced across the street where Clyde sat in the Hudson, poised as if ready to move. Joe peered around into the brick alley where Ryan had Williams backed against the building. The man was totally submissive. Was he enjoying himself? Getting it on with this woman's rage? Torn between disgust and amusement, Joe settled down between the trash cans to watch.

Ryan looked like she was about to pound Williams when the scuff of shoes made Joe spin around. Clyde stood with his fists clenched as if he wanted to pile into Williams. But Ryan's display of anger held him frozen.

The hint of a grin ticked at the corner of Clyde's mouth as he studied Williams's pallor and Ryan's businesslike grip on the man's collar. She glanced at Clyde, her face coloring.

"What was he doing?" Clyde said, amused.

She said nothing, but turned back to Williams. "If I *ever* hear that kind of talk *anywhere*, I'll know it came from you. I swear I'll pound you, Williams, then sue your pants off for slander. I have four top attorneys in the city, and I would like nothing better than to see them take you down."

Jerking Williams away from the wall, she shoved him hard. He stumbled and half fell out onto the sidewalk. "Go home, Larn. Go back to San Andreas. I don't know what your purpose is. But you pull anything more—*anything*, and you'll be cooling your ass in the slammer."

Larn rose from an off-balance crouch, stared at Ryan and at Clyde, his face unreadable, and headed away fast. Ryan watched until he reached his car and had driven off, then she collapsed against Clyde, her face buried against him. Her shoulders were shaking, whether shivering with nerves, or rocking with laughter, Joe couldn't tell. The gray tomcat, sitting among the garbage cans in the dark alley, was sorry that Dulcie had missed this one.

23

A WEEK EARLIER, JOE GREY WOULD HAVE SWORN that this would never happen, that he and Clyde would never go undercover together running surveillance, tooling along in Clyde's old Hudson behind Larn Williams's Jeep like a pair of buddy cops. But here they were, slipping up the hills through the night behind Williams's white SUV.

Clyde had waited, in front of Burger Basher, as patiently for Joe as Holmes waiting for Watson while Joe played electronic bug underneath Ryan's table. Then that little affair in the alley that had left Joe weak with laughter, and left Clyde wired for action, ready to move as Ryan headed for Clyde's place to pick up Rock. Clyde had told her, in the alley, that he was just passing, that he had an errand. Whatever she believed, she'd grinned at him and thanked him nicely for coming to her rescue; no harsh word for following her. Gave him a buss on the cheek and said she'd see him in the morning.

So here they were following Williams, Clyde dawdling in traffic so not to be noticed, then panicked when Williams turned a corner for fear they'd lose him. Joe did his best not to laugh.

Watching Clyde practice his surveillance skills was an absolute and entertaining first.

And it was, as well, an occasion that Joe suspected he would deeply regret. First thing he knew, Clyde would be telling him exactly how to conduct every smallest detail of his private business.

"*Where's* he headed?" Clyde said, frowning.

"I could be wrong. I'm guessing the Landeau cottage. Watch the road," Joe hissed as Clyde turned to look at him.

"Why would he go there?"

Joe himself was surprised. But maybe he shouldn't be. There was nothing to show a connection between Williams and the Landeaus, but they did live in the same small town of San Andreas, they could know each other.

Or, Joe thought, maybe this was the meaning of Gramps Farger's remark, *Them San Andreas people.*

The Fargers and the Landeaus? Talk about an unlikely mix.

Once they were above the village the residential streets were black, where the moon had dissolved above pale clouds. Joe glanced at Clyde. "Better turn off your lights."

"I'm not driving with my lights off. And hit some animal?"

"He'll make you, otherwise. There's not a car per square mile moving up here."

Clyde cut his lights. The street went black.

"Drive slower. *I* can see the street, *I* can see if there's an animal. Maybe he'll think you turned off. He's not moving very fast."

"Why would he trash her father? Why would he go to the Landeau place? What's the connection? What's this guy up to?"

"Slow down, he's turning in."

Easing to the curb a block before the cottage, Clyde cut the engine. Williams had pulled onto the parking close to the cottage door, making no effort to hide his car. On the dark granite paving, the white Jeep stood out like snow on tar. "Roll down your window," Joe said softly. "You'll stay in the car like you promised?"

"Didn't I promise?"

"That's not an answer." Joe glanced at Clyde. "He sees you, you could blow everything—and could put me in danger." Before Clyde could answer, he leaped across Clyde's legs, dropped out the window, and beat it up the street. He had no idea how long Clyde would remain patiently behind the wheel or, in his new investigative enthusiasm, come sneaking along the street like some two-bit private eye. Surveillance was easier with Dulcie. No human in their right mind would suspect a pair of cats.

He was just in time to see Williams let himself in with a key. Swiftly Joe slipped into the house behind his heels, just making it through as Williams slammed the door, and sliding behind the Mexican chest.

Williams didn't pause as if getting his bearings, nor did he turn on the light. He headed straight for the bedroom, knowing his way. Moving up the four steps he sat down on the bed and pulled off his shoes. The bed was unmade, the brightly patterned designer sheets and spread tangled half on the floor. Dropping his shoes, Williams picked up the phone. As he dialed, Joe crept past through the shadows, and hightailed it into the kitchen.

Leaping to the dark granite counter, slick as black ice beneath his paws, he searched frantically for the extension. The counters were nearly empty. A set of modern canisters. Nothing behind them. Bread box, but no phone inside. Did they keep the phone in a cupboard?

Or was there only one phone, and Williams had moved it to the bedroom at some earlier time?

Yes, behind the bread box he found the empty jack. Was the guy staying here with the Landeaus permission? Or without their knowledge? Why else would he not turn on the lights?

Dropping to the floor as silently as he could manage, he slipped into the bedroom in time to hear Williams say, "Yes, but I don't see the point. So the Jakeses sue her. So what does . . . ?"

Pause . . . Behind Williams's back, Joe slid across the room and under the bed.

"Why is it none of my business! If I'm going to do the work, I . . . Does this have to do with her divorce?"

Joe could make out a faint metallic reverberation from the other end. Sounded like a woman's voice, sharp with anger. Creeping along under the bed, gathering strands of cobwebs that made his ears itch, he crouched directly beneath Williams. Amazing how fast these little busy spiders could set up housekeeping.

"Of course I did. *Yes*, a code she won't find. What do you think? So the Jakeses hit the fan, what then? So what's the purpose?"

Angry crackling. Definitely a woman.

"Thanks. *I* go to all the trouble, to say nothing of the risk, and all you can say is, *Don't sweat it! You* tell *me* don't sweat it!"

Crackle, hiss . . .

"She's what? What time in the morning?"

A terse response.

"*What* time? That's the crack of damn dawn. *Well, isn't that cute* . . . Of course I'll be out of here. When did you find this out? Why didn't you . . . Well, all *right*. Don't be so bitchy . . . No, I won't leave anything lying around!"

Crackle, crackle . . .

"All right. And what if I spill about *Martie*?"

The voice at the other end snapped with rage. Williams listened, drumming his fingers on the bedside table. "Well, it's just between you and me," and he brayed a coarse laugh. "Just between us and *Martie! Martie Martie Martie*. He pounded on the night table. "*Martie Martie Holland* . . ." then banged the phone down, giggling a laugh that made Joe's blood curdle.

This guy was one weird player.

And Ryan had gone out with him. Ryan had, Joe thought with a sharp jolt, Ryan had beat up on him . . . this guy who was, in Joe's opinion, first in line for the nut farm. And, first in line as having killed her husband.

For instance,what would most men do if a woman tried to beat up on them? Grab her arms and get her under control—or knock her around and pound her. Williams had done neither. How many men would just stand there and take it, as limp as a decapitated mouse? No, Larn Williams, in anyone's book, was a long way from normal.

And what did he mean to do to Ryan later? What might he be saving up to do?

Furthermore, if that was Marianna on the other end of the line, why would she want to cook Ryan's books? What did Marianna have to gain by framing Ryan?

And who was Martie Holland?

Above Joe on the bed, Williams shifted his weight, still giggling and muttering. Joe heard him pick up the phone again, heard the little click of the headset against the machine, heard the dial tone then a fast clicking as if Williams had hit the redial.

Laughing that same crazy laugh, Williams shouted the name over and over, *"Martie Holland Martie Holland Martie Holland,"* then he slammed the phone down again, rose, and padded into the kitchen. Joe heard him open the refrigerator, then the cupboard, heard the icemaker spitting ice cubes into a glass, and could smell the sharp scent of whisky. While Williams mixed a drink, Joe lay under the bed trying to make sense of his phone conversation. Williams brought his drink into the bedroom, set it on the nightstand, and stretched out on the bed so the springs creaked above Joe's head. He heard Williams plump the pillows then straighten the covers as if perhaps preparing for sleep. The tomcat was about to cut out of there when he heard, outside the window, the faintest rustling of bushes.

Scooting on his belly to the window side of the bed, he peered up at a familiar shadow dark against the glass—then it was gone.

He didn't wait to find out if Williams had seen Clyde. Leaving the bedroom fast, he leaped at the front door, praying the dead bolt would give before Williams heard him—wondering if he'd be *able* to turn the bolt.

There was not a sound from the bedroom except Williams

shaking the ice in his glass. Joe leaped again, and again. Dead bolts were hell on the paws, most of them stronger and with less leverage than a cat could manage. Had Williams heard him? Why was he so quiet? Joe was swinging and kicking when, glancing across the living room where moonlight slanted down against the mantel, he saw something that made him drop to the floor, looking.

Something about the three smooth black indentations that held the three pieces of sculpture wasn't right. Two were smooth and properly constructed. But in the angled moonlight, the right-hand rectangle looked rough and unfinished. Someone had taken less than the required care in smoothing the concrete, had left a ragged line and rough trowel marks.

Considering the perfection of detail in the rest of the house, that did seem strange. Considering Marianna Landeau's reputation for demanding perfection, it seemed more than strange. He was about to slip closer, for a better look, when beyond the front door he heard Clyde's whisper. *"Joe? Are you there? Joe?"*

In the bedroom, Williams stirred, sending a shock of panic through Joe. He turned, watching the man. He didn't think he wanted to play innocent lost kitty with this guy.

Leaping for the lock in huge panic, driven by desperation, he just managed to turn the dead bolt, seriously bruising his paws—the door flew open. Clyde loomed, his familiar scent filling Joe's nostrils. Joe glanced to the bedroom again, but Williams had turned over and seemed to be dozing off.

"Wait," Joe said. "Pull the door to and wait, I just want to . . ."

"Wait, hell. Come out of there *now*."

"One second," Joe said, and he was across the room rearing up, staring up at the moonlit mantel.

Yes, definitely flawed. Sloppy work that Marianna should never have permitted, or for that matter, Ryan either—though possibly you couldn't see this in the daylight; Joe hadn't seen it then. Only now did the sharply angled light pick out clearly the thin, ragged line that ran diagonally across the black concrete.

Wondering if such a flaw *could* have gone undetected, he heard Williams stir again and push back the covers. Taking one last look at the rough black concrete, Joe fled for the door. Clawing past Clyde's feet, he was out of there racing ahead of Clyde across the yard into the dark, concealing woods, where they crouched together among the bushes like two thieves.

"What was that about?" Clyde snapped, snatching Joe up in his arms. "Why did you go back? That guy . . ."

"I . . . something I needed to look at."

Behind them there wasn't the faintest sound, the front door didn't open. Rising slowly, holding Joe half-concealed under his jacket, Clyde slipped out of the woods and headed fast for the car. Jerking open the driver's door of the Hudson, he tossed Joe on the torn seat, slipped in and locked the door behind them. "You're risking your neck in there and risking mine, you sound like a herd of bulls jumping at the door, but then you just have to go back—for another look at what? Did it occur to you that this guy might snatch up a cat and . . ."

"It occurred. It occurred. It was something urgent."

Clyde started the engine. "I endanger life and limb playing bodyguard to a demented gum-paw, and something in there is so important you risk both our necks, going back."

"We didn't risk our necks. That guy's a wimp. *Ryan* beat him up."

Clyde sighed and headed down the hills, turning his lights on the instant he was around the first curve. Watching him, Joe felt almost bad that he wasn't sharing what he'd seen with Clyde.

But for the moment he wanted to keep that puzzling glimpse of the fireplace to himself, wanted to think about it without Clyde's take on the matter, without anyone's input. When something strange nagged at him, he liked to let it fall in place by itself. Let it rattle around with the rest of the mismatched facts and see how they shook out; see what his inner thoughts would do, without outside influence.

He'd had the feeling, when he looked up at that black recess, that this was the moment of truth. That he stood teetering on the brink of one big, momentous discovery.

Beside him, driving down the dark and narrow, twisting streets, Clyde was nearly squirming with curiosity. "So besides whatever you went back for, whatever you're keeping so secret, what else went on in there? Did I hear him talking on the phone? I thought sure he'd find you, I was ready to smash a window." He looked sternly at Joe. "This stuff's hard on a guy's blood pressure, you ever think of that?"

Joe smiled. "He was talking to a woman. I'm guessing it was Marianna, that he's here with her permission, that they're friends."

"That would be a twist. So what was he shouting about?"

"I think the guy's crazy. Kept shouting the name Martie Holland, over and over, wasn't making any sense. You ever hear of a Martie Holland? Harper or Dallas, or Ryan, ever mention that name?"

"Not that I recall."

Joe frowned. He didn't like when the pieces wouldn't add up. Heading home in the Hudson beside Clyde, he thought he'd catch a few hours' sleep until Williams left the Landeau cottage and then, if Ryan or Hanni *was* to be there early in the morning—and who else would it be?—he'd play friendly kitty with those two, and get a closer look at the flawed mantel.

24

WHEN RYAN LEFT BURGER BASHER HEADING FOR Clyde's place to pick up Rock, she was still steaming with anger; playing back Larn Williams's words about her dad, she was mad enough to chew nails. Clyde had hurried away in his old Hudson on some errand, and just as well. She was in no mood to be civil for long, even to Clyde, though she had greatly appreciated his coming to her rescue—he might have followed her, and that was okay. He might have rescued her from killing Williams, the way she'd felt at that moment.

As she pulled to the curb before Clyde's house, Rock heard the truck and began to paw at the gate. Hurrying back to release him, reaching to open the latch, she stopped. Rock had backed off from her, snarling with a cold, businesslike menace.

"What's wrong?" She reached for him. "Come, Rock." He dodged away growling. She thought of rabies, and shivered; but quietly she moved toward him. He showed his teeth, focused on something she couldn't understand.

Last night he'd been this way. Leaving Lupe's Playa after Williams switched the contents of the envelope on the seat of her truck, following Clyde home, opening this same gate, Rock had been delighted to see her—but when she opened the truck door and told him to load up, he'd pitched a fit, smelling the scent of someone strange in the cab. And when they got home and Rock encountered the stranger's smell there in the apartment, he'd nearly torn the place apart, looking for the intruder.

The smell of the intruder, of Larn Williams. Now that smell was on her. She stared at her hands where she had marched Williams into the alley and shoved him against the wall. And, stepping into the yard past the growling, puzzled weimaraner, she moved around to the outdoor sink and washed thoroughly, scrubbing to her elbows.

Then again she approached Rock.

He cringed low but came to her. He sniffed again at her hands, and he grinned up at her and began to dance around her, all wags and kisses, whining and licking and loving her.

Putting him on the lead and shutting the gate securely behind her, she settled him in the truck and headed home. He watched her seriously, his pale yellow eyes puzzled, as if he couldn't understand about the smells. In the passing lights, his sleek silver coat gleamed like satin. She scratched his ears. "You not only have a very good nose, my dear Rock. Considering the source of your anger, you have superior judgment."

At her lighter tone, Rock grinned and wagged, his long, soft ears thrust eagerly forward. Smiling to herself, she wondered what Rock would do, face-to-face with Williams. And again she saw Williams in the alley, his white, shocked expression as she backed him against the wall. The incident, thanks to Clyde, hadn't turned as nasty as she'd expected. She really wasn't sure how the encounter would have ended if Clyde hadn't appeared so suddenly.

She didn't often lose her temper like that, and tonight was certainly not the time or the place. She would most likely regret later her public display of rage.

What was the source of Larn's remarks about her dad? There

could be no source. Sick words from a twisted mind. Williams was riding a loose rail.

Or was it more than that?.

And what a bizarre twist, that Clyde's tomcat had been in the restaurant with her and Larn, then had apparently followed them to the alley; she'd caught just a glimpse of him as Clyde snatched him up, heading for his car. "A very peculiar cat," she told Rock. "I don't like to insult present company, but he really does act more like a dog, if you could manage to take that as a compliment."

Rock grinned and wagged, happy for her improved mood. But then as she turned into her drive he stiffened again, watching the stair and her studio windows and glancing at her as if for direction, the hair along his back rising in a harsh ridge.

Scanning the yard and the upstairs windows, she slipped Hanni's gun from her glove compartment. She wondered if she dare let Rock out of the truck? If someone was there, would she be able to control him?

Or was he simply wired again after sniffing the scent of last night's intruder on her hands? She would have to learn to control the dog, and *soon*, if she meant to keep him.

Slipping the loaded, unholstered gun into her jeans pocket and putting Rock on leash, she moved quietly up the outside stairs. Rock, walking at heel, almost slunk along, silent and wary. She had unlocked the door and stepped in and turned on the light when the phone rang. She didn't pick up but stood looking around the apartment, letting the machine answer.

The room didn't seem disturbed. The kitchen was as she'd left it, cups and glasses in the drain, an inch of stale coffee in the pot. The studio windows all closed and locked. She moved with Rock to the hall, approaching the closet-dressing room and bath. Together they cleared the apartment, and she checked the lock on the door of the inner stairs. When all seemed secure she released Rock. He continued to prowl, perhaps making certain the intruder's scent was not fresh. Sitting down at her desk, she hit replay.

It was Hanni. She was wired, laughing with excitement. "The rug's in! Delivered this afternoon while I was out installing the Brownfield house—I just got home. Starved. Exhausted. The kids hardly know me, I haven't had time to breathe. Jim and the kids unpacked it, we couldn't wait. It's in the living room, one end draped over the couch. *It's fab, Ryan! Just fab! Are you there? Pick up the phone!* Can you meet me in the morning? I was going over anyway, early, to take some Mexican planters. I'm glad we ripped out the old carpet. It won't take us a minute to put this down, just a little two-sided tape. It's going to be sensational. Eight o'clock too late? Call me. I know you've started a new job. Call me please before I go to sleep, and let me know!"

Stripping off her jeans and sweatshirt, Ryan washed her face and brushed her teeth then pulled on her robe and crossed the studio. Pulling the curtains, she made herself a drink, and turned her bed back, removing the hand-printed spread to reveal its matching comforter. Carrying the phone to the bed, she made herself comfortable propped against the pillows. Immediately Rock stepped up onto the foot of the bed looking questioningly at her.

"It's okay," she said softly. Who would know if she spoiled him? If he was going to be her dog, she could spoil him as she pleased. All her childhood, one or another of the hunting dogs had been allowed to sleep on her bed. After her mother died, that nighttime companionship had been important. A warm, caring creature to lie across her feet or to snuggle with.

Easing back into the pillows, sipping her drink, feeling the last of her gritty anger at Larn Williams ease away, only then did she pick up the phone and call Hanni.

Hanni had turned off her tape. Letting it ring, Ryan sat enjoying the high-ceilinged studio, taking pleasure in its plain white angles and tall, open space. Someday she'd want paintings, more furnishings, bright and intricate accessories maybe to the point of crowding. But right now the open, nearly empty interior was deeply soothing. The only real luxury items were her hand-blocked spread and quilt in shades of black and white and tan, a primitive Australian pattern on which, at the moment, one long, lean, silver-coated freeloader reclined, his short pointer's tail gently thumping as he looked shyly at her, not totally certain that she meant to let him stay. Hanni answered.

Ryan said, "We're working on Clyde's attic, ready to jack up the roof first thing in the morning. Can the rug wait?"

"I can't stand to wait. It's so beautiful. You can't imagine how elegant and rich. I've already added it to Marianna's insurance policy, and I . . . I could lay it myself, but I don't want to use the stretcher. Could we do it at seven? You don't start work until eight."

"If I can be on the job by eight."

"It won't take long. You'll be so thrilled. See you at seven."

Ryan sighed and hung up. She had to remember that Hanni had designed that rug, that she had indicated the placement of every hand-knotted piece of yarn, that the rug was Hanni's painting, her latest masterpiece. Of course she was excited—and Hanni was never one to quell her passions.

Turning out the bedside lamp she sat going over tomorrow's work to see if she'd forgotten any detail. Against her feet Rock was like a furnace. The fact that he was taking half the bed, that she would likely sleep with her feet hanging out, or twisted up like a pretzel, didn't off-balance her satisfaction at having him there. Maybe, when she had a little break in Clyde's job, she'd put a couple of her men up here to fence that steep backyard, maybe bring some heavy equipment in to terrace it. Finishing her drink she stretched out with her feet tucked securely against the big weimaraner.

But then she couldn't sleep.

She lay wondering if Larn had killed Rupert, wondering if she had had dinner tonight with the man who murdered her husband.

She had gone out for that casual dinner drawn by curiosity, just as Larn had meant her to be. Manipulated like a puppet. And she had learned nothing true about her father, had learned only that Larn Williams was driven by motives she didn't yet understand.

Dad had had woman friends over the years since her mother died, good friends, women he'd dated and whom he'd brought home for dinner or picnics or to hunt with them. Maybe in all those years, no more than four or five woman friends. He'd never been serious enough to think about marriage, he'd always let his daughters know that no one ever would replace their mother. And certainly none of his dating had been of the kind that would embarrass himself or his children. He had never, *would* never have dated any parolee or probationer. Her father was too much a stickler for professional behavior to do such a thing, he would fire any of his officers caught in such a situation.

So what was Williams trying to accomplish?

Larn Williams was, as far as she knew, no more than a small-town realtor who had, she'd thought, been interested in her work in San Andreas. She'd made it clear that she'd only just left her husband, and wasn't dating. That she would have dinner with him to discuss possible remodel work for his San Andreas clients.

What if it turned out that Larn had killed Rupert?

But what connection could there have been?

If Larn were arrested for Rupert's murder, how would that look to the dozens of people who had seen them having dinner, and heard them arguing? Two conspirators having a falling out? She had turned on her accomplice in anger?

She imagined she was drifting off, she was trying to drift off, when the phone jerked her up and startled Rock so he stood up on the bed with one hard foot on her leg barking loud enough to break eardrums.

Hushing him, she picked up the phone, answering crossly, wishing she'd let it go on the tape. Rock, watching her, hesitantly walked up the length of the bed and lay down beside her.

"It's Clyde. I just . . . wanted to be sure you're okay."

"I'm fine. Was nearly asleep. Thanks for pulling me out of that, no telling what I might have done. That man . . . I'll fill you in later, more than I did. I may be late in the morning, would you leave a note for Scotty and Dave? I have to meet Hanni at the Landeau place at seven, to lay the new rug. She's so excited, I couldn't put her off. Do you have company? Who are you talking to?"

"The damn cat. Insists on hogging the bed, sprawling all over my pillow. Guess he likes the sound of the phone."

She laughed. "Don't knock it. It's nice to have a four-legged pal to warm your feet. What ever made me think I wouldn't keep Rock?"

"I never thought that," Clyde said, laughing.

Hanging up, she burrowed into her pillow. She was deeply asleep when the phone rang again encouraging another round of barking. Hushing Rock, she wondered how long it would take to teach him the futility of barking at the phone, while not discouraging his other alarm responses.

The voice at the other end was Dallas. "You asleep?"

"No, not now."

He chuckled. "Thought you'd like to know that Davis and I picked up the old man, up at the Pamillon place. That we've got enough on him, for drug making, to go to the grand jury and maybe enough for a bomb-making charge."

"What did you find?"

"Has a lab up there, all right. We had to suit up like astronauts to go down into it. Talk about stink. It's in a cellar under some chicken houses." Ryan could hear the smile in his voice. "All kinds of stuff with his prints on it, glass jars, retorts. Old man must have thought we'd never find the place.

"And he'd dumped mountains of trash down in the estate, in a cellar, again with his prints on everything—including some electrical parts and a bag of ammonium sulfate that could relate to the bomb. We're taking prints from samples of the trash, and listing the brands, to compare with Max's list of purchases in San Andreas. Should tell us quite a lot."

240

"That's really great news. That's one down . . ."

"And one to go. I'd sure like to thank our tipster. Hope we have as good luck with the murder, with these women we're talking to. You can be sure that Wills and Parker are getting all they can."

"You don't have anything, this soon?"

"In fact, I think we can scratch three. Parker called me an hour ago. Three of them have pretty solid stories. That leaves seven, with two of those out of the country, as far as we know."

"I'm keeping my fingers crossed. I'm sure glad you have capable friends when you need them." She yawned, and rubbed Rock's ears.

"Go to sleep," Dallas said, laughing. "Keep the good thoughts."

She hardly remembered hanging up. She was deeply asleep when the phone rang again. Again, the loud, frantic barking jerking her awake along with the ringing, making her cringe at what her neighbor, on the other side of the duplex wall, would be saying—she hoped they didn't call the department.

"Ryan, it's Dad. Sounds like I woke you. I'm in San Francisco, just got back, checked into an airport motel. Catching the early shuttle down to the village in the morning. You want to meet my plane?"

"I . . . I'd love to. You're coming because of me, because of the murder. You haven't been home." How strange she felt, talking to her own father. How uncertain—because of what Williams had said. But how silly.

"I'm coming because I have a few days leave and need to rest up after running that training session, before I go back to work. Can you meet my plane or shall I . . . ?"

"Yes, I can meet it. What time?"

"If it's *on* time, five A.M.."

"I'll be there but I can't wait past six-thirty, I promised Hanni. An early installation, one she refuses to put off."

"If you're not there, I'll take a cab or call Dallas. You sound—

tired? A bit stiff. You okay? You're not letting this thing get to you? I haven't talked with Dallas. What kind of leads is he getting?"

"It's not that. I . . . He's working on it, has a couple of guys in the city checking out Rupert's . . . Rupert's women. And, they know my gun didn't kill Rupert."

"Then you should sound very up, not like you just lost your last friend."

"I'm fine, really. Very very up. Just . . . dead tired, Dad. That's all. I'll see you in the morning, bright and early. We can have breakfast, if you're on time." But her voice caught, and the tears were just running down. What was wrong with her?

"Ryan? What?"

"Nothing. Honest. Pancakes and bacon. See you at five. G'night." She hung up, choking with tears. She wanted to bury her face against her father's chest and hear him tell her that everything Larn said was lies, that everything about her father was just as she had always believed, just as it should be. She felt like she was six years old again, badly needing comforting by her dad. Did anyone ever get too old for such comforting?

But the worst thing was, he'd heard exactly how she felt. He'd heard all the dismay and uncertainty that she didn't even know was there, all the stupid questions.

This wasn't *like* her, to let Williams lay this kind of trip on her. Williams was lying, there was no way she was going to believe *him*.

And, suddenly, she buried her face against Rock and bawled.

25

It was **4:40** in the morning when Ryan pulled into Peninsula Airport, parking in the short-term lot. She left Rock in the cab of the truck, cracking the windows and locking the doors, and hurried into the lobby hoping Dad's flight was on time. She didn't like leaving Rock very long on that expensive leather upholstery.

The big dog hadn't offered, so far, to do any of the damage his breed was famous for, but she couldn't forget the horror stories. Before she entered the small terminal she removed a police badge from her purse and pinned it on her jacket, a procedure highly irregular and illegal. Entering, she nodded to several security people, gave over her purse for perusal when requested, glad she'd remembered to remove Hanni's gun. She stood reading the schedule, then approached the security desk. The guard on duty was maybe thirty, good-looking, clean shaven, with nice brown eyes and no wedding ring.

"I have a security dog in my truck, I'm meeting his handler." Ryan widened her eyes, looking deeply at him. "This is . . . a sort of surprise for him. Mike worked with the dog for a year and then . . . well, he was wounded on the job and now he's coming home." She took a step closer to the counter. The guard did the same. "Would it . . . would it be okay if I bring the dog inside, just until flight six-oh-two-seven lands? My boss will be so thrilled. I promise the dog won't be a problem, I've been training him since Mike was hurt. . . ."

The guard grinned at her and waved her on in. She touched his hand briefly, smiling up at him and headed for the truck.

Rock was as thrilled to see her as if she'd been gone for weeks. She hugged him extravagantly because he hadn't torn up the upholstery then leashed him and slipped the yellow vest on him that she had made with felt and a marking pen, neatly lettering *Working Dog* on both sides. Commanding Rock out of the truck she told him to heel, praying that he wouldn't let the strange sights and sounds of the terminal undo him. She didn't yet know this dog very well, he might have all manner of behavior problems that could surface suddenly in the very different environment of the airport.

Before taking him into the terminal she walked him a block up the sidewalk and back. He honored every command. Heading for gate B she glanced across at the guard. He gave her a bright smile and a thumbs up, openly admiring Rock. Outside the gate she settled down at the end of a bench, feeling strangely nervous at meeting her dad, trying not to hear Larn Williams's words: *I don't believe the gossip . . . I thought of course you'd heard . . . It's common knowledge . . . The women . . . you have to know about the women . . . I can't believe you never heard . . . Flannery had plenty of women . . . affairs with more than a few female parolees . . .*

None of that was common knowledge, none of it ever happened. Not Mike Flannery, who had been totally committed to raising his girls the way their mother would want, totally committed to their high morals and to keeping alive the memory of their mother. Not this thoughtful man who had said to them a thousand times, *What would your mother have done at your age, in that situation?*

Not Mike Flannery who had spent every free minute with his daughters working the dogs or hunting or riding, who had never had any free time unaccounted for, not Mike Flannery who had never given Ryan or her sisters any tiniest cause to doubt him. Growing up in a law-enforcement family, Ryan and Hanni and their older sister were not naive, they had all three been wise beyond their years, any of them would have noticed, would have known if their dad was fooling around.

She startled suddenly when Rock whined. Looking down at him, she realized she'd been rubbing his ears so hard she'd hurt him. She stroked his head softly and apologized. He whined in return, never offering to move from the sit-stay command she had given him almost ten minutes ago. Ten minutes . . . and as she looked out at the empty runway here came a plane landing.

As it taxied out of view to the south, she waited, heart pounding, for it to return up the long field. Watching it slowly pull up to gate B, she felt queasy in her middle.

This wasn't going to be easy, telling him what she'd heard. But then it wouldn't be easy, either, facing her dad with a murder charge hanging over her, a charge that, even if it was a setup, could affect both Dad's career and Dallas's, could ruin both their futures.

Standing out of the way she watched people flock as near to the doors as they were allowed, watched and waited nervously with her hand sweating on Rock's leash. She felt far more nervous than when, at twelve, she'd struck a ball through the neighbor's window, or when she'd let one of the pups run off and nearly get hit by a car, or the time she had accidentally fired a round through the roof of the firing range. She was far more nervous now, at seeing her own father.

Make a fuss over him, Rock. A fuss and a diversion. And don't make a liar of me, in the eyes of that security guard. Who knew when she might need to rely on that guard for some yet unimagined emergency? When he looked up, watching her, she smiled and petted Rock.

Her dad was among the first off the plane, right behind the first-class passengers. She waved to him but kept Rock out of the crowd, letting Dad come to her winding his way through, his tall, lean frame easy in a suede sport coat and jeans and boots, his familiar grin, his pleasure at seeing her.

He didn't hug her or touch her until he knew what the dog was all about.

"Make a fuss over him, a big fuss, he's supposed to be your dog. I'll explain later. His name's Rock."

Mike Flannery took in the badge on her lapel, and Rock's vest, and let Rock smell his hand then talked softly to him until Rock was dancing around him, whining and so happy with this new friend that any minute he might start barking. Dad glanced at her, laughing. "This better be good. I'll get my bags. Where's the truck?"

"New . . . red Chevy king cab. Short-term parking, aisle three." She grinned at him and headed for the door, the big dog looking back longingly at Mike Flannery—and so did she. Just being with Dad had chased away her stupid doubts.

She had settled Rock in the backseat when Dad came across the lot with his all-purpose, scarred and battered elk-hide bag. She stowed it in the backseat beside Rock, but where Mike could keep an eye on it so the big dog wouldn't chew. "We have plenty of time for breakfast. We'll go to the Courtyard where Rock can lie under the table—he doesn't need elk-hide for breakfast." Wheeling out of the airport, she headed for the freeway.

"So why is he supposed to be my dog? What's with the working dog getup? All that fuss just so you could take him into the airport?"

She grinned. "Weimaraners are famous for tearing up the inside of a car."

"So I've heard. This is the stray Dallas told me about? Looks like he's not a stray anymore."

"I guess."

"You've had him vetted? Had his shots?"

246

"Um . . . Not yet. Haven't had time."

Her father looked at her sternly.

"It's just two days. Maybe I can—"

"You want me to do it? I'm hanging around for a few days. I can drive one of Harper's surveillance wrecks."

She turned off the highway into the village. "Would you? It's Dr. Firetti, up near Beckwhite's Automotive."

"I know Firetti. Shall I have him check for an ID chip?"

She was surprised at the sinking feeling that gave her, that maybe Firetti would find Rock's owner with that simple electronic scan. "I guess you'd better." As she pulled up before the Courtyard, Flannery looked intently at her, and patted her knee. "It'll be all right. Outside of being afraid you'll lose your fine hound, what else is bothering you? Besides, of course, Rupert's murder?"

She swung out of the truck, saying nothing, and unloaded Rock, moving ahead of her father into the restaurant. When they were seated, he gave her a questioning look. "You don't want to talk about it, this early in the morning."

"Not really. Not here. Just . . . gossip." The longer she put it off, the harder it would be.

"Gossip about you, because of the murder? Well I wouldn't—"

"Could we talk about it tonight?"

"Shall I pick up some steaks?"

"Perfect." Fishing in her purse, she found the extra key Charlie had given her, and watched him work it onto his key ring. They talked about the remodel she was starting for Clyde, about Scotty moving down to the village to work for her, about the rug she and Hanni were laying and how excited Hanni was, about all the inconsequentials. They enjoyed waffles and sausage and quantities of coffee then she dropped her dad and Rock at the police station. But, heading for the Landeau cottage, she was again tense with unease. Too many things going on, too many problems butting at one another.

Scotty said life wasn't full of problems, it was rich with decisions. He said a person was mighty lucky to have the privilege of making choices, even hard ones. That the more carefully you thought out your decisions, the more the good times would roll. All her life Scotty had told her that if you did nothing but worry, if you were indecisive and scared to make decisions, then the good times would escape like a flock of frightened birds.

She guessed she'd better listen. If she got herself into a knot, she wouldn't conquer any of the present tangles. They would conquer her.

IT WASN'T YET DAWN WHEN THE THREE CATS ARRIVED AT THE Landeau cottage, Joe fidgeting and pacing, consumed with getting inside for a look at the mantel. The kit too was wired, so excited to be out and free again and on an adventure. She had been home at Wilma's since the night before, when Cora Lee reluctantly returned her and was pleased to stay for dinner. Now that Dallas had arrested Gramps Farger, now that the old man was safely tucked away in jail, it had seemed all right to bring the tattercoat home.

The kit loved Cora Lee, and certainly she had loved Cora Lee's extravagant attention, but the kit easily grew restless. Cora Lee said she'd been peering out the windows with far too keen an interest. Having promised not to let the kit out, Cora Lee had worried at her unrest.

Now behind the Landeau cottage in the dark woods where the three cats crouched, the kit's tail lashed with excitement. Her eyes burned round and black, she could hardly remain still.

"Cool it, Kit," Dulcie said softly. "We're not set to charge that cottage like a platoon of commandos."

The kit eased the tail action to a slow twitch. But her eyes remained wide and burning. If they'd been hunting rats, her enthusiastic vibes alone would have cleared the premises. As the cats watched for Ryan and Hanni, above them the sky faded from black to dark pearl. The moon hung low in the brightening sky, circled by a nimbus of mist. Within the cottage, beyond the floor-to-ceiling glass, there was no sign of Larn Williams. The bed was neatly made. The sunken sitting area shone like a softly lit stage. Joe watched intently the flawed black niche in the fireplace, but the moon's diffused light, from a different angle at this later hour, showed him nothing. He could smell on the breeze the stink of exhaust from the departed Jeep. The cats were dozing when Hanni pulled onto the granite parking.

She wasn't driving her powder-blue convertible but a white van with the dolphin-shaped logo of her design studio. Certainly the Mercedes wasn't made to haul the ten-foot rug that stuck out the back where the rear doors stood open and tied together. Swinging out, she began to unload some huge, Mexican ceramic pots that were wedged in beside the rug. She was dressed this morning in faded designer jeans and a tomato red velour top that set off her short, windswept white hair and her flawless complexion and dangling gold earrings. *"Smashing,"* Dulcie whispered. Hanni Coon had a wonderful talent for elegance. If Dulcie were a human, she'd kill to look like that.

Hanni had the pots unloaded when Ryan's truck turned in. Ryan swung out dressed in her usual nondescript work jeans, a navy flannel shirt over a cotton blouse, and rough work boots. Hanni looked her over, a quick assessment of how Ryan *might* dress herself, how Ryan *might* look, a hasty glance that seemed to the cats little more than habit. "Where's Rock?"

"Dad's back, he called last night, I picked him up this morning. He's getting Rock vetted. "

"He came directly here? Because of Rupert! We could have dinner. He's staying at the cottage?"

"I . . . There's something I need to talk with him about."

"Personal? About the murder?"

Ryan looked at her helplessly. "That okay?"

"Of course it's okay. Can I help?"

"No, just . . . Could I explain later? It's . . . Makes my stomach churn. I'm trying to be cool."

Hanni looked at her quietly, and began to ease the wrapped rug out of the van. They carried it into the house, one at each end as if, Joe thought, they were toting an oversized cadaver. Ryan opened up the sliding glass walls of the sunken sitting area while Hanni vacuumed the wood floor. Then, kneeling, they unwrapped the rug, stripping off the heavy brown paper. When at last they had it laid out on the wood floor, even Joe was dazzled. Dulcie caught her breath, creeping closer to the window through the fallen branches.

"I've never seen anything so beautiful," she whispered. She and the kit stared and stared at the medley of brilliant colors, the thickly woven, intricate patterns. The kit crept closer still, watching the rug and watching Ryan and Hanni where they knelt in the middle pressing the rug gently toward the walls securing the edges with two-sided tape. Kit was so fascinated that her nose was soon pressed against the screen of the open window. Hanni's masterpiece, handwoven in England at a fortune per square yard, made all three cats want to sink their paws in and roll with purring abandon. Silently Dulcie reached a paw, as if hypnotized, sliding the tall screen open, and padded delicately into the room.

The kit followed. They were poised among the pillows looking down at that sea of colors and sniffing the scent of clean wool when Ryan and Hanni looked up.

Ryan lifted her hand as if to stop them, but Hanni laughed. Any other designer, confronted with cats on her costly installation, would have shouted and chased them away. Hanni simply watched them, watched Joe Grey pad in too, stepping diffidently among the pillows.

"What harm can they do?" Hanni said. "Come on, cats. Are your paws clean?" She looked where they had trod and saw no dirt. "Come on, have a roll before the grande dame arrives. It's your only chance. Marianna would eat you alive." She grinned at Ryan. "Can you imagine? Cats on her hundred-thousand-dollar masterpiece?"

"Don't you worry they'll pull a thread?"

"It's a well-made piece, the English know how to make rugs that last—the English *know* there'll be cats on them. And Joe *is* a perfect gentleman. Kate and I kept him for a week, at the cottage, when we were down looking at the Pamillon estate. Something about Clyde painting his place. The cat had perfect manners then. Why would he be different now?"

Beneath the cats' paws, the wool was softer than a featherbed. Dulcie and the kit rolled deliriously, wriggling, sinking into the thick pile, the kit flipping back and forth lashing her long, fluffy tail.

But Joe rolled for only a moment. He came to rest lying on his back, his white paws waving in the air as if in total abandon while he considered the flaw in the fireplace.

In the morning light, from this angle, he couldn't see that out-of-place, ragged scar. Rolling across the rug as if crazy with play, he looked again.

Nothing. The rising dawn light coming from every direction showed the black recess as smooth as the other two. But last night he *had* seen the diagonal scar running down the right-hand rectangle, as sure as his name was Joe Grey. Rolling again, he tried another angle.

"See," Hanni said, "they're not doing any harm. But, oh boy, wouldn't Marianna flip!"

"You love doing something that would enrage her."

"She'll never know, as long as they're out before she gets here."

"She's coming down? This morning?"

"She's in Half Moon Bay—or was, last night. She called me about something, I told her the rug was here. She sounded pretty excited, for ice queen Marianna. Said she'd be down early, that she had some business in the village. One of their rentals, I suppose." Sullivan had, several years before when the real-estate market was soft, made some excellent investments in Molena Point.

"There, that's the last of it," Hanni said, smoothing the corner of the rug. Standing, she stepped up to the tiled entry with Ryan for a full view. They could see, even with the three cats sprawled across the rug, that it lay smooth and flat, a perfect fit, a meadow of color as fine as any painting.

"I'd like to roll on it, myself," Hanni said.

"Go ahead, you earned it. It truly is magnificent. You can—"

Both women turned as a car pulled into the drive. They couldn't see it from the entry, that wall and the door were solid. Hanni, stepping into the bedroom to look through the window, hurried out again. "Get the cats out! Come on Joe Grey, Dulcie. Move it, she's coming."

Her excited voice would have startled even the dullest cat. But as Joe and Dulcie leaped for the open screen, Marianna, with her usual dispatch, was out of the car and through the front door, her tall, slim figure frozen in the doorway.

The cats, crouched among fallen branches, looked for the kit, but she had vanished. They peered back toward the bright room, where Marianna stood on the landing. She was dressed in a severe black suit, long gold earrings, black stockings, black sandals with four-inch heels. Her eyes were fixed on the fireplace, her expression unbelieving.

Staring back at her from among the freshly split logs, the kit crouched unmoving, her black-and-brown coat hardly visible against the pine bark, but her yellow eyes wide with fear.

Having apparently, in her panic, bolted straight through the mesh curtain, she was trapped. When Marianna approached the firebox, the kit backed deeper, shivering, too frightened to bolt past her and run.

26

KIT STARED OUT OF THE FIREPLACE AT THE TALL, black-suited, spike-heeled blonde with all the fear she would exhibit facing Lucifer himself. And from the woods outside, Joe and Dulcie watched with the same fear of the woman. Even Ryan looked uncertain.

But Hanni moved into the empty silence, laughing. "One little cat, Marianna. Look at her, she couldn't resist your lovely new rug. Your English weavers would say that's good luck, to have a little cat bless their creation."

Marianna gave Hanni a look that should have reduced her to a grease spot. Hanni took Marianna's hands in her own and tried to ease her down the steps onto the thick, bright rug. Marianna resisted as rigidly as if cast from stone; and Hanni smiled more brightly. "Slip off your sandals, Marianna. Come, sit on it, isn't it a wonder?" Hanni sat down cross-legged on the bright weave. "I am just so thrilled. Tell me you're as pleased as we are."

"There was not one cat in here, Hanni, there were three. I can't *believe* you would let *cats* into my home to make their messes on a brand-new, hundred-thousand-dollar, one-of-a-kind hand-made rug, to leave filthy fleas, and very likely ticks."

"We didn't *see* them come in," Hanni said, smiling. "We didn't see them until just as you pulled into the drive, they can only have been in here for a second while our backs were turned."

Beyond the screened windows crouched among the forest's foliage, Joe and Dulcie looked at each, laughing at Hanni's chutzpah, but frightened. The kit was still trapped in there, crouched in the firebox staring up at Marianna. From the look in the kit's eyes, Marianna would not be smart to reach into the fireplace meaning to snatch her out and evict her.

As they watched, Ryan knelt, reaching in to the kit. The kit came to her at once. Ryan picked her up, carried her to the long windows, set her through and gave her a little pat, then closed the screen.

Kit was a streak, fleeing to them. Behind her, Hanni laughed. "What harm did she do? Just a pretty little neighborhood cat."

Pressing between Joe and Dulcie, the kit shivered with the residue of fear, but lashed her tail with anger. "I would have slashed her, I would have bloodied her." But soon she began to wriggle, to scratch at something in her fur. Turning, she licked her back, fidgeting as if she itched all over.

"What?" Dulcie said. "What did you do? *Did* you pick up a tick? Don't get it on me. Let me have a look."

"Hard," the kit said, licking again and spitting something into the dry leaves and pine needles. "Not a tick. Rocks in my fur."

Joe nosed at the bit of debris that had fallen among the leaves, and peered closely. He turned it over with his nose, then looked at the kit. "Are there more of these in your fur? *Don't shake them off!* Come out to the drive. Don't spill any! Walk carefully. Hurry, Kit! Come *on!*"

Puzzled but obedient, the kit followed. Joe nudged her to a spot on the drive not visible from the living room, and licked at her fur until he had dislodged three more rough pebbles. On the smooth drive he pawed at them, turning them over until each piece lay with its smooth side up, the surface painted jet black. They were bits of broken cement, each with one smooth surface.

"Did you feel those before you hid in the fireplace?"

The kit shook her whiskers. "No."

Carefully Joe pawed the fragments onto an oak leaf, and slid that beneath a bush. When he turned to look at them, his yellow eyes burned with excitement. And quickly he moved to Ryan's truck. "Watch for me, Dulcie, in case anyone comes."

"But you . . ."

"It's the only phone handy." Slipping under the truck to the far side, he was up through the window in a second and punching in information. Another minute and he had rung the Coldiron number and was talking with Eby. "This is a neighbor of the Landeaus . . ."

He peered out once, but the three women were still inside; and Dulcie sat watching the door, the tip of her tail twitching. When he'd finished explaining to Eby Coldiron what needed to be done, he dropped from the window. "Go home, Dulcie. Go call Dallas, I'm afraid to do that from this phone. *He* has caller ID. I'll be along soon."

She looked at him with suspicion.

"It's safe, trust me. Would I do something foolish?" He brushed his whiskers against hers.

She widened her eyes, and cuffed him. Of course he would do something foolish.

"Tell Garza, if he'll get over to the Coldirons pronto, they'll give him a rug from the Landeau cottage, that it's vital evidence. They're waiting for him. Tell him to look for little bits of concrete with black paint on them, and to check for blood. My guess is, the DNA will match that of Rupert Dannizer. Tell him the rug has been sponged, then doused with wine."

"You're building a lot on a few little bits of concrete."

"And a scar on the fireplace. Go on. If Dallas isn't there, talk with Davis."

"Of course I'll talk with Davis." But she gave him a whisker kiss, and a nudge for luck. "Come on, Kit, get moving." And as she and the kit headed at a gallop toward the village and home, Dulcie wondered: with Garza checking on Rupert's lovers, would this call about the fireplace tie in somehow? Would it, she thought shivering, tie in with his ballistics report?

JOE WAS NOT THE MOST PATIENT OF TOMCATS. WAITING IN THE bushes by the front door, he kneaded the dry leaves, and scratched his ear. He wanted to yowl at the three women to get on with it, finish their business and leave. But when at last Ryan's truck pulled out, Marianna and Hanni stood in the doorway—not three feet from him, just above the holly leaves—indulging in incredible inanities as both women tried to smooth over their earlier confrontation. Hanni would make amends because Marianna was her client. Marianna's motive, in being nice, was less clear.

He tensed as Hanni turned to leave, and crouched.

The instant Marianna turned back inside he was through the door behind her like a shadow easing behind the Mexican chest.

He heard Hanni's van start and pull away. He was alone with Marianna Landeau, locked inside the cottage. Any route of escape would take at last a few minutes to accomplish, perhaps under conditions he didn't want to consider. He could hear her rummaging in the bedroom as if she was shifting the clothes in the closet, maybe one of those pointless rearranging orgies to which all women seemed addicted. When he heard her go into the bathroom he strolled through the bedroom door and slipped under the bed, frightening a little spider, wishing someone would dust under there. Didn't she have a cleaning crew?

A light shone under the bathroom door, and the closet door stood open, the big walk-in space all fitted out with sleek white shelves and drawers and zippered garment bags. Absolutely neat. No place in there for a cat to hide. The hanging rods contained minimal wardrobes, his and hers. He supposed if one had three residences, it would be convenient not to cart suitcases back and forth.

The bathroom door opened and Marianna's elegantly sandaled feet appeared inches from his nose, her stiletto heels suggesting formidable weapons. He listened to her rummaging in the closet again, heard a zipper close.

Stepping out, she dropped a small duffel by the bedroom door then crossed the tile entry to the sunken sitting area. He heard her close the long windows and lock them, then she stood at the top of the steps with her back to him, as if admiring the rich new rug.

But then she moved swiftly to the kitchen, returning with one of those little plug-in hand vacs designed for quick cleanup, for those moments when someone scatters coffee grounds or cookie crumbs across the kitchen floor. With the brand-new rug, what was there to clean up? Joe went rigid, watching.

Kneeling before the fireplace, her tight skirt hiked up around her thighs, Marianna slid the mesh curtain back and reached in to vacuum the corners of the firebox behind the clean, stacked logs. Surely removing the same debris that the kit had picked up on her fur.

She did a thorough job, forcing the nozzle into the back corners. But when she returned the little machine to the kitchen, Joe smiled. She'd forgotten something. Retrieving the duffel bag from the bedroom, and shutting the closet door, she jingled her keys and was out of there, locking the front door behind her.

Not until he heard her car pull away, did he come out from under the bed.

First he tossed the bedroom, working open the night table drawers, then the drawers of the television armoire. He checked between the mattresses, poking a wary paw in, then crawling deeper, but he found only lint. Swinging on the closet-door handle, he was in within seconds, leaping at the bank of built-in drawers, gripping and kicking.

Forcing each one open in turn, he pawed carefully through.

Dulcie would love Marianna's expensive lace undies, the silk and satin perfumed with fancy little sachets. The last drawer contained half-a-dozen evening bags and as many compacts, all of them expensive looking. Crouched on the edge of the drawer, Joe frowned. Should he?

Well, why not? What could be more opportune? Pawing half-a-dozen compacts into a quilted evening bag, he snapped closed his prize and carried it in his teeth to the front door. There he began the tedious, paw-bruising, leaping contortions necessary to slide the dead bolt, turn the knob, and escape from his self-made prison.

LASHING HER TAIL WITH AMUSEMENT, DULCIE PUSHED THE phone back onto its cradle and rolled over on Wilma's bed, her paws in the air, a Cheshire cat-smile lighting her tabby face. Oh, she did enjoy these anonymous phone calls. Dallas had not only assured her that he would drive over to the Coldirons' cottage at once, to pick up the brown shag rug, but he thanked her. He knew as well as she that it was futile to ask her questions.

Though at first, he had argued with her. He said the concrete crumbs in the rug could be simple debris left over when the fireplace was built. Dulcie reminded him that the black recesses had been painted some time after the fireplace was built, and the fragments had black paint on them. Then Garza said that the three sculptures had been installed in those niches only recently, and *that* probably accounted for the black-painted chips. He'd gone silent when Dulcie informed him that the sculptures were fitted with special tension brackets at the back, so they had no need of bolts to hold them in place.

Garza hadn't asked how she knew so much about the sculptures and about the interior of the Landeau cottage. Like Max Harper, Detective Garza had learned that it was useless to ask such questions, that he'd best take what he was offered and run with it.

So far these anonymous tips had been 100 percent; both cops knew that. And maybe, she thought, this information might dovetail with lines of investigation that Garza was already pursuing. That would be interesting.

And, she thought rolling over and purring, *this* morning, with *this* phone call, Detective Garza had almost taken orders from her. He had agreed to collect the rug right away, absolutely trusting her, never once making light of her instructions. Oh, she couldn't wait to tell Joe.

THE QUILTED EVENING PURSE, STUFFED WITH ITS SIX COMPACTS, was hellishly heavy. But Joe wasn't willing to jettison even one bit of possible evidence. Why a woman needed a dozen compacts was beyond him. Well, he never claimed to be an authority on female vicissitudes, cat or human. He could track a rabbit through rocky terrain, could dispatch the biggest wharf rat that ever snarled in a cat's face, could leap six feet between rooftops. But he couldn't tell you much about a lady's love of finery. Gripping the quilted bag firmly between determined teeth, he hurried through the bright morning along the less frequented lanes of the village, avoiding passing cars and pedestrians. Dragging the bag up three trees and across innumerable rooftops, he arrived home at last with aching neck muscles and tired jaws.

Crouched on the front porch, he listened to the racket above him, from the attic, hammers pounding, nails being forced from old wood with tooth-jarring screams, human voices sharp with tension. *"Hold it. There. Back a little. Whoa—Put your level on it. Up . . . A little more . . . There! Nail it!"* Above him, the porch roof shook. Sticking his head through his cat door, he looked around the living room.

Empty and safe. The house had that hollow feel that heralded deserted space. Shoving the satin bag in onto the carpet, he followed it, collapsing beside it.

He didn't want to drag it over to the station or to Garza's cottage in the daylight, he'd had enough trouble getting it home without alerting some nosy citizen. *Oh look, what's that cat got? Come here, kitty. Let's have a look . . .*

Right.

He sat contemplating the several options he could employ as a safe hiding place until dark. He considered his battered easy chair that Dulcie and Clyde and several other insensitive folk said resembled the hide of a molting elephant. He had hidden several valuable items in that well-clawed and fur-coated retreat. The purse need remain there only until dark, until he could carry it unseen across the village and slip it into the police station, or maybe into Garza's car—if he didn't rupture a neck muscle, getting it there.

Shoving the little bag between the cushions, he stretched out in front of his chair across an African throw rug, wondering what Clyde had left him for breakfast. And praying that his evidence would nail Marianna Landeau. Praying that Ryan's ordeal was about to be resolved.

27

THE PAN-BROILED STEAKS WERE TWO INCHES thick, crisp and dark on the outside, deep pink within, so juicy and tender that Ryan almost groaned. She had left the curtains open so they could enjoy the sunset that blazed beneath the dark clouds. Sitting across from her dad at the kitchen table, tasting her first bite of steak, she sighed with a fine, greedy pleasure. "You can do, with a plain black skillet, what most chefs can't manage even with their fancy grills."

Mike Flannery grinned. "I've heard that line."

She laughed, but she watched him carefully too. He wasn't even home yet, this was only the last leg of his trip, he had come down here to help her, worried about her, and she was going to dump these ugly rumors on him, lay out all Larn Williams's lies to cheer him.

But she had to talk about this if she were to resolve her own uncertainty, her own fears. Thinking about Williams's vicious story, on top of his tampering with her billing, she had grown increasingly frightened of what else he might plan to do, of what his ultimate goal might be.

Was Williams's mind simply twisted, was he an impossible

mental case? Or had he killed Rupert? But why would he draw attention to himself?

Maybe his actions were a carefully planned harassment designed to keep her off-center and perhaps complicate the murder investigation? Designed to throw the police off track and protect someone else?

Her father put down his fork, watching her, his expression half amused at her fidgeting, half a frown of concern. "Whatever's bothering you, Ryan, spit it out. Before you choke on it."

"Something someone said. It's all lies. But . . . Well, lies that are hard to repeat."

"If it makes you this edgy, if you're embarrassed to say it, it has to be about me. What have I done? What did someone say I did?"

She looked at him helplessly.

"It wouldn't be the first time someone told a lie about law enforcement."

"He said it was common gossip in the city but I never heard anything like it, in the city or anywhere else."

He waited patiently, buttering his baked potato.

Hesitantly she began, repeating Williams's accusations. Flannery listened without comment, without interrupting. When she finished he asked only, "Do you believe him?"

"Of course I don't believe him. But—what's he up to? Is there some strange little thread on which he could build such lies? And there's more."

She told him about the break-in, about Larn cooking her books and switching the bills. "What's scary is, this has to fit in with Rupert's murder. That's what's scary."

"What makes you think that?"

"You and Dallas always say, never believe in coincidence."

"Have you told Dallas what Williams said, and about the billing?"

"I called him about the bills, the night it happened. But what Williams said . . . I didn't tell him that."

"Why not?"

"Partly because I made a spectacle of myself in the restaurant when he told me those things. I lost my temper, big-time. Strong-armed him and marched him outside. I just . . . I suppose Dallas has heard that, by now. If Clyde hadn't come along and stopped me, I *would* have pounded him. What a weird bird. He just went limp, didn't try to fight me, didn't do anything. As if—"

"As if he likes the ladies to pound him?"

"That's sick."

"Can you make any connection between Williams and Rupert? Or, even between Williams and the bombing on Sunday?"

"No, I can't. It's such a muddle. Except, it all seems to connect to San Andreas. Williams lives and works there. I just finished the Jakes job there. And Curtis Farger was staying up there before the bombing. He came down from San Andreas in *my* truck, hidden in the back with the dog." She sighed. "Maybe one thing just led to another, but . . ."

"Go over it step by step, the relationships. Begin with your job in San Andreas."

"I had remodeled a house for the Jakeses in the city, so it was natural for them to come to me for their vacation addition. They approached me, in fact, before I left Rupert. After I left, I told them I didn't want to take the job away from the firm, but they said they wanted me, that they didn't want to deal with Rupert. So I agreed.

"Then when I moved down here to the village, the Jakeses recommended me to the Landeaus because Marianna and Sullivan had bought a teardown here. The Landeaus came down and we talked. She sort of scared me, she was so . . . austere. One of those gorgeous natural blondes, but without any warmth. Intimidating. We went over the property, I gave them my assessment, and I ended up remodeling the teardown.

"As to Larn Williams, he just showed up when I was working

263

on the Jakeses' place. Wanted me to bid on a job for one of his real-estate clients." She looked helplessly at her father. "I can't see a connection. I didn't realize then how strange Larn is, I didn't see that." She studied her dad's preoccupied frown. "What?"

Flannery was quiet.

"Do you know something about Larn Williams?"

"Would you have a picture of Mrs. Landeau?"

"No. Why?"

"How old would you say she is?"

"I . . . Maybe a beautiful forty-some."

"I had a parolee who would fit that description. Let me do some checking. What do you know about her?"

"That they'd been living in L.A. for some years before they moved to the Bay Area, maybe a year ago."

"Did she say that she'd lived in San Francisco before?"

"Marianna doesn't chitchat. But she does know the city. She didn't ask directions when Hanni and I sent her to various out-of-the-way shops and decorator supply houses."

"What does Hanni think of her?"

"Cold fish," Ryan said, grinning.

"I had a woman on my caseload a few years back who would fit her description. She came out on parole after serving a conviction for bank fraud. I hadn't had her a month when she was into a complicated embezzlement operation. I told her to clean it up or she was going back. When she tried to make trouble, I *sent* her back. A vindictive sort. Served the balance of her sentence, when she came out I had no reason to keep tabs on her. I heard she'd moved down to L.A. and married into a fair amount of money, not all of it clean."

He cut some scraps from his steak and put them on a plate for Rock. Ryan watched him spoil the big weimaraner in a way he would never have allowed for his own dogs. "Seems far-fetched," he said, "but let me see what I can find out."

"But why would she—"

"Let's see what I can turn up. If this *is* Martie Holland, I'll tell you the rest of the story." Watching her expression, he laughed. "No, I wasn't involved with her."

"No," she said. "But Rupert was. Right?"

Flannery nodded.

"Dallas knows her, she's on the list he's investigating. I think she's one of the two supposedly out of the country. The Bahamas, I think he said." And she felt cold again, icy.

THE GARZA COTTAGE CLUNG TO THE SIDE OF A STEEP HILL north of the village, its front windows looking down on rooftops and oak trees that now, at night, were a black mass broken by only a few scattered lights from the houses tucked among them. At the back of the cottage, the kitchen windows faced the rising hill, the steep backyard softly lit by ground-level lamps that Joe and Dulcie avoided as they approached the back steps—two neighborhood cats checking out the garbage cans.

No lights were on in the kitchen, but a glow from deeper in the house suggested that Garza sat at his desk, perhaps catching up on paperwork.

Approaching the back door, with quick paws Joe tucked the little purse under the mat. And as Dulcie curled down on the cool earth beneath the bushes to watch the door, Joe nipped down the hill to the lower-level guest rooms—family bedrooms from the time when they all came down for weekends.

Crouched on the windowsill he reached a paw through the burglar bars and through the hole in the screen, product of his own handiwork some months back, when he'd done serious spying on Garza himself. Flipping the latch and sliding the screen open, he jiggled the window until its lock gave.

He was through the bars and inside. Leaping to the small desk, he touched the phone's speaker button. This was the only phone in the house with two lines. The upstairs fax, and the main line, were on different instruments, the fax tucked away, he hoped, in a cupboard in the desk where Graza wouldn't see it's telltale light blinking. Hitting line two, he pawed in the main phone number that he had long ago memorized. Joe's talents didn't extend to writing down phone numbers, he was forced to keep all such urgent information in his head—a living computer that, over time, had become strong and reliable.

Garza answered on the second ring.

Dispensing with polite formalities, Joe kept his message short. "I've shoved a little purse under the back doormat; it contains items taken from Marianna Landeau's closet that I hope will reveal her fingerprints.

"You may find the prints are also those of a Martie Holland. I don't know who this person is, but perhaps that information will be of interest when the lab has finished with the rug—the one you picked up from the Coldirons. And when you've had a look at the mantel in the Landeau cottage.

"You should find four more chips from the mantel on a leaf under a lavender bush just south of the Landeau front door. Those were removed from inside the fireplace before Marianna vacuumed there. She used the hand vac from the kitchen, and I don't believe she emptied it when she finished."

He felt as if he was spelling the steps out too clearly, insulting Garza's intelligence. But if Garza nailed Rupert's killer, that was all that counted. Police work was a cooperative undertaking, a team effort—even if part of the team was irrevocably undercover. He had hardly hit the speaker button to end the call when he heard Garza cross the room above him, and hit the stairs. And Joe was out of there, out the window sliding it closed, diving into the bushes as Garza switched on the light. Had the phone made a telltale click? Why did Garza suspect the caller was down there?

Checking out both bedrooms, and bath and closets, Garza cut the lights again and turned to the window. Standing just above Joe behind the burglar bars, looking out, he was still for a long time. Below him, crouched in a tangle of prickly holly, patiently Joe waited until at last the detective turned away. Joe heard him mount the stairs.

He waited until he heard the kitchen door open then close again. When he knew that Garza had the little evening purse and the compacts, he beat it up the hill to Dulcie.

Above them the kitchen light was on. Rearing up in the hillside garden, they could see Garza sitting at the table wearing cotton gloves, opening the little purse.

He didn't touch the compacts, he simply looked. He looked out the window at the rising yard, and sat for a long moment doing nothing. At last, rising, he fetched a folded paper bag from a kitchen drawer, dropped the purse inside, and marked the bag with his pen.

"What now?" Dulcie said. "Can he send the prints to AFIS electronically?" She thought the automated fingerprint identification system that California used should take only an hour or two.

"I think he can. But it will show only a California record. Maybe he'll send it to WIN too, for the western states. But if she had only a federal rap, it could take weeks."

The Western Identification Network, which supplied fingerprint identification for the eight western states, was usually prompt, as well. But if an officer got no results there, and had to go through the FBI that covered the entire country, he'd better be prepared for a wait.

"You think Marianna and Martie Holland are the same person?" Dulcie said softly.

"I'm betting on it. I think Larn Williams either works for Marianna, or they're good friends."

"You think she planned the bombing? But why? And how does that connect to Rupert? She knew Rupert in San Francisco, but . . ."

"My guess is, the bombing was all the Fargers' doing, payback for Gerrard's prison sentence." He turned to look at her. "But my gut feeling, Dulcie, is that Marianna killed Rupert. We just don't know, yet, why she killed him.

"Something tore up that fireplace, after the three niches were painted. If the mason had left it like that, she'd have pitched a fit. I think she installed those three pieces of sculpture to hide the flaw in the concrete that she tried to fix."

"But the woman is a stickler for perfection. Why didn't she do a better job?"

"If she was trying to get rid of the body, maybe she didn't have time. She wanted to be gone, out of there before anyone knew she was at the cottage. Maybe that plaster job was the best she could do, in a hurry to get it dried and painted. Maybe, in the artificial light, she didn't see the flaw. I didn't see it until the moonlight slanted at an angle. And remember, she had to sponge his blood out of the rug too. And dump that bottle of wine, trying to cover her tracks."

"But how did she get the body out of there? She looks strong, but—if she dragged it to her car, then dragged it into Ryan's garage, there'd have been marks."

"There were marks—those narrow tire tracks along Ryan's drive. Dallas photographed them. By now he has to know those weren't bike tracks. Maybe a wheelbarrow, or more likely a hand truck. Maybe she brought it with her from the city."

"Grisly. She loads a hand truck into her expensive car, knowing she'll soon have a body to haul away. If the cops find it, and check out her car too, there should be plenty of traces for the lab."

"And before that," Joe said, "there should be replies on Marianna's fingerprints, and the lab report on the rug. I wonder how long that will take." He narrowed his eyes. "And what was the dog on about, when he pitched that fit there in the driveway? It sure wasn't Eby Coldiron who made him so mad."

28

Police dispatcher Mabel Hammond saw the gray tomcat slip into the station on the heels of two officers returning from lunch, strolling in behind them through the security door with all the assurance of the chief himself.

Glancing down over her counter, Mabel grinned at him. "Come on up, Joe Grey. I have fried chicken." The officers looked around laughing, and went on down the hall.

Mabel was fifty-some and inclined to be overweight. Her curly white hair was dyed blond. Her thick stomach didn't allow her to lean too far over the dispatcher's counter that defined her open cubicle on three sides. On the back wall was an array of computer and video monitors, radios, and other state-of-the-art electronic equipment that Mabel commanded. She not only handled emergency calls and dispatched officers, relaying all urgent communications, she juggled incoming faxes and the computers for vehicle wants and warrants and for wanted persons, and indexed officers' reports.

Joe Grey, never one to refuse fried chicken, landed on the counter among the in-boxes of files and papers, just inches from

Mabel's face, smiling and purring up at her, laying on the charm. Mabel's hair smelled of perfume or maybe cream rinse; he wasn't an authority on these matters. Rubbing against her outstretched hand, he made super-nice in deference to the promised snack, and in keeping with his and Dulcie's commitment to improved public relations.

Ever since Harper had remodeled the station, increasing security and locking all outside doors, Joe and Dulcie's only sure access was the quick leap inside behind a returning officer. Their previous technique of pawing open the unlocked front door was no longer an option. Everything had changed. The new, efficient reception area was totally empty of desks to hide under. Upon entering, one faced only the dispatcher's cubicle, the booking counter, the holding cell back in the corner, and in the other direction a long, blank hallway. And the dispatchers didn't miss so much as a fly coming through the glass doors. Fortunately, those good women were all cat lovers.

Mabel had three cats of her own and, having recently married, shared her home as well with her husband's two dogs and his parrot. But despite her domestic menagerie, Joe Grey always amused her. The tomcat seemed to Mabel the epitome of cool feline authority. Mabel's work could get stressful; to have a four-legged visitor smiling and purring, sharing a few free moments, seemed to make her day shorter.

It interested her that the tomcat and his two lady pals liked to prowl the whole department, slipping in and out of the various offices. And, as cats were among the few visitors that could present no breach of security, most of the officers made a fuss over them. No one knew why the cats had grown suddenly so friendly to the department after the renovation, but the little freeloaders did like to share the officers' lunches.

Reaching to a low shelf, Mabel opened the paper bag containing her own lunch and removed a fried chicken thigh. Tearing the chicken off the bone into bite-sized pieces, she laid these on a folded sheet of typing paper, on the counter.

The tomcat scoffed up the chicken, licked his whiskers, then padded along the counters investigating her cubicle as he often did. Pausing, he peered across the entry to the holding cell, which to a cat must smell to high heaven. *She* could still smell the lingering scent of the last occupant. Oh, not the boy. He'd smelled okay. But after they took the boy out to the regular cells, and brought that old man in, *he'd* stunk up the whole building.

The tomcat, returning to Mabel's in-boxes, began intently to watch the piles of papers that she'd set aside to index, patting and feinting at the reports as if maybe he'd seen a spider. Hot weather always brought out a few harmless spiders. The deadly ones stayed more in the dark, but did not live long if she spied them. Pawing at the papers, Joe went very still, staring as if he would grab whatever had crawled underneath. He remained for some time fixed on Gramps Farger's arrest sheet and then on the AFIS fax that had just come in for Detective Garza. It was wonderful, these days, how quick you could get back fingerprint information, to speed up the department's work. She watched Joe turn away at last, as if losing interest in the spider. What a strange cat, so deliberate in his actions. Now suddenly his attention was totally on the front door where he could see, through the glass door, Detective Garza returning from lunch.

She buzzed the detective through. "Captain Harper's back, he just came in."

Garza nodded and headed down the hall; and Joe Grey dropped from the counter and followed, making Mabel smile. Too bad the captain and Charlie had to shorten their honeymoon, though it was nice to have him home. The department had seemed just a bit off-kilter with the captain gone, not quite steady or comfortable.

FOLLOWING DETECTIVE GARZA, JOE COULD HARDLY KEEP from turning flips; he was as high as a junkie from the fingerprint report on Marianna Landeau giving her real name as Martie

271

Holland. *Martie Holland Martie Holland Martie Holland* . . . Joe thought, grinning. And the sight of Gramps's arrest sheet had almost made him open his mouth in a wild and unsuitable cheer.

Though even without the arrest sheet he'd know that Gramps had recently occupied the holding cell, by the stink that emanated from that corner. Didn't the old man ever bathe? Did the shack where Gramps lived have no running water? But it must have, if Gramps was making drugs up there. He guessed the old man was just naturally slovenly. You wouldn't catch a cat, even a very old cat, stinking that bad. A dog maybe. Never a cat.

The time of arrest was recorded as 7:15 last evening. The place of arrest was that cliffside shack up the mountain above the Pamillon estate. The charges on the arrest sheet were possession of explosives, evading custody, and manufacturing illegal drugs.

Well done, Kit! Joe thought, smiling. The kit had fingered Gramps Farger all by herself. Had practically wrapped him up, helpless as a slaughtered mouse, waiting for Garza to come find him. Phoning Garza, placing her first call, her first hard-won and important tip, she'd been so excited she hadn't thought how scared she was. She'd given Garza the facts just as skillfully as he or Dulcie would have done. And she'd hit gold. She had helped nab the bomber that Garza might never have found—that old man had ditched the law once, as slick as if the shack in the hills wasn't his only place to hide.

The tattercoat was growing up, Joe thought with a twinge of sadness. That fanciful youngster capable of such wild and passionate dreams was developing a solid, hardheaded turn of mind. This was all to the good, the kit was learning to take hold of a problem and deal with it. But he was going to miss her scatterbrained enthusiastic plunging into trouble that had so far marked the kit's approach to life.

Following Garza to Harper's office, Joe lay down in plain sight in the doorway. Garza had already seen him on the dispatcher's counter, so why not? Might as well try a little feline indolence, play the four-footed bum.

Harper glanced out at him, and shook his head. "That cat been hanging around?"

Garza laughed. "Off and on. I let him stay, he doesn't do any harm—keeps the mice away."

"You get Curtis to talk?"

Garza shook his head. "Tight-mouthed. He's been an unhappy kid since we brought Gramps in. You can bet he's scared of the old man. Well, he wasn't too happy before, either. He blames us and the whole world for his dad being in prison. But he wasn't like this, we need to move him somewhere. Even separated the way they are, the old man's been threatening him, hinting as much as he dares, figuring we have a bug on him, back in the jail."

Which of course they would, Joe thought. It was perfectly legal, once a man was arrested, to bug his cell.

"You think the boy's scared enough, now, to talk if we get him away from Gramps?"

"He might. I'm sure he could use a friend. I was thinking of bringing Ryan back with the dog, try that again before we send him to some juvenile facility farther away."

Harper said, "I was thinking of taking him over to drug rehab, give him a tour of the juvenile section, let him see what his daddy's and grandpappy's drugs did to those kids."

"Might work," Garza said.

Why, Joe wondered, would a boy who tried to kill several hundred people care about the suffering of drug addicts, even if they were kids his own age? Still, though, what could it hurt?

Garza said, "You find Hurlie?"

"He found us. I arrested him on obstruction of justice, sheriff took him in. We tossed his place. Didn't find any link to the bombing, but I have a nice list of purchases in the area, and three shopkeepers made Hurlie, from his brother's mug shot. Sheriff says

Hurlie works sometimes for the Landeaus. At first, Landeau said he couldn't place him. Then I pressed a little. Not a friendly welcome."

Garza nodded.

"I left Charlie in the car with the keys and phone and radio. She was more scared than she let on. Landeau's guard dogs watched her the whole time, while Landeau jived me along. Sheriff said the feds are spotting marijuana patches up there, that they took out a couple last week, over in the national forest. The sheriff was . . . maybe holding something back. Telling me what he knew I'd learn anyway."

Max leaned back in his desk chair absently reaching for a cigarette though it had been more than a year since he quit. "I talked with DEA. They think the Landeaus have been backing small meth labs in several counties, using the take to finance some marijuana operations. Good chance Hurlie could be involved."

"As could the sheriff?"

Harper grunted. "I hope not. Maybe intimidated—that's a political appointment, you well know. Important thing is, you have enough on Gramps to go to the grand jury."

"I have more than that. I might have Rupert Dannizer's killer."
"Oh?"

"I ran prints on Marianna Landeau. Her real name came up Martie Holland."

"That's one of the women we couldn't get a line on, supposed to be in the Bahamas. Some years back, Mike had her on parole."

Dallas nodded. "That's a long story. Your snitch got her prints to me last night. Don't know how. Don't know why," he said quietly.

Harper listened, saying nothing.

"I came down last night, ran them through AFIS. Had a warrant for her issued on information, and called San Francisco."

"She was in the city. Well, I sure missed that one."

"As did Wills and Parker. Well, the woman has a whole new identity. If you'd never seen her . . . San Francisco picked her up at her Nob Hill address early this morning. All packed, said she was going up to their country place. But she had a ticket for Caracas."

Harper grinned.

"They took her in, impounded her car. Searched the house, found a hand truck in the garage that, from its dust tracks, had been moved recently. Track marks match those from Ryan's driveway. I thought I'd send Green and Davis early tomorrow, to pick her up. D.A. has called the grand jury for her, and for Gramps Farger. They're able to meet day after tomorrow."

"Very nice."

"I'll rest easier when Ryan's completely in the clear. We'll all rest easier when this bomb trial is under way."

Harper nodded. "Ryan doing all right?"

"Keeping her head."

"When did you talk with Mike Flannery?"

"He's back, he came straight down here, got in yesterday morning, worried about Ryan. He didn't know then about Martie Holland's prints, the snitch hadn't delivered them yet. Brought them right to my door, last night. Half-a-dozen compacts the guy apparently lifted from the Landeau cottage." The two officers looked at each other, a *Don't ask, don't try to figure* look. And out in the hall, Joe Grey turned to scratch a nonexistent flea, then appeared to collapse once again into sleep.

"Mike says he has enough on Martie Holland to establish motive," Dallas said. "He'll testify before the grand jury. I remember a good deal about her from when he had her on parole; I was working in north Marin then, never ran into her. Don't remember seeing a mug shot. But I knew then, through Mike, that she was involved with Rupert. I don't think Ryan ever knew about that. Mike will be by in a while, to fill you in. Where's Charlie?"

"Up at the house getting settled. And seeing her cleaning crews. We'll bring the horses back down tomorrow. You going to let that cat sleep in your door all day?"

"Why not? Well, now look. You woke him."

Yawning, Joe Grey rose and headed up the hall in the direction of the locked security door. If no officer opened it, he knew that Mabel would come out from behind her counter and oblige. He had a lot to tell Dulcie, and a lot to tell the kit that would please her.

He'd like to have one more look at Marianna-Martie, at that cold piece of work, before she went to prison.

He could watch the trial, of course, if it was held in Molena Point. He and Dulcie had, during past trials, enjoyed a private and uninterrupted view from the window ledge above the courtroom; they wouldn't miss a thing providing the weather was warm enough so the windows were open.

But he'd like a look at Marianna *now*, when they brought the woman in. He didn't know why, or what he expected to see. Call it a hunch. What he'd *like* to see was how Rock responded to Marianna Landeau-Martie Holland.

It *was* only a hunch, but a hunch so strong it made the fur down Joe's spine rise and prickle.

29

THE ROOF HAD BEEN RAISED; ITS TWO LONG slanting surfaces stood upright, forming the new walls of the bedroom suite. The new roof trusses overhead were covered with tar paper and plywood and shingles, weather tight. Where the fresh studs of the end walls were still open the setting sun slanted in, turning the late afternoon light golden with floating dust motes. The forty-foot space was otherwise empty, or nearly so. The carpenters were gone for the day, the two younger men heading home as Ryan and her uncle Scotty descended the stairs to the kitchen, brushing off sawdust. Joe and Dulcie wandered the sun-warmed space alone, relishing its vastness and the challenge of unconquered heights.

Leaping to a sawhorse then atop a ladder they gained the soaring rafters. From that vantage they could see, through the open ends of the vast room and beyond the tops of the dark oaks, the ocean's breakers blowing with foam. Nearer, just below them, the village rooftops angled cozily, inviting a run across those slanting shingles. On a neighbor's roof a flock of bickering crows shouted and swore. From the outside stairs, Scotty looked up at the cats, and laughed, taking pleasure at the sight of them. The redheaded, red-bearded giant had told the younger carpenters that cats were just as lucky at the site of new construction as were cats on shipboard.

Close around the cats, the warm air smelled sweetly of fresh-cut lumber—and of hickory-scorched beef from the back patio, where Clyde had the rotisserie turning over glowing charcoal, preparing a welcome-home dinner for the newlyweds. But when, from the rafters, the cats spotted Harper's truck turn onto the narrow street they galloped down the stairs, pushing into the kitchen through Rube's dog door.

They watched Ryan throw her arms around Charlie then hold her away. "You got back yesterday! You look great! How was the wine country? Did you have lunch at Beaudry's? Isn't it beautiful! You're sunburned."

Charlie laughed. "Like a patchwork quilt. We saw the Jakeses' new addition. We love it, Ryan. It's beautiful. When can you build my studio? Maybe redo the kitchen and enlarge the master bedroom. Or maybe—"

"Anyone home?" Dallas shouted, coming in through the front door with Mike Flannery. Wilma entered just behind them carrying a bakery box under one arm, and the tattercoat kit balanced on her shoulder. She set the box on the kitchen counter, but the kit made no move to jump down or to leap to the top of the refrigerator beside Joe and Dulcie. She clung to Wilma, tucking her face beneath Wilma's chin and would not look up at the two cats. Wilma looked highly amused, the laugh lines around her eyes crinkled. Her long white hair was escaping in tendrils from its clasp and her lipstick was worn away as if she'd hardly had time to tend to her own concerns.

Full of uneasy questions, Joe and Dulcie followed the party as everyone carried plates and silverware and beer out onto the patio. Charlie and Ryan were still deep in conversation. The cats liked seeing Charlie find a woman friend she truly cared for, she'd always been such a loner. They had observed Wilma and her older contemporaries long enough to see the warmth and strength that could evolve from such a sisterhood, a friendship very different from Charlie's solid friendship with Clyde—and now of course her most enduring friendship of all, with Max himself.

Well, Joe thought, Charlie had liked Kate Osborne too. They could have been close friends if Kate had stayed in the village. They had in common, for one thing, the privilege of the cats' own secret. But Kate had abandoned Molena Point for San Francisco and abandoned Clyde, leaving the field wide open to Ryan—humans, one had to admit, could be every bit as fickle as the randiest tomcat.

Yet despite human vicissitudes, Joe found himself deeply purring as he watched Charlie and Max. Mr. and Mrs. Maximilian Franklin Harper, he thought, grinning. A name that very few people had ever heard, Max himself finding his full name far too fancy and formal.

Joe had missed the chief.

Well, I missed needling Harper, he thought, embarrassed by his sentiment.

And he *had* missed Charlie, missed her steady support. Because Charlie knew the cats' secret, she had been there for them in the same way that Clyde and Wilma were there. She knew what they were up to, and was ready to help if she could. Joe had, in fact, found Charlie, just a few months ago, snooping among the same incriminating books and papers that he himself had found suspicious, evidence that had ultimately helped convict a killer.

He watched Charlie and Ryan and Wilma set the table and lay out, on the edge of a planter box, a place mat and three small cat dishes, causing Max to give Charlie a sour look. Little did Harper know that Charlie was setting the supper table for his three best informants. But Joe's eyes grew round with surprise when Dallas took the kit from Wilma and held her, gently stroking her, his dark eyes laughing.

"Since when," Ryan said, "were you so fond of cats?"

"Since I had to arrest this little terror," Dallas said, settling the kit on his shoulder. "Talk about chutzpa." He looked into the kit's yellow eyes. "This one's a regular little burglar." He didn't seem to notice Charlie turn pale, or Clyde stop speaking. The kit closed her eyes, hiding her face against Garza's shoulder.

"You arrested her where?" Ryan said. "What could a little cat do?"

Garza sipped his beer. "You know how secure a grand jury room is. No one's allowed in except the prosecuting attorney and witnesses, and the court reporter.

"I was called in this morning to testify, but also to evict the cat from underneath a chair. I had to haul her out by the nape of the neck before I could give testimony. No one knew how she slipped in. The jurors were not amused. Clerk of the court took it as a personal affront that a cat had sneaked past her into that part of the building. I took Kit to the dispatcher, and she called Wilma to come get her."

Wilma said, "I found her on the dispatcher's counter lapping up a carton of milk. I don't know what got into her," she said innocently. "Why would a cat . . . ? Well, I kept her in the house the rest of the day, shut in the bedroom."

Clyde had turned away to check the prime rib, hiding a laugh. Joe watched him, scowling. Why were the kit's adventures so entertaining, when his own serious surveillance and information gathering drew nothing from Clyde but insults? Joe supposed that the kit, because she was responsible for Gramps Farger's arrest, had wanted to be in on the kill. He watched Clyde remove the roast from the rotisserie to a platter and, with a lethal-looking carving knife, begin to cut off paper-thin slices so juicy and pink that the tomcat began to drool. He watched Dulcie wind around Clyde's ankles with the three household cats, and the two dogs crowd so close their noses were scant inches from the carving board. It was only when everyone was seated, tying into the delicious meat and two vegetable casseroles and salad, and the animals all had their own plates, that Clyde said, "After the grand jury evicted Kit, what did they find?"

"With the evidence we had," Dallas said, "they indicted Martie Holland for Dannizer's murder. And they indicted Gramps Farger. Four charges of manufacturing drugs, two of attempted murder for the bombing, two on inciting a juvenile."

Behind Dallas, the kit looked incredibly smug.

"What *about* the boy?" Ryan asked.

"We're still holding him," Dallas said. "He'll be remanded over to juvenile. There'll be a hearing. I expect juvenile court will either put him in a foster home and maybe a trade school, or send him to one of the boys' ranches if they think he's a good enough risk. I doubt it. I don't like to think we'll be seeing that kid back in jail in years to come, but you know the statistics.

"No one knows for sure what was in the kid's head—whether he was as hot to blow up the church as his grampa says, or whether the old man forced him to climb up on the roof, maybe threatened him."

Garza frowned. "Some kind of grandfather. He laid as much blame as he could on the boy, said Curtis wanted to set off the bomb." He looked at Ryan. "If the defense attorney can get the boy to lie, on the stand, to protect Gramps, that could complicate matters. Would you want to talk with him again? See if he'll open up? He's scared now, since we arrested Gramps. The old man *has* threatened him. But maybe if we can convince him Gramps will stay locked up, and with the dog to comfort him, maybe he'll open up, tell us what happened."

"I could try," Ryan said doubtfully. "It can't hurt to try."

"I took makings for the bomb from that shack where Gramps was living, and from the trash bags he hid at the Pamillon estate, along with the stuff from his underground meth lab. Empty containers of Drāno, white gas, alcohol. Propane cylinders, you name it. The old man's prints all over everything. And the Jag is registered to Curtis's mother, she's been driving the old man's broken-down truck." He looked at Max. "I'd sure like to thank your snitches.

"I'm guessing the old man waited until we checked that area up there, before the trial and again last month, waited until he thought we'd lost interest, then moved in."

Max nodded. "Checked every out-of-the-way house and shack in the county. *And* the Pamillon ruins."

"It's called egg on our face," Dallas said, laughing. "Anyway, the grand jury had a full and productive day. Davis will have Holland back here safe and sound, early tomorrow."

Ryan looked at Clyde. "That's what Larn Williams was talking about when he accused Dad of having affairs with his caseload—a parolee named Martie Holland, alias Marianna Landeau. Only it wasn't Dad she was involved with. It was Rupert."

Flannery said, "Martie came out of federal prison ten years ago. Beautiful woman, could have had anything she wanted. But she couldn't stay out of trouble. She wasn't out two months, she was into an extortion racket. When I told her to clean up her act or I'd send her back, she came on to me. She thought she could buy the world.

"When she understood that *I* wasn't buying, she decided to target my family. She wasn't used to not having her way. She settled on Ryan, I guess because Rupert was . . . accessible. She was soon in bed with him and teaching him how to skim the company books. When I found out, I revoked her, sent her back.

"She came out with no time to serve. Was in L.A. for a while, got married. Became Marianna Landeau. I didn't keep track of her, didn't know they'd moved back to the Bay Area or that she'd laid a false trail under her own name to the Bahamas.

"Apparently she got involved with Rupert again, perhaps out of spite. Martie was never what you'd call forgiving. They began skimming the books again, before Ryan left him. We've talked with Ryan's attorneys. If I'd known that Martie was back in the city . . ."

"The woman I built that house for," Ryan said angrily, "the

woman I created that beautiful cottage for. That was their love nest. Hers and Rupert's love nest. She killed him there, to pin the murder on me. To destroy me."

"To destroy *me*," Flannery said, "by destroying you."

"She shot Rupert in there," Ryan said. "A love nest as lethal as the web of a black widow. Luring the male in, to kill him."

Dallas said, "The lab found blood in the rug that was taken from the cottage, the rug Ryan and Hanni gave to the Coldirons. That too was a tip from one of Harper's snitches. The lab came through right away. Since the county allotted more funds, they've been able to do some hiring. We're waiting for an answer on the DNA. If it's Rupert's, we've got a closed case.

"She shot him in front of the fireplace," Dallas said. "Shot into the niche where the right-hand sculpture is placed. Where the concrete had been patched and repainted, Davis and I dug out two spent bullets. I have no idea how the informants knew about the damaged fireplace. Maybe I don't want to know. The important thing is, their information dovetailed in nicely with our investigation."

"We're not sure yet," Harper said, "what else the Landeaus were into. The feds will be dealing with that. Could be, we'll be able to nail them with backing the Fargers' meth labs, we don't know yet. As to the bombing, from the evidence we now have, that was strictly a Farger family project."

"And what about the dog?" Clyde asked. "With all the threads that stretch from San Andreas to Molena Point, everyone's guilty but the dog."

Mike Flannery laughed. "He's the only innocent."

"Maybe," Dallas said, "Rock can help convict Gramps, if he and Ryan can get Curtis to talk." He glanced at his niece. "And maybe Rock's some kind of compensation, for Ryan having to go through this mess."

Ryan grinned, and rubbed Rock's ears, where the big dog leaned against her.

30

WHEN RYAN LEFT THE JOB AT NOON WITH ROCK,
heading for the PD, she had more stowaways than she'd accommodated coming down from San Andreas. Hidden under the tarp in the truck bed the three cats crouched as warm and cozy as three football fans snuggled under blankets in the bleachers awaiting the big game.

Despite the hard bouncing of the truck, Dulcie and the kit purred and dozed; but Joe crouched tense and excited, ready to scorch out the minute Ryan parked, and slip inside the station. If their luck held, if the timing worked, this might be the game of the season.

He had placed one phone call just after breakfast. Using the extension in Clyde's bedroom to dial Ryan's cell phone, where she worked in the attic above him, he had suggested that today at noon might be the optimum time to have that talk with Curtis Farger, and he had shared with Ryan his take on the matter.

"Have you wondered why Rock pitched a fit, the day you took him to the Landeau cottage?"

"Yes, I have," she'd said softly. She didn't ask how he could know about that. Like Max Harper and Dallas, she kept her answers brief, and she listened.

"Davis and Green will be bringing Marianna in from San Francisco around noon," Joe said. "Would it be instructive to let Rock have a look at her—kill two birds with one . . . stone?"

She was silent, as if thinking about that.

"Couldn't hurt, could it?" Joe said.

She remained quiet. But then when she spoke, there was a lilt of excitement in her voice. "I'll be there at noon," she said softly. Then in a faintly seductive voice, "You know a lot about this case. I can keep a secret, if you care to tell me who you are."

Joe had hit the disconnect, pushed the headset back on its cradle, and left the house by his cat door. Slipping along beneath the neighbors' bushes, he'd followed a route away from the house that he well knew was invisible from the room above.

And now as he rode into the courthouse parking in Ryan's truck, he was highly impatient, tense to fly out. Ryan found a parking slot just to the right of the glass doors, one of those spaces marked *Visitors Only, Ten Minutes*, where the cars nosed up to a wide area of decorative plantings. Stepping out of the cab, commanding Rock to heel, she locked the door behind her. While she stood waiting to be buzzed inside, Joe dropped from atop a toolbox into the bushes. Behind him, the kit and Dulcie would take another route. As Ryan moved inside, Joe slipped in behind her and under the booking counter. Rock rolled his eyes at the tomcat, but didn't make a wiggle.

The shelves under the counter were stacked with rolls of fax paper and computer paper, cartons of pens and pencils, and all manner of forms, neatly arranged. Slipping in between boxes of printer cartridges and computer disks, he crouched where he could see both the front entry and the holding cell, but could pull back quickly out of sight. Curtis sat in the cell looking glum. He had apparently been brought up where he could speak freely, out of earshot of Gramps. Joe could hear from above the ceiling the faintest rustle of oak leaves as Dulcie and the kit swarmed up like a pair of commandos to the high, barred window that looked down into the cell.

But where the sun shone in against the cell wall, silhouetting the oak branch, it silhouetted, as well, two pairs of feline ears, sharply pricked. Joe prayed Dulcie would see the reflection, that she and the kit would back off.

Ryan stood outside the cell with Rock waiting for an officer to unlock the door. Rock stared in at the boy, whining. And beyond the glass doors of the front entry, a police unit pulled into the red zone. Talk about timing! Joe could see, behind the unit's wire barrier, the golden-haired passenger. He watched Detective Juana Davis and Officer Green emerge from the car observing the area around them, then quickly unlock the back door and order Marianna out.

She slid from the car maintaining her grace despite being shackled by handcuffs. Immediately Davis marched her toward the glass doors. The dispatcher hit the admittance button. Joe glanced to the cell's telltale shadow again, and saw that the two pairs of pricked ears had vanished. The officers and Marianna were hardly inside, with the door locked behind them, when all hell broke loose. A roar of anger greeted Marianna, and a leaping gray streak went for her, held back only by Ryan, crouching with the leash across her legs. The dog fought the leash snarling and barking. Joe glimpsed, in Ryan's eyes, a terrible hunger to let the dog loose. She held him as he fought her trying to get at Marianna, ignoring her command to sit.

Marianna did not back away. "*Hold!*" She snapped at him. The dog froze stone still, his lips drawn up over killer teeth.

"Rock, sit!" Marianna commanded.

Rock sat, but he kept snarling, torn between hatred and what he'd been trained to do. So, Joe thought. So they had indeed found Rock's owner. Ryan stepped to the dog's side, taking hold of his collar.

But a catch of breath made Joe look past the rigid tableau to the holding cell where Curtis Farger stood at the bars, his face white, his dark eyes burning not with anger but with fear. The boy's knuckles were white where he clutched the bars.

Marianna-Martie, drawn by that hush of breath, turned. The look between Marianna and Curtis was so filled with hatred that Joe Grey backed deeper among the boxes, shivering as if their mutual rage were daggers flying or lethal gases ready to explode.

The keys, Joe thought. Curtis *did* take those keys for Marianna to copy. Somehow he did it and brought them back again. And now . . . now her look has warned him, Don't talk, Curtis. Don't dare tell them . . .

At the sound of Rock's barking, Garza and Harper had appeared in the hall with several officers. The whole station seemed to be gathering, crowding down the hall, all the officers watching the dog, Martie, and Curtis. Only Davis and Green remained focused totally on their prisoner. Rock, though still sitting as he'd been commanded, was tensed to leap, his gaze fixed on Marianna's throat.

"Down, Rock. Back and down."

Now, he defied her. He backed one step, but he wouldn't lie down for her. He stood snarling as, beside him, Ryan turned to look at Curtis.

She said no word, just looked. Curtis looked back, his eyes huge.

"Whose dog is this?"

"Her dog. He's *her* dog." His voice was unsteady.

"Shut up, you little bastard!"

"Hers. She tried to train him like the others, like those rottweilers, but she only made him mad, made him turn on her." Curtis looked terrified. "She beat him, beat him bad. She shot at him with a shotgun. You feel his skin, the little lumps? Buckshot where she shot him to run him off the place because half the time he wouldn't mind her. He wouldn't attack for her so she didn't want him anymore."

Marianna swung around, fixing on Detective Garza. "You have

no right to allow this dirty little boy to say such things. I still have rights. My lawyers will take you apart, officer. Get that little bastard out of my sight, get him out of here."

Dallas looked at Curtis. "How do you know who owns him?"

"I . . . Someone I know works up there. I went with him sometimes. I saw her try to train Rock, her and that real-estate guy. It takes two to train a guard dog. That Williams was the . . . I don't know what to call it. He wore the padded suit."

"The agitator?" Dallas said.

Curtis nodded.

Marianna was very white. "I've heard enough of this. If you insist on arresting me—and you will ultimately be very sorry for that, officer, then I insist on being shown to my cell or whatever you call it, and afforded some modicum of privacy—if your little hometown jail can offer such a thing."

"Larn was good friends with her?" Dallas asked Curtis.

"I *said* . . ." Marianna began. But Davis gripped her arm in a way that silenced her.

"He was all over her," the boy said. "Her husband never knew, he was gone half the time. Hu—my friend saw Williams sneaking around."

Dallas said, "Why didn't you tell me before, who owned the dog?"

"Afraid you'd take him back to *her*."

"And what about the sheriff?" Dallas asked Curtis. "Did he know where the dog belonged?"

"He knew. He didn't want him taken back there and penned up. She'd have killed him. So Sheriff just . . ." Curtis shrugged. "Sheriff keeps his mouth shut. Maybe he hoped Ryan would take him. Then when you didn't," he said, looking at Ryan, "and my gramps told me . . ." He stopped speaking, and his face reddened. "When I decided to hitch a ride home to Mama, I brought Rock with me. Well, he wanted to come. Couldn't drive him away if I'd tried. Couldn't leave him there."

"And your gramps wanted you to come back," Ryan said softly.

"No! I told you, I decided to come back to Mama."

"Then why didn't you go on down the coast to your mama?"

"I called her to come get me but she wasn't home, she didn't answer the phone. I thought to stay with Gramps for the night and call her again."

"Did you take my keys?" Ryan said. "Did you give them to Marianna?"

"I want my lawyer *now!* You can't question that boy like that. I want . . ." Davis twisted her arm, hard.

Curtis glanced at Marianna and looked away. He nodded. "Yes," he said softly. "I got them for her."

"Do you know what she did with them?"

Curtis shook his head. "She said she'd keep her mouth shut about . . . certain things, if I'd get the keys."

Ryan, keeping Rock close to her, had moved nearer to Curtis. She stood just beside his door, her back to the gathered officers and to Marianna. Rock stuck his nose through the bars, licking Curtis's hand. Looking around at Dallas, Ryan nodded. Dallas nodded to Davis, and the detective led Marianna away, down the hall toward the jail. Ryan stayed focused on Curtis. She spoke quietly, as if they were alone.

"Would you testify for me, Curtis? This is a murder charge. I could be facing life in prison. Or worse." She reached through the bars, to touch his hand. "If Marianna killed my husband, she should be convicted. If she is, she'll be locked up for a long time where she can't get at you."

She looked at him deeply. "Would you tell a jury the truth? That you took my keys for Marianna? Things . . . might go easier for you, at your grampa's trial," she said softly. "No one could promise such a thing, but the judge or jury might look on you more kindly, if you've already told the court the truth about Marianna."

Curtis looked back at her. "Would you keep Rock? For good? For your own dog?"

"I promise I'll keep him for good. For my own dog."

289

"Could I visit him?"

"You could visit him," she said softly. "Or he could visit you."

Curtis nodded. "If you'll promise to keep him, I'll tell . . . testify."

"Please understand, Curtis. I want you only to tell the truth."

Curtis nodded. "If you'll keep him, I can do that."

And Joe Grey heard, from high above him, the faintest mewl echoing through the roof, the kind of murmur Dulcie or the kit made when they got emotional, a plaintive cry too soft for human ears. A tenderhearted mutter that made him frown with male superiority.

Licking his own salty whiskers, the tomcat did not consider that he was emotional. *He* was only wired, only congratulating himself that his timing had worked out for optimum results. Worked out in a manner that seemed to him to cap both cases—testimony to help hang Martie Holland, certainly. But in the process, perhaps a change of heart in Curtis Farger? A greater willingness to tell all he knew about the church bombing as well as about Martie Holland?

Perhaps, Joe Grey thought. He hoped so.

But in the case of young Curtis, the only proof would be time—and what Curtis decided to do with that time.

For a long moment, the uncertainty of a boy's life, heading either for good or for the sewer, left Joe a bit testy, as if he had a thorn in his paw.

And it was not until later that night that Joe began to look with equanimity upon the unanswered questions regarding Curtis Farger. When, as Clyde and Ryan sat in the expanded attic watching the stars through the newly cut windows, Joe began to unwind and take the longer view.

Dulcie and the kit lay on the rafters looking out at the sea, their paws and tails drooping over. But Joe prowled among the beams looking down on Clyde and Ryan where they sat on the floor leaning against the newly constructed wall, sipping coffee. Rock lay sprawled beside Ryan, deeply asleep, his coat silver in the faint light.

Moving restlessly along the heavy timbers, Joe tried to work off the tangle of thoughts and events that crowded inside his head, as irritating and insistent as buzzing bees. Maybe he needed some down time, needed to slaughter a few wharf rats, some uncomplicated bit of sport to get centered again, now that the human rats were locked up.

But when he glanced across to Dulcie, she too was restless, the tip of her tail twitching, then lashing. Joe, leaping from rafter to rafter, brushed against her and led her along the center beam and up into his small, private tower that rose above the new structure.

The cat-sized retreat was still only framed, its six sides standing open to the night. It would have glass windows that Joe could easily open. Its hexagonal roof was fitted with pie shapes of plywood, and shingles. There would be cushions later, and a shelf to hold a bowl for fresh water.

Sitting close together beneath the little roof, Joe and Dulcie watched the ocean gleaming beyond the dark oaks. They were mesmerized for a long moment by the endless rolling of the white breakers, by the sea's beating thunder. Nearer to them humped the village rooftops, the cats' own exclusive world, its angles and crannies and hiding places far removed from human problems and human evils—though Dulcie, as usual, could not divorce herself from human needs.

"Tomorrow," she said, "I'll go into the library early." She gave him a guilty look. "I've made myself too scarce." She was, after all, official library cat, and she had let her chosen work slide. "Tomorrow is story hour. I'll snuggle on the big window seat with the children, let them pummel and pet me." She smiled. "Too bad I can't read to them, Wilma says I have a lovely reading voice."

"The kids would love it. Probably triple attendance."

But then she shivered. "I keep thinking about the bombing. And about those drug labs that might have killed as many people as the bomb would have done."

"It's over, Dulcie. Everyone's safe. Those people are locked up."

"And I was thinking about Marianna—Martie Holland. About

her cruelty to Rock, to that sweet silver hound." Dulcie turned to look at Joe, her green eyes wide and dark. "That woman cares for no living thing. She cares for nothing but her own destructive schemes—as if she's linked to all cruelty in the world. As if hate and cruelty are one massive force that she's part of, a force that can shape itself into a million faces."

Joe Grey licked his whiskers. "But there's more that's *good* in life, Dulcie. Clyde and Ryan down there, so right and comfortable with each other. Charlie and Max at home together, safe and happy. The ladies of senior survival tucked away in their new home. Wilma, and our good police and detectives." Thinking about their human friends, he grew almost mellow. He looked hard at her, the starlight catching a gleam across his pale whiskers and dark eyes. "What *they* have, Dulcie, is way more powerful than evil." And the tomcat looked, not predatory then or teasing as he so often looked, but only wise. "The force of goodness is stronger, Dulcie."

"Goodness," she said, "and the little droll things, the humorous turns of life."

"Such as?"

Dulcie laughed. "Silver tomcat and silver dog like mirror images."

Joe Grey smiled. He guessed, in this case, comparison to a dog wasn't an insult. He purred deeply. "Despite bombs and lethal drugs, despite all the evil, there's far more that's good. The humorous things," he said, smiling. "The positive things."

And it was true. At that particular moment, their own bit of the world was safe and right. They were all together in their small village, the three cats and their friends. Those who would harm them were otherwise occupied, and no matter what disasters might visit among them in future, they were there for each other. Nothing, Joe Grey thought, nothing even in death could separate their closeness, could change the fact that they were family.